TENDER CAPTOR

———— ⟬⟭ ————

"EAT," RAFAEL WHISPERED TO HER, AND BROUGHT
his hand up to her mouth, pressing something to her lips.
Bread. She opened her mouth and accepted it, tasting
nothing, feeling only his fingers, so light against her. He
did not move them away but altered his touch, following
the shape of her lips, skimming softly over her cheek, her
chin, and Serath felt the heat of the room swim over her,
taking her reason away and leaving only this newness, the
texture and marvel of this man.

She swallowed the bread.

"Yes," said Rafael, very softly, and then leaned his
head close to hers and placed his lips where his fingers had
been, a gentle caress over her cheek, his breath warm
against her. Serath blinked and pulled back, astonished,
and he followed her, closing his lips over her own.

Nothing in her life had prepared her for this. . . .

A KISS AT MIDNIGHT

Shana Abé

ℬANTAM ℬOOKS

New York   Toronto   London   Sydney   Auckland

A KISS AT MIDNIGHT

ISBN 0-7394-0821-6

Published simultaneously in the United States and Canada

Bantam Books are published by Bantam Books, a division of Random House,
Inc. Its trademark, consisting of the words "Bantam Books" and the portrayal of
a rooster, is Registered in U.S. Patent and Trademark Office and in other
countries. Marca Registrada. Bantam Books, 1540 Broadway, New York, New
York 10036.

PRINTED IN THE UNITED STATES OF AMERICA

*For the dazzling Ruth Kagle,
my remarkable agent, who listened
and believed in me. Thank you.*

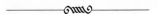

*Endless gratitude also goes to
Wendy McCurdy, Stephanie Kip, Mom and Dad
and the rest of the family, and of course, to Darren.
I could not do this without you.*

A Kiss at Midnight

Prologue

———————— ⟨₥₥⟩ ————————

*O*NCE, MANY YEARS AGO, THERE WERE TWO BROTH-
ers. One was very good, and one was very, very bad."

"I beseech you—do not do this thing!"

The nursemaid addressing the children gathered near
her feet appeared not to notice the distant voice that interrupted her tale. A few of the children exchanged looks,
but only one small girl dared to scoot back a little from
the group, so that she could see a corner of the shuttered
window beyond the woman in front of her.

Nurse, sitting high on a stool, pinned her gaze on the
girl and talked on.

"The good brother was all that made God smile: fair
of face and heart. But the bad was the devil's delight: dark
and brooding. Together they traveled to many strange
lands, for despite their differences they were partners in
blood and adventure, until at last they came to a place like
none other. It was wild and unfamiliar, it held magic and

promise like no land they had seen before. The brothers named it Alderich—the land of forgotten dreams."

"*Injustice! Cold hearts! Spare me this!*"

"What was that?" asked the little girl, but her nurse-maid hushed her.

"Do you want to hear the story, Serath Rune? Yes? Then you had better listen to me." The woman threw one quick, nervous glance over her shoulder, toward the sole window in the nursery, before continuing.

"Both brothers were captured by Alderich, by the spell of the land and the ocean and the mists. Each was enchanted by the beauty of this place, each was held in its charm, and each vowed to make it his own. Since they were brothers, they agreed to split the land between them—half and half, a fair share each."

"*I am wronged! I am betrayed!*"

The little girl named Serath leaned around the figure of her nurse, craning her neck to see the shuttered window where pieces of daylight crept through the wooden slats.

"But after they made the bargain the evil brother found he was not content with this deal," the nurse went on, speaking loudly over the noise outside. "And so he brewed a plot as wicked as his own soul: he would steal the castle and the rest of the lands from his brother. The beauty of Alderich had turned sour in him, had turned him darker and more lost than ever before."

"*My children!*"

"It sounds like Mama," said Serath, turning to look at her older brother.

"Listen!" commanded Nurse sharply. "If you don't, I'll not finish the tale, and you're to bed without your meal, I promise you that!"

The girl subsided, though she did not stop staring at

her brother Raibeart, who, full of the importance of his eight years over her six, frowned at her and shook his head. The other children seemed to hear nothing unusual, enthralled in a story they had all heard many times before.

"Tell us more," urged one.

The nursemaid went on. "The good brother had built a fine castle on his portion of the lands, you see. He had worked very hard to build it, day and night, night and day, until it stood as we see it now, our fine Fionnlagh. And he married and had his sons here, and all was well with him."

"Stop—"

"But the wicked brother had done none of this, choosing instead to live in sloth and wastefulness. His lands fell into ruin, and his crops were not tended to, until the soil became naught but rock and brush. Yet he had watched his brother's castle with envy, and his brother's fruitful lands. And because he was so wicked, he went to the king with his complaint."

"No, no, my lord, I beg of you—"

Nurse spoke louder still, her voice strained, and Serath watched as the cords in her neck began to bulge.

" 'Heed me, O King,' said the wicked brother, 'for my kin has stolen my land, and taken from me a fine castle! Give me back what is rightfully mine, for I am the elder brother!' "

"Pity! God's pity, I ask for mercy! I have children to care for, your own grandchildren—"

"And the king said, 'You are indeed the elder. I know it to be true. Your brother has built this home, and deserves the right of it. Yet you are the elder, and so I cannot dismiss you.' "

"Serath! Raibeart!"

"It's Mama!" exclaimed the little girl, jumping to her feet, but to her astonishment Nurse leaped up from her stool and pushed Serath back down to the floor, very hard. There was a hot flush to her face, and beads of sweat on her forehead.

"Sit here!" hissed the woman. "Listen and obey me, child! You hear nothing else, do you understand me?"

"Please, no!"

Serath looked again to her brother, who stared back at her, wide-eyed. Thin ribbons of sunlight fell across him and lit him in stripes, golden blond and shadow, worried blue eyes.

Nurse crossed to the window and pulled the shutter hard against the stone wall, though Serath thought it was already tightly closed. She then turned to the children, keeping her back to the wood, and the sunlight became part of her, dark and light around her.

"So the king said, 'Though your heart is wicked, by law I cannot refuse your claim. Hear me now: The castle of your brother's labor is your brother's, and his crops are his own, although Alderich should be yours. So they shall be his until the end is come, until the heavens fall and our years turn into the next thousand. On that day, the first day of the new millennium, Fionnlagh shall pass to you, and all the lands of Alderich shall be yours, as well. Until then you must live in Leonhart, the lands you have wasted. So shall it be.' "

A new sound was edging past the shutter and the solid form of Nurse—the sound of a fire burning, and a woman's sobbing.

"Please, please, don't do this. . . ."

Despite the threat of her nursemaid Serath rose again to her feet, staring at the sunlight and wood, feeling something cold and tingling running across her hands, her shoulders, her spine. The air left a strange taste in her mouth, heavy and unpleasant.

"And so we have Fionnlagh, children," said the nurse, her voice shrill over the fire sound, "and here we stay! And we are the right and true people of Alderich, and we are the sons and daughters of that good brother!"

"I curse you!" came a scream now, drowning in the crackling of the flames. *"I curse you all!"*

"For the end of our days here shall be the end of the world!" exclaimed Nurse, and the sunlight behind her was turning a strange color, sooty and poisoned. "The beginning of the next thousand years shall be the end of time, and our reign here at Alderich shall be complete, and the wicked brother will be thwarted in his devil's plan!"

"I curse you! You think me a witch, so believe me in this— I curse you now, you and your castle and these lands!"

"Mama!" cried Serath, and ran to the nurse, to the window and the scary air of soot, the sound of death so clear in the courtyard hidden behind the shutter.

"Away!" shouted Nurse, and shoved Serath back, her face a terrible mask.

Serath turned and darted through the children huddled together on the nursery floor, all of them staring at her, a few beginning to cry. She made it to the door and yanked at the handle, but it was locked tight against her.

"Mama! Mama!"

Raibeart was beside her, pulling with her, their hands overlapping, tugging with equal fervor.

"And in the end the devil will come," said Nurse softly, watching them, unmoving. "But it will be too late. For we will all be done here, joined with the purity of all the good—for the beginning of the thousand years will be the end time for all of us."

Serath released the handle, turning to stare at Nurse,

at the poison smoke seeping into the room, the smell of fire curling into every corner. Raibeart took her hands in his, holding her close as they both looked at the woman at the other end of the chamber.

"It will be," stated Nurse simply, "the very end."

Chapter One

⟨❦⟩

*T*HE OMENS ARE ILL INDEED."

The bishop leaned back in his chair and allowed the novice to refill his goblet of wine. The young woman did so with steady hands, head bowed, and then stepped back into the shadows of the prioress's private chamber, keeping her jug of wine ready.

"Think you so?" murmured the prioress, taking a bite of her evening meal. "The new year is still weeks away."

"What is a matter of weeks to the mind of God?" asked the bishop. "Mere weeks are nothing to Him. I tell you, God is warning us. He is showing us these signs to prepare us for the end times. How else do you explain the curious weather we've been having? The heat of August on a day so close to winter?"

"You are correct, of course," concurred the prioress.

"One of my villages has reported the birth of a lamb to a cow. How do you explain that, I ask you? And another has had its well dry to dust overnight. Overnight!

From a well that was plentiful just the day before. Every day of my travels brings me to a new village with new portents, each one more severe than the last. The Day of the Lord is nearly here!"

The prioress nodded thoughtfully.

"Expect miraculous things," whispered the bishop, his voice low and thrilled. "Showers of fire! The earth opening up! The red dragon himself come to plague us! Yet we will be strong, and be blessed for it!"

"We are grateful you have come to warn us," said the prioress.

"These are strange times," muttered the bishop, and waved his goblet for more wine. The young woman came forward, tipping the jug to the goblet, but the wine splashed out too quickly. A splattering of red fell onto the sleeve of the bishop's robe.

"Clumsy girl!" exclaimed the man, and pushed back his chair, holding out his arm in front of him.

The novice quickly set the jug of wine on the table. She grasped the stained cloth of the robe and began to blot up the wine with the edge of her own sleeve.

"Leave it," grumbled the bishop, jerking away from her. "You're spreading the stain, child. Leave it be!"

The young woman bowed her head again, hiding her face, and curtsied deeply before backing away once more.

"What?" said the man, watching her. "Have you no repentance to offer, child?"

"She cannot speak," said the prioress calmly. "She is under an oath of silence."

"Ah." The bishop studied the girl again, curious. "She's a bit too old to be a novice, isn't she? Most her age would have taken their vows by now."

"Serath has . . . special problems," said the prioress with a needle-sharp glance to the novice, who remained motionless. "She has not done well with discipline, I'm sorry to say. She is willful and disobedient, a great trial to us all."

"Ah," said the bishop again, nodding. "So this is Serath Rune, granddaughter of the Lord of Alderich. I understand."

"Indeed. I'm certain your lordship has heard of the black history of this girl. It is all we can do to control her."

"The Lord of Alderich is a faithful man," commented the bishop meaningfully.

"He is," responded the prioress. "It is due solely to his good faith that the girl remains here."

"Look at me, child," said the man, and slowly the young woman raised her face. "Come forward," instructed the bishop. "My eyes are old. I cannot see you in the shadows."

And the novice walked toward him, until the light from the lamps on the table fell across her figure and lit the gray of her veil and gown to the color of smoke.

The bishop seemed startled, throwing a look to the prioress before turning back to the novice. He leaned forward in his chair, examining her.

"Remarkable," he announced. "She is her very image, is she not?"

"It is not so strange for a daughter to have the look of her mother," said the prioress.

"Yes, but this—her eyes, her face . . . I remember Morwena Rune. I remember that darkness about her."

"Yes," said the prioress, but nothing more.

The young woman before them had her gaze focused somewhere beyond them, as if she were not really in the same room but rather someplace very far away.

"The devil's beauty," remarked the bishop, frowning. "I can understand how she might trouble you. It's in her

blood, is it not? Coldness. Pride. She is tainted with her
mother's spell."

"So it is said," agreed the prioress. "Yet her grandfather . . ."

"A faithful man," finished the bishop, still staring.
After a while he turned away again, waving a hand at the
novice. The young woman spared a glance to the prioress,
who nodded, allowing her to fade back into the shadows
of the chamber.

The bishop continued eating. "I had forgotten he
sent his granddaughter here. I saw him just a few months
ago, in fact. He is preparing for the end, as well."

"Oh?" remarked the prioress.

"Fionnlagh is as fine a castle as I've seen," said the
bishop. "But Jozua Rune knows it will not be his much
longer. He is preparing for the Lord."

"Alderich and everything in it goes to the other
branch of the family with the turning of this year. Everyone knows that."

"They will not have the chance to claim it," replied
the bishop, serene. "It *is* the end."

The prioress nodded again to the novice, lifting her
goblet. "So what does he think to do?"

"Naught but the will of God," said the bishop.

The prioress watched her goblet being filled. "Jozua
Rune thinks to challenge Rafael of Leonhart for the
land?"

The jug of wine slipped from the girl's fingers, this
time falling to the table and then to the floor of the chamber, where it shattered into fragments of clay, wine froth-
ing over the stone.

Serath Rune stood back, hands apart, staring at the
mess, wine spreading to her feet.

The prioress slowly rose from her chair.

"Clean it up," she said, her voice deceptively mild. "And tomorrow there will be fifteen lashes for this."

The young woman looked up quickly, opening her mouth to protest, then closed it again, her face going blank. She nodded and bent to the ground amid the wine, gathering up the shards of pottery in her hands.

Both the bishop and the prioress watched her work.

"A great trial," said the prioress again, almost to herself.

"You may not have time to save her soul," pronounced the bishop. "It is most likely too late for her."

————— ༄ —————

SERATH HELD HER BREATH AS SHE EASED OPEN the door to her cell.

The hinges were old and rusted, and she took care to go as slowly as she could manage, although the excitement was singing through her, and it seemed her entire body was ready to run.

But no, the door crept open as slowly as a prayer, and to her credit there was not one squeak from the hinges. She slipped past the opening and into the narrow hallway, unlit but for a faraway torch near the end. When she turned she bumped the edge of the door and it closed too quickly; a high-pitched creak filled the air.

Serath stopped, heart racing, listening for movement from any of the other cells. Nothing. She was fortunate— none of the other novices stirred.

She picked up the bundle of cloth that contained her few possessions—a change of gown, her mother's brooch, some food she had managed to steal—and crept down the hallway, moving swiftly.

The small windows set into the doors of the other cells showed only darkness upon darkness. Everyone should be asleep by now. It was very late, and the nuns and novices would all be up in a few hours.

Serath had figured this to be the most ideal time for escape: the dead of the night, when the torches would be burning low and even Sister Peninnah, notorious for her light sleeping, would be drowsy and lost in her dreams.

She had thought she might have had problems remaining awake herself. Her days were full of work and meditation, and the prioress made certain she was never idle. Yet to her relief Serath had felt nothing like exhaustion when she finally lay down for the night on her hard pallet. Even when feigning sleep for the sake of the final check through the cells, she had felt her senses sharp and ready, eager to begin her final hour here.

She was leaving. She was truly doing it. She was leaving this place, this prison of hers. She was going to use her voice again and sing to the ocean, sing as much as she liked, and there would be no one to stop her, no one to strike her or punish her. . . .

The end of the world was looming close, but Serath would beat it. She would find her peace outside these walls before it came.

Sister Peninnah always slept with the door to her cell open, and the torch was just outside of it. It was her duty to watch over the novices, to ensure they were where they were supposed to be when they were supposed to be there. Serath aligned herself beside the door and cautiously peered in.

A blur of a form on the pallet. Steady, even breathing.

Serath passed the door as lightly and as quickly as she dared, her cloak flaring behind her.

The bishop had been correct about the weather—it was unseasonably warm, and Serath wore the cloak only because the dark color of it would blend better with the night than the pale gray of her novice gown.

Done! She was out of the dormitory, at the long, open walkway that led from the cells to the main buildings. The sky above her was vast and remote, studded with stars, the moon hidden behind a bank of clouds. Only part of her noticed that the light seemed peculiar, smeared the wrong color, but that was nothing to think about now. The gate was just a short walk away.

Serath did not walk. She ran, holding her cloak and her belongings as best she could, jumping over the uneven stones of the path until she came to the great gate itself, tall iron and three heavy locks.

Tucked away in the bundle of cloth was the most vital element to her freedom—the prioress's master key, normally hung prominently on a hook in that woman's private chamber. Her hands found it without the need of sight; it was heavy and ornate, thick brass polished to slickness.

It had taken Serath nearly two months to find a key close enough to it in style to risk making the switch. The key to the wine cellar now hung in the prioress's chamber. One close look would reveal the deception, but Serath was betting that the prioress was too distracted with the visit from the bishop to worry much about that key tonight.

She found the first lock and fumbled with it, shoving the key in place and jiggling it until she was able to turn it. The lock clicked open. Serath removed it from the gate and tossed it to the ground.

She reached for the second lock.

A faint glow of yellow light fell on the stones to her left. Serath whirled around to see the unmistakable movement of torchlight growing brighter from the open doorway of the dormitory. She heard voices. They were saying her name.

She knew as soon as she turned back to the gate that

she was too late. She would not be able to open the remaining two locks in time.

It can't be over this quickly, she thought, desperate. *It
can't.*

Her body was moving without her will, instinct alone
saving her, making her grab up her bundle and bolt from
the path, through the knotted undergrowth of the convent garden, throwing the key aside to land in the dirt.

The garden was large and varied; Serath had spent
more time here than anywhere else on the grounds, and
so knew which way would hold the most promise for
hiding.

The lights were becoming brighter, the noises of
women's voices growing louder. Serath heard her name
being called, exclamations that were almost too dim to
make out.

The far wall. She had to reach the far wall, with its
thicket of bushes and vines. A good portion of that corner
of the garden was skeletal and dying, and the prioress had
decided to let it go fallow for a season. It was there that
she should hide.

"Serath! Serath Rune!"

So close, so close. . . . She was running bent almost
in two, crashing through bare branches and exposed roots,
and surely they could hear her, surely they had seen her
by now, darting through the starlight—

"There!" called someone, and Serath threw herself to
the ground, scratching her hands and face, barely feeling
it. She came up hard against the outer wall of stone; it
knocked the air from her, leaving her dazed.

They were swarming everywhere now, calling out for
her, talking to each other. Even the other novices were
joining in.

She crawled to a sitting position, then leaned her head
back, taking in the height of the crumbling stone wall.

"Where *is* she?"

It was the prioress, very near. Serath closed her eyes and covered her face with the hood of her cloak, trying to control her breathing. She heard footsteps pause in front of her, the crackling of a torch.

"She cannot be far. The gate is still secured. Sister Damaris ensured that right away."

The second speaker used a calm, consolatory tone, perhaps not wishing to witness the prioress's infamous temper. Serath knew it well.

"Wayward," the prioress was muttering, directly in front of Serath's hiding place. "Willful. Disobedient, wretched girl. . . ."

She couldn't bear not to witness the end of her careful plans, so Serath opened her eyes, finding the shadowed shapes of the two women in front of her. Torchlight slipped past the tangle of the bushes, glancing off the woven cloth of her cloak. At least she had that much protecting her.

"We shall find her," the other nun said, facing away. "She cannot go far."

The prioress was still muttering. Serath could picture the scowl on her face, the deep furrows of displeasure worn into her forehead beneath the wimple.

"I am beginning to think she is not worth the coin her grandfather sends," the prioress said. "I am too old to be chasing ungrateful, spoiled novices into the night. Especially this night."

Both women paused, looking up to the sky, and Serath finally gave in to the urge to do the same, staring past the twisted stems and vines to see what they did.

A blood moon, free of clouds now, full and round and deep red. It hung low and sullen on the horizon, an orb of ominous proportions, disfiguring the night.

She felt the hair on the back of her neck rise, understanding now why the night seemed so strange, why the air felt so heavy in her lungs. The light around her was growing redder by the minute. Sweet heavens, how had she not seen it before? The end was closer than she had dreamed—she would be trapped here in her final hours, after all—

The prioress crossed herself. The other nun did the same.

"Hurry," said the prioress. "We must find this cursed girl and get back inside. The sooner the better."

The other woman murmured agreement, and together they moved away, taking the betraying light of the torch with them.

Serath waited anyway, just to be certain they were gone. She remained perfectly still, listening to the sounds of the convent roused, voices calling her name in tones that ranged from sleepy to irate—thirty-seven women in search of one. It seemed the bishop could not be bothered for the hunt.

Slowly she inched her way up from her position, keeping the rough stones against her back.

The wall was most dangerous here, farthest from the main buildings, ill-tended and falling to rubble. She imagined it would not be too difficult to scale; the danger would be in the time it took her. The height of it was still impressive. Eventually, she would be seen. Even though the walls of the convent enclosed a significant amount of land, once above the bushes, she would be open to discovery by them all.

Serath took a deep breath of the warm air, calming herself, then turned and faced the stone.

She had not climbed in a very long time. In fact, she had not done much in a very long time, it seemed, except meditate on her sins, pray at a cold stone altar, and duck blows from her superiors as she scrubbed and cleaned and implored forgiveness for faults she was not truly sorry for.

She had guessed correctly about the wall: the loose stones made for easy handholds, if precarious ones. She took one step up, then another. The hood of her cloak fell away but she had no means to fix it. She could not afford to let go. She had to hurry.

The bundle of cloth tied over one shoulder bumped against her with each move, a heavy weight that made her balance that much more uncertain. But she must not stop.

The wall was so tall, taller than she had anticipated. It had been built to repel raiders and pagans, and even after climbing what seemed like an eternity she was barely half-way up. The menacing moonlight washed her in red shadows, turning her fingers to the color of rawness, the stones to dark crimson. Perspiration made her grip tenuous.

She should have removed her boots for this. How stupid not to—she was having difficulty feeling for holds through the heavy leather of them. Why hadn't she thought of that? Stupid, stupid—

Serath heard a group of women off to her left, coming toward her. Her breath grew shorter, almost panicked. She moved more quickly, careless, and felt her foot slip on a stone that broke free of the ancient mortar, rolling and clattering down to the dirt.

Serath froze.

"What was that?" asked someone—Alva, new to the convent, younger than Serath. Her voice was sharp and fearful.

"An animal," suggested someone else, in a voice even more filled with fear.

"Or Serath Rune," said a nun tartly. "Keep moving."

It was finished, so very quickly. Her last hopes, her last prayers unanswered, cut short by one betraying stone.

They would find her and keep her here until it was all over. She would never see the sun again; her remaining days and nights would be spent in this hard and unforgiving place—why had she ever thought it would be any different. . . .

Serath closed her eyes against the wash of crimson moonlight, paralyzed with despair, unable to move to save herself.

"Oh, sister, what if it was a demon?" Alva's panic was becoming more apparent. "We should go to the chapel! Look at the moon! God is warning us! This night is cursed!"

"God will protect us," retorted the nun, though some of the tartness of before had faded, turned less certain. "Keep searching, child."

Serath heard them begin to walk toward her again. When they passed the birch marking the corner of the path, they would find her.

She would *not* die here, in this place she loathed. Serath unclenched her hands and found the will to climb again, as swiftly as possible, uncaring of the falling stones now. It was too late for subtlety.

At the new clatter of stones one of the novices let out a shriek, prompting more from the others. But the nun had more sense, Serath knew, and she couldn't help but look behind and below her as the woman came into sight.

"Serath Rune! Get down from there!"

Serath ignored this, climbing faster.

Others had sounded the call of her discovery, but it might not be too late—she was close now, so close, she could make it to the top and leap down if she had to—she would take that chance, because now that they had found her they would open the gate with the spare key and run along the outer wall to stop her—

And Serath reached the top of the wall and found this

was what was happening. The prioress and a core of followers were already stalking toward her outside the convent grounds, fluttering gowns and veils tinged dusky crimson. If she didn't jump right now they would have her, and they would take her back inside and lock her up again, and there would be no next time—they would keep her locked away until the final gasp of this life, kept in unending silence—

Serath glanced behind her, at the women gathered near the base of the wall amid the thicket, staring up at her. Most of them were young, wide eyes and open mouths, pure astonishment. Beyond them stretched the compound of the convent, her prison for the past nine years.

And on the other side of the wall, precious freedom: dark woods glimmering with red-fire moonlight, beckoning her.

She might break her bones in the fall. Surely she would. But they weren't close enough yet to stop her, and perhaps she could limp away to hide—

"Serath! Climb down immediately!" The prioress was coming so near, wrath and fury in every line of her.

Serath placed one hand on the bundle still slung over her shoulder, so that she would not lose it in her leap. A heated wind came and pushed her cloak and skirts in front of her, drenched red.

Someone screamed, and the girls on the other side of the wall shrieked again, pointing up into the sky.

Slowly, reluctantly, Serath looked up, past the blood moon, and saw the stars begin to fall around her, streaks of silver and gold against the indigo night, raining down around them. It was the bishop's shower of fire, a true portent, unfolding right now as dizzying threads of beauty shot across the sky.

Serath felt the last of her courage desert her. She

stood still on top of the wall, caught in the terrible splendor of the moment, watching the heavens fall to earth.

From the woods erupted noise and movement where there should be none, a commotion spilling out into the clearing by the wall. The turmoil became riders, many of them, men wrapped in metal and weapons, scarlet and stars glittering off them—the demons Alva predicted made awfully, completely real.

The prioress and her group stopped, clustered in a tight knot, gaping at the riders.

Moonlight revealed the crest on the shield of the leader: a red dragon writhing against black.

"Lord save us, it's the devil himself," gasped one of the nuns.

Serath gazed down at the apparition before her, surrounded by the falling sky, feeling strangely calm at this, what would be the end of everything after all.

The devil broke away from his group, taking his crimson steed up to the base of the wall.

"Serath Rune," said the devil, looking up at her, his face alternately masked and then lit by the blood light and the falling stars.

She heard the deep command in his voice, felt her body move in response. She sat down on the top of the wall, staring at him, and the unnatural breeze came again and played with her hair, loose and blacker than the night, bringing it up to dance around her face.

"Come," the devil said to her, and her feet obeyed him, beginning to descend the wall, and then her hands, and the climb was almost easy now, effortless. Simple.

She made it down in what seemed like no time at all, her feet touching the soft earth again, and then she turned to face him.

The devil towered above her on his demon steed, and the blood moon was his, and the streaking stars outlined him to show her only shape and form: huge and solid, utterly black but for the gleam of red on his shoulders and hair.

"Come," said the devil again, and he leaned down from his saddle to reach out one hand to her.

"She *is* cursed," whispered one of the women loudly.

There was nothing else to do. With all the nuns watching, still as death, Serath Rune accepted the devil's invitation and took his hand, allowing herself to be pulled up into his saddle in front of him.

The world below her now seemed so small, more distant even than it had from the top of the convent wall. The nuns of Saint Basilla's dwindled to a shrunken terror, each face only a pale oval of crimson.

The devil placed his arm around her waist, securing her against him. Serath took the bundle of cloth from her shoulder and moved it to her lap, holding it with both hands.

And he wheeled the demon horse around in the clearing, carrying her to his dark group and then beyond it, out into the blooded woods, the sky still hailing silver and gold around them.

Chapter Two

---⟨∞∞⟩---

*H*E HAD BEEN WAITING FOR HER TOO LONG.
To anyone else, the passing time had been no more than a day and a night, camped out in the woods surrounding the convent, a quiet scrutiny of the situation before the attack. Just a day and a night, and then suddenly the girl was there, and she was theirs.

But to Rafael of Leonhart, the waiting time had spun out to years—thirty-two of them to be exact, the sum of his entire life.

Thirty-two years of waiting to take this novice from her safe convent, thirty-two years to gain access to this girl and steal her away to suit his needs.

Thirty-two years waiting for the turn of this century, when the land of Alderich and the castle, and the wealth they represented, would become his. And now this granddaughter of his enemy would ensure it for him.

So while his soldiers had remained in the woods with him for that day and night, had met with him and discussed how best to breach the walls of a holy sanctuary, most of them felt mere hours slip by. But Rafe had felt his lifetime come sliding to a sudden and final countdown, each second bringing sharp anticipation to his blood.

And in the end, there had been no need to violate the sacred rules of the church. No need to force open the convent gate and take what he wanted, because—as God or the devil would have it—Serath Rune had come to him.

They had immediately noticed the commotion of women echoing beyond the walls. They had converged in silence, watching and waiting, ready to take advantage of whatever mishap this might be to rouse nuns on such a night.

When Rafe had heard her name being called, he knew the time was his—now, at last. He knew it so surely that he had already brought his mount up to the edge of the woods before the nuns emerged from the shelter of their walls. He was already in place by the time he caught sight of Serath, standing high and alone on that old stone wall, a figure of woman and dark mystery against the falling stars.

And now she was his.

Part of him doubted the perfection of it still—Serath Rune come to him so easily, sitting here in front of him so docile as they rode like madmen through the woods. Was she touched? Did she not understand what was happening to her?

Rafe had heard such contrasting things about the woman he now held. He had expected a shrew, a wild woman, filled with wrath and feminine wiles. . . .

A witch, it was said. A witch with the allure of an angel from Lucifer, with hair of pure ebony, and eyes to steal a man's soul—not that he was in any danger of *that*.

Still, that was what he had heard, and such persistent rumors were hard to dismiss.

But here was merely a woman—eighteen? nineteen?—of studied silence, making no move to escape him and his contingent of men, making no protest at all to her abduction. Granted, she was fair enough, or so he thought from what little he had seen of her features. And her form was pleasing, he considered, neither too plump nor too thin, the warmth of her body reaching him even past his chain mail.

Perhaps it wasn't her.

Rafe glanced down at her, glimpses of smooth skin beneath the shadows of the forest, her hair flowing down her back, around him, looking like . . . he didn't know what. Like magic, mayhap.

He hadn't truly seen her eyes yet, but yes, this was her. The nuns had been shouting her name for what seemed like ages before he had made it to the convent wall. But more than that, Rafael could *feel* that this was her, that this was the maiden Serath Rune, the key to his future. And it felt *right*.

The night was spinning on. Another thing to be pleased about, to see the last of that red moon. Slowly it was paling, turning bone white above them, and with it the shower of stars began to taper away to nothingness. Rafe felt something in him shift, grow even sharper and more precise. Everything was coming together as he had planned. Better.

He had Serath. Rafael broke into a fierce smile that no one could see, unable to help himself. He had her. And so he had Alderich.

"This way, my lord." His cousin Abram took the lead momentarily, showing Rafe the correct path amid the autumn grasses.

The woman in front of him started at the words. She

turned her head to see Abram, who spared her only one quick look before turning away.

Rafe followed the faint trail, pushing his mount to a gallop as they entered the smoothness of a valley. Serath's black hair flew up with the new wind, brushing against his chest, curling along his neck with surprising softness. Rafe ignored the sensation, concentrating on the land ahead of them.

This area was largely unfamiliar to him, which is why he allowed Abram to direct him. Rafe wasn't used to taking orders from anyone, but he was wise enough to exploit every advantage he had. It was how he had been raised, how he had survived. Abram had scouted the convent for him weeks ago, had traveled this route more than anyone in his contingent, and would guide them back to familiar territory on their way to their goal. But there was never any doubt about who was in charge of this group: Rafael had been their leader for years, and each man here would bow to his authority without question. It was the only reason they were with him now.

And although he allowed Abram to direct them all, Rafe thought privately that he could find Alderich no matter where he was in the world, even blinded and lost. It was a constant pull deep within him.

Come to me. Come home at last.

The valley ended, became a forest again filled with spindly pines and old oaks, and the horses slowed to manage the narrowed path. The light faded farther in; moonlight turned murky, clouded beneath the canopy of limbs.

Rafe slowed his steed even more, waiting for the rest of his men to catch up, and the figure in his arms shifted and then slipped down and away, leaving nothing but empty space where a warm woman had been. It happened so quickly and so effortlessly that it took him several seconds to comprehend it—as if she had transformed into the very air before him.

Dammit! Rafe reined in completely, looking left and right before catching sight of her running through the trees, swift and nearly gone already.

"Where did she go?" one of the men asked, dumbfounded.

He didn't bother to answer, though several others did, shouting and pointing at the diminishing shape. Rafe was already lunging after her, his stallion picking his way through the trunks of the trees with surety. She would not be able to outrun a horse.

There—there she was, sprinting through the woods, not bothering to look back at him at all. Thin moonlight slid over her in eerie slivers, flashes of movement against the night. Her path became serpentine, random, difficult for him to follow past ferns and brush.

Clever, Rafe thought. But it would not be enough to save her. She was nimble and supple in her movements— he almost admired her just for the sight of such grace fleeing before him, rushing through groves and bushes and low-hanging limbs. . . .

Then, all at once, she was gone. Vanished.

Rafe pulled in again, searching the shadowed woods, scowling. But there was nothing—no sign of her, no betraying rustle of leaves, no movement in the air, no flickering of light over a living figure. The woods fell into a dark stillness, deep and secretive and hushed. It was as if she had never set foot there at all.

Witchcraft.

The unwelcome thought took hold of him, refusing to be banished. He would not believe in this—but still it burned through him.

Rafael was not a man who placed his faith in the whispers of rumor. The world was solid and predictable as far as he was concerned: might conquered meekness. Intelligence ruled foolishness. Strength over weakness. Bravery over fear. Fact over hearsay. The land and seas and forests were of value because they were real; empty gossip was not. Serath Rune would not be a witch simply because such a thing was not credible, and thus was of no use to him.

But how to explain the fact that she had disappeared right in front of him? If Rafe had not been the man holding her in his own arms, he would not have believed that such a complete and sudden vanishing was possible. He had been trained in the tricks of warfare for years, had practiced and honed his skills at tracking and stealth until they resonated deep in his bones. How could an ordinary woman—a nun—so completely elude him?

Abram and others came up beside him, horses snorting, men talking over each other. Rafe held up one hand and his soldiers quieted instantly, watching him, turning to look for her.

"Serath," Rafael called, his voice low and carrying. "It does you no good to hide. We will find you. Come back, and save us this trouble. You will not be harmed."

Nothing. Either she didn't believe him—he couldn't blame her—or she truly was already beyond his reach, off to her own ensorcelled realm.

No, Rafe thought, the sharpness he had felt before churning into something close to anger. *She is here.*

"I've never seen a woman so fleet," whispered a soldier.

"A witch's trick," muttered another.

Rafe glared at the two men, who fell back, silent and chastened. He stood in his saddle, taking in every detail of the surroundings, letting his gaze linger on any spot that might hide a full-grown woman.

If it *was* a witch's trick, it was a damned good one.

And if she was not a witch—*she isn't,* he reminded himself firmly—at least she had wits enough to hide well when her enemy was so near.

Rafael dismounted, walking away from his soldiers, his steps slow and sure on the mossy ground. He examined the brush and dirt by his feet. None of it looked disturbed. He couldn't even spot any animal tracks. In fact, the woods before him appeared completely bereft of life. A slight tinge of disquiet crept up his back.

Leaves stirred above him; a light breeze brushed by, warm against his skin, rustling through the trees with quiet mockery of his efforts.

"I have no patience for this, my lady," he called out now, still walking. "I am pressed for time, and you are only serving to delay us."

Where? he thought, searching, searching. Where would she be? Where would *he* be, if he wanted to hide?

"It is not a good idea to displease me, Serath," he continued, still examining his surroundings, careful, methodical despite his underlying uneasiness. "You'll find me a much better man when I get my way."

Rafe stopped, closing his eyes, listening. The obvious came to him first: men behind him, completely silent now but for the creaking of saddles . . . the bare, metallic clinks of shields and swords against chain mail. Horses, a few shifting with impatience. Wind through pine needles, a ghostly murmur of sound . . .

. . . faint breathing. Muted, nearly imperceptible. Off to his left.

Pure relief made him release his own breath, close to a sigh. Rafe opened his eyes and found her immediately— or rather, found the spot he had figured to be just another bramble of bushes, exactly the same as the multitude of others that dotted the forest floor. He walked past it, the relief becoming close to exhilaration, then stopped again.

"Serath," he said, not raising his voice. "It was a good effort, my lady, but now it is done. Come back. My patience is ended."

And since she did not move, he reached through the brush and grabbed what was there—a mass of cloth, the woman beneath it erupting from the branches and dead leaves with complete and sudden fury, striking at him, struggling as he wrapped his arms around her and tried to contain the unexpected strength of her. It was a strangely silent battle, no sound from her other than the raggedness of her breathing, and his own harsh gasp as she landed a blow to his cheekbone.

"Enough!" Finally he had her restrained in front of him, her arms pinned, her tousled head just below his.

"Enough," Rafe said again, more subdued, and held her there until she was still at last, that blanket of silence about her shrouding them both.

There were leaves in her hair. They stood out against the black even in this dim light, papery ovals, a few twigs enmeshed in otherwise glossy locks. Her panting was slowing but the heat of her body seemed to grow against him, uncomfortably warm.

Rafael scowled again, fighting the unexpected appeal of this, a soft woman so near.

"Will you obey me, Serath Rune?" he asked her, his voice rough.

She said nothing, only turning her head to see beyond him, out into the wildness of the night.

"Do not force me to unpleasant measures, my lady," Rafe said now. "And do not doubt that I can be most unpleasant, indeed. I have no qualms about tying you up for the rest of the ride."

Slowly, slowly, he felt the tension from her body begin to fade, begin to melt, ever so slightly, against him. His own body responded with a completely unwelcome rush of hunger for her, for the sweet curves and ebony hair and the scent of some unknown spice that haunted her.

This was bad. He could not allow himself to feel for her, not even this basic, overwhelming lust. He could not allow anything so petty as passion for a woman to disrupt his plans, no matter how fair or enthralling she was.

"Will you obey?" he asked again, gritting his teeth.

And at last she nodded her head, just once, a short jerk. He turned her around in his arms, not releasing her completely, because he didn't trust a nod; he needed more from her—and he wasn't at all certain even that would be enough. But the absolute lack of sound from her was beginning to worry him. Could she be a mute?

Rafael tried to remember if any of the gossip had mentioned this. He thought not. But it might have happened since she had been sent to the convent, the result of some illness, perhaps, that had silenced her forever. Something inside him twisted painfully at the thought.

Serath kept her head lowered, the lines of her body stiff again.

"Say it," he instructed her. "Tell me."

Rafe saw her lips purse, a frown beneath the fall of hair that covered half her face. He still couldn't get a good look at her. She could have been anyone to him, a stranger, her face so carefully concealed—and this, oddly enough, bothered him most of all. He needed to see her, to hear her voice. He needed to know this mysteriousness about her could be banished.

"Tell me," he said once more, almost—but not quite—shaking her.

Her head lifted; she shook away the curling strands of hair. Rafael found himself staring into a pair of blue eyes paled with moonlight, a face of such delicate and unlikely beauty that it left him winded for a moment, mute himself.

I know you, Rafe thought, shock running through him.

Aye, there was a profound and telling recognition in him at the full sight of her, those eyes, that look. It was as if he had just discovered a part of himself in this person, a missing part that only now pained him for its loss.

He stood there gaping at her, knowing how inept it seemed, unable to help himself. She was a vision from a forgotten youth, a young woman with a face of timeless sorcery, dark brows, perfect nose, full lips, eyes surrounded by thick, black lashes. Her skin was utterly colorless in this light, her gaze the color of silver on heaven. She was the sun and the moon together, she was smoke and desire made real.

He could understand now the rumors that surrounded her, the slinking accusations that always seemed to accompany her name: if ever a witch might be born a noble maiden, this would be she. It was not merely the beauty of her features—it was all of her, the air about her, the tangle of black hair, the shape of her eyes, the moonlight glistening on her lips. Every bit of her spoke of magic and dark dreams, the promise of the forbidden to be revealed . . . and savored.

She had the face of an enchantress, yes, but the blue of her gaze told him something more: she had pride, and spirit—and what might have been fear. Rafe fought his reaction to that, the desire to comfort her.

He became suddenly, acutely aware of his hands on her, the burning heat of his palms against her upper arms, where he held her. The firm but giving flesh of her, so close her body nearly brushed his. He felt a kind of insanity from it, touching her, realizing all at once that here in his grip was more than a prize he had won; this was a woman, warmth and familiar succor, and he wanted nothing more than to pull her the rest of the way to him, to feel the whole of her pressed to his body. To bury himself in her.

It *was* a spell—a mortal spell to be sure, but a terrible and disastrous one, and Rafael of Leonhart was, for the first time in his adulthood, helpless to combat the emotions that raged through him.

Her frown came back, staring up at him, the arch of her brows turning doubtful and troubled. He watched, mesmerized, as her lips formed the shape of a word.

No sound came out.

She stopped, then gave a little cough before trying again.

"Who—" Her voice was raspy but lyrical, strangely sweet. At the one word she broke off with a slight cough again, blinking and looking away before reluctantly turning back to him.

"Who are you?" she asked at last, again with that rasping music.

Aye. She must have been ill. It would explain her pallor, the huskiness of her voice.

"Who else would I be?" he answered her quietly. "I am Leonhart, of course."

Her eyes widened—terror or amazement, he couldn't tell which. But then she did the last thing he would have expected: she laughed. It was odd and chilling, because she made no sound as she did it, only closed her eyes and leaned away from his grip, which did not loosen. Yet it *was* laughter, he was certain of it; real mirth that seemed coiled around her now, causing her head to tilt back. Moonlight caressed her face and shoulders while her body shook silently, a gorgeous smile offered up to the treetops.

"Is she mad?" asked Abram, hushed.

A few of his men had come to stand near during their exchange. Rafe hadn't even noticed.

Serath had ceased her laughter but shivers still ran through her body. Her head dropped forward again, one hand brought up to her face to hide it.

"Not mad," Rafe said. "Ill, I think."

"A witch's illness," said someone.

"A fever," Rafe snapped. "Nothing more. Mount up. We're off again."

He led her back to his stallion, had Abram help her up into the saddle and she settled there against him with a limpness that worried him, even though he told himself she would be fine. The granddaughter of Jozua Rune could not be made of anything but cold strength, after all.

Yet he found himself cradling her against him, softer than he had to be, gentler than he should have been, trying to make the ride easier on her. Serath Rune allowed him this, her head tucked down and low, her hair blowing again in the wind, silent once more, an enigma to him.

She seemed a creature of contradictions, one moment so poised and proud he might mistake her for his imagination, a winter faerie queen revealed before him high atop that convent wall. But in the next heartbeat she would change—youth and inexperience, novice—then back to enchantress, woman. And all of it was somehow amazing to him . . . each aspect of her held a dark, sparkling appeal.

Her hands clutched at the lumpy sack of cloth she had not dropped. Rafe tried not to notice how small and frail they seemed, phantom white in the darkness, slender and fine.

She is a tool, he reminded himself grimly. *Nothing more. A tool to gain that which should have been yours long ago. Do not forget it.*

Too late, too late, sang a voice in the back of his mind. Too late to ignore her, too late to pretend she was nothing but a hostage to him now.

Rafael had looked into her eyes. He had seen the bottom of his own soul reflected in them, and it had shaken him to the very depths of his black heart.

---

*W*HEN THEY STOPPED TO REST IT WAS BENEATH a sky that was glowing pink with morning. Already the land around Serath was foreign, blended to the steady sameness of woods and valleys. Her devil captor and his men were careful to skirt all the villages, even the small ones. But Serath had watched the sky and eventually found her guidance—Venus, shining bright on the horizon. And so she knew in which direction they headed. It gave her some comfort.

Leonhart had pushed them on until the horses were sweating and exhausted, and only stopped when the sun had broken free from the line of trees beyond them, blinding.

Serath was beyond exhaustion. She felt awake and nerveless, buzzing with edgy incredulity.

When the riders had first emerged from the red-fire woods last night, she had truly thought Satan himself had come for her. Yet it wasn't so; it was, in fact, even worse than that.

Of all the people to stumble across, she had to surrender herself to Rafael of Leonhart the very instant she had finally found freedom. But no, she thought, considering it. She had never actually touched freedom at all. At the verge of it—on top of that convent wall—she had stepped instead into a new sort of bondage, right into the grip of the second to last person she had ever wanted to see.

Laughter bubbled through her again and Serath fought to control it, to suppress the hysteria that wanted to rise up and take over her.

Rafael of Leonhart. Dear God. Surely he planned to kill her.

Yet he was doing a fine job of ignoring her now, moving among his men as they set up the camp, leaving her well guarded on the fringes of the activity. She could pick him out easily, even in this uncertain new daylight, even though the padded tunic under his hauberk was no different from any of the others around him, red and black mixed.

Brown hair, very dark . . . almost black, but not quite. When a shaft of sunlight fell on him she could see the chestnut tones of it, subtle and splendid. Shadowed gray eyes, rugged features—not handsome. Not really.

Not that she was any proper judge of men, Serath thought wryly. Save for the passing monk or bishop, she had not seen a man since entering the convent nine years ago; even those men she had seen had been mostly from a distance. And before that . . . before that, she preferred not to think about.

But none of those churchmen had held the command of this lone warrior. None of them were so tall, she thought, nor so menacing. None had his somber look, the unmistakable lines of power and determination shaping him. None had hair that brushed such broad shoulders, nor such big, rough hands. Chiseled lips. Eyes of a falcon, alert and brightly dangerous. Even a convent novice could recognize the air of threat about him.

She had seen him only once before in her life. And that was another time that didn't bear thinking about.

The campsite was simple and ready very quickly, men working with brisk efficiency, obviously well trained in this sort of task. The horses were contained—Leonhart's steed was not an unholy crimson, as she had initially thought, but rather a dappled silver—a group of sentries set up to patrol.

Serath stood with her hands clasped together in front of her, unmoving amid the commotion. A man guarded either side of her, both watching her as if she might wave her arms and fly up to the clouds at any moment.

Leonhart himself staked a small tent and then came over to her, taking her arm, leading her to it.

"You will rest here," he said, with the same effortless command in his voice that he used with his men. He held back a flap of the tent for her, waiting.

Serath didn't move. The strange buzzing in her grew lighter, lodged in her throat. To her surprise, the words came easily now. "If you mean to kill me," she said, "I ask that you do it now, and not later."

Nothing about him really changed, yet she could sense the impact of her words on him, a slight tightening of the lines around his mouth.

"Inside," he said, and that was all.

The strangeness hummed stronger, giving her the will to defy him. "Can you not grant me this simple request, Rafael of Leonhart? I would die now, in the open, rather than continue this game with you."

"I don't play games," he said, and pushed her lightly forward, into the tent.

She stumbled and landed on her knees against darkness and something soft, a blanket. Before she could move she felt him behind her, against her, and she pulled back a little more quickly than she meant to, suddenly frightened in spite of her bold words.

He was nothing but hulking shadow and shape in the false darkness of the tent, hunched over beneath the low ceiling.

"Sleep," he said to her. "You're going to need it. You have an hour."

And as soon as he said the words Serath felt a remarkable weariness settle into her, drenching her. She fought it, the feel of the soft blanket against her palms, beckoning her to slumber, to forget all this madness. . . .

"When do you mean to kill me, then?" she asked, resisting it all.

His face was masked to her, but she could make out the gleam to his eyes, no mercy at all.

"Not until after my meal," Leonhart replied. "I am loath to slay nuns on an empty stomach."

When she remained frozen at this, he made a curt gesture with one hand, exasperation in his voice.

"I did not take you to kill you, Serath Rune. I told you that you would not be harmed."

"The word of a killer," she retorted.

He said nothing in response; she thought she saw him shrug, and then he turned to leave.

"Wait—" Despite her effort at calm her voice cracked. He paused, outlined against the gradually increasing light outside the cloth. Serath's fingers found the blanket again, holding it up to her lap to disguise her nervousness.

"Then why did you take me?"

"I have need of you, lady."

She started back again, and this time there was no mistaking the flash of his teeth in the darkness, his wicked amusement.

"Need of you as a hostage, that is."

"You think to ransom me?" she asked, disbelieving. "To nuns?"

"Not nuns."

His face was still shaded with soft lavender shadows, yet clear enough now to show her the darkened gray of his eyes. He seemed to be examining her just as intently as she did him, from the farthest recesses of the tent.

"Then to whom?" she asked him, genuinely confused.

"Serath Rune," he said softly. "Lady of Alderich—to your grandfather. To Jozua Rune."

Her mind went smooth and blank, his words as simple and beyond her as the moon might be, or the joke of a worldly man. He could not be serious. He could not.

But he did not smile again, and there was no hint of jest about him, so the thing she had fought to repress overtook her again—her own silent laughter, lighter than the air, floating up and away from her, beyond her control.

He had her by her shoulders, suddenly too near too quickly, his face above her own, and she struck him away.

"Are you ill?" he asked, releasing her, not retreating.

To her grandfather. Sweet Mary, what a fix.

The laughter faded and Serath turned away from him, still holding the blanket.

"You waste your time with me, Leonhart. The Lord of Alderich will pay you nothing for me."

"I doubt that."

"I do not. You might as well kill me now as hope to gain coin from him in exchange for me."

He sat in front of her now, blocking the only exit with ease, one knee up, an arm casually resting across it. It was plain he did not believe her, and the idle drawl of his voice confirmed it.

"It's not your grandfather's coin I desire, my lady. I want far more than that."

She eyed him warily, waiting.

"I want everything," he said to her, slow and sure. "And it is everything that I will have from him. His home, his castle, his fields, and livestock. That is what you will gain me, lady. Everything."

She couldn't stop the smile again, and didn't try. "My grandfather despises me. He would as soon pay *you* coin to have me dead."

For a moment she thought she had convinced him. He remained motionless, staring at her, the light around him slowly taking on a golden glow. His gaze was closed, speculative.

Serath had no further words to offer, though she tried very hard to think of something. She feared she had spent so much time in silence that she had lost the sense of her own voice, of what keen power sounds might yield. So instead she merely met his stare, her smile fading as the uncertainty washed over her again.

She was weary. She was sore and spent, and the past few hours had been nothing short of incredible. Perhaps she was dreaming.

It wasn't like her to dream so vividly—Serath couldn't recall a time in her life when she had felt such things so clearly in a dream. But this might be the first time, for how else could she explain what was happening to her now?

It could not be Rafael of Leonhart sitting across from her. She could not be his prisoner, trapped in this tent, escaped from her convent only to be stolen by the demon-man himself.

The demon stirred, roused from his study of her with just a dismissive turn of his head. Without another word he rose and left the tent. Serath found herself alone, still clutching the blanket, sinking slowly and wondrously to the ground, where she tucked an arm beneath her head and breathed in the scent of the rich earth.

Her eyes closed, and more dreams came.

Chapter Three

⸺ ◯〰〰◯ ⸺

SHE WAS ALONE IN THE WOODS, STRETCHED OUT
on the ground with her hands behind her head. Serath was
wearing the new bliaut she had been given to mark her eleventh
birthday a sennight ago, a fine gown of rose and violet with
golden piping. She should most likely not be lying on the ground
in it. She would be dirty, her gown stained. Nurse would be
angry.

But Nurse was always angry with her, Serath decided, staring up at the sky through the trees. So what did it matter if it
were over the gown or her tardiness or merely the tone of her
voice? It took nearly nothing to incur her wrath, in truth.

Heaven was heavy and close, gem blue past shifting leaves of
orange and scarlet above her. It felt nice to be alone, away from
the castle, away from all the other people of Fionnlagh. Away
from Nurse, with her quick slaps and constant scolds. Away from
the other children, who would not play with her unless Nurse
first lectured to them in hushed whispers and much shaking of her
finger.

Away, most of all, from Grandfather, who seemed to turn red with rage each time he saw her, no matter how prettily she behaved.

Her brother Raibeart, sole ally in the maze of her life, was gone on a hunt. He would not return for days. So why not sneak away from the castle, and steal some time for peace and lazy dreaming?

The day was lovely indeed, with crisp autumn changes surrounding her, and crackling leaves to nestle in, and Serath supposed that she must have drifted off because when she woke up, she was no longer alone in the small forest clearing.

She sat up too quickly, making her head spin some, but when it cleared she saw the same scene as a moment before:

Strange men in front of her, immense and tight-lipped, standing in a rough line just past the trees. They were not from Fionnlagh, she could see that right away—their colors were wrong, red and black tunics, not the familiar blue and white. They did not bow their heads to her, as the serfs of Fionnlagh still did, short nods of deference to her station that they could not ignore. These men simply stared at her, and Serath stared back, appalled, a knot of fear expanding in her stomach.

She should run. She should scream and flee back to the castle, back even to Grandfather, who would protect her, and banish these scary men. Yet she did nothing, and the men did nothing, and the only movement around them was the fall of a single crimson leaf, floating in slow circles to the ground.

The men parted; someone new came forward, no farther than where the others stood. He was slightly younger than the rest— but even in this youth he carried about him a manner of powerful fierceness. He held something in his arms, an oddly bent shape covered with a rough blanket.

"Girl," he said to her, in a terrible and fearsome voice. Serath couldn't stop staring at his face, so dark and forbidding, gray eyes like a clouded night.

"Girl of Fionnlagh," said the man. He knelt and placed

his burden on the ground, amid the leaves near her feet. "This belongs to you."

She tore her gaze from his, down to the lumpy cloth, a shape that looked too familiar. The knot of fear bloomed to something uglier within her—quick painful panic—her heart was beating too fast, she could not take a full breath, she didn't want to see what this was—

The man with the nightcloud eyes paused, his hands stilling over the form for a bare second; then he pulled back the cloth, and Serath saw the blank and white face of her brother Raibeart, his head at an awkward angle, his mouth and eyes open, vacant.

She felt her heart stop. She felt the world stop. She felt her entire self separate from her body, stunned and shrunken, even as she crawled forward on her knees to him, touched him with her own hands.

Raibeart. Dead. Raibeart, Raibeart . . . her only hope, her only love, dead, dead, dead—

"We found him on our land like this," said the man, watching her, not moving. "No sign of his horse nearby, although there were prints. His scabbard is marked with the emblem of Alderich, so tell your master this. Tell him this boy died by no hand of ours."

"Raibeart," Serath whispered, the only thing in her head.

"Girl!" The man used his hand to lift her chin, to make her see his face. "Do you understand me? Tell the Lord of Alderich this lad died alone on our lands. We think he was thrown from his horse. Can you remember this?"

She was empty and dry, staring at the stranger, unable to comprehend.

"He is dead?" she asked, a foolish question, but she couldn't help it—she knew the only answer but it couldn't be true. . . .

Something in the man's face gentled.

"Aye, girl. He is dead."

She shook her head at this, yanking away from his touch,

throwing her body down over her brother's, her cheek pressed to the coldness of his.

"No, no," Serath was murmuring, stroking him, "no, no, Raibeart. . . ."

After a long while the man stood, then moved away from her. A part of her heard this, heard him confer with the others in a low voice, but it was so distant. So unreal.

"Listen to me, child," said the man to her, crouching again in front of her. "Go back to Fionnlagh. Fetch some men to carry this boy, and give your master my message. Tell him Rafael of Leonhart told you these things, and swears by them. We'll not set foot in his demesne, so you're going to have to go get help."

She looked up at last, bewildered, the whole of her world taken and turned utterly wrong, incomprehensible. Perhaps the man could see it, for he softened his tone.

"I'm certain it was an accident," he said now. "The boy should be buried in consecrated ground. Remember that, as well."

He waited a moment, examining her with his nightcloud gaze, then turned and walked away with his men, all of them melting into the depths of the forest.

Serath looked down again at the form beneath her. She cupped Raibeart's face with her hands and felt the dry heaves begin, his death at last coming real.

Remember, remember, remember. . . .

HE LET HER SLEEP UNTIL THE SUN WAS NEARLY at the apex of the sky.

It was much longer than he should have, Rafe knew. It could prove to be a dangerous delay, although he didn't think the nuns of that tiny convent would be able to do much more than protest to the nearest church council about the loss of their novice. It was highly doubtful there was any serious pursuit.

No, it was not what lay behind them that burned at Rafael; it was what lay ahead. Alderich was not far from them now. He hated the delay. He hated every second spent out of sight of Fionnlagh Castle, away from the old man secluded away up there, plotting the ruin of all that should be Rafe's.

Yet when he went to awaken Serath she was so deeply asleep that even his touch to her shoulder did nothing. The cloak she wore had come undone, spread beneath her in a fan. She slept on her side, hands curled up beneath her chin, lips parted, face calm. There was a smudge of dirt over her cheek. The blanket he had set aside for her half-covered her hips, draping her figure with unintentional allure.

There was an air of captured innocence about her now, overlying the sensuality he had found in her last night. She looked less like a witch in this moment than merely a remarkably fair young woman, sleeping soundly, gone to her dreams. Rafe had pulled back, reluctant to disturb her, then annoyed at his reluctance.

She would drowse the day away if he allowed it, no doubt. They had to leave soon. Everyone was ready to go, especially him.

But he had retreated from the tent, and Serath slept on, immersed in her innocence. When Abram and the rest had looked at him expectantly, Rafe turned his back on them, refusing to explain.

He found himself contemplating the ripped, bulky bundle of cloth Serath had carried with her. When they camped he had taken it from her, handed it off to someone else, and now he saw it again by the rest of his things near his mount.

Rafael walked over to it and knelt down, untying the

series of knots to open the cloth. She had secured it well but it was a simple thing to undo, the rough material falling away in tight wrinkles. Inside he found what appeared to be another gown—pale gray, like the one she wore now—and a few bits of food.

"No weapons," he noted out loud, for the benefit of the men who had come to stand around him.

"Check for charms, my lord," suggested Abram.

"Witching things," added Nils.

"Such as what?" asked Rafe mildly. "Do you expect her to carry a bag of hexes with her, mayhap?"

"Stones," stated Gerold. "Witches cast stones. Look for those."

"Nightshade, for poison," suggested another man.

"Dead men's bones!" added yet another, prompting uneasy murmurs of agreement.

Rafe stood. "There is none of that here. She is no witch."

"She is the daughter of Morwena," said Gerold, looking sullen but stubborn. "You cannot deny it, my lord."

"Why should I deny it?" Rafe kept his tone even, but many of the men noticed the edge of ice to it. A few stepped back. "She is indeed the daughter of Morwena Rune. And Morwena Rune was burned for witchcraft by the father of her dead husband. Think you that I am unaware of the doings of my enemy, soldier?"

"No, my lord," said Gerold hastily.

"Perhaps then you doubt my judgment, to think I would bring a witch so readily to us, one who might harm us all?"

"No, my lord," said the man again, eyes lowered.

Rafe paused, letting the silence speak for him, until the soldier began to fidget and flush red, eyes still averted. No one else moved.

"I want no more talk of this," Rafael said at last, to all of them. "I know the rumors. I know what we've all heard about this woman. You are my men, and you are with me because you are proven warriors. I am leading us to Alderich. Serath Rune will help us gain what is ours. She is only a woman, blood and flesh, same as any other. No witch."

He met each look with his own, until he was satisfied that all of them understood him. It would not do to have grown men cowering from this novice nun. It would not do to have them shy from her glances, giving her power. He had too much at risk to let it all unravel now because of this woman, no matter what her history.

Rafael bent to retrieve her bundle, and as he did so something hard slipped from the layers of the gray gown, falling to the grass. Several of the men began to mutter.

"A charm," hissed someone.

It was a rectangular stone of some kind, no longer than his thumb, thin and smooth with a strange silver luminescence. Two flattened bars of gold bracketed it, holding it in place, many tiny rubies set amid them in a looping pattern. Rafael picked it up, keeping it in the sunlight.

His mind found the name for it, an unexpected recollection: *moonstone*. And then something more associated with it, women's chatter about talisman jewels—something about prophecies. And lovers.

"Jewelry," he announced, showing them the back of it, where a straight pin had been fixed to the metal. "Naught but a woman's thing."

"It is mine!" came a clear call. Rafe turned to see Serath emerge from the tent, her hair wild and twisted around her, her gown creased. She began to run toward him, but two guards grabbed her arms and held her back.

"Give it to me!" Serath demanded, tugging at their

grip, her eyes on Rafe. She sounded impassioned, almost distraught. He felt himself unwillingly responding; to overcome this reaction he deliberately turned his back to her, dropping the bit of jewelry back into the cloth of her spare gown. His men watched, silent, their glances going from him to her to him again.

Rafe gathered up the bundle and walked to where she stood. He nodded to the guards, who released her, stepping back.

"Awake, I see," Rafe said to her.

Serath snatched the bundle from his hands, searching until she found the strange stone. Her fingers closed over it, rough possession.

"I wasn't going to take it from you," he said.

Her look was scathing, regal cold. He could see now, in the full flush of daylight, that her eyes were a true, striking blue, not the pale reflection he had seen last night. They glowed against the stark white of her face, beneath the ebony of her brows and lashes, intensely beautiful.

He had seen eyes like hers before, he knew it. Rafe frowned, trying to place the memory.

"So the killer tells me he is no thief. How amusing." Her voice was anything but amused.

It stung, sharply so, and Rafael answered her in a bored tone to conceal it. "I am pleased to entertain my lady. But since it appears you are full rested"—he let his eyes roam up and down her disheveled form, insulting—"it would please me further to have you mount up. We have much ahead of us."

"Kill me, killer," she replied.

Rafael felt the beginning of a headache coming over him. "Mount up."

"I'll not travel anywhere with you, demon-man," Serath declared, hugging her pathetic cloth rags to her.

Rafe eyed her wearily. It had been a very long while since he had slept. He had given her the luxury he had denied himself and most of the other men, and right now it was wearing hard upon him.

She stared up at him, a brittle smile in place, as if she actually expected him to follow her ridiculous order. The blue of her eyes was very bright.

"If you do not mount up," said Rafe carefully, "then I will bind you, Serath, and toss you over my horse, and we will ride that way, if you prefer. It matters not to me. You decide."

The edges of her smile dimmed, apprehensive, and again he watched that fleet change come over her, from winter faerie queen to young girl, vulnerable and pained.

It found some tender spot in him he didn't want to consider. The woman was already pushing him to insanity.

"Mount up!" he ordered again, impatient. The men around them dispersed, going back to the horses. He raised one brow to her, an unspoken choice, and watched her wrestle with the idea of her rebellion.

"I have close to two hundred men with me total," he said indifferently. "Scattered from here all the way to Alderich. No matter where you might think to go, my lady, I will find you."

"Alderich?" she echoed, and he thought he saw that bafflement in her again.

"Aye."

"You're going to Alderich?"

"*We* are," he corrected her.

"But—why should you go there?"

Rafael took a step nearer to her; she didn't move away. "Because it pleases me to do so."

It was a challenge, Serath knew. He meant to test her will, to bend her into following his order merely because he ordered it. He had come and captured her and ridden halfway across the kingdom with her, and now—when she thought she had at least understood his reasoning—he claimed to be taking her to Alderich instead of his own home, where surely it would be best to hold a hostage. It was completely mystifying to her, and just as completely dismaying.

Her mother's brooch was warm in her hand, the familiar corners of it a comfort. She held it tighter, keeping it close as she met the demand of his stare.

He looked so much like the young man he had been all those years ago, that fateful day in the woods, she thought abruptly. His face was almost unchanged, a few more lines, his hair slightly longer, his tan deeper. Only his eyes remained exactly as she remembered, the color of clouds at night.

He moved suddenly, one hand coming up to her face, surprising her. Before she could pull back she felt his touch against her cheek, a gentle brush—heated and strangely welcome—and then it was gone.

"Dirt," he explained, unsmiling.

Serath felt a slow blush begin, cursing herself. She looked down, away from him, ashamed that such a small thing from this man could provoke such a strong response in her.

"Why Alderich?" she asked again, and was sorry that her voice was so soft.

He waited to reply, but finally said, "Your grandfather has barricaded himself in Fionnlagh Castle."

This caused her to look up again, startled. "What?"

"Jozua Rune has locked himself in my castle," said Leonhart. "You are going to help me get him out."

She reacted more to his tone than his words, his confident assurance. "It's not your castle yet."

His smile was short and mirthless. "A matter of

weeks, Serath. A small amount of time until the *Christes masse,* and the turning of the century. And then all of Alderich falls to me."

"I know the legend," she said, biting. "Your wicked family tricked my own to gain what was not yours."

"Hardly a legend," he replied evenly. "And that is hardly the way it came about. Your family was the one that did the tricking, Serath, but that is finally about to be remedied."

"My family! Yours was the brother that complained to the king, betraying his own kin to steal the land and the castle—"

"To rightfully *regain* the land and the castle that he had built *along* with his brother—your own ancestor who turned on his elder brother and baldly lied to the king, claiming all the labor as his own. My ancestor was merely trying to claim his rightful share. It is fitting that we take all the land now, after these long years of want due to your treachery."

"You are utterly mad!"

"And you are stalling. But it amounts to this, my lady: I don't give a damn who stole it from whom. However you want to believe the story went, the fact remains that our ancestors had an agreement with a king, and very soon that agreement is to be fulfilled. It is certainty, pure and plain. It is law by command of our own king now. Alderich and Fionnlagh Castle will be mine. I'll not have Jozua Rune destroy what I've so long waited for."

Serath shook her head, irritated. "As I've said before, you waste your time with me, demon-man. I have no sway over my grandfather. I'll not go."

Rafael took her arm. "You seem to think you have a choice about this, Serath. I assure you, you do not." She tried to pull away from him and he tightened his grip, holding her easily. "I've told you your options. Come bound, or come free. But you will come, lady. I promise you that."

Two hundred men—a good portion of them surrounding her now, staring down at her from their mounts with awful, empty faces. Two hundred reasons to walk with Leonhart to his own giant silver steed and ride back to the place that used to be her home.

Oh, God. Alderich. She never wanted to see it again.

Leonhart gave a low whistle and the silver beast came forward, standing ready. Serath gazed up at Rafael and he released her arm, turning to mount his horse. When she looked around a young man knelt in front of her, forming a cup with his hands. Rafael leaned down from the saddle, one hand out, exactly the same position he had held when he stole her from the convent. His face was impartial, but she could already see the controlled victory in his eyes.

Two hundred men.

Serath lifted her chin, stepped forward, and reached for his hand.

ⲚOW SHE KNEW THE LAND, ALL RIGHT.

As they rode it grew more and more familiar, becoming wilder, more lush, the mountains steeper, necklaces of fog draping them. She had been born amid these hills, and despite all that had happened, some part of her still considered herself a child of them.

Too bad no one else from Alderich did.

So many years had passed since Serath had seen these slopes, these trees. When she had traveled here last it had been under the protective cover of a litter, hidden away, as if the shame of her face and her past could be so easily concealed.

She had been sent from Fionnlagh in punitive silence, and now—with so many years of silence to her credit—it seemed she was destined to return the same way.

Rafael of Leonhart disdained to speak to her. She had tried to reason with him again on this journey, had tried sense and logic, and then heart and emotion to reach him, and all of it had failed.

He had merely kept his resolute look, his arms still firm around her, his hair sometimes grazing her cheek. He led them on while ignoring her, and all the other men had pretended she was not there, not trying to enlighten them with the rediscovered power of her voice:

"I will be of no help to you," she had said to him. "I will hinder you. I am to your disadvantage," she had tried.

Then, "They will not deal with you! They will not want to see me!"

And, "Release me now and save yourself your precious time!"

At last, the final, desperate truth: "Don't you understand? I am not welcome at Alderich! They hate me there!"

But Leonhart had done nothing, said nothing, remained as solid and vexing as any boulder in a field. His horse plodded on, taking her closer and closer to that dreaded place.

"Simpleton," Serath had cursed at him, and then fell into a bitter silence herself, focusing on the mists around them, the winter pines still green.

Yes, she knew this land. In spite of all the years away it still thrilled her blood, as familiar as the imprint of a vital memory. She remembered this air, its particular scent— ocean and fields, bluebells and clover. Even now, with most of the land turned gold and orange and brown, she could catch the faint ghostly bouquet of summer, and those meadow flowers.

Or not. Perhaps she was only wishing it into being—as firmly as she wished not to be here at all.

She saw the furrowed fields first, neat plots of land divided into squares, straight lines in brown dirt. Slowly they grew closer and closer together, the trees regimented into long clusters.

Leonhart felt more comfortable once they reached Alderich, Serath noted; he was no longer avoiding the tell-tale signs of civilization. Along with the fields there were occasional huts of sod and thatch—curiously silent, no smoke wafting up from the roofs, no movement at all, not even from chickens or pigs.

Leonhart and his men passed without pause, a few examining the huts as they rode by, none slowing.

Serath alone frowned, twisting in the saddle, straining to see, until Leonhart moved her back into place again with one arm, his look ominous.

More fields, more huts, even whole villages. No people. No animals.

The hills here were sharper still, and the land had been worked to accommodate them, steep ledges like stair steps winding down the sides of them, rings of soil amid the dried grass and trees.

Still no people. No shepherds, no flocks feeding on the hay she could see fallow in some of the fields, unharvested.

She remembered the bishop, his words of doom about the future. Perhaps it had happened here already. Perhaps the Lord had come to Alderich and taken everyone in preparation for the end, just as she had been told as a child, and only they were left—she, alone with these savage men of Leonhart, cursed and belonging to the devil, left abandoned and behind in the ill-fated world. . . .

Serath closed her eyes, fighting the bud of panic in her. It couldn't be true. She would not believe it was true.

To be sentenced to spend an eternity with this man, with his unyielding gaze and his hard arms and devil's looks, his lips so finely shaped, his form so solid and pleasing—

Her eyes snapped open again. What was she doing?

"Halt!" It was Leonhart, shouting just behind her ear. Serath winced and shifted away from him, but his arm tightened around her. He looked to one of his men, still holding her firmly.

"Abram," he said, and the other man dismounted, walking ahead of them down the road.

Serath saw it now, and wished she had not: pools of blood in the road; dirtied wool; terrible, severed shapes. She turned her head away but not before seeing the glazed eyes of a lamb, most of its head already eaten.

"It's fresh, my lord," reported the man. "Not more than a few hours dead, by my guess. Two ewes and a lamb."

Serath kept a hand over her eyes, refusing to look again.

The man behind her continued breathing steadily, no sign of disquiet over this gruesome sight.

"Serath," he said to her, his voice calm. "Do you know of wolves at Alderich?"

She nodded, her head still lowered.

"That sounds right," said the other man, who must have walked closer to them. She could see the lower part of his hauberk, his boots stained dark red on the soles. "There are tracks heading back into the woods. Must have been a pack, my lord—five or more. We probably ran them off just now."

Again Leonhart said nothing, everything about him hard and composed. Serath waited, along with the other man, until finally her captor said, "Move on."

Abram walked away, out of her sight, and she felt Leonhart press his heels to his mount. Serath closed her eyes once more and kept them that way, until she hoped they were long past the carnage.

Carefully she opened her eyes, looking first to the sky, then cautiously lower, seeing only the empty road again, the barren fields and the mountains and the deep woods, where wolves would live.

"Where was the shepherd?" she heard herself ask.

Leonhart did not reply.

"Why weren't the sheep protected?" Serath went on, almost to herself. "Why didn't the shepherd at least salvage the loss?"

"Because he is not here," Leonhart said at last.

"Where would he be?" Serath asked, drawn into this mystery despite herself.

Leonhart gestured to the misted lands beyond them.

"Out there," he said simply. "Gone."

THEY RODE BOLDLY INTO THE VILLAGE AT THE base of the cliffs, right into the center of the town. Serath remembered it to be a prosperous place, filled with people and animals, dogs chasing sheep, cats chasing chickens. Children chasing all of them.

She remembered the well, its vine-crusted sides rising up from the cobblestones, the simple bucket and rope that watered the population of this village named after the castle it served.

Out of habit she looked up into the cliffs slanting above the village, finding the glowing white stone of

Fionnlagh Castle, unchanged from her memory, a perfect wish amid the autumn colors of the land around it. It was set near the top of the mountain, remote and starkly radiant even on this clouded day. A thin sweep of steel blue hugging the cliffs beyond was all that she could see of the ocean the castle overlooked.

She used to think it beautiful, with its walls of nearly pristine white, a thing of rarity and exquisite proportions against the dramatic frame of the cliffs and sky. A twisted path climbed up the mountain, weaving through the trees to reach it—the only way in or out of this stronghold of Alderich.

The land of forgotten dreams, it was called. Yet Serath had never forgotten it in her own dreams, no matter how hard she tried.

She used to be proud that her ancestors had labored to tame the land and build this castle. In her girlish fancies she imagined they had taken the very foam from the ocean to create its form, that pearls lined its crenellated towers, that seashells made up its turrets and eaves. It was indeed an awesome thing to behold. Even the freemen and serfs in the villages boasted of it to their neighbors, proud of the castle as if it were their own.

But there was no one here to do that today.

The village of Fionnlagh, like all the others they had passed in Alderich, lay deserted, fallen to empty brush and winds, doors and windows gaping open to reveal nothing but blackness.

Leonhart and the others gathered near the well, the horses' hooves very loud on the stones—the only sound around them.

Serath was helped down by the same man that boosted her up, and then Leonhart was right behind her, holding her arm again. His men milled about, searching the area without moving too far from their horses, cautious in this unnatural place.

Far in the distance a pair of bells began to toll, unearthly and remote. As one the soldiers looked up to the castle on the hill.

"Mayhap it's a ghost," Serath suggested heartlessly, and Leonhart gave her his grim stare. She looked away, lifting one shoulder to hide the effect he had on her. "Grandfather has always had the hours tolled."

"Abram," said Leonhart in that tone that meant action, and the other man responded, brushing past her, taking a group of soldiers into the nearest cottage. They came out again almost immediately, shaking their heads. They moved on to the next home.

Leonhart shifted his grip to her hand, pulling her with him as he walked toward a building at the other end of the village, more men behind them. Serath moved as quickly as she could, her legs sore from all the riding, her feet tingling.

He stopped before the largest structure in the village—the tavern, Serath recalled. All the windows were shuttered, the door firmly closed.

Rafael pushed on it; nothing happened. He pushed again, harder—still nothing.

"Locked," he said, throwing a glance over his shoulder to the other men. He released her hand and Serath stepped backward, until someone took hold of her arm and kept her still.

Leonhart turned back to the door, motioning to some of his soldiers to follow suit, and on his mark they threw themselves at the aging wood, causing a great crashing sound.

Serath thought she heard voices from inside the tavern, but couldn't be certain, because the soldiers were at it again, and after a few tries the wood buckled completely.

Two of them kicked down the remains of it; the rest stood in a half circle behind them, swords up, watchful.

The last of the shattered wood fell to the dirt, bringing up a swirling cloud of dust and splinters.

Rafael drew his sword and went inside. A score of others followed and the rest crowded close, trying to see, blocking her own view.

There was a terrible cry, and then many of them—cries from men and women both, children too. Words were lost to her, but over the chaos Serath heard the familiar tones of her enemy, loud and commanding, still calm, still cool. Eventually the other noises quieted, but for a faint, occasional sobbing.

"Outside," Leonhart was saying. "Everyone, outside. You are safe, I promise it. We will not harm you."

The soldiers around the doorway backed up. Serath saw the huddled shapes of the villagers emerge, cowed and shaking, a few of the women still weeping. Children, red-eyed and staring, clung to their parents. It had to be close to a hundred people, perhaps even more, and she wondered how they had managed to fit themselves into the space of the tavern.

When the last of them had come out into the daylight, Leonhart himself followed, stern and so tall he had to duck away from the frame of the door.

"People of Fionnlagh," he shouted, and every face turned to him. "I am your new master. I am Rafael of Leonhart, and if you are good and hardworking folk, you have naught to fear from me."

If the circumstances had been less dire, Serath might have laughed at so obvious an error. Announcing his identity caused nothing but further alarm among the crowd. A swell of sound came from them, the people gasping and turning to one another, jabbering in fear and confusion. The sobbing grew louder and a few of the children took it up, wailing. The men were trying to get their women in the center of a ragged circle. A few carried sticks, hoes. Serath shook her head in pity.

"I will not harm you," Leonhart repeated firmly, the steel of his sword shining deadly bright in his hand.

"Spare the women!" one of the men shouted, and a few of his fellows took up the cry. "Spare the women! Spare our children!"

"I am going to spare *all* of you!" Leonhart yelled, and then remembered to lower his sword. At last they subsided to a low murmuring, still clustered together against the threat of the soldiers.

"Peace, good folk," he said now. "I am here to help you, in faith. You are my own people—you will be, soon enough. I have no quarrel with you."

They did not believe him. It was clear to Serath even from this distance. She could see it in the way they hunched their shoulders, the way they stared at one another and the ground but never at Leonhart himself. And certainly she could not blame them—they had heard the same stories she had, that this man was nothing less than a minion of the devil, out to rape and kill and destroy all he could of Alderich, heralding the end of the world.

Aye, everyone knew the appearance of Leonhart was an irrevocable omen of the Last Days.

Perhaps the demon-man knew what had been said of him, as well. He turned, looking past the crowd until he found her, and then he deliberately sheathed his sword.

"I grant you peace, Fionnlagh," called out Rafael of Leonhart. "My men and I will do no harm here. To prove it to you, I bring you back one of your own. I bring to you the very daughter of your land." And he lifted his empty hand and pointed straight to Serath.

The people turned, following his gesture. Serath took

a single deep breath, gazing back at them, emotionless, unmoving.

A woman raised one trembling arm and pointed to Serath as well—then she screamed. It was shrill and stunning, and it provoked a rash of others, piercing cries of sheer horror and panic from the people as they caught sight of her. The crowd pushed away from her, everyone howling now, mindless and terrified. They rushed past Leonhart, back to the shelter of the tavern, shoving away the soldiers who attempted to restrain them. Rafael stood back, arms raised, battered but not falling.

In seconds there was only him and his men and Serath left in the courtyard, and a kind of whimpering silence coming from the depths of the tavern.

Serath met the astounded look of her captor.

"I told you," she said.

Chapter Four

———— ⟨ww⟩ ————

A<small>T NIGHT AT LEONHART, THE CHILD RAFAEL</small> would fall asleep listening to the mournful sound of the wind skimming over the bare rocks that made up his homeland. It became a lulling constant for him over the years, never ceasing, but for some reason with the setting of the sun it grew particularly noticeable.

It had comforted him in the small chamber he had shared with his cousins and comrades growing up. It had sung to him below the frequent arguments of his parents when everyone else was abed. It had become almost a friend, or at least no enemy—the one fixed certainty in his life, when all else seemed as stable as quicksilver cupped in a palm.

When he left Leonhart, it was the wind he had missed more than anything. Just that—the steady, sweet groan of it, echoing tones that crossed miles of inland plains to reach the rough fortress that held the population of his land.

Traveling all those years, wandering the country, meeting peasants and princes and rogues as reckless as himself, Rafe had only to close his eyes to remember that sound, and the strange solace it could bring him.

Wind had no serious barriers at Leonhart, nothing to push against there besides the rocks; only flat fields, and wasted soil, and thin crops that never offered up too great a yield. Were it not for the generosity of the sea, there could be no doubt his kin would have starved several times over.

In fact, Leonhart was as different from the land it bordered as could be. At almost the exact line of the boundary between Leonhart and Alderich, trees grew in abundance, the soil turned fertile again. To stand on that line was to gaze at all that the people of Leonhart had been cheated from—sweet pastures and hills, fine crops, clear streams and pure lakes. It was a forbidden paradise to his own empty purgatory.

It was why he had left; it was why he remained away. Almost immediately after Rafael had reached the age of twenty-two, his father had died, leaving behind a legacy of a land and people impoverished. Rafe had realized years before that there was only one obvious answer to their woes, and once his father was gone, there was no one to stop him from implementing it.

He had gathered together the hardiest of his cousins and friends and set out to express some of the anger that had marked his life. Aye, and they had done a fine job of it, forming one of the most feared bands of mercenaries the kingdom had ever seen.

Or so he had heard.

To Rafe they were no different than any of the other men roving the countryside, eager for battle and reward. For a price they would join lords in skirmishes, seize strongholds, or release the hostages they took. They gained coin and a reputation for fury, which suited Rafe exactly.

If he ever grew tired, if he ever felt worn, he deliberately thought of the wind, the crops, the hunger of Leonhart—and it carried him on.

The passing of the years had offered Rafe an unexpected gift: for all the envy of Alderich that dwelled in his heart, he came to the realization that no matter where he roamed across the lands, he was a stranger, and always would be. There was only one place in this vast world that truly belonged to him at that time—Leonhart. Despite its desolation, it was his birthright, and his obligation.

The rewards he and his soldiers gathered they sent back home, each man keeping only a small portion for himself. For as many times as he let the jealousy of Alderich consume him, Rafael made efforts to ensure the care of Leonhart twice over. Every drop of blood spilled was for the people—families and friends—still there. Every day, every night, was devoted to them, to enrich what he and his men had left behind. Seed for the land, livestock, coin. . . .

And weapons. Many, many weapons, to defend a land with an absent lord from predatory mercenaries, from men just like him. The irony of that observation was not wasted on Rafael. Aye, he was always certain to send weapons when he could.

The reports that came back to him from his demesne were gratifying for all of them. The last ransom had ensured his people enough food for the winter. The successful siege of a baron's castle had earned extra clothing for each family. The next battle might bring a measure of surplus grain, or a few new horses, even cows.

It was a slow growth for Leonhart, but then, Rafael had always expected it to be. They would never be as wealthy as Alderich, and he knew it. But each gain was a satisfaction for Rafe and his soldiers. Each new year meant he was one year closer to his destiny—Leonhart and Alderich united. Once that happened, his people would not suffer want again.

Sometimes he would imagine what his mother might be doing with her portion of the bounty. New dresses, perhaps. Jewels. All the things she had claimed to deserve but had never had.

He hoped she had them now. The price was dear enough.

They lived short lives, many of his group; Rafe had buried more men than he cared to remember, and he regretted each loss. Yet more would arrive from home—always more kin ready for adventure—and somehow it kept their band together. They were united in pride and a sort of desperate hope for a better life. It was a dangerous existence and it was foolhardy. But it kept everyone fed.

Sacrifice and pain and miserable death. But it was always worth it. It had to be.

Ten years of that. Enough time to thicken the calluses on his hands from the hard hilt of his sword. Enough time to lose three horses, two of them to battle, and one from simple exhaustion. Enough time to burn off some of the raging helplessness he felt whenever he considered the plight of his family, his people, trapped back at Leonhart.

And enough time to let the century come cascading down to its inevitable conclusion—the time he had been waiting for his entire life.

It was a message from his mother that brought Rafael back toward home. A strange message delivered by word of mouth, no doubt garbled by the series of men who passed it along until it found him in a port town one day at the tip of the southern coast, watching his men get drunk to celebrate some victory or another.

Hie you to Alderich, his mother had commanded. *Stop Jozua Rune.*

He had no idea why she had gone to such trouble to reach him with such a cryptic communication. She had not bothered to contact him for years . . . but then, he had not made it easy to be found. Yet this short message had a ring of sincere urgency to it.

His men were between engagements, spending their money perhaps too freely these days, enjoying too much mead and town air, so Rafe had obeyed her summons. He had reckoned it was about time to begin the journey home, anyway. December twenty-fifth—the birth of the Lord, the end of the century—was looming near.

As they traveled closer to Leonhart—and Alderich— he had picked up the ever-increasing gossip: a lord gone mad with the end of time, the world thought to be about to spark into a flaming cinder with the new millennium. Serfs and freemen alike fleeing to the woods. Turmoil, desperation, insanity.

The Lord of Alderich was abusing his demesne. He had hidden himself away in his fine castle, neglecting his people, his land, his animals, losing more and more each day—except that they were to be *Rafael's* people, *Rafael's* lands and animals. It infuriated him, as no doubt it was meant to do.

It soon became clear to him that to counter this he was going to need more than just the brute force he could enact, no matter how adept he had become with it. When some serfs his men questioned whispered a name he had long forgotten—*Serath Rune*—Rafael thought he had discovered an instant solution to the problem at hand.

He wasn't used to making mistakes. He still didn't quite see how this one had befallen him.

She sat alone at a scarred table in a cottage in the nearly deserted village of Fionnlagh, drawing one finger down the lines in the wood, silent, staring at nothing. Serath had barely eaten any of the food they had scraped together for her evening meal, and most of it lay untouched on the table, cold and forgotten. A small fire in a pit in the center of the dirt floor was the only illumination in the room. Smoke curled around her, caressing her body, becoming lost in her hair, and then—when she glanced up at him—her eyes.

Her lips took on that brittle curve; she looked away again.

Rafael walked from where he had been lingering in the doorway to sit across from her at the table. She wouldn't spare him another glance, so he examined the crude cottage of mud and stone, neat but small, all signs of occupancy gone: no blankets, no utensils, no animals or even scraps of food, save what Serath had left on the table. They had found the stones circling the firepit kicked out of line, the benches and table pushed aside, as if someone had left in a great hurry.

Rafe supposed the table and benches themselves were too heavy to cart off to the wilderness by whoever used to live here.

"What now, Rafael of Leonhart?" he heard Serath ask, and turned to see her staring at him again, bewitching eyes and unrelenting beauty. "You did not heed my warnings to you, and so here we are in the place I told you I should not go. Now these people fear you more than ever."

"Fear is not necessarily bad," he responded.

She shrugged. "So say you. I'm not surprised you would think as much, demon-man."

He had to smile at this, although she did not see it, since she was looking down at the table once more. "We demons can use fear most effectively."

"I know it," she said gravely.

"Tell me what happened out there today, Serath," Rafe said. "Tell me why the people of this town fear you."

She gave a little half laugh, again to the table, but otherwise said nothing.

"They won't come near you," Rafe said, watching her closely. "They speak your name in whispers. They turn away from you, and won't walk by this cottage because we told them you are in here. Why?"

"I owe you no answers," she said sullenly.

"No," he agreed, after a moment. "But you will give them to me, nonetheless."

"It's so easy for you, isn't it?" she sneered, startling him with her sudden venom. "You wish it, and so it becomes truth. You command, and others obey. Well, not I, my lord. Command away. I have nothing else to say to you."

She stood and paced away from him, although there was nowhere much to go. The hut consisted of a single chamber, no windows. The lone door was guarded by his man; she veered away from that. The table and the fire took up most of the space, so she walked to a flat mound of dirt in one of the corners, foundation for what used to be a sleeping pallet. He watched her stand there for a moment, her back to him, her hair loose and long, like midnight rain down her back.

"Is it the stories of witchcraft?" he asked her. "Is that it?"

He truly thought she would not answer him. She remained so still, her head bowed. The firelight showed him her slender frame, the pride in her shoulders, the subtle curves of her waist, her hips. Right then, seeing her like this in her solitude, it came to Rafael how truly alone she must feel—abducted from her convent by a horde of strangers, only to be rejected by her own people.

It was an unsettling thought, and bothersome. He was not used to feeling guilt over his actions. His life had not allowed much of that luxury.

Rafe was trying to think of some way to coax her to speak when she surprised him yet again, her voice very light and thin.

"You know of my mother, I suppose."

"Aye," he said, and then stopped himself from saying more.

"They burned her," Serath noted impartially, as if this were a discovery.

"Aye," he said again.

Once more she paused, her hands clasped behind her now, fingers interlocked near the small of her back. He found himself watching them, their fine shape.

"I was very young at the time," she went on, in the same voice. "But I remember that day. I remember the fire."

"They made you watch?" Rafe asked, jolted.

"No. But I heard it happen. And I saw the bailey afterward, the wood and ashes, the blackened ground. Grandfather showed us."

"Showed whom?"

"My brother and me." Now she faced him, her gaze clear and distant. "My brother Raibeart."

Something in him was arrested, caught for a bare moment in a sensation that felt like a warning, deep and uneasy.

"They tell me I have her look," Serath continued, dispassionate. "Her hair, her eyes, her features, her voice. As I grew older they said I could *be* her, Morwena Rune, so closely did I resemble her. I suppose I might even have her soul—I've heard that said, as well."

Pity washed over him, remorse for her, for her simple words and their terrible meaning.

"You have your own soul, Serath," he said gently.

She laughed, low and quick. "Now, that is an unlikely thing, coming from you. I've heard you have no soul at all, Rafael of Leonhart."

"Aye," he replied. "I've heard that, too."

She stared at him again, the firelight casting a golden hue over her, showing him the elegance of her cheekbones, the seductive line of her lips.

"Is it true?" she asked him, tilting her head.

"It doesn't matter," he said roughly.

"I suppose you're right." She sat on the mound of dirt, slowly, carefully, as if it were an uncertain thing. She was no longer meeting his eyes. "Your life is none of my concern."

"So the villagers see your mother when they see you, is that it?" Rafael asked, curt. "And that is why they fear you?"

"One day, many years ago," said Serath with her lyrical steadiness, "I was alone in the woods, very near your own land, as it happens, though I did not realize it at the time. I had slipped away from Fionnlagh, from my nursemaid and my grandfather and all the rest. I enjoyed being alone as a child. I did not know I was to spend so much of my future in such a state," she added reflectively, again with that half smile. "But on that day, I fell asleep in the forest, and my world was at least whole, if not friendly. When I awoke, everything was different. Do you remember it, my lord?"

And abruptly, he did. Rafael remembered that girl in the woods, the sight of her pale and stricken face when he had revealed the body of the boy to her. *Raibeart,* she had cried out. And now Rafe knew, with a sense of awful awakening, who that little girl had been, and who it was that she had mourned.

Her brother. Of course.

He had heard of the death of the heir of Jozua Rune. Everyone at Leonhart knew that Jozua had lost his son—his only child—in a boating accident during an ocean storm many years ago. But that son had been married, and had produced two children of his own. Rafe had never even been certain of their ages, only that the boy was the eldest, and the only likely danger to his own claim to Alderich when the century ended.

In the years since he had heard that Rune had chosen another man to take over for him, in case he died before the end of the millennium, Rafe had supposed. That was no matter to him. Only the blood of Rune could truly rule in his stead, Rafael knew that. Only blood was a certain threat. And that blood was gone.

It had taken days for Rafael and his men to realize that it had been the grandson of Rune that they had found dead on their land—at the time none of them had even suspected it.

There had been no obvious signs of the boy's lineage other than the imprinted crest of Alderich on his scabbard—and even that had been small and elusive, almost hidden. His clothing had been plain and serviceable. He wore no jewelry, no heraldry, things the grandson of such a lord would have been entitled to. It was a mystery as to why he had been traveling through Leonhart at all.

And certainly there had been no reason to suspect that that girl had been his sister. She looked nothing like the boy—who, as Rafe recalled, had been blond and gangly, the opposite of her delicate darkness. True, she had been well spoken, and _her_ clothing, at least, was too fine for the child of freemen. He had assumed that she was just the daughter of minor nobility from the castle, perhaps strayed from a picnic or other outing. Never would Rafe have guessed that the Lord of Alderich would be so careless as to allow his own granddaughter to wander the woods alone.

Rafe had left Leonhart almost immediately afterward, anyway, gone on his quest. Over the years that followed, the strange fact of the dead boy had sunk away to become one of a great many deaths, all of them wrenching, none of them anything he preferred to dwell upon.

All this time, it had been *her*, lurking in his memory. He knew now why he had recognized Serath's face, why the pure blue of her eyes had been so familiar. Indeed, now that he had captured that memory, it was easy to see in this woman the same haunting refinement that had shadowed her then, that girl whose life he had ravaged that day.

Of course, he thought again tiredly.

"You told me to fetch men to carry him back," Serath said, watching him. "You told me to get help, for you'd not step foot on our land."

"I remember." Rafe kept his own voice even, no hint of what her revelation had done to him.

"But I couldn't do that, you see. I couldn't leave him alone—it wouldn't be right. He was my brother . . . fair of face—all that made God smile. I loved him. I couldn't leave him, not like that." She stared off to the side, a frown barely creasing her forehead, then said again softly, "It was not right to leave him."

"Serath," he began, but she cut him off.

"I carried him myself. I dragged him, rather—he was older than I, and heavier. It took a very long time. By the time I reached the village I was fair spent. It had taken hours, my lord, to move him. I did the best I could. I tried to . . . protect him."

Her words ended high and wavering, so she hesitated for a moment, then went on, stronger. "I can only imagine how it seemed to them, the people here. They feared me already, of course—they thought I was unlucky at best, or at worst that I had Morwena's charms and spells. They tolerated me solely for my position. Even Grandfather would not bear my presence, and all knew it. So when I arrived dragging my dead brother—best beloved, most cherished child in the land—holding him in my arms, too weary and numb to call for help, even . . . I suppose that is when it happened."

Rafael let out a sigh and passed a hand over his eyes, trying to rid himself of the vision.

"From that day forward, they would not suffer me," Serath said. "They would not speak to me, they could not even take in my face. They kept their animals and children from me, would not allow me near their food—serfs and nobles alike."

"You must have told them," Rafe said harshly, feeling that unwanted guilt again. "You must have explained to them what happened, how we found you—"

She dismissed him with a disdainful sweep of her fingers through the air. "My explanations were useless to them. Grandfather claimed to believe me, but I knew he was lying. I could see it in his eyes. Because of his power no one attempted to retaliate against me, but my life here was over. It was said I was certainly a witch like Morwena, that I had killed my own brother. Within a year my grandfather sent me to the convent, there to spend my life in solemn penitence."

She stopped at last, lying slowly back onto the dirt as if it were still a pallet, her hair becoming a pillow beneath her, her arms lax by her sides. Her next words were addressed to the heavy thatch of the roof.

"And now you have come yet again, demon-man, all these years later. Twice you have ruined me. So do forgive me; I really must wonder what it is you plan to do with me next."

Rafael stood silent, hearing the beating of his heart in his ears, feeling the uncomfortable mixture of remorse and defiance provoked by her words, the almost gentle accusation that he had somehow done this to her, had brought her to this state. Either she was a complete innocent or else the most accomplished liar he had ever come across. Either way, it boded ill for him.

God's truth, Rafe thought reluctantly, she looked too thin and fragile to be what the villagers said she was. She sounded too candid to bear false words. And worst of all, she reached too deeply into some unknown part of him for her to be what he so desperately needed her to be—his pawn.

So he did not know what to do with her, how to answer her question, and it left him feeling angry on top of these other unfamiliar emotions, tying up his tongue. All he could do was glare down at her.

She was supposed to be the key to gaining him all that he and his family had ever wanted. She was supposed to be used to ensure his destiny, to ensure that he ruled the land he had been raised to think of as his. But all she appeared to be, in fact, was a noble maiden, tragically misused, exquisitely out of place in this rough room . . . and very, very defenseless.

From her supine position on the dirt Serath slowly turned her head and gazed up at him, calm blue brilliance. Tendrils of smoke glided between them, partially masking her, opening without warning the tight lock he had managed to keep on his imagination up until this very moment. Rafe saw her on a bed of furs instead of dirt, her hair still loose and inviting beneath her, sultry eyes, her skin like cream, her arms out, welcoming—

He clenched his jaw and turned away, exhaling slowly. When he thought he had regained control, he spoke to the wall ahead of him, not bothering to turn around again.

"Tomorrow morning you and I are going up to the castle. Your grandfather is going to grant us an audience."

"It will not happen," she said with languid certainty.

None of the replies he had were fit for speaking. Rafael stalked out of the hut, leaving her alone with her damned convictions.

And after the night's business was done—guards posted, horses stabled, men fed and bunked, peasants calmed and controlled, tomorrow's plans made—Rafael spent a long and restless night in one of the many deserted cottages of this village, staring up at the stars past the holes in the thatchwork roof, listening to the distant tolling of Jozua's bells . . . and pondering the puzzle of Serath Rune.

THE CLIMB TO FIONNLAGH CASTLE WAS LESS STEEP than Serath remembered, though it did seem longer.

She rode a dun mare Leonhart had given her, which was a relief. Days of being pressed so near him in his saddle had left her with an aversion of getting too close to him again—not because it had been as horrible or as shocking as it should have been. By heavens, she was a noblewoman despite everything, practically convent-bred. Such intimacy with a man should have been nothing but disgusting to her.

But it had not been. Instead of shock there had been heat. Instead of horror there had been something that came close to comfort, being shielded by his body, held tight against the firmness of him.

That was the truly terrifying thing. Perhaps she was no better than her mother, after all. Surely a true gentlewoman would rather have died than be subjected to such treatment again.

Yet Serath had dreamed of him last night. Dreamed of those moments with a hot and exciting acuteness, feeling him against her again, just as they had been on the ride, resting against his strength, allowing the scent of him to envelop her. It had left her flushed and bothered, and she had awakened with a sense of loss, a vague fear that his touch had been naught but thin illusion.

So yes, Serath was glad to have her own steed now. Anything to purge that dark part of her that yearned for him, terrible though he was.

And perhaps he felt as uneasy around her as she did around him. This morning he would not meet her eyes. Even when ordering her to get ready to leave he had let his glance skid over her, as if she were something disturbing, painful to see.

His aversion to her did not extend to complacency— Leonhart made certain to keep her near him on the ride by keeping her steed in check; a rope tethered the bridle of her horse to the saddle of his own. There was no chance she could bolt.

Besides, a contingent of men surrounded her. Rafael of Leonhart would not risk losing her now, it seemed.

The road to Fionnlagh was well traveled, packed dirt with ruts from the weight of passing carts. Closer to the castle it became stone, even and unbroken, mottled cream and gold to offset the white of the stronghold.

There were no other sounds besides the passage of their group, not even birds singing. Certainly no other people. Even the ocean seemed muted, suppressed beneath the weight of the anticipation around them.

None of the men spoke. They rode in almost the same formation as usual, with the same expressions of wary caution, hands ready to reach for their weapons.

Only Leonhart, beside her, appeared unaffected by the hushed surroundings. His face was carefully impassive. But when he glanced at her his eyes seemed full of coming storms.

The castle towered above them, more and more of it revealed above the trees as they drew closer. Their party would have been spotted by now, Serath knew. The sentries of Fionnlagh Castle would have seen them the moment they began up the path from the village—before, if they had been watching the village from the south tower yesterday. Clearly this was not to be a surprise assault.

Leonhart did not need surprise, after all. He had Serath, and so he thought he had the advantage.

Nervous laughter threatened her. She swallowed it, focusing on the rough mane of her horse for long minutes until it was under control.

Something went crashing through the woods to their right; the horses started, sidestepping with anxious snorts. In an instant Serath heard the hiss of steel against steel, saw the flash of swords being drawn, shields being raised. Leonhart had one hand on his sword and the other on the rope that held her mount, standing in his saddle, scanning the area.

A tremendous bird rushed from the branches of a pine with great clamor—a rook or a crow, Serath wasn't certain which—screeching wildly as it flew past them.

Leonhart sat back again, though he did not resheathe his sword. Serath lifted her head and watched the bird become a pinpoint against the sky.

"Forward," Rafael ordered, and the line of men moved on.

Now she could make out the separate blocks of stone that made up the outer wall of Fionnlagh, an even layer of lines. Sunlight glinted off the glass of the few windows near the tops of the turrets, diamond panes that otherwise showed darkness. She could see no men along the wall-walks. The castle looked as deserted as the village had looked.

The road became almost level near the gate, and it was here that they gathered, not too close to the walls, out of reach of obvious traps—boiling water, or pitch, poured through the murder holes would not reach them.

Arrows still would, she thought.

Leonhart might have been considering the same thing; he positioned himself in front of her, lifting his shield to cover her as much of her as he could. The rest of the soldiers remained behind them. Serath could hear only the occasional echo of a horse's restless step.

"Jozua Rune!" shouted Rafael. "You know who I am! Come forth to meet me as the lord of this land should!"

Nothing happened. There was no movement along the walls. The gate remained sealed.

"Come forth!" demanded Rafael again, his voice ringing off the stones. He lowered the shield and tugged at the rope he held so that Serath's mount came up even to his own. Grasping her wrist, he lifted her arm up to the sky, forcing her to face the gate.

"I have something of yours, Lord of Alderich!"

A cold wind came and blew around them, sifting through her hair, bringing strands of blackness across her eyes to tangle in her lashes. She reached up to clear them, too proud to duck her head and hide from this moment, the way she truly wanted to.

The arm Leonhart held up was growing numb, although she was extremely aware of his grip against her skin—calluses, strength, control. He glanced back to her just once, but Serath kept her focus on the west tower of the gatehouse. It was there that the sentry would be. That was the most fortified location along the wall. Yet there was still nothing, no betrayal of any presence, and after a moment, Leonhart released her arm.

Minutes passed. From the corner of her eye she saw him shift in his saddle, no doubt getting ready to shout again, but before he could someone appeared at the top of the tower. A sentry.

"Who trespasses against our lord?" called out the man.

"Tell Jozua Rune that the new master of this land is here. Tell him Rafael of Leonhart will speak with him."

"The Lord of Alderich will see none of you! Begone, afore we take offense!"

The threat seemed hollow enough. Serath doubted anyone inside the castle would truly attack this group— not while knowing who their commander was, and not without knowing how many men total there might be behind him. The leader of Leonhart was nothing if not feared and reviled among her people.

"Tell Jozua Rune that I have his granddaughter! Tell him to come out and see her for himself, if he values her!"

Serath lowered her head after all, crossing her arms to her chest to fight the chill that crawled over her. Her hair fell down around her face, hiding her. She knew what would happen next.

The sentry's answer floated back down to them, no uncertainty at all in his voice.

"My master says to take her and go! He will not see her, nor you! Leave us, Leonhart, unless you desire combat!"

Despite herself Serath turned to take in Rafael, seeing the hard reality hit him—a wrathful scowl, narrowed eyes, dawning outrage. It was absolutely the face of a killer. That dark, forbidding aspect of him grew fiercer, hardened into something that spoke of wars and bloodshed, and countless battles won.

He was so suddenly like everything she had ever heard him to be: ruthless death, gleeful chaos, the devil's minion out to destroy all that belonged to her family, only evil, only wickedness—

"Do you not understand me, fool?" Leonhart shouted back to the castle. "I have the maiden Serath, the daughter of his son! She is my hostage! Do you wish to see her die?"

Blood rushed from her head, panic rose in her throat. She had to grip the mane of her horse to stay on it, closing her eyes. This was a nightmare—worse than that, worse than the worst day of her life so far, to be left for dead here before this castle, before all that used to be hers, scorned and discarded. . . .

Serath became aware, at some point, that Leonhart had taken her hand, keeping it lowered between them now, and he was squeezing it, very hard. When she tried to pull away she couldn't, and so she raised her head again to see him past the haze of tears clouding her vision.

Leonhart was not looking at her. His profile remained distinct against the velvet greens of the woods beyond, the intensity of his expression unchanged.

"Breathe deeply," he said in an undertone, his lips barely moving. "Serath, don't faint. You're fine. You're fine."

The sentry had vanished. She only noticed it because in that moment he reappeared, a helmeted head behind one of the large white stones of the tower. Her grandfather's man bellowed a new message down to them.

"My master the Lord of Alderich says to tell you to kill the witch if it suits you. He cares not, and he will not speak with you. Begone, devil of Leonhart!"

---⟨∾⟩---

*A*RE THEY LEAVING?"

"Aye, my lord."

The old man paced unevenly, his steps broken by the grooves in the fitted stones of the inner hall of the gatehouse.

"Was it she?" he asked, pausing, turning to face the soldier behind him.

"Aye, my lord. I believe so."

"I could not see her." The old man's voice was fretful, quiet. A beam of sunlight from the nearby archer's slit scored down his side, rippling over the cloth of his tunic. He placed one hand against the stone wall beside him, leaning against it. "The distance—I could not *see,* and be certain. Tell me the truth, Olivier. Was it my granddaughter?"

The soldier watched his master, his eyes drawn to the richness draped over Jozua Rune's thin shoulders, a cape of brilliant yellow and garnet. The bright line of the sun shone down it like a lance.

"She had the look, my lord, I can tell you that most certainly. If it was not she, it was such a copy as to fool anyone."

"Indeed."

Jozua Rune stood up straighter, coming closer to the slit in the wall, and the sunlight slid up his form to light his hair to gleaming silver. His tone turned musing. "So the devil of Leonhart has found himself a hostage, has he?"

"Shall we attempt to gain her back, my lord? I could have my men ready for attack by tonight, should you wish it."

"Nay. Better not to waste men now, not for this.

They are trapped down there in the village until we will it otherwise. Let us use our advantage. We may regain my granddaughter another way."

He looked now at the soldier, his eyes small and narrowed. "How did she appear?" he demanded.

"Your pardon, my lord," Olivier said, hesitant. "Appear?"

"Aye," snapped Jozua. "How did she appear, man? Was she wan? Was she frightened? Pleased? Stout? Thin? Did she look abused at all?"

"No, my lord—that is, I did not think she looked harmed."

"Then what?"

"Well . . ." The soldier hesitated again, and Jozua's eyes grew smaller.

"Can it be I have named such a simpleton as my heir? A man who cannot even recall the most basic facts of warfare? Examine your enemy! Learn from him. Use every situation to your advantage, manipulate it."

"My lord, I was watching Leonhart!"

"But not, apparently, my granddaughter."

A heated flush began to work its way up Olivier's neck. "I did not consider her to be an enemy, my lord."

"Didn't you?" asked Jozua, his voice careless. "Then you are a fool, after all. Know this, Olivier. Women are unpredictable and untrustworthy. Never think otherwise."

The old man lowered his head, examining his clasped hands. "By her very nature, her loyalty must be in question. We cannot know." He nodded thoughtfully, then repeated his words. "We cannot know."

Olivier spoke again, cautious. "Leonhart did not hurt her. Not even after we told him he could."

"There, you see? Perhaps you've learned something

from me, after all. The devil would not kill her here in front of us. Interesting."

"If I may ask, my lord—how did you know he would not kill her?"

Jozua Rune shrugged. "I did not." He appeared not to notice the startled expression that crossed the other man's features. "But now at least we know he was not willing to harm her. So tell me, Olivier. What might it mean?"

"He is waiting for a better moment?"

"Mayhap. Or—she might not be his hostage, after all."

"My lord?"

Something about the old man grew subtly tighter, a strange shifting from within that echoed across his body, twisting his body farther, his fingers gnarling into knots.

"Mayhap," he said, very softly, "she has grown up to become her mother's shadow. Mayhap she is no better than a whore."

The soldier had no reply for this; the hard glitter to his master's eyes choked off his surprise. He swallowed, and said nothing.

"If she has given her body to the devil of Leonhart," continued Jozua, in that same chilling tone, "then better to dispatch her at once than allow her to continue to defile my name and land."

"Perhaps," suggested the soldier cautiously, watching the bent form, "a test, my lord. . . ."

Jozua Rune looked up at him, the lines of his face deeply carved in the light.

"Aye," he agreed slowly. "A test."

"If she fails?"

"If she fails," Rune responded, "then we have lost nothing. You may kill her for me yourself."

⌐◦◦◦¬

$\mathcal{T}$HE JOURNEY BACK TO THE VILLAGE WAS NEARLY as silent as the one going up had been.

Serath heard occasional snatches of conversations between the men riding behind her, words too low to catch, tones deep and serious. Someone would say something; another man might respond, and then they quieted again, letting their anger simmer.

There was one word she did manage to distinguish from the rest, perhaps because she had heard it so often before: witch.

The devil of Leonhart, still beside her, did not bother to join in these intermittent dialogues. He seemed wrapped in his thoughts, almost brooding.

In contrast to the mood of the group, the last of the clouds had thinned from the air, letting bright sunlight splash down upon them, lifting the colors of the woods to ruddy reds and browns, soft moss, emerald greens. It was a welcome diversion to Serath, and she lost herself to it, shutting out the men, the castle, even Leonhart himself to take in the hidden beauty around them. She had taught herself this trick at the convent and perfected it over the years, a powerful, singular focus that could block out nearly any unpleasantness, from aching knees from kneeling too long to extended days and nights locked alone in her cell.

So she did not see the new men on the path, riding up to greet them from the village. Enraptured by the colors of the trees that they passed, she did not even hear them. It was only after her horse stopped that she realized there was something amiss.

"My lord!" called the man Serath recognized as Leonhart's second-in-command. When he was close enough he pushed near to Rafael, his voice urgent. "We have a problem, my lord."

"What is it?" Leonhart asked, with no suggestion of emotion.

"The serfs. They're fleeing the village."

Chapter Five

———— ⌣ﬀ⌣ ————

THE DAY WAS CLEARLY NOT GOING THE WAY he had anticipated.

As Rafael rode back into the town he took in the remaining villagers as they huddled near the well, plainly terrified. It did not help that his men surrounded them with weapons out, hostile, intimidating. Many of the women were weeping again, loudly and nervously. Somewhere in the crowd an infant cried, a baleful, hitching sound.

Aye, there were quite a few less people here than he had seen yesterday, there could be no doubt of that. And God knew how many more had fled before they had arrived at Fionnlagh, Rafe thought acidly. All this, the ill work of Jozua Rune and his vindictive madness.

He dismounted and walked to stand in front of the group, surveying the mass of them.

"Have you a leader?" he asked.

After only a brief hesitation a man pushed his way to

the front, thickset and with a shock of red hair, about as old as Rafe's father would be. He stood in front of Rafael almost rebelliously, but said nothing, staring at his feet.

"Are you the leader?" Rafe asked him, curbing his impatience.

"Aye," said the man.

"Come with me." Rafe walked away from the group, over to an afternoon shadow cast by one of the buildings.

The man followed, carefully staying a few steps out of reach. Rafael crossed his arms over his chest, leaning against the wall.

"Your name?"

"Calum," said the man.

"Well, Calum, it appears that people are missing."

Again the man angled his gaze down to the ground, and he did not reply.

"Where did they go?" Rafe asked, temperate.

Still Calum said nothing.

"To the woods, I should think," Rafe answered himself. "There's nowhere else for fleeing serfs to go, is there? So I suppose a better question would be, when did they leave, Calum, and how?"

Silence.

"Do you or do you not speak for your people?" Rafe demanded.

Calum looked up. "I do."

"Then answer me, man, or else I'll have to start asking some of the others among you."

"I won't betray them," Calum said suddenly. "I won't!"

Rafael studied him for a minute, then let out a sigh. "I know what you're thinking," he said quietly. "I have an idea what you have been told of me. Let me assure you once again that I am not here to harm any of you. I need you—all of you—to stay and work this land for the benefit of us both. You belong here as much as I. As your new master I am sworn to protect you, don't you understand that?"

Rafe watched as Calum's eyes darted to the left, very quickly, and then back to him again. He turned slightly to take in the same view.

Quite a few of his men had not yet dismounted, no doubt waiting for his orders to begin combing the woods. But square in the middle of them was Serath, also still mounted. From here she held a distant loveliness, faerie queen again, a cloud of black hair flowing free, sapphire eyes and rose-pink lips.

In the course of the few days he had known her, Rafael had discovered in Serath Rune an inherent paradox. She was a maiden of such fairness she might move men to war; yet she had been hidden away—indeed, abandoned—by her own family.

He knew better than all the people here—aye, and knew it well—that she was a woman, sweet flesh and layers of vulnerability. But in this instant Rafael could also imagine how she might appear to the eye of a superstitious man: a fey beauty too perfect to be natural—her hair too shining dark, the blue of her eyes too intense for mortal gaze. The stoic expression Rafe suspected hid her true feelings could be seen as disdain and secret sorcery.

She stared over at them, ignoring all else.

"Ah," said Rafael. "You worry about the woman, is that it?"

"If it be so, my lord, that you do not harm us," whispered Calum, "then why did you bring her here? She will curse us all!"

"She is no witch," said Rafe, with as much conviction as he could muster.

"She is!" countered the man, almost frantic. "I know

it, my lord! I saw them burn her mother! I was here the day she killed her own brother!"

"Where did your people go, Calum?"

"My lord—your pity, your mercy, I beg you! She will ruin us all!"

"Your people, Calum."

"Her mother placed a curse on us, my lord, as she burned! I heard it with my own ears, and now it has come to truth, right now, today! The daughter is here to steal our souls, just as she did to her brother and all other innocents she finds! When the world ends, when the Lord comes for us, He will pass us over for our sins! I pray you, great lord—Rafael of Leonhart—send her away! You have the power to do this! Do not let her bewitch us!"

Rafe felt his temper beginning to fray. "Listen well to me, for I don't want to say this again: Serath Rune is no witch. She will not harm you, not any of you. But if you do not answer my questions I cannot promise you any safety from *me*. Now, tell me this, Calum of Fionnlagh— *where did your people go?*"

Calum dropped to his knees with his hands over his face, shudders running through him. He began a low, babbling moan that sounded like a plea for mercy. Rafael watched him with fatigued acceptance. Of course the man wouldn't answer him. He was either too frightened or else too stubbornly loyal to give in to what he surely thought would be the death of his people.

"Enough," Rafael said. "Enough, Calum. Go back to your family."

He didn't wait for the man to come to his feet. Instead he found Abram again, standing ready nearby, a hand already on his mount.

"Find them," Rafe ordered, and without a word Abram vaulted into his saddle and led a line of men out of the village, fanning into the thickness of the trees beyond.

Serath watched him as before, regal atop her horse. She was as compelling as ever, as complete a mystery as a woman had ever been to him, but right now the sight of her only filled him with irritation, reminding Rafael of the impossible difficulty his life had become. He walked away from her, throwing an offhand order over his shoulder as he moved toward a circle of his men.

"Confine her," he said, and then went to deal with the rest of his problems.

* * *

SERATH SPENT HER TIME PACING AT FIRST, wearing a path in the dirt floor of the squat room she was trapped in. Skeleton stick shadows fell past bits of the thatched roof, disorganized lines of light and dark sliding across the ground, the table, her hands, and gown.

She was hungry but the food did not appeal to her.

She was tired but could not sleep.

She was worried and anxious and filled with foreboding, but there was no one to grant her solace.

The guards at the door would ignore her unless she tried to leave, so she had only herself for company, which was hardly unusual. But right now Serath did not feel comfortable isolated from what was happening around her; too many of Leonhart's plans revolved around her. He had not come by at all—she didn't know whether to be relieved or incensed about it.

He had threatened to murder her, after all. He had shouted out to all the world that he would kill her unless her grandfather spoke with him—this, after all his hollow assurances that she would be safe.

The word of the devil, she thought tartly. Why had she ever listened to him at all?

Yet he had not done it. He had backed away from his

threat, allowing Jozua the victory, at least for the moment. So she still lived thanks to him. For how much longer, she had no idea. Perhaps until the end of the world—perhaps not.

He had held her hand so tightly. He had whispered consolation to her, even as he threatened to slay her. He had looked like a warrior, spoken as a warrior, but for his own unfathomable reasons he had chosen to comfort her at the same time, a secret between them, binding them together for the space of a few heartbeats. Serath didn't know what to make of it. And here she was, trapped again, waiting for whatever he might try next.

To fight her sense of helplessness she decided to change her gown, shaking out the folds of the fresh one, which was wrinkled but at least clean. Her old dress looked truly beyond repair. It was torn in more places than she could count, and dirt streaked it almost everywhere. Still, it was one of only two gowns that she possessed, so she brushed it clean as best as she could and folded it up carefully, then repeated the process, because she had so little else to do.

She had not taken any of her veils from the convent. She had not even noticed this until now; Serath supposed it was because she hated wearing them, their confinement, their wispy fluttering in her ears. She had not worn her hair down like this since she was a little girl, but now Serath devoutly wished for a ribbon, a comb—anything to tame the mess it had become.

She sat down at one of the benches and used her fingers to untangle the knots, starting at the ends, working her way up. It took time, but that was all right. It appeared time was the one thing she had in plenty. When she was finished she braided it all back into a single plait, looping a strand over the end to keep it tight.

With the setting of the sun the lessening warmth began to bother her, so she paced again. What was left of the fire from this morning was just ash, no flames at all.

She watched the patchy sunlight turn from pale gold to dusky amber, growing richer with the advent of the night. If she glanced up at the smoke hole in the center of the ceiling, she could see the changes saturating the sky as well, thin blue deepening to purple dusk.

At night it might be difficult to see a person on top of the thatched roof. At night, with the moon beginning to wane to a crescent, the light would be poor at best—much as those fleeing serfs must have discovered.

Serath stood up on her bench, examining the roofing. It might hold her. If she tread lightly . . . if she spread her weight as evenly as she could, and stepped only on the support beams, then yes . . . it might work.

And the woods were dark and endless. She knew that very well.

Voices outside the door warned her to jump down from the bench, taking her seat quickly, just in time to look up and see Leonhart stoop to enter the room.

Serath folded her hands in her lap, hoping she looked composed.

He raked her with his gaze, his look cool and impersonal, then motioned to the bread and fowl she had left on a plate.

"You did not eat." He did not sound pleased.

"I am not hungry."

"I don't care," he said, coming close. "Eat what I give you. I won't have it said that I starved you."

Her eyes widened, her temper flaring despite her resolve to stay calm. "You threatened to *kill* me today, but you worry about others saying I *starved* in your care?"

He eased himself down to the bench beside her, just a little too close.

"It was a bluff, Serath," he said bluntly. "Obviously."

"Oh, a bluff! How foolish of me to think you meant what you said! I forgot you are the master of deceit."

"Now, there's a title I haven't heard before." He actually smiled at her, sharp and wickedly handsome. "Master of deceit. I must remember that."

"I thought you said you don't play games," she shot back.

"I don't play games I cannot win," he amended, and kept that dangerous smile.

She set her lips, turning her head just slightly away from him.

"Eat, Serath," Leonhart said.

"I am not hungry."

"So you said. And again, I don't care. Eat your meal."

When she still did not move he leaned closer to her, stone hard again, the teasing edge banished. "Listen to me, my lady. Do you think I want you to fall ill? Do you think I would risk such a thing, after all I have done to bring you here? I have every reason to keep you sound. I've given you the best portions of the meals—and it's hard enough taking food from these people, they have so little already."

She stared at him, dismayed.

Leonhart pushed the plate in front of her; the sound of it scraped across the wood. "God's blood, Serath, eat the food before I have to do something neither of us will like. Do you fathom me, my lady?"

The threat was simple and clear. She would not win this contest against him. Both of them knew it.

Tonight, Serath thought. *Freedom tonight.*

She reached out and picked up the bread, breaking off a small piece. He watched her closely, not leaning back again until she was chewing, trying to swallow the dryness of it.

"Good," he said, and then closed his eyes, inhaling deeply.

She noticed then how tired he looked, how the lines around his eyes seemed deeper than before, the new growth of beard dark against his skin, the rich brown of his hair mussed. He was unkempt and scruffy, reeking of sweat and horses and green woods, and somehow he became, all at once, overwhelmingly appealing to her. Compassion struck her in a rush, followed by complete disgust with herself.

He was tired because he had been busy trying to impose his will on an entire land held hostage to his whims. He was violent and ruthless. He did not deserve tenderness from her—no, he deserved nothing but scorn, in fact.

But right now, seeing him in the twilight of the cottage, Serath found she could not summon scorn. He looked worn and guileless, more man than demon, exhausted, resting after a long day.

He needs help, came the thought, and then she forgot to eat, so startled was she by the depth of her sympathy for him.

His eyes opened, catching her scrutiny. The night-cloud gaze was almost invisible to her now—they had no light besides the dusk beyond the roof—and in the approaching darkness she imagined she saw yet another new aspect to him. He did not seem angry with her any longer, nor exasperated, nor even indifferent. The fatigue of before fell away. What Serath saw in him now was something she had never seen before from any man, and she didn't even know the words to describe it.

His look left her feeling odd, flustered, the room grown suddenly too hot despite the night. The very air felt different, as if a summer storm of lightning had come and gone in a single breath, leaving behind a glowing burn that singed her skin.

He was very near. When he shifted their thighs touched, and the heat became real to her, the solid muscle of him pushed against her. His gaze turned from hers and then came back, trapping her. She could not move away to save her life.

"Eat," Rafael whispered to her, and brought his hand up to her mouth, pressing something to her lips. Bread. She opened her mouth and accepted it, tasting nothing, feeling only his fingers, so light against her. He did not move them away but altered his touch, following the shape of her lips, skimming softly over her cheek, her chin, and Serath felt the heat of the room swim over her, taking her reason away and leaving only this newness, the texture and marvel of this man.

She swallowed the bread.

"Yes," said Rafael, very softly, and then leaned his head close to hers and placed his lips where his fingers had been, a gentle caress over her cheek, his breath warm against her. Serath blinked and pulled back, astonished, and he followed her, closing his lips over her own.

Nothing in her life had prepared her for this, the sensation of a man so intimate with her, the contrast of hard and soft against her, the heat of his lips, the rough scrape of his beard. His hands slid up her arms to hold her shoulders, and then her neck, the back of her head, and she moved with him now, harmony to his lead, pliant and cautious together as this uniqueness filled her.

His kiss changed again, becoming more severe, an urgency now controlling his hands and the rest of him. He pulled her closer, awkward on the bench, and Serath had to balance herself by placing her own hands on his shoulders, feeling the unyielding form beneath the tunic he wore.

Rafael made some sound deep in his throat that sent her senses reeling, making her gasp for air against him. He took the breath back, an exchange that felt like honey to her, or mead—stinging drunkenness. His tongue stroked hers; Serath felt the sting turn to fire.

He murmured her name, hoarse, and his palms cupped her cheeks as he traced the kiss across her face . . . to her eyes, closed tight in wonder, her breath coming in short pants.

"Serath," he said again, tasting her, "sweet, sweet Serath. . . ."

"Oh," she said, or something close to it, more of a sound than a word, stunned and shaken.

She felt him pause then, hands still firm on her, his own breath rapid and rough. When she opened her eyes he was close enough for her to see the faint, lost look to his eyes, a man coming awake from a dream.

"Serath," he said once more, but it was different now, unsettled.

She pulled away from him and he let her. The air that took his place felt like cold numbness against her, the exact opposite of what he had been. Serath raised a hand to her cheek, pressing hard, fighting the strangeness.

Rafael stood up quickly, backing away from her, gloom and night surrounding him.

"My lady—I . . ." His sentence faded off into perplexity.

"Why did you do that?" Serath heard herself ask, and then couldn't believe she had said it.

But all he did was bow to her, quick and terse, and then he was gone from the room.

$\mathcal{T}$HE THATCH OF THE ROOF WAS NOISY.

It was a difficult thing, moving quietly, but as Serath

struggled out the hole of the roof, what worried her most was falling.

Directly below her burned the embers of the fire they had lit for her earlier, chunks of wood still hot enough to glow with orange menace in the night. She could feel the heated air wafting up around her even now. Falling would be painful and permanent. She would probably not be able to stop herself from screaming.

Serath had to hope the bench she had used to boost herself up here was far enough from the heat not to start smoldering itself. The last thing she needed was for the cottage to go up in flames.

She wasn't certain how late it was; she had tried to count out the hours by her grandfather's bells but had drifted in and out of sleep anyway, falling off only to jerk awake minutes later, sick with dread that she had missed her chance to escape.

Beyond lighting the fire for her, no one had come to check on her that night. Just in case, she had finished the meal that had led her to such an unexpected place in the arms of her enemy. But Rafael had not returned to her, and eventually she had given up expecting him to.

Serath kicked her feet up and found a support, crunching through the dry reeds, wincing and hanging still as she listened for any sound of alarm—all she heard was the distant call of crickets, or perhaps frogs. No voices.

Aye, Leonhart had kissed her and then vanished, leaving her to mull what had happened between them in shocked silence.

He *kissed* her! Not just once, the way she had always dreamed a kiss might happen, a single tribute of chaste admiration, but several times, over and over—and each had scorched to ash any thoughts of chaste modesty. Rafael of Leonhart, the demon-man himself, had held her and kissed her, and it had felt like a rain of stars upon her head, making her weak and blunted, a victim of the wild glory of it. Heaven have mercy on her.

She never would have guessed that a man so capable of the most brutal of crimes would ever touch her in such a way—or that she would have allowed it to happen. But he had, and she did. Her flight tonight took on an added imperative; Serath *must* escape him, or else risk betraying herself with him again.

There—she had managed to make it out of the smoke hole, miracle of miracles. She crawled until she lay flat over the tilted slant of the roof, noticing the paleness of her sleeves and hands against the thatch. It wasn't so bad. The night was very dark, like the inside of a cellar, but that was good. She could do this.

She had to leave the extra gown behind—perhaps she should not have worn her new one after all, she reflected wryly. But it was too late now. Even just her gown and her cloak were bulky enough to come close to hindering her. Carrying extra weight would have doomed her plan. Besides, there was nothing left in that cottage that she needed. The extra gown was ruined. She had no spare food. And her mother's moonstone was pinned close to her throat. That was everything.

The woods would protect her until she reached her destination. And after that, none of this would matter, anyway.

The pitch of the roof was surprisingly steep. She had not considered it before, but now it left her at an ungainly angle, trying to work her way down without falling. Thankfully the back of the cottage was part of a long, narrow alleyway; she had noticed that before they had taken her in. Unless the pattern of the town had changed drastically while she had been gone—and it would not have—that hidden alley would lead to a few more buildings at the outskirts of the village, and then to a field, and then to freedom.

It was slow going. She had to freeze in place when she heard a noise nearby. It faded almost immediately to silence—perhaps one of the guards moving about, or a horse.

Not wolves, Serath thought resolutely. *Not wolves.*

At the convent she had once overheard a conversation between two novices, discussing in animated, trilling whispers the dismemberment of a peasant woman from one of their villages. The baker's wife, the girl had said. Eaten alive, a mess of blood and bone—and the girl's father had gathered the men together and found the wolves and slain them all. But not before they had managed to maim a little boy. His entire arm was chewed off—

The noise came again, subtle and sly and very close, from the depths of the alley directly below. Serath clenched the reeds of the thatch and felt a chilled sweat come over her.

Not wolves!

Stupid girls—they probably made up the entire tale, knowing Serath had been near enough to hear it. They had been teasing her, of course. It had happened occasionally, knowing she was bound to silence, saying the most outrageous things just to try to get her to react. Yes. Now that she thought upon it, it was this very same girl who had regaled the other novices with the story of a kiss the son of some visiting lord had stolen from her—and her words had been nothing but lofty and scornful. That proved it. The girl was a liar. Had she actually been kissed, her story would have been far different. Instead of scorn she would have spoken of fire, and lightning, and delicious sin.

Serath knew that now for herself.

She eased herself down to the end of the roof, crouching precariously at the edge, trying to peer through the blackness. No further noises came.

Of course there were no wolves in the village. Not with all these men about. It had been a mouse. A fox, mayhap. Something harmless.

Serath steadied herself with her hands beside her, then slid feetfirst to the end of the thatch, until there was nothing but air beneath her. The ground would not be that far away. She released the reeds.

Something soft and gasping broke her fall, making her land in a clumsy heap on the ground. A loud scream split the air beneath her, followed by more screams all around, a cacophony of them—her own now joining them—and the world around her heaved and turned, ramming into her, pushing her back and then down until her head struck something hard and stars filled her vision.

The noises became distorted, madness filling her ears, and when a light blinded her Serath raised her hands and protected her eyes, near deafened from it all.

People were shouting, men and women both, stepping on her and over her, and then someone pulled her upright again, and she heard the familiar growling tones of her demon-man, holding her roughly in his arms.

"Stop them!" he was shouting above the noise. "Over there—by the mill—"

Serath yanked away from him and was immediately pulled back, an arm around her neck.

"These people here—bring them to the courtyard! Do not harm them! Hurry!"

And the chaos began to separate into torchlight and groups of faces: frightened peasants and the soldiers of Leonhart surrounding them, pushing them out of the alley to the relative brightness of the town center, where tents had been set up, and fires lit, and men rushed frantically about to capture the remaining serfs who were trying to run.

Leonhart pulled her along with him, dragging her to stand by the well, where he grabbed both of her shoulders.

"What were you doing?" he demanded, storm and fury. "Leading the escape, Serath?"

"No!" she protested, hands up to push against him, against the irresistible force of him. "No! I didn't even know they were there—"

A group of villagers huddled together now in front of them, most of them kneeling, pleading loudly for mercy.

"Wake the others!" Leonhart ordered, not releasing her from his stare. "Bring them here with the rest!"

This demon was as far from the man who had kissed her as could be. How could she have been so naive as to think he might have an ounce of gentleness? *Here* was the man she had wanted to forget.

Here indeed was the man who had killed her brother.

Serath pushed at him again and was rewarded with her sudden freedom, stumbling backward. In an instant he had her by the flesh of her upper arm, bruising close. They watched together as the rest of the serfs were ushered toward them with muffled cries, a sea of worried faces, guilty looks, and shivering children.

"Count them!" Leonhart commanded, and a man appeared at his shoulder, muttering a number. She heard Leonhart swear under his breath, and then he set his teeth and glared at the tableau in front of him.

In that moment silence fell over the village—a heavy and strained thing, as all the people, peasants and soldiers alike, slowly looked to one another and then to the man that faced them, camplight licking at him with golden tongues. Even the children stopped crying, subdued.

"You know who I am," Rafael said to them, in a

voice that made the steel of his sword seem dull. "You know the law, and what I may do to serfs fleeing the land."

Serath took a step away from him and he pulled her back easily, not even bothering to look at her.

"Six more of you fled tonight. I know at least a dozen of you were trying. Although I am not yet your master, I know the king would grant me this right as your future lord: I could slay each of you who tried."

A keening wail broke out from the crowd, a lone woman's voice, quickly smothered.

"I am not going to kill you!" Leonhart shouted, his anger even more marked. "I will not even punish you—but you must stop this foolishness! There is nothing for you out there!" He used his free hand to gesture to the darkness. "There is only lawlessness, and hunger, and no peace or safety for any of you! *This* is your home! *This* is where you live, and work the land, and tend your animals! Would you leave this place to suffer the deaths of your families by thieves and wild beasts?"

No one answered him. Rafael paused, and Serath felt his words settle over them all, chilling. His men eyed the group with hostility, then looked to their leader.

Leaping shadows from the scattered fires tricked her eyes, hiding faces and then revealing them, creating phantom people against the night. Only Rafael stayed etched in the light, almost seeming to absorb it.

"Fionnlagh is where you shall live," he said now, and his voice was dark and dangerous. "Fionnlagh is where you shall stay. Work with me, and all will be well. Oppose me—and suffer the consequences."

Something happened at the back of the crowd; the shadows became turmoil and quick-moving shapes. More people had chosen to run—three men and two women, but they were not fast enough, and were brought to the

ground with more screams and cries. The rest of the villagers began shouting again. Leonhart's men drew their
swords.

She heard Rafael make some inarticulate sound—fury
again—and then he was speaking to her, forcing her to
look at him.

"Talk to them," he said. "You were with them tonight—tell them what I say is truth!"

"I was not with them! But even if I *could* reach them,
I would not. Let them take their chances in the rest of the
world. I would not wish them to you!"

"Oh, lady of mercy, are you now?" The flames lit his
eyes to an unholy hue, neither gray nor gold, but both.
"Well, look around you, Serath! Look at my men! We are
not farmers, not any of us! We will not survive without
these people, and they will not survive without us!"

"They will!" she cried.

"There are wolves out there, Serath. You saw their
work for yourself. Would you condemn these people—
these *children*—to deaths like that? It is the least of the
dangers they will face, homeless and unarmed. You may
believe me on that. There are outlaws and thieves who
will not hesitate to slit their throats for their meager belongings. Talk to them!"

"I will not help you." She pulled as far from him as
his grip allowed. "I will not!"

"Then they will die," he said flatly. "If not by my
hand, then by your own stubbornness in letting them go.
But hear me well, Serath: beginning tonight I *will* use
force to gain what I want—what has been sworn to me—
until either it is mine or else we are *all* dead."

He gazed down at her, his voice lowered to gravelly
conviction. "I am weary of war, my lady, and that is a
truth. But this place is mine, and I will battle to the end to
gain it."

She stared up at him, speechless, and nothing at all about him gave her any hope: he remained a demon, lethal amid the night and the quick licking flames of the fires. He saw her waver. The warlord aspect of before grew sharper; he crushed her arm in his grip.

"Say it," he murmured. "Or they will die."

Serath faced the crowd.

"Stay," she called out, and felt the simplicity of the word echo around them, sinking into uselessness. She struggled for something more. "He speaks the truth. There is nothing out there in this world for you beyond danger, and peril. Stay here, in your homes. Be protected."

She heard the shape of the word before it became distinct; familiar and dreaded:

"Witch," they were muttering, trading it back and forth among themselves. "Witch, witch, liar, don't listen. . . ."

"No—" Now, of all times, the ache of the word buried into her, the falseness of it a slap to her face. "No—listen to me!"

But they would not. Instead there was a new fervor taking them, carried by the strength of their belief. It was turning powerful and bright amid louder voices, stirring bodies. The men of Leonhart were beginning to step back, swords aloft, eyeing the crowd with fresh alarm.

"Witch!" someone yelled, pointing to her, and the others took up the cry, pointing, trembling with rage or fear or both.

"Get them to stay, Serath." It was Rafael, very close. She turned, startled, and met the shadow of his look. "Say what you must. Get them to stay."

She knew what he meant by it, what he wanted her to do. He would sacrifice anything to gain hold of this place, he had already told her so. The small matter of her reputation—her sanity—would be nothing to him. Serath felt the trembling of the crowd beginning to affect her as well, and her stomach lurched.

"I am no witch!" she hissed at him.

"It doesn't matter if you are or not. Say it. Or people will die."

"I am not . . ." The rest of her sentence slipped away, drowned against the new noise around them, and she had to wipe a hand across her eyes to clear her vision.

"Look at them," Rafael said, fierce. "Look! They will riot soon, and my men will defend themselves! It will be a slaughter! Say what you must, Serath!"

Two serfs tried to breach the wall of the soldiers and the armed men rebuffed them, pushing them back at swordpoint, snarling.

The trembling had taken control of her entire body, stable only because Leonhart still held her, pressed so near now, the rush of his breath in her ear.

"*Serath!*"

"I curse you," she said, her voice small and unheard.

Nothing changed; people were beginning to panic, pushing, shoving.

"I curse you!" she said again, much louder.

A few in the crowd noticed. They stopped what they had been doing and turned to see her, mouths open, looks of horror.

"*I curse you!*" Serath screamed. "*I curse you! I curse you all!*"

"Nooo!" A woman's voice pealed forth, silencing all the rest with its anguish, and it faded off to become sobs.

"You think me a witch, so believe me in this—" Her voice broke, snapped by the trembling, which felt like tears, thick in her throat.

"God shield us!" someone cried, but everyone else had fallen into a terrified silence, gaping at her.

"Stay on this land," Serath said, and felt the tears in her eyes now, painfully hot, "or else I curse you and all of yours!"

She caught sight of the woman who was weeping, kneeling with her arms wrapped around two children who clutched at her and stared at Serath. A boy and a girl—a blond-haired boy, and a dark-haired girl. The boy reached out and took his sister's hand, holding it to his chest. The little girl buried her head against her mother's shoulder.

"Stay," Serath implored them in a voice that she could not make loud, and the tears fell like bitter embers down her cheeks, burning her, scarring her. "Please. I pray you . . . stay here."

The people before her either knelt or fell to the ground, overwhelmed, hiding their faces from her, crossing themselves against her. None would raise their heads.

Leonhart had his arm around her shoulders now, supporting her. He nodded, his face distant, unmoved.

"Fine," he said to her, and the rest. "Excellent."

Chapter Six

*T*HE DAY SHONE WITH FALSE SUMMER; EVERY-thing about it was bright and sunny, and even the shadows seemed to hold a faint warmth against the truth of the season.

Christmas was but a few weeks away, and with it the new year, and all the turmoil that the end of the world would bring. But today, fair and temperate, seemed like a promise from God, a reminder of the slumbering peace of this land.

Another falsity, Serath was certain.

Far and away, she sometimes caught a drift of smoke rising up in the distance, sooty clouds that marked a fire somewhere, fields or woods or villages, no one could say. They appeared to be another unnerving consequence of the abandonment of the countryside, lone fires sparking and burning with no one left to stay them. Light rains at night seemed to control them; eventually, the feathered plumes of smoke would fade off, until the next day, when someone would spot a new patch of it snaking up to the sky.

Serath walked alone near the edge of a plowed meadow, trying not to watch Leonhart and three of his men attempt to coax an ewe from a tangle of brambles.

Two more men ignored the fuss—they watched only the space around her, their eyes even with her pacing, ever vigilant, ever cautious. The meadow behind her stretched out open and plain. There would be no easy place to hide.

The ewe let out a distressed call, no doubt unhappy with her plight, no doubt even more unhappy with the rough attention she was gaining because of it.

There were precious few animals left in their pens at Alderich. Even as Serath overheard the peasants' explanations—*the lord had told them to release them, the animals were not needed, God would see to their needs when the Rapture came very soon*—she found it difficult to believe that these people would abandon and set loose one of the few things that meant their security in this world, even when their master had told them to do so.

But then again, who would dare to disobey Jozua? No one from Alderich, certainly. Even Raibeart, her grandfather's favorite, had hurried to follow his orders whenever Jozua spoke, for fear of his displeasure.

And Serath, raising a hand to shield her eyes, could see the proof of her grandfather's lasting influence even from here. Scattered throughout the hills and fields, clusters of woolly white dappled the dark brown earth. Flocks of sheep roamed the land in complete abandon, moving in and out of the distant woods and vales. Leonhart had sent out men to round up what they could, but Serath knew it would be no easy task. The sheepdogs would not obey the soldiers. And the serfs were too petrified to step foot from the village, not even to gather the sheep.

She had overheard that exchange this morning from her place in the cottage. The peasants spoke her name, and of the threat of her curse, and their fear was so plain that even Leonhart could not, apparently, surmount it. No doubt it had infuriated him, having his plan turned around so abruptly, the people he longed to rule so quick to disobey him. There could be no mistaking the undertone of danger to his voice as he spoke to them. Serath had half expected him to come to her and order her to recant her curse, to tell them to gather the flocks. But he had not.

She felt a tight, spiteful satisfaction in her chest. He had demanded her obedience that night, in the most painful and irrevocable way possible. Well, now he had it, and a town full of people unwilling to leave, not even for a moment, lest the curse fall upon them.

He deserved it all.

Killer. Demon. Impossible man, with his cruel threats and soft touches.

The ewe bleated again, and Serath turned her gaze back to it, troubled.

Leonhart had let her out into the sunshine this morning because she had insisted upon it, sick with the tension of staying blind and deaf in the little hut. The sheer nothingness of her captivity bothered her already—she, who had lived for years with next to nothing, and no words or song to soothe her. But here it was worse somehow, this ringing emptiness. Even the table and benches were gone from her room now; only the mound of dirt and some blankets remained. Clearly he did not trust her enough not to try the same trick again.

So this morning she had stopped him from simply depositing her meal on the ground and leaving, as she knew he would do. He had listened to her request with his body half-turned from the door, staring at the floor. In the end, all he had done was give a slight, distracted frown, as if he heard something off in the distance rather than her, and then just a jerk of his head in assent.

And here she was, tethered to him with an invisible line, for he had not let her stray more than twenty paces away from him, even with all the others around. When she tried once to go farther, the guards had crowded close to her, not meeting her eyes, and told her to stay where she could be seen.

How they were to see her if they would not look at her seemed to be something only Serath wondered at. Only the demon-man, only Rafael, would look square into her eyes anymore. Everyone else turned their heads away when she drew near, soldiers and serfs alike. It was dismally familiar.

". . . two, three—*ho!*" came Rafael of Leonhart's voice, and all four men grunted and strained to push the captured ewe forward through the thorns. The animal called out again, in clear distress.

"Stop." Serath walked to them, unable to bear the pain of the ewe any longer.

Rafael straightened up from the brambles, sweating and scratched on his hands and wrists. His tunic was darkened with moisture, clinging to the outline of him. A lone, thin line of blood marred his cheek; he swiped at it impatiently.

"What?" he asked her, the impatience now directed at her.

"Let me try," Serath said, and motioned them all to move away. The other men backed off at once, but to her private surprise so did Leonhart, after only a moment's hesitation. When she passed him he nodded his head to her, almost taunting. She ignored it.

The ewe was wide-eyed and panting in the tangled brush. Wily, supple vines and branches like taut stings held her bound in place, firmly caught. She watched Serath approach with trembling fear.

Serath advanced slowly, calmly, holding out her hands in a gesture of peace, letting the animal see them. She spoke in a soothing voice, saying things that were nonsense, childish talk, using her tone instead of words to ease them both. She did not touch the ewe but kept up her soft nonsense talk, until the whites of the animal's eyes receded, and its breathing slowed. All else faded away, the men, the field, until there was just her and this unfortunate sheep, alone with the problem of the brambles.

When she could Serath knelt in front of the brush, examining the bonds that held the ewe. She made certain to stroke its nose, calming again, and then began to tug at the vines and thorns, pulling apart the puzzle bit by bit. The ewe stood silent before her, her head drooping down to Serath's shoulder with trust and exhaustion, her breath blowing against Serath's neck.

The final strands of the brambles bent free; suddenly the ewe darted forward, knocking into Serath but stopping and skipping back to her, shaking, pressed to her skirts. Serath stroked her nose again, praising her.

The men came forward, seizing the animal, leading her off down the path to the village. Leonhart, now next to her, watched them go.

"Mutton tonight," he said, sounding almost cheerful.

Serath turned to him, appalled. "You're going to eat her?"

He glanced down at her, brilliant with the sun, tanned and heartless. "We have to eat," he said, and shrugged.

Serath crossed her arms over her chest. "I won't."

"The hell you won't."

"I won't do it," she said.

He gave the field a small smile, a bare curving of his

lips. "I hear that from you a great deal, my lady. And yet I think there is always a way around your resolve."

She ignored his quiet mockery, caught between frustration and consternation, and the only thing she could think to say was: "It's not fair."

He studied her now, his nightcloud gaze intent on her, slate gray. That frown he had worn before was back, distant and pondering, as if she confounded him in some deep way. Yet when she searched his eyes she saw he was anything but distant—that what greeted her there was something warm and shamefully familiar, that unspoken intensity between them. It reached out and found its complement blooming in her heart, distinct and undeniable.

She remembered his kisses, her own shaking reaction to them. Serath bent her head, pretending to examine the brambles.

"No, it's not fair," said Rafael now. "But that's our lot in life, Serath. Fairness is mere fantasy, both for us and them." From the edges of her vision she saw him gesture to the village, and didn't know if he meant the ewe, or the serfs, or both. "We each have our roles. You must understand this by now."

"I won't eat her," Serath repeated, watching the broken vines.

"Then starve," he said, and walked away.

How did she manage it? Rafe gave a shake of his head to the trees, half of him still listening for her behind him, left at the brambles.

She had done it again, found that persistent pang in him that echoed her emotions, that left him feeling things he never thought to feel again—compassion, pain. Pity for a creature meant for nothing but wool and food, and for her, for Serath and her gentle heart. It left him angry and baffled and stirred, all at once.

He did not want to feel these things. He did not enjoy feeling them. They hampered him, they constricted him in ways he had not even imagined. They reminded him of wants he preferred hidden away—*trust, need, comfort*—bits of him long ago buried by time and his own command of his destiny.

There was no room in his life for such emotions. Too much depended upon his strength; too many expected him to reign in this place with complete and total confidence. Anything less would be an affront to Leonhart, and all the suffering his people had endured over the years. He would not sacrifice his future, nor theirs, for these soft and sliding feelings.

After all, Serath Rune had grown up with all the things denied to him, the bounty of Alderich—what right had he to overlook such a fact? If she suffered some now, surely it would be worth it, to ensure the peace of the new, united land he would rule.

Yet she did affect him. And Rafael had never thought to fall so completely into touch with another person, least of all a maiden. *Last* of all a maiden from Alderich.

He had been so proud of the way she handled the crowd that precarious night. He had been impressed, even, hearing her words, observing her mastery of the hysteria that had seemed certain to drown them all.

But no. Serath had tamed the volatile mood of the people, just as she had this bedraggled sheep, and both times he stood near and simply admired her for all that she was—all that she didn't know she was: courage and insight, light and clarity.

It had hurt her to cast her false curse, Rafe knew that. She had wept as she spoke and he had watched that as well, the gleaming paths of her tears.

His own practical spirit had dismissed it as inconsequential—if the people were going to fear her, at least *use* the fear—but another part of him, that hidden part . . .

. . . had ached for her. And with her. Had wanted to hold her to him and kiss away that pain, and kindle in her a forgetfulness of her misery with the desire that lived between them. And it did live between them. He knew that now.

It was a damnable thing.

Rafael came out of his contemplations, back to the field, the bright day. A glance behind him showed him Serath still where he had left her, watching him. The urge to return to her was nearly overwhelming.

Strangely enough, it was this final realization that made Rafael understand the danger of her, why he had to stay away. If he was not careful he would slip away to such pleasant daydreams that he might find himself doing almost anything for Serath Rune. And he would not grant her that kind of power over him. He could not afford that. Not now. Not ever.

He turned away from her again, and kept walking.

"My lord."

Rafe found Abram ahead of him, with a few of the other men.

"You sent for me?" his cousin asked.

"Walk with me," Rafe said, and the men fell in behind them.

They crossed the path to the village, headed for the edge of the fallow field beyond them, a mountainside of green and gold at the end of it blocking out the sky. He was not surprised to hear the bells of the castle begin their song, a brief series of notes to mark the midday.

"How fare the villagers?" Rafe asked.

Abram, younger than he by five years, had the look of a man older by a dozen. He had always been this way, Rafael thought, sober and sturdy during all the hardship and the violence of the years. When his cousin had reached twenty, Rafe had finally allowed him to join their roving band, and it had been Abram—always Abram—who had kept calm amid the plentiful storms, and had a level head when everyone else turned rash and reckless.

So Rafe was not surprised when Abram did not grin, or even smile at their mastery in keeping the peasants at Fionnlagh. All he did was speak to the air in front of him, deliberate and plain.

"No new losses. No threat of it, either, at least as far as I can tell."

"A measurable success," Rafe noted. "And what of the stores of food?"

"Hard to say. They've managed to put away a fair amount—some of them, at least, were thinking of the future. But they let too many fields go fallow."

"Jozua Rune will not have shut himself off without adequate supplies. We can hope he has more up at the castle."

"Aye," agreed Abram, and then sealed his lips closed.

"Is there something else you want to say?" Rafael asked him, just as plain.

Abram's brown eyes were frank. "I don't like our situation, not any of it. I don't like the woman, and I don't understand why you allow her such ways. It cannot be good."

"You said yourself the serfs are staying. How else would you have had me do it? You saw how close it came to ending the wrong way."

"Aye," said Abram again, reluctant. "They fear her now, right enough. And so do your own men, Rafe. Now there is a weakness among us."

"Do you fear her?" Rafael asked, mild.

"No," he answered, only a shade too quickly. "But

you cannot deny that air of sorcery about her. I wonder at the rumors now, if they weren't more truth than not."

"Listen," Rafe said. "I'll tell this only to you. She is no witch—nothing like that at all. She only said those things because I forced her to."

"They said it was the same spell her mother used. The very same words."

Rafael had a flash of appreciation for Serath again, for her quick thinking and sharp wit.

"And that's not the end of it," Abram went on, lowering his voice. "I saw what she did with that ewe, Rafe, and so did quite a few others. One of the villagers next to me said it's exactly what Morwena would do, that she cast some sort of spell over the beasts, taming them, so that they would become docile as pets."

"It's just talk, Abram."

"Well, talk or not, it's more trouble than we need, I say. She's got these serfs caught up in something—if not a spell, then at least the power of fear."

"All the better. Whether you like the means or not, Serath persuaded these people to stay. We need them, you know it as well as I. We cannot tear away the population of Leonhart to toil this land. It would weaken our defenses on both sides. There are not enough of us."

"Aye." Abram sounded gloomy.

They had reached the end of the field. Rafe stopped, gazing up at the stunning blue of the sky, and then ahead of him, to the mountain, and the remote white fortress at the top.

"It's going to have to be a seige, I think," he said.

Abram stood beside him, silent. After a moment he said, "News from Leonhart, my lord."

Rafe turned to him.

"Your mother," said Abram. "She has heard of your arrival here. I think perhaps she comes."

Rafael closed his eyes. "Jesu. Just what I needed."

"Aye," agreed Abram in his gloomy voice.

THE TOLLING OF THE CASTLE BELLS FILLED THE chamber, echoing off the stones with such sharp clarity that the captain of Jozua Rune's guard fought hard not to wince as he stood at attention, waiting for the Lord of Alderich to acknowledge him.

Jozua was standing by the lone window in his solar, staring out. Sunlight spilled past him into the room, warming it, and Olivier passed the time by watching motes of dust whirl in slow circles across the air, carried by a lazy draft.

At last the old man spoke, still facing the view.

"Your report, Olivier?"

"Leonhart and his men seem scattered thin, my lord. They spend their time in the hills, chasing animals. The villagers do not appear to be aiding them."

"No," said Jozua. "They would not. They know who he is."

Olivier cleared his throat. "There are only occasional glimpses of your granddaughter, walking in the village or fields. Mostly she is kept hidden."

He paused, waiting for further questions on the subject of Serath Rune, knowing the lord's burning interest in her. But time passed again, unbroken, and Jozua said nothing at all, only stared out the window at the sky and clouds beyond him.

Olivier shifted his balance from his left foot to his right. He did not move otherwise.

"Do you believe in evil, Olivier?"

"Aye, my lord," he replied. "The church declares it so."

"The church," said Jozua, and nodded to the sky. "Yes." Still without turning, he asked, "And would you say you have led a virtuous life? Shall the Lord find you deserving when He comes?"

"I pray it will be so, my lord."

Jozua seemed to give a small laugh. "Pray very hard, Olivier. You do not have much time left before you will know most certainly." He turned now, moving over to sit at a table of darkened wood, motioning the captain nearer. "So you believe in evil. Very well. What say you to the existence of sin?"

Olivier stammered, "Sin must, perforce, exist, my lord."

"Aye, perforce. Is it a sin, would you say, to aid in evil?"

"Aye, my lord."

"So that which helps evil, becomes evil itself?"

Olivier shifted again. "I—suppose it is so, my lord."

Jozua Rune said quietly, "Evil lives down in that village, Captain. Evil is thriving down there. Whom do you suppose is aiding it?"

Olivier swallowed, not replying.

The old man smiled. "We both know, do we not? She is only a woman."

Jozua stood up from the table, coming very close to Olivier, so close that the captain could make out the particular shade of green of his eyes, the flecks of hazel within them. Despite the worn face of the man, those eyes shone brightly.

Jozua's next question was spoken at near silence, his breath stirring Olivier's hair.

"Would you die for me, soldier?"

"You know I would, my lord."

"Are you certain? Is your loyalty so strong?"

From nowhere a knife appeared in Jozua's hand. With a quickness that belied his age it was suddenly at Olivier's throat, cold as winter. A faint quiver from the hand that held it sent subdued sparks of pain into his skin. The captain did not dare look away.

The blade pressed harder against him, Jozua's face very close, examining him impartially.

Time stretched out. Olivier felt his eyes begin to water—fear or strain from not blinking, he didn't know, and still Jozua did not move, but kept the knife in place, taut beneath his chin. The green of his eyes was hard and clear, revealing only remote curiosity as he stared at his captain. Olivier was reminded of nothing so much as a cat contemplating the torture of its meal before the final blow.

A swelling of fear began to form in his throat, laboring his breath.

"My life for you," the soldier whispered. "My life for you. . . ."

When his body began to tremble, when Olivier thought he could not remain in place a second longer, Jozua at last stepped back, lowering the blade.

"Your loyalty speaks for you," said the old man, still with his remote green look. "It's why I chose you for Alderich, to complete my rule here should I die before the new millennium."

Olivier spoke around the thickness in his throat. "You shall not die before that, my lord."

"No," Jozua agreed, placidly. "I don't think I shall." His hands cradled the heavy knife; Olivier could see now the wicked shape to it, polished and deadly. A thin gleam of red lined its edge—his own blood, sacrifice to the blade.

He heard Jozua murmur, "I have no time for death yet. There is too much to do before the new year."

———— ⟨⟡⟩ ————

$\mathscr{C}$ONTRARY TO THE DEMON-MAN'S THREAT, SER-
ath did not starve during supper. While everyone else ate
meat stew from the doomed ewe, she had bread. And
cheese. And even a salted dish of leeks and onions, cooked
to wilted lumps. Rafael had made certain of it, that she
had been given a meal despite his curt words this morning. He even came inside her hut as she ate, and Serath
had not tempted fate again by shunning her plate. She
consumed everything before her.

Leonhart, standing by the fire since there was no
bench, studied her, inscrutable. She did not need to look
up at him from her pallet to feel his stare.

"How is it?" he asked her, after a few minutes.

"Well enough," she answered, which was a lie. The
bread was stale, the cheese too hard, and the vegetables
left a strange taste in her mouth, metallic.

Rafe watched her take another bite and chew with
determination, as if she could will him away just by concentrating on this one thing.

It almost made him smile, but he conquered that. She
wouldn't appreciate a smile from him, and for some reason he had no wish to rile her. It was somewhat pleasant,
actually, just to contemplate her where she perched on
the edge of the pallet amid her blankets, her plate bal-
anced on her lap. She moved with a spareness that fascinated him, simple grace, nothing grand or unnecessary.
He supposed she might have learned it in the convent, but
then he thought not. It seemed too natural to her.

Her silence—that she had learned. And perhaps the
way she kept her eyes lowered but not shuttered, leaving
the impression she saw things no one else did, a careful
deference that shielded her intelligence. Even the slow

bites, the steady breathing—no rush, just calm, just seren- ity—he could envision being the products of her life with the nuns. But not her grace, not that special air about her, mysterious and fey and divinely feminine.

No, that part was uniquely Serath, and Rafe found himself admiring it all the more, recognizing it for what it was.

Her lips had been so soft. Innocence was what he had tasted there, untried, and it had left him in a tempest of desire, the want to have her—to take her as his own— nearly overcoming him.

Rafe looked away from her, toward the gentle fire in the room. It had been a perilous moment for him. Per- haps she had no idea. Perhaps she never would.

Don't do it.

He should not kiss her again. Despite her heritage she was a noblewoman, and he was no country oaf, despoiler of anything so rare and fine.

Don't.

And he definitely should not have come here tonight. He should have listened to that flare of warning he got whenever she was near, and stayed away from her, as he had meant to do this afternoon. But it was too late for regrets now. He had wanted to ensure that her wishes for her meal, however impractical, had been seen to. He had wanted to see for himself that she would eat the food given her. It would not do to have her wasting away over some damn foolish notion of nobility toward an ani- mal. . . .

Serath raised her hands to her lips, taking another bite. The firelight gleamed over her skin, inviting.

No. He would not kiss her again. She was bound for her convent. As soon as he had what he needed from her, and her grandfather, he would release her. She could spend her life with nuns and prayers for all eternity, if she wished.

It was this thought that finally moved Rafael forward into the room, circling past the pit of the fire, to the only thing he had left her at all—her pallet, soft comfort, blankets already molded to her shape. Large enough for two, he thought, easily so. Aye . . . and with just the slightest, slightest slip of his imagination, Rafe could feel how it might happen, how he would run his hand underneath her hair, to the heat of the back of her neck, and then lower her to the covers, until her arms circled up around him, bringing him down to her. . . .

Stop now.

Serath lifted her head and gazed at him warily, hands frozen over her meal, a lock of hair waving free from the braid she had made.

"You did well the other night," Rafe said to her, trying to break through the caution that marked her entire body.

She didn't reply; he thought he saw a new tension come over her, the opposite of what that hidden part of him wanted, her willing softness.

Stop.

"I was . . . impressed," he said, and found the beating pulse in her throat, light and rapid. His own speeded up in response. In anticipation.

"To what are you referring, my lord?" she asked coolly. "Your threat or your kiss?"

The mere word from her increased his lust, the shape of her lips around it, pink and succulent. But the boldness of her direct attack made him want to smile again, and he had to speak around the conflicts in him.

"Raised in a convent." He let the smile come. "You're not what I expected."

"While you are exactly what I expected," she retorted. "Excepting your lack of horns."

The smile turned to laughter, soft and buried, and even her response to this scorched through him: the narrowing of her blue eyes, the haughty disdain that hid her true self. To control himself he looked up, away, and found the smoke hole in the roof, the telltale shattered reeds hanging from part of it.

"That night I found you—not with the villagers," he added, with a sideways look at her, "but at the convent, you had scaled the wall. What were you doing there, Serath?"

The haughtiness of before increased, a regal queen too proud to answer. She lifted her hand and ate a bite of cheese instead, chewing, facing away. Firelight slid along the line of her jaw, delicate and smooth. Her lashes were lowered, sable dark against her skin.

Don't think of it.

"You went to escape," Rafe said. He sat down beside her, very careful not to touch her. "But I am wondering, my lady—why?"

She took another bite, ignoring him.

Don't think of her hair, loose and long, fragrant.

"Why?" he asked again.

Her mouth, perfect, luscious, her hands against him, touching him—

"I was tired of being struck," she said at last. "It grows wearisome."

His fantasies spun down to nothing, halted flat against her words.

Serath did not pause in eating, very controlled, still so regal. "So I decided to leave."

In all of his years of roving and plundering, not once had he used violence against a woman. Not once had he suffered any man of his to do so. His father's lessons had stuck to him well even after his death: guard the women. Protect them. Defend the meek.

He would not make the mistake of thinking Serath Rune meek, despite her lowered lashes. But she was a woman, gossamer and fancy, and the idea that anyone had hurt her in such a way—*anyone*—built up in him a boiling rage.

She mistook his silence for further inquiry, mayhap, for after a moment of deliberation, she said, "I had thought it such a fortuitous thing. The bishop was visiting, distracting the prioress. I had gained the key to the gate." She shook her head, thoughtful. "So many elements fell together in one perfect moment. I could not resist it. And then you came—so I suppose it was not so perfect, after all."

"On the contrary," he replied. "I commend your timing."

"You would," she said darkly.

Her plate was empty. She rested her hands beside it, her fingers touching the edges, pale flesh against pewter.

"I am sorry I did not come sooner," Rafael said, a sort of offering to her, but she only gave her own smile to the night, derisive.

"Oh, yes—and you would have battered down the walls of a convent to steal me? Was that to be the way of it, my lord? The king and the church would hardly overlook that, no matter how many aged decrees you had on your side."

He answered her slowly, letting her gauge his utter sincerity. "Serath, there is nothing that would have stopped me from taking you. Know that now. Not convent walls. Not church decrees. Nothing."

When she glanced up at him he was nearly lost in her again, her sapphire and midnight radiance, her oval face and full lips.

He said to her, "I always get what I want. Eventually."

Don't. . . .

Her eyes dropped down to his mouth, unwillingly, he could see, but still caught there, leaning into him just so slightly. She probably had no idea she was doing it. His will began to crumble.

No one will stop you. Even she wouldn't stop you. . . .

He stood quickly and Serath started back, a tint of rose sweeping high over her cheekbones.

"Where did you think to go?" Rafael asked, trying to stem the temptation of disaster.

Don't do it, don't even look at her. . . .

She took a long breath—just the sound of it held an enticing allure—and he looked at her anyway, watched her raise a hand to the brooch pinned to her gown, her touch light against her throat. The moonstone gleamed silvery smooth, the rubies around it glowing in crimson points. Once again, she did not answer him.

"You had food for only a day or two, at the most," Rafe said, still standing from his safe distance, his gaze fixed on her hand, those stones. "So you could not have meant to go far. But where?"

And to whom? he wanted to add, but stemmed that, as well.

He did not think she could have had a suitor, not locked away as she had been—and not judging by the way she had kissed him, the shocked purity that had defined her. Rafe knew it was highly unlikely that she had been able to form an attachment to any man, even if one had been desperate or foolish enough to test Jozua Rune. Certainly he had never heard of such a rumor, and God knew there were rumors enough about her.

If she had had a secret lover, they would have met clandestinely, away from nuns and all others—a near impossibility, he knew. But just the remote prospect of it pricked at him with unexpected force.

"All I wanted was to see the ocean," Serath said softly.

"The ocean?" His attention swung back to her, surprised. "Why?"

Her hand released the brooch; she lowered it to her lap again, grasping the plate.

"When I was a child, my mother used to take me there. It was the one place where she could find peace, watching the water, the waves. I wanted to see that again."

"Just that?" he persisted. "The ocean, that's all? You'd risk your life for it, my lady, this whim to see the water?"

She looked at him askance, assessing. "I've spent nine years behind convent walls. Nine years of solitude, and marble and prayer and cold hands. I wanted the ocean, one last time. I wanted that peace. It was no whim."

"And then?" he asked, not looking away from her face.

She didn't reply.

"Serath—what then, after the ocean?" he asked, hushed.

She gave a half smile down to her lap, almost wistful. "Well, the world *is* about to end."

For a moment Rafael did nothing. Then he laughed again, unable to contain it, feeling a strange elation at her words.

"It's not," he said. "I won't let it. I have waited too long for these lands and this place to let it end here, with just this."

"Think you to control the will of God, demon-man?" she asked quietly.

"Aye," he replied. "In this instance—depend upon it."

Chapter Seven

T HE VILLAGE WAS A JUMBLE OF DISORDER.
Rafael could not deny it any longer; having the people constrained to this plot of land was no longer a good thing. They walked about in a kind of nervous torpor, huddled together in coves of gossip, and fearful shapes. Subtle whispers caught his ear: truly they had displeased the Lord, to be forced to spend the last of their days here, trapped with a devil and a witch. Curses, omens, portents, catastrophe—they were doomed. . . .

He noted Calum out and working, a few young men with him, at the mill, the slaughterhouse, occasionally the smithy. But that was all. Everyone else just hid.

Rafe knew it was his own doing, an incantation brewed and served up through the inspiration of a black-haired, blue-eyed faerie queen—or novice nun, depending upon her mood—and it had worked so effectively that this afternoon Rafe stood hip deep in a noisy mass of

animals, all of them skittering madly across the meadow
that rimmed the eastern part of the village.

Goats and sheep and a few stout pigs ran around him
and into him, the meager success of his soldier's shepherd-
ing abilities. They had almost gotten them to the village.
But, perhaps the result of weeks of freedom, the animals
would not be chased into the pens.

Men on foot and horseback attempted to impose order on the chaos, with little effect. Dogs barked frantically
on the fringes, exciting the flock further.

Villagers watched from the end of the town, or else
from their homes, behind windows and doors.

And Serath Rune, a sylph perched on a stone in the
meadow, appeared to ignore it all, although sometimes
Rafael caught her looking toward him, a faint curl of
victory to her lips.

Damn her. She had been like this ever since he had
come so close to kissing her again in her cottage. They
had not spoken of it again since; every moment between
them after that night had been marked by nothing but
frigid politeness. Rafe himself had initiated it. At the time
it had seemed a wise, even inspired, idea. Putting emotional distance between them, he had reasoned, would
help sever this unwelcome link to her. Remembering and
enforcing their roles here—ruler and hostage—could do
naught but good for his troubled mind.

Why wasn't it working?

Still she haunted him. Still he found himself looking
forward to seeing her, talking to her, even if it was the
most perfunctory of comments.

And Serath herself had acted as if none of it mattered
to her. Her icy facade never broke; she never seemed
relieved to see him, or chagrined, or anything at all. Indeed, this slight mocking smile from her now was the
most revealing sentiment she had offered him in days.

It was as if he truly was nothing to her, and this was what irritated Rafael most of all.

At night he dreamed of her. By day he found himself straining to catch sight of her, to relish her beauty, aloof as it was. No matter how hard the work, or how tired he might be, the image of her would always revive him to exasperation, or admiration, or just plain lust.

A goat ran into him, bucking painfully, followed by another, which paused to take a swipe at him with its teeth.

"Enough of this!" Rafael said out loud, and Abram and two others looked to him in harried inquiry, all of them wrangling with sheep. Rafe strode over to Serath on her stone, the sun on his back, ire in his steps.

"Tell them to work the fields," he said to her, when he was near enough.

"Tell who?" she asked innocently. "The sheep or your men? Both seem to be doing a fine job of it as it is."

"Do not test me now, Serath. You know what I speak of. Go to the serfs and tell them they must work the land."

She turned her head away, chin up, that irksome smile still in place.

"Very well," he snapped. "I find I have need of a shepherdess, my lady. I think you will do nicely."

He grabbed her by the arm and hauled her off the rock, pulling her into the confusion.

"Enjoy your task," he invited her, his own wrath nearly as cold as hers. "I have heard that animals heed witches. This should be little effort for you."

Her spine straightened. Serath yanked her arm free, picked up her skirts, and waded through the bent grass to the center of the meadow, chin still high. There she stopped and turned, black fire and blue ice, and slowly, majestically, she lifted one hand to the sheep in front of her.

He watched, as enthralled as the rest of the men, all of them pausing to stare at her.

"Cease!" Serath intoned, in a rich and ringing voice.

And then she remained that way, surveying the sheep, which only pranced and darted around her.

Somewhere in the distance a cock crowed.

She glanced back at him, and there could be no mistaking the expression on her face now.

"Why, look, great lord, they heed me not," she called out sweetly. "Alas, I cannot command the animals for you."

A lamb toddled up to her, followed by its mother. By chance or good fortune, both halted just in front of Serath, then started to graze. Another ewe followed them, turned away but still quiet, its head bent down to nibble the grass.

One by one, bit by bit, the animals bunched together in the meadow, calming nearly docile. Even the billy goat that had tried to bite Rafe hung near the edges of the herd, offering a yellow glare to the world around him.

Serath, hand still raised, stared down at them all, and Rafael could see the slow, bewildered look come over her, quickly followed by something he could only describe as complete dismay.

Rafe started to laugh. A man behind him uttered, "By all the saints," in impressed tones, and then others began to speak, low and amazed.

Serath met his look, and her hand came down. She picked up her skirts again, saying nothing, and walked past him and all the others, back up the hill to the village. He followed after her, just as the animals did, all the way to the nearest pen, made of rickety wood with the gate gaping open. People had begun to gather near the brink of

the meadow, drawn to the spectacle. All stood silent as
Serath entered the pen as any true shepherdess might,
turning and making little *hep! hep!* sounds to the sheep
and goats, which, with just a few exceptions, ambled in
behind her.

Some levelheaded fellow remembered to shut the gate
after they were all in. Peasants and soldiers alike stood
around the pen amid the rising dust, looking at her and
then at one another.

Serath came to the gate, reopened it, and left the pen.
She found Calum in the crowd—she must have remembered him from before—tall and red-headed. As she approached him he showed no fear—rather admirably,
Rafael thought.

"Work the fields," she said to him, clipped and precise. "These are your lands, and your animals. Do not
neglect them. God disparages waste."

The man bowed his head to her, immediately deferential; she nodded to him and walked away again. The
crowd parted for her with rapid respect.

Rafe began to walk after her.

"A rider!" someone called then, and Rafael looked
toward the road that led out of the village, scanning the
countryside, seeing nothing.

"There, my lord!" said the same man, behind him,
and when Rafe turned the other way he saw what his
scout had: a lone man on a horse, picking its way slowly
down the path from the castle.

Not a rider from the outside world—his mother or
the king or the church. A rider from Fionnlagh Castle. A
man from Jozua Rune.

Everyone gathered at the base of the mountain, waiting, some mounted, some on foot. All armed and bris-
tling with nerve, eager for whatever their enemy had to
offer them.

Rafael had forgotten to order Serath back to her cottage; he saw her now with her guard standing too far away for his peace, and he motioned his men to bring her closer to him.

The messenger from the castle wore the colors of Alderich, a tunic of blue and white, a combination that had always brought out a seething resentment in Rafe as a child, and even as a young man. But he faced this stranger with no emotion, knowing well enough now how to hide any hint of himself, disguise all weaknesses.

The man approached, coming no closer than a stone's throw, remaining mounted. He was older than Rafe, blond and ruddy, eyeing the group from Leonhart with clear suspicion. Rafe tried to remember if this was the same guard he had dealt with before, at the top of the gatehouse. Probably not. Probably Rune had an army of such men tucked away up there.

"I have a message from the Lord of Alderich," announced the man, looking straight at Rafael.

"Deliver it," Rafe responded.

"My master says to tell you to come to the castle this night. He will meet with his granddaughter after the setting of the moon."

--------⟨∞⟩--------

𝒯HE MOON SET TOO QUICKLY.

It seemed to drop from the sky in no time at all, swallowed up by the blackness of the night, hidden away, perhaps, behind coy stars that winked and glittered at her.

Serath locked her hands on the saddle in front of her, eyes raised to the path ahead, already at the stone road of the castle. Already at the star-shadowed boundary of the keep.

It was an eerie repetition of the scene they had played

out days ago, transposed to night instead of day. Rafael
was still beside her. Her steed was again secured to his
own. More men rode up behind them, an army ready for
attack.

And her grandfather was still up ahead, cloistered
from the world in her childhood home.

Only this time, they would gain entry.

This time, she would see him.

A greasy sickness rolled up inside her and Serath
closed her eyes against it, quelling it. She would not be
the one to break now. Everyone else seemed so ruthless,
so brutal. She would not be the one to dissolve into tears
or laughter with her apprehension.

Calm, she silently chided herself. *Stay calm. Mayhap it
won't be that bad. . . .*

But it was worse.

Worse to hear the clinking of the chains that lowered
the gate, and then raised the portcullis of Fionnlagh Castle. She had heard that sound countless times in years
gone by, and never once had it given her gooseflesh.
Never once had it sent waves of trepidation rushing
through her.

Worse still to ride into the bailey—so familiar!—a
hostage where she had once been a princess, handed
down from her dun mare by the men of her enemy, surrounded by them.

To walk through the thick, dark doors of the keep, to
feel that stone-cooled air brush her cheeks, to inhale the
scent of rushes, and woodsmoke, and beeswax. To see the
shapes of the rooms unchanged, shadowy ceilings and intricate frescos on the walls, a checkered tile down the
hallway that she remembered—vermilion and cobalt, distinct and colorful.

To hear the resounding silence that surrounded them
as they were escorted across the great hall, past hanging

tapestries and tables bereft of people, eyes watching from the corners and shadows, their own footsteps the only relief to the emptiness.

And now, worst of all: to see his face. Jozua Rune himself, white-haired, seamed and gaunt and looking exactly the same as the very last time she had seen him, when he had banished her from this land and all that she had ever known or loved.

"Grandfather," Serath greeted him, with fragile composure. She walked to the head table where he sat alone in a splendid chair of gilt and emerald cushions, then dipped a shallow curtsy.

Jozua spared her a flicker of a glance, nothing more. She saw his gaze move instead to take in the man beside her. Rafael had not strayed more than a pace from her side.

"So," Jozua said to him, his voice echoing in the room. "You come to me."

"You knew I would," Rafael replied.

Only one of the great hearths held a fire; three others were hollowed out of the walls, dead and cold. No torches were lit. Yet Serath could see, as her eyes adjusted to this dimness, that a good many men stood lined up around the edges of this room, more men than she had initially thought. Their chain mail gleamed in the cheerless light, faint curves of sword hilts barely visible.

One man in particular caught her notice. He stood closest to her grandfather, tall and blond. The rider of before, she thought. She vaguely remembered him from her childhood, captain of Jozua's guard.

Unlike the others, this man seemed nearly uninterested in Rafael. He kept his hard stare on her alone, hooded, appraising.

"How do you know I have not set you a trap, Rafael

of Leonhart?" her grandfather asked, and the demon-man beside her only smiled in response, cryptic.

She knew how carefully he had prepared for this. She had noted the squadrons of riders leaving the village at different times, in different directions, all headed into the mountain woods, scouts and attack forces ready for anything. She knew the leader of Leonhart would not walk blindly into a trap, and so did Jozua.

"A strange hour you have chosen to meet, Jozua Rune," said Rafael evenly.

Her grandfather had his own smile now, thin against his face. "I am an old man. Daylight is too uncharitable for me. The night is my time. And you, Leonhart, with all your youth and boldness—surely you do not cower at the dark."

"You will find I cower at nothing."

Jozua leaned back in his chair. Serath saw the light pick out the gold on his tunic, rich ermine in the folds.

"Such a brave warrior," he commented in the same neutral tone Rafael had used. "You offer a woman as your shield."

"Not just any woman." Now Rafael had a new smile, plainly insolent. "Only the one that used to be yours."

Serath sucked in her breath at this; a suspended hush swept over them all. She blinked and clasped her hands in front of her, then released them again. When she dared to she looked up at her grandfather, and found him finally looking back at her, grave.

"Serath," he said to her, in such a gentle voice that her heart nearly shattered with hope. She took a half step forward, filled with yearning, and then he motioned to something on the table beside him.

"Pour the wine, child."

Her world came crashing back into place with breathtaking disappointment, bitter swift. She barely even felt the restraining hand on her arm, Rafael holding her back.

"I did not come here for wine, Rune."

Jozua's eyes noticed the touch between them; he did not look away from it.

"Oh?" he drawled. "What did you come to my demesne for, Leonhart?"

"For what is rightfully mine. For what you seek to destroy—with madness or simple spite, I cannot say."

Jozua bared his teeth, a warning. "I am not mad, Leonhart."

"No," Rafael responded. "I thought not."

His hold on Serath's arm had not abated. She felt his strength, the tension in his fingers.

"Nor do I have aught of yours," Jozua continued, still watching the two of them together, his eyes bright and venomous.

"Will you defy the king, then?" Rafael asked smoothly.

"Not I. Only God may do such a thing. I am but His servant."

Serath made some small movement at this, a reflex of nerves, recalling with sudden force the nursery tales repeated to her, over and over. That terrible day was coming—smoke and death.

"Ask my granddaughter what the new year shall bring." Jozua stared at her again, a challenge. "She knows full well."

Rafael slanted her a look, buried inquiry, but she said nothing. She could not speak of it. She would not. It was too real here in this place, too deeply embedded in her to deny it, as she wanted, or to treat it with disdain. No matter how she wished it were not so, Serath knew she believed in it with her whole heart.

. . . the devil will come, but it will be too late . . . for

the beginning of the thousand years will be the end time for all of us—

Rafael spoke over her fears.

"All the new year shall bring is the proper lord to rule Alderich."

"On that we agree. The Lord shall indeed rule here soon."

Serath glanced at Rafael, to see if he understood the meaning of her grandfather's words. The narrowing of his eyes showed her he had.

"This place *will* be mine." His words were clear and deliberate.

"Only the worthy may rule here, Leonhart."

"Why should that be—when the unworthy has held it for so long?"

A murmur took the room, faded.

Jozua had his thin smile again. He said lightly, "You amuse me, Leonhart. You do. Such arrogance. Yet I know your true place will be revealed soon enough."

"My true place," Rafael echoed, and then nodded. "Aye, indeed." His hand swept the room, a gesture of possession. "Yet it will not be soon enough for me."

"Nor me," said Jozua, in a voice that used to make Serath quiver as a child.

They were silent for a moment, these two adversaries, each one staring hard at the other. To Serath, caught between them, the tension felt so thick and strong it seemed to bend the very air.

In the end it was her grandfather who broke the moment.

"Come now, a drink," exclaimed Jozua, indicating the wine again, a golden ewer and two goblets lined up on the table. "Let it not be said I refused to play host to anyone, not even the devil of Leonhart."

Rafael slowly shook his head. The men behind him shifted, cloth and metal rubbing together.

"Don't trust me?" Jozua gave a cackling laugh. "Very well. Fair enough. My granddaughter will drink first, to prove my goodwill. Won't you, girl?"

"No," Rafael said instantly.

"Won't you, Serath?" pressed Jozua, focused on her.

"Yes, Grandfather," she said.

When she attempted to move forward Rafael restrained her again, until she looked back at him, defiant, feeling wildly dauntless in this moment. His face was closed and harsh. He did not release her arm.

"What!" Jozua laughed. "You think I would actually sacrifice my only living blood to this feud of ours, Leonhart?"

Serath pulled again at her arm and Rafael let go abruptly. His eyes were dark and unreadable.

She approached the table, stepped up on the dais, and grasped the ewer—pearls lined the handle, crystals studded the bowl of it—and poured the wine as she had so many times before, quickly and evenly into the two goblets, filling them a little over half each. She picked up one, and handed it to her grandfather. He took it from her and their fingers brushed—his hand was cold and dry.

The remaining goblet was cool, heavy. She gazed down at the surface of the wine, almost black in this light, showing only a burnished crescent reflection of the rim. The liquid dipped and swayed in her grasp, inky and dense. When Serath lifted it to her face she could see her own eyes shining there, and then her lips.

Close behind her, she could hear the breathing of Rafael, long and sustained. It seemed to be the only sound in the room.

She drank.

The wine tasted strongly of spices and wood, the

richness of it almost overwhelming, an assault on her tongue; she could not tell if there was poison in it or not. She swallowed carefully, lowering the goblet.

"I might," murmured her grandfather now, casting her a small smile. "I might just do it. . . ."

Rafael had moved closer to her still, gazing at her with tightly coiled emotion. Serath looked away from him, back to Jozua and his sinister smile. She raised the goblet to her grandfather and took another drink.

Mandrake, hemlock, nightshade—it could be almost anything . . . she shut out that thought, tilting the goblet higher, until she had drained it completely.

When she finished, panting, all were intent upon her, every man in the room seeming to wait for her to grab her throat, or fall to the ground, or simply die where she stood.

Serath placed the goblet back on the table, looking at no one. She wiped a hand across her lips and saw the smear of maroon left there, garish against her skin.

The wine burned its way down to her stomach, gurgling, the aftertaste turning sour in her mouth.

"Pour for my guest, child," said Grandfather softly.

She did, using the same efficiency she had developed long ago, and the metal ewer felt surprisingly warm to her palms now, not as heavy as before. She handed the filled goblet to Rafael, who took it from her with care.

"A toast!" called out Jozua, standing and raising his goblet. His face was skeletal in the firelight. "To the end of the world!"

"To the end of the millennium," Rafael amended, and—watching Jozua—drank to that.

Only when he was finished did Jozua take a sip of his own wine.

Serath felt heated, almost dizzy. Not poison, no—surely not. Just the effect of wine on her empty stomach, clashing with her nerves, bubbling through her. It heightened the sick feeling of before, and she had to breathe slower, deeper, to control it.

Rafael handed her his goblet and she took it back to the table, setting it down exactly where it had been before. She paused there, waiting, and when Grandfather finally met her eyes all she saw in him was cunning and blight, no hint of welcome—not even pride at her blind faith, a show of bravado put on solely for him.

He sat back in his cushioned chair, became naught but sharp colors to her . . . white hair, yellowed skin, a tunic of purple and gold. Even the emerald cushions around him became more vivid to her now, too bright, painful to see.

All at once it was too much to bear: this place, this room, these people and this man, the last of her own kin, one she dreaded and loved in spite of herself. She had missed it all, she had missed it so much that it had become like a wound to her over the years, day in and out, exiled, forsaken. And now here she was amid all the things she had thought never to see again—and the rejection was still here, still living and thriving—she had tried to expect nothing from this and instead had ended up wishing for everything. For hope. For acceptance. For her grandfather's love.

She wanted to run away. She wanted to die here. Why hadn't he poisoned the drink?

Rafael took her arm again, pulling her back to his own people; once more Jozua followed the move with ardent interest.

"Serath," whispered Grandfather, holding her with his gaze. "My sweet child. My only son's daughter." He leaned forward, toward her, almost beckoning. "Years ago I sent you away to safety, to modesty. Look at you today, my lovely girl."

Tears brimmed up in her eyes, reaction to his unexpected softness.

"Look what you have become here, before me now," he continued, so tender. "A harlot, betrayer of your own family."

Serath felt the air leave her chest. "No," she protested—appalled, stunned.

"You consort with him," accused Jozua.

"No—"

"You stay with him, you aid him—"

"No!" she said again, shaking her head.

"She is my hostage, old man," interjected Rafael, hard. "Nothing else."

"Betrayer," Jozua whispered, locked on her. "Consort. No better than your mother, that witch who would have given us all to evil—"

"Stop!" Serath said, louder than she had managed before. "Stop!"

"Jezebel! Bathsheba!" hissed Jozua. *"You nurture the beast who murdered your brother!"*

"No!" she cried, but this time it was only a strangled gasp.

Rafael felt her pull her arm free from him, backing up blindly, her breathing ragged. She ran into Abram, who steadied her.

"What are you saying?" Rafael demanded, swinging back to Jozua. "I had nothing to do with the boy's death!"

"Mur-der-er!" wheezed Jozua, the sound long and drawn out, and some of the men behind him picked up the syllables, echoing it, a chant that filled the room and then died away in uneven reverberation.

"Murder!"

"Murderer!"

Jozua Rune had not stopped staring at Serath.

Rafe looked back at her and saw, in one blinding instant, her thoughts revealed, the truth behind the deep blue of her eyes.

Killer, she had called him. *Demon-man.* And he knew now that it was not merely her childhood hearsay she was throwing at him, to bait him. They were not empty insults she was repeating because she thought to gall him.

She believed it. She believed he had killed her brother.

It left him sick and angry, filled with rage and even despair that she could contemplate such a thing, that she had misunderstood him so completely, and in such a horrific manner. When she faced him, heaving and wide-eyed, Rafe saw the helpless panic seizing her—and the loathing she had for him.

Rafe rounded on Jozua. "You are a lunatic *and* a liar. I will not suffer your insults to me or to her."

"Arrogant butcher! *You* suffer *nothing* for her!" Jozua stood once more, triumphant. "She is still mine!"

"Wrong." Rafael came to the table, close enough to make out the green of the other man's eyes, light and feverish. "I came to caution you, old man. I claim all that was yours, including this woman. Do not cross me. Do not attempt to stop me. I have no qualms about war. It is my ally."

They stood there, nearly matched at eye level despite the dais, and Rafe felt his rage whipping through him.

"The change of the millennium is near," he said, deadly soft. "Soon all of this will belong to me. And then you and your lies will be vanquished."

"Vanity," scoffed Jozua. "Defeat for you. God will see to it!"

"I think not. I do not lose, old man. Best remember that."

Jozua Rune eyed him a moment longer before sitting

down again, sinking back into the emerald cushions of his chair, looking suddenly frail and battered. Rafael was not fooled.

"Begone with you, then," Jozua said, his voice thin. "Begone, Leonhart, and take your consort with you. I'll have naught to do with any of you."

"Do not cross me," Rafael warned once more, unmoving. "Do not think to thwart me, or hide away up here forever, Rune. I will come again at the dawn of the new century."

Jozua gave a huff of laughter, his hair a little wild now in the night, the shadows deep on his face. "Begone," he repeated, and dismissed them all with a wave of his gnarled hand.

"I have warned you, Rune." Rafe stepped away from the dais, his steps strong and unhesitant. "It is more than you deserve."

As he turned he saw Jozua fix on Serath, ashen pale in the crowd. The old man's smile turned forbidding.

"We will see who may win this game, Leonhart. We will see."

Chapter Eight

⊶∽∙𝒎∙∽⊷

$\mathcal{S}$HE RODE BACK IN UTTER SILENCE, WHICH WAS hardly unusual for her. But now Rafael felt it with an acute worry, knowing the turmoil of her thoughts, a secret part of her revealed to him, even though perhaps neither of them would have wished it to be.

He followed her into her cottage. If she noticed him she gave no clue, moving slowly across the enclosed space, a sleepwalker with tragic steps.

She lay down on the pallet, on top of the blankets, not bothering to pull any over her. Her eyes closed.

"Serath," Rafe said, standing on the other side of the room.

She did nothing. She could have been formed of wax.

"I didn't kill him, Serath," he said.

He waited, then added, "He was just a boy. I would have no reason to harm him. Even if I did, I would not have killed him."

She rolled over, turning her back to him. The outline

of her figure became dramatically curved beneath her gown, dips and swells of feminine elegance.

"I would not have done it," Rafael said to her once more, but was not surprised when she continued to ignore him. He left her alone.

The remainder of the night held a blur of dreams for him, a mix of war and home, anxiety eating away at him, men dying in his arms—friends, family, all of them too young.

The boy, Raibeart. Rafe clutched at him and tried to stop the death, cursing, praying, running, but nothing changed. The boy still died, his golden hair shining like an accusation through the mists of the nightmare.

You did it. Treacherous killer.

Serath, standing alone in the middle of a tempest, her hair blowing around her, her voice filled with pain and wrath.

I hate you for it. Demon-man!

And all his protests were swept away in the wind, unheeded. She turned her face away from him until there was nothing but the blackness of her hair around them. Bells tolled, relentless, echoing, and it seemed to Rafael that even they were condemning him, a ringing chant to haunt him:

DEmon! DEmon-DEmon-DEmon-DE—

"—mons in the fields last night. We did not dare go see. . . ."

Rafael struggled to understand the new voice, hushed and nearby. It was not Serath now, not bells, but a man—

"Which fields?" asked another voice, almost as hushed. Abram.

Rafe opened his eyes and saw the sky above him, watered gray with leaden clouds. He had not slept in a cottage last night. He remembered now, he had wanted to sleep beneath the endless sky, where dreams and night-

mares might not be trapped so near him. He knew they
would be coming—

". . . by the mill. Barley field by the stream. More
down near the western woods. . . ."

Rafael sat up, pushing off his blankets.

Abram and Calum, standing together a few feet away
amid the tents of still-sleeping men, turned as one in the
tepid light of the dawn.

"My lord," said Abram, and came to him. "You need
to hear this."

Rafe stood. His fatigue weighed on him like a suit of
mail. "Demons in the fields?" He frowned, trying to
shake off the nightmare and the dregs of sleep.

"Aye, my lord," muttered Calum. "Last night. They
danced and cavorted. We did not dare approach."

"Demons," Rafe said again, wondering if he was
hearing the word right. It was too close to his dreaming,
he couldn't make sense of it.

"Many!" assured Calum. "Silent as death, they were,
and black as the devil! They rose up from the ground with
the fog and danced around, to every corner of the fields!
Then they vanished again, my lord, just as quick!"

Abram and Rafe scowled at the man together.

"It's God's truth," Calum said now, defensive. "I'm
not the only one who saw them. At least a dozen others
did, too."

"Did any of my men see them?" asked Rafael.

Calum looked away, then shrugged. "I know not.
Most of your men were gone, my lord."

Rafe felt a chill run through him, colder than the
breeze that was beginning to pick up through the camp.

"Gone?" he echoed quietly. "Up to the castle, you
mean?"

"Aye," said Calum.

He didn't need to meet Abram's eyes to confirm the

uneasiness in him. Rafael moved instantly to the brink of the village that overlooked the nearest field. Both of the other men followed, Calum with great reluctance.

"Where?" Rafe demanded, pointing to the land.

"Not this field, my lord. None so close in. Over there, farther out. And there, next to the woods. More on the other side, I was told."

Rafe ran a hand over his face, wide awake now, staring at the brown earth before him. He could see nothing strange. Most of the crops had been harvested, some plowed under already. It looked perfectly normal. But he knew, deep in his bones, that it was not.

"Wake Serath," he said to Abram. "Bring her to me." He did not wait to see his order followed, but began walking to the field Calum had indicated, out on the far side of a creek.

Cold dew from the grass soaked his boots. The air was turning brisk, a taste of winter finally strong upon it. Yet Rafael barely noticed these things, because as he drew closer to the field the unease in him was growing keener, his instincts all but shouting at him that something was very, very wrong.

He reached the field. It was one of the shorn ones, brittle stalks of wheat, or perhaps oats, scythed clean at his ankles, dried to straw. He could still see nothing amiss, but as he walked deeper into it he noticed the tracks of something large—not deer, or even wolves. Not demons, but men.

Rafe crouched down, examining them. Just footprints, nothing else; nothing dragged behind or pushed ahead, for instance. There could have been no more than two or three men here—but Calum had said there had been many, all told.

The stalks had bent to mark the men's trail, and Rafe could see no evidence of cavorting or dancing. Indeed, it seemed to him that these men had followed a very deliberate pattern: emerging from the woods, each going to a separate corner of the field, then back to the woods again.

He heard others approaching behind him, and did not bother to turn around.

"Serath," he said. "Why would Jozua Rune send men out to these fields at night?"

When she did not answer he turned his head, impatient, and then stood.

She looked around them sleepily, her arms hugged across her chest. Apparently she had not been given time to take her cloak, but he couldn't worry about that now. He took a step nearer to her and her look focused on him, disconcerted.

"I don't know," she said, sounding truthful enough.

"He waited until we were gone. He sent them here while we, like perfect fools, answered his summons at the castle. He knew we would be out of sight of this place, and most of my men with us." Rafe paused to control the anger, scanning the field again, the paths of broken reeds. "He played on the fears of these people, and on our own stupidity."

The wind came once more, rattling the severed stalks, whistling like mournful laughter.

Abram spoke. "He knew full well the serfs would not challenge demons."

A party of men had come down to the field, his soldiers waking and joining the scene. Rafe could hear them trading questions.

"What did you do here, old man?" he muttered, almost to himself.

A whisper of gray moved beside him; Serath walked out into the field, examining the ground, the reeds, just as he had done. During the night her hair must have become loosened from its plait, and when the wind blew again long curls stirred around her, showing him her thoughtful frown. She gathered her skirts and bent down, touching the dirt. Rubbing it. She lifted her hand, then tasted the tip of one finger.

She raised her eyes to his. Vivid blue. Worried.

"He did not poison the wine," she said to him, surrounded by the whistling reeds. "He did not need to."

"What did he do?" Rafael asked her, above the wind, above the hard knot in his throat.

"Salt," she said, and showed him the brown dirt dusting her palm. An unnatural sparkle flashed there for an instant and was gone, invisible except with the exact tilt of her hand.

"Salt," he repeated, and felt that familiar rage begin.

Laughter threatened him, completely inappropriate, disbelieving.

"Salt," said Rafe again, closer to a shout. He stood up, staring at the vast expanse of the field, the dead plants.

"Salt!" he yelled in fury, turning to glare at the castle behind him, the sides of it dull white beneath the clouds.

Fionnlagh remained as it had always been to him— distant and shuttered, closed off, perched too high on its cliff for his shout even to be heard. Completely unattainable.

"It's ruined, all of it," Rafe said. He closed his eyes against the sight: the disaster of the tainted soil, the lone woman watching him.

"That was the dancing," said Abram, right behind him, marveling. "That's what they were doing. Spreading the salt. Sweet Jesu!"

"How many fields did Calum say?" Rafael asked him, eyes still shut.

"At least seven, my lord. Mayhap more."

Seven. He felt the number stab through him, knowing what it meant—disaster, starvation. Seven fields.

Enough to ensure the hunger here would not abate. Enough to hurt them all—perhaps fatally. When spring came, seven of the good fields of Alderich—his new home—would be fallow and useless, perhaps for years to come. God's blood! Even assuming that Jozua Rune had stores and stores of food up at the castle, there was no way of knowing if it would be enough to cover such a loss. What would they do? How could he feed them all, when Leonhart was so close to lack as it was?

"Sea holly," said a small voice below him.

Rafael opened his eyes. Serath was gazing up at him, hesitant, her regal shroud momentarily gone. He saw the girl in her again, shy and uncertain.

"What?" Rafe asked.

"Sea holly." Her gaze was bottomless blue. "I know a little in the way of plants. Sea holly might do. It likes the salt."

He felt despair sweeping over him, and tried to cut it off. "You want me to plant sea holly here—what is it? A weed? Kelp? You think *that* will help us?" His voice was turning sharper in anger, so he stopped.

"None of that. It's flowery, thistlelike. But you would need to remove the top portion of this dirt, to rid it of most of the salt. You could take it to the ocean."

He stared down at her, wrathful, silent.

"Sea holly is edible," she added, matter-of-fact. "For man and beast both."

No one said anything. Rafael felt his mind consider it, almost removed from the moment, from his anger, this meager token from her little consolation.

Serath stood, brushing her hands free from the salted dirt. "You'll need to act quickly. It's going to rain soon."

He looked up to the sky, galvanized, realizing the truth of her words with fresh shock.

The clouds hung lower and lower, already turning a

malevolent black near the bottoms. It was going to be a storm, no light drizzle. And the rain would melt the salt into the ground permanently, saturating the fields, perhaps even spreading it to nearby areas, land that had not been poisoned, or the network of streams that fed into them—

"Get every able-bodied person you can," he barked, facing Abram and the rest of them. "Bring wagons or carts—whatever there is to haul away this mess. Check with Calum to confirm which fields. Hurry!"

Men scattered, running back to the village. Only Serath remained beside him, watching them go. The wind took her skirts and her hair in teasing gusts, a dance of black and gray at the edges of his vision.

Her black hair, blowing. . . .

Amid the wreck of the field, Rafael suddenly remembered his nightmare, the not-so-subtle message behind it. *Treacherous killer.*

She believed he had murdered her brother, a despicable act that would most certainly call for revenge, were it true. For one long, breathless instant he had to wonder at the neatness of his entire situation: Jozua had forced a crisis upon the land where Rafael's only bloodless solution would be a hostage—and there could be only one hostage who mattered.

And Serath had come to him so easily from her convent, remarkably easily, in fact. She had stayed with him with hardly any protest, and only two quickly foiled attempts to escape. She had boldly drunk the wine Jozua had offered—surrendering her trust to *him* without hesitation.

It was all too convenient not to question. Had it been naught but a trap all along? Had he been fooled by her from the beginning?

Rafe felt the doubt begin to eat away at him, deep

and unpleasant. He turned to take in her face, pure beauty. Serath's eyes lowered, and then raised, to his. He could see nothing of herself revealed in her gaze. Her look remained cool and hidden; her entire body seemed to be wrapped in careful restraint.

Perhaps it wasn't really even salt in the fields. Perhaps *here* was the poison, seeded in the dirt, and she had not actually tasted it at all, only pretended to, in hopes that he might follow suit. . . .

No. Absolutely not.

But Rafael bent to touch the earth before them, rising again to bring the speckles of brown close to his face, trying to catch the scent of it. He smelled only the soil.

Serath watched him, expressionless. He could not even begin to guess at her emotions.

Without releasing her eyes, he tasted the dirt on his finger, exactly as she had.

Biting, pungent, and familiar—salt. Just that, Rafe told himself. Just that.

He dusted his hands clean, a faint cloud of brown that blew away with the breeze.

"You didn't know about this," Rafael said, not a question.

"Of course not," she responded, but instead of anger there was a weariness about her, as if she had expected him to ask. A look at her now showed him only the lowered fan of her lashes, her arms again crossed over her chest. The cold tinted her cheeks a becoming pink.

"A good guess, to think it salt," he said, and wondered if he might be testing her.

"It wasn't too difficult." She tucked a strand of hair behind her ear. "I know this land. And I know my grandfather. Salt is plentiful at Alderich. It was quick and devious."

The village was stirring; people rushed about, talking,

waving their arms. The first of his men were already headed back here, pulling one of the wagons from his own procession loaded with tools, a line of serfs behind them.

"You need a cloak," Rafe said to Serath.

She shook her head. "I don't want to dirty it. I'll be fine."

He understood, without asking, that she meant to stay and work. He thought briefly of refusing her, confining her again, but then looked around once more at the vast field, rows and rows of hollowed straw.

She was not truly his enemy, despite their circumstances. She would not betray him so readily. He knew, for some reason, that he would not be able to bear that.

"As you wish," Rafael said.

―――――――――― ⟨∞⟩ ――――――――――

THE DIRT WAS THIN AND LOAMY, WHICH WAS fine, because it meant she could dig it up easily with the spade they had given her. Serath held a rough-woven sack, identical to the ones all the others carried, and filled it as quickly as possible with the tainted earth. The difficult part was hauling it back to the wagon. Once filled, the sack became impossibly heavy.

Rafael was suddenly beside her, taking it from her, lifting it himself to the flat of the wagon. When he turned she saw the dirt and sweat streaking him, his hair untamed, the gray of his eyes silvered in this light.

She accepted an empty sack from someone and returned to the field, back to where she had stopped work, and began to take up the soil again. Her two guards toiled near her, watching more of her than the earth. Winter wind pushed at her back.

They were not going to be in time. She knew it as

sure as she knew anything. The clouds were growing darker, heavier, their curves more swollen. It would not be long before the rain came.

How well she remembered it, the storms pushing in off the sea, clouds racing to the land, surging and changing colors before her. The ocean, striving to reach up to the sky, to touch that turmoil, whitecaps and faraway waves.

On stormy days Morwena would find her, wherever Serath was, and take her up to one of the turrets to watch the show begin. Sometimes Raibeart came along, sometimes not. But always Serath and her mother, holding on to each other in the wild wind, delighting in the sky and the water, and the taste of salt and rain mingled.

No doubt it had only served to feed the rumors about her mother's witchcraft. It had been said she could control the very elements—that rain heeded her, and lightning sparked at her command.

Serath herself had never seen such a thing. As far as she recalled, watching the storms from the turrets had been full of nothing but joyful innocence.

She lifted the spade again. Dirt sifted down from the sides of it, sparkling back to the ground.

Look! Morwena would say, her arms tight around her daughter. *Look, beloved! It's God, talking to us! It's heaven come to earth! It's your father up there, watching us. Listen— you'll hear him laughing with us. . . .*

Scoop up the dirt. Drop it into the sack.

Take off an inch or two, no more, Serath had instructed them. That should be enough to ease the hold of the salt. Any more than that, she knew, and the new plants would not grow well. The top of the soil was always the richest.

See the lightning? That's truth, my angel, from us to God, from God to us. It's blinding, isn't it?

At the convent, Serath had been assigned to garden-
ing, at first as a punishment for some infraction she could
not even recall. But instead of wilting under the sun, she
had blossomed as her plants had, and even the prioress
could not deny enjoying the fruits of the garden. Peas and
onions, Serath had nurtured. Herbs and spices. Fruit trees,
from sweet cherry to pear. She gained solace from touching the earth, from breathing it and feeling it against her
hands. It had taken years for the prioress to notice it; once
discovered, her new punishment became solitude in her
cell, away from her plants and the warm sun. Away, even,
from the rain.

Today Serath could take consolation in this sad field.
She could lose herself to the work, to the feeling of helping the ground—and aye, even the people who had
spurned her. It was why she dragged her sack behind her,
why she did not cease, even though her knuckles became
red and chapped. Even though the wind was now like a
knife slicing around her.

*Watch the water, Serath. See it? See the foam? Mermaids
frolic in it—they dance in these storms. They put pearls in their
hair, and sing with the rain, and play games with the
fishes. . . .*

Far away, over the hills, thunder rumbled through the
clouds, announcement of the show to come.

Bend. Scoop. Sack.

Simple work. Simple thoughts, realizations.

All of Serath's past fell into place with easy clarity.
Every aspect of her life had a link to this moment: from
Morwena's death to her own banishment, to the convent
garden, to this field. Which, when they were done, would
take her to the ocean, her final aspiration. She would see
it again at last. The one last thing left to do in her mortal
life, the one final vision to realize before the end.

Peace and song and her mother's ghost, all waiting for her there. . . .

A raindrop plopped to the ground just in front of her. Serath looked up, then around. Haze misted the horizon, deep violet, the storm rushing toward them. Another raindrop hit her on the cheek, and then her shoulder.

The men and women around her were peering up at the sky, seeing what she had seen, pointing with alarm.

Rafael was yelling orders at everyone, directing them to the cart with their sacks, and the people began to move toward him as the rain picked up.

Serath bent down and scraped up more of the field. Water began to sting her back.

The soil turned black. It grew weighted in her spade, clumped, but this only made it easier to gather. She moved in half steps through the row. She blinked to get the rain out of her eyes. Her breath became frost.

A hand closed over her own—rough, as dirty as hers, holding her gently but firmly, taking the spade from her. Serath straightened, feeling the aches take over her body.

Rafael gazed down at her, soaking wet, a sheet of rain between them.

"No more," he said. "It's over now."

She looked around—it couldn't be over, they hadn't finished the field, though they had come so close—but everyone else had fled. Even the wagon loaded with dirt was being hauled away, men hunched over against the rain as they pulled it.

"The sea," she said, watching them go. "We need to get it to the sea now, before it's too late."

"Aye," said Rafael. "They're off to join the carts from the other fields. Calum will show them the way to the ocean."

"No," she said, startled. "I need to go, too!"

He gave her a look of shaded speculation. His hand tightened over hers.

"Not you. You're to get inside, and dry off."

She pulled her hand away from him and he let her. The rain grew stronger against them, pushed by the wind, plastering her skirts to her legs.

"I have to go," Serath tried. "They—they need me there, to show them the holly."

"Calum claims to know the plants you mean," he said. "If there is time, he will see to it."

"No, I should help! It must be done as soon as possible, to gather the roots and the seeds that are left, before the rain washes them away."

"Later."

"Idiot!" she cried, suddenly furious. "You don't know what you're doing! This cannot wait!"

"I know exactly what I'm doing, Serath," he replied, finding her hand again. "And I know that you will obey me."

She hit him with her free hand, outraged, and her fist bounced off his shoulder harmlessly, pain cramping through it. It enraged her all the more, so she hit him again, and again, and all the while he merely stared down at her, perfectly calm amid the storm and her own temper, not even trying to defend himself.

"Fool!" she cursed at him over the crashing of the rain. "Simpleton! Demon!" Each blow hurt her hand more; she put all her might into the next strike, hitting him hard enough so that he took a step back. Her triumph was short-lived—as he moved she lost her own balance, her feet skidding out from beneath her. Serath landed hard on her thigh in the mud, Rafael's hold on her hand now painfully tight.

"Serath!"

He was leaning down over her, trying to pull her up,

and still she fought him, crying now, tugging at her hand, which he did not release. He bent closer to lift her up and she struck at him again, slapping mud on his tunic.

"Serath." His voice was soothing, an arm around her shoulders.

"I have—to go—" she choked out, wiping away the tears with blackened fingers, the rain mixing mud and water together down her face.

"Come up," he was urging her, his touch not so rough.

"You must—let me—*go*—"

"No," he said, almost gentle. He had stopped trying to lift her to her feet and instead crouched down beside her, against her, sheltering her from the lash of the torrent.

Serath raised her head against the rain and met his look, his face inches away from her own. His body supported her now, the only warmth in the world.

"I have to go," she said again helplessly, pleading. "You don't understand. I have to go to the ocean, before it's too late. . . ."

He shook his head, unyielding, but here in this muddy field, in the midst of this downpour, there was something new in him that she had never thought to see: compassion.

She turned her head away, defeated, brimming with frustration. His hand reached up, cupped her cheek. He moved her chin back to him, until she met his eyes again.

"Later, Serath," he said to her, solemn. "We'll go later. I promise it."

And with everything turned to water and wind around them, he kissed her, just as he had before, what seemed like years ago.

The rain flowed over them, cold and wet, but what Serath felt was the strength of Rafael, his lips against her own, creating a heat that even the storm could not douse. His fingers splayed across her cheek, cradling her closer, and the arm around her shoulders became a support so that she could lean back into him, head tilted.

He dragged his lips across her own and their breath made mist between them, magic in the rain. She felt his tongue against her, surprising and soft, allowing her to discover his taste, something masculine and undefined. It did strange things to her stomach; it made her legs feel weak but her heart strong, beating fast, thrilled.

His hand moved down her neck to her shoulder, finding and skimming along the delicate bones there, the center of her throat, beneath the brooch, where his thumb circled and caressed her. Serath raised her arms and held him closer, her own fingers exploring the rain-smoothed strands of his hair, the muscles in his neck. He shifted until she was sitting up, held pressed against him, their chests together. His kisses moved to her cheek, her jaw, her temple. She heard his breathing in her ear, deep and uneven.

When she opened her eyes she saw his face cleansed of dirt, water shining on his skin like purity. The darkness of his lashes clung together to frame the gray of his eyes, now the color of the storm. Once more his hand came up to her face; a caress that guided her, that showed her how to move, where to kiss him—his mouth, the corners, her tongue touching them, the roughness of his new beard.

His hands grew harder against her, less careful. With just a slight move he took control of the kiss again, fiercer now. Excitement caught at her, pinned in his embrace, panting, taking in the cold air and making it fire inside of her.

For a long, sweet moment Rafael leaned into her hard—but then he pulled back, allowing the rain between them. Serath let out a little sound of protest, but it only pushed him away farther, his body leaving hers, his hands only on her shoulders.

He had that look again, bemused, turned in to himself, as if slowly rousing. She wanted to howl in aggravation, sitting there in the mud.

"No," she heard him say, very quiet. "Not here."

Numbing despair, shame, and humiliation flushed through her. She yanked back from him, on her hands and knees in the field, and then stood, trying to catch her breath, inhaling raindrops.

He stood as well, darkened with the storm. His face was lost to her. Serath ran her hands across her eyes, fighting the downpour and her own sense of doom.

"Does it make you happy, demon-man, to seduce the sister of the child you murdered?"

Rafael didn't seem to react to her vengeful tone, aimed perhaps more at herself—her own weakness—than at him.

"It would not, even if I were guilty of such a crime." His words were still quiet. "But I did not kill him, Serath."

Nothing helped; not her own bitterness, not his denial. Nothing halted the desire still filling her, that lightning heat she felt for him. Serath scowled at him, wordless now, and fought the tremble that wanted to bow her mouth.

"Come back up to the village, Serath," said the demon-man, and he seemed close to kind, which was the most awful thing of all.

She stood there, shivering, muddied and wretched, wrapped in this betrayal of her own senses.

"Come," he repeated, but did not try to touch her again.

"Please," he added, when she still did not move.

Madness. She was surely going mad, when such a simple word from him could break her, could make her heart constrict to a painful tightness in her chest. Oh, she was turning mad, and there was no one in the world to stop it.

Raibeart, she thought helplessly, and the pain in her chest expanded.

She lifted her drenched skirts and walked past him, slogging through the field, and the mud sucked at her boots, and the torrent pounded on her head. But all she could focus on was Rafael, walking beside her, matching her pace.

Relentless, horrible ruin.

As they drew closer to the end of the field she could make out a long line of figures standing in the village, facing them. The forms were blurred, dusky purple in this light and weather, but there seemed to be something odd about them—most stood beneath what appeared to be an awning of some kind, held up at the corners by men. She watched, trying to understand it as she drew even closer, close enough to see that some of the people were women, with brightly colored skirts. And the men wore the colors of Leonhart—red and black tunics, official heraldry that Rafael and his men had abandoned for plainer clothes days ago.

He remained beside her, his steps unbroken, but she could have sworn she felt something in him retreat. The only clue he gave was a sort of sigh. When she glanced at him he looked grim, his hair now sculpted against his cheekbones. Rain slid over and down him in shining streamers.

New people. New people from Leonhart, obviously. Serath wanted to stop and walk the other way. She wanted to ignore them, to pretend these encroachers were not here, but Rafael headed straight to them, and with a kind of listless acceptance, she went as well.

It was a group far too grand for the moment. Ladies in fine gowns stared at them with avid eyes. The men stood motionless, until Rafael was but a few feet away. Then the whole of them—the men holding the awning included—bowed or curtsied to him.

Only one woman did not. She stood at the center of the group, an older lady with hair swept up behind a veil, rings on her fingers, and a peculiar pinching around her mouth.

"Leonhart," the woman greeted him, the only person to speak.

"Mother," Rafael replied, with a curt inclination of his head.

The woman's eyes moved from him to Serath, surveying her from the top of her head to the muddied and torn hem of her gown, then back up again. The pinch around her mouth increased.

And Serath, with rainwater washing over her and her gown clinging to her in indecent curves, remembered with extreme mortification that the field they had come from was in perfect view of this site; that anyone who wanted to might have seen what just happened between her and the man beside her. Yet when the woman looked back at her face, Serath managed to raise her brows slightly, a look she copied from the prioress when confronted with outrageous impertinence.

"So this is Serath Rune, I suppose," said Rafael's mother. Serath could hear nothing but steely calm in her voice.

"You suppose correctly," Rafael said. "Excuse us, Mother. We need to get dry."

Rafael took her arm and now Serath allowed him

this, and together they brushed past the staring group, all composure. From the corner of her eye Serath watched the woman, her steady contemplation as they passed by.

Ruin, Serath thought again, and felt it shaking through her.

Chapter Nine

⟨⟩⟩⟩

NANWYN OF LEONHART WAS NOT A WOMAN who appreciated being kept waiting.

Of course Rafe knew this. He had grown up with her, after all. He had witnessed her moods and the looks that spoke volumes. He had seen for himself the effect of her quiet, constant displeasure at her life, at her husband and her home, and, over all, at her son.

She was no shrew, no ill-bred fisherman's wife. Blood from kings and conquerors flowed through her, a fact she never even had to mention. When he was a child, all it took was a single freezing look to wither him. His father had remained equally cowed by her; the unhappiness of their marriage was an accepted truth at Leonhart. They had wed as they were supposed to, uniting blood and nobility in preparation for the advent of Alderich. Both had known, his father would tell him, that their heir would become the leader of a newly combined land, and the way out of the barren state of Leonhart. Rafael had grown up knowing his role, and never once had he wanted to shirk it.

He still did not now. But how much easier it would have been if his mother had been content to stay home, out of his way, at least until after the century ended.

She had taken over one of the more spacious cottages, and Rafe wasn't even certain if the serfs who had lived there were still in the village or not. Hopefully not. It would not be an easy task to evict Nanwyn from where she had settled in.

The rain had lightened by the time he strolled out of his own shelter, into the heart of the village again. He did not bother to duck his head against it, but instead examined this new group of arrivals—more tents set up, more horses clogging the alleys, overflow from the stables. More people huddled about, bowing to him, staring at his back. He thought he recognized some but certainly not all. It had been so long since he had seen Leonhart. It was almost a dreamland to him now, just memories.

He paused outside Nanwyn's abode, still looking around, bracing himself for what waited for him within. Best to finish it now.

Faint music came to him from inside the cottage, jarringly out of place, an elaborate melody, strings and a soft voice, singing. He opened the door.

He certainly would not have recognized this chamber as a part of this plain village. No rustic simplicity here: inside were warmth and bright colors, fine chairs and tables set up, a pallet with feathered ticking, embroidered fabrics, and multihued furs. Heavy trunks lined up against one wall. Someone had scattered rushes, for pity's sake, on the muddied dirt of the ground. Even the fire seemed civilized in his mother's presence.

The music jangled to an abrupt halt.

Nanwyn looked up in tranquil concern from one of

the chairs as he entered; the two women on either side of her immediately stood, curtsying to him. Rafe stared at them, momentarily distracted by the formality. They kept their faces lowered. One of them held a lute.

"My lady," Rafe said, tearing his gaze away from the unlikely scene.

She lifted one hand to him. He walked over to take it, bowing, marveling again at the etiquette that seemed so foreign to him and this place.

Nanwyn murmured his name back to him, much softer than she had at the verge of the meadow. Rafe lifted his head.

"Why did you come?" he asked bluntly.

Her fingers stayed lax in his hold. "To see you, naturally," she replied.

His gaze skipped again to her two waiting women, and now Nanwyn granted them a short look, nodding her head. They left in swishes of fragrance and pastel colors. He had a glimpse of the falling rain outside, and then the door closed.

"Please, sit," invited his mother in her mannerly tone.

He did, choosing a chair not far from hers, a place where he could see the firelight playing off her features.

She seemed much older than he knew her to be, though he could not say what it was about her that had changed so much. Her hair remained chestnut brown, just a few silver threads now near her temples. Her eyes were as dark and observant as ever. Nanwyn was still a handsome woman; it was more her air that was unfamiliar to him, a kind of caution in repose.

"I want you to leave," Rafael said.

She showed no change of expression, said nothing in response.

"This is not the place for you, Mother. Jozua Rune is

a dangerous man, and I don't know what he might do next. You're not safe here."

"I know his madness," Nanwyn replied. "I was the one who sent for you, Leonhart."

"Then you understand why you must go—now, today. I have enough on my hands as it is."

"Indeed," commented his mother. "I had a glimpse of what was on your hands today in that field."

So much for her caution. Rafael felt a slow, uncomfortable burn begin in his chest, and had to exhale around it.

"Salt," exclaimed Nanwyn, shaking her head, so refined. "What a travesty it could have been."

"Pack up," said Rafe. "Now. Hurry."

Her look became one of gentle hurt. "But, Rafael! I have only just come. You know what a rough journey it is—and in such a storm! Surely you are not so cruel as to refuse me the simple favor of rest?"

He rolled his eyes up to the ceiling, leaning back in his chair. Why did he bother talking to her? The heart of her had not changed a bit; she could still maneuver around him in emotional circles without even raising her voice. He should have just told Abram to send them off. He should not have even tried—

"I've missed you, my son," said Nanwyn.

He looked back at her, skeptical.

"It's been years," she added, with a tiny, tiny fracture to her voice. Rafael stood and turned away from her.

"It's not safe," he said again, for the benefit of them both.

"Safe enough for the kin of Jozua Rune, however," said Nanwyn softly.

He didn't move.

"She is a great beauty," Nanwyn continued, after a bare hesitation. He could read nothing at all in her tone.

"My hostage," Rafe responded, clipped. "It benefits me to keep her close to the castle."

"I see," said his mother.

The sound of the rain was muffled by the thatch of the roof, a few leaks coming through near the corners of the room. Rafael watched a slow drip, the fall of water to the dirt.

"Does she dwell with you?" Nanwyn asked, indifferent.

He turned. "No, she does not. She stays alone, as do I. She is a nun, Mother. When this matter is done she's returning to her convent."

Nanwyn looked down at her hands in her lap, their delicate interlacing. "It's being said she was stolen from the convent by the devil himself. That she actually flew over the walls of God's sanctuary into Lucifer's embrace, off to plot for the end of us all."

He felt a cynical smile overtake him. "Is that what they're saying?"

"Aye. And that, of course, the destruction of the world is at hand. Atone for your sins. Pray. Cleanse yourself from all evil. That sort of thing." She gave him a look that might have held humor. "I suppose none of that applies to you, since, apparently, you have become Lucifer."

He shrugged. After a moment, Nanwyn returned her gaze to her hands.

"If it's true what you say, that Serath Rune is merely your hostage, then it is hardly proper to keep her without attendance."

"Proper?" He couldn't believe this. "Are you joking?"

"Of course not."

"I don't think that you understand that this is *war,*

Mother, not some idle quest. Serath Rune is only here to aid me. I don't give a damn about what's proper."

"Still. . . ." began Nanwyn, and Rafe heard a wealth of intricate plans in that single word.

"No," he said, final. "I won't have it. You will not stay here, not for any reason. I have too much to defend without the added worry of you. You may return to Alderich after I settle the land and the people here, perhaps this spring. Not before."

She tapped one finger against her lips. "You cannot be considering all the consequences."

"The hell I'm not. Don't think to tell me how to handle this. This is not Leonhart, Nanwyn, nor will it ever be. You are not mistress here."

"No," she agreed, too easily. "Who is, my son?"

There was only one answer; he didn't have to say it.

"Such a great beauty," commented Nanwyn again. "And I've heard she has quite a hold over this place—the people. Men. Even outside of Alderich they're speaking of her spells."

"She has no spells."

"Oh?"

"It's all gossip. I'm surprised you even listen."

"I always listen, Rafael. I always listen to anything that mentions my son—most especially anything that ties my son to the granddaughter of Rune."

He felt frozen at this, the notion of what rumors must be circulating around them, what even Jozua Rune might be hearing; he had not considered it before now. Nanwyn watched him keenly.

"Is it true, Rafael? Has this—nun—cast some sort of charm over you?"

"Don't be foolish," he said harshly.

"I should hope that the last thing that *I* ever am is a

fool," she replied, with just the right emphasis to goad him.

The burning in his chest grew hotter. Rafe found the drip of water again and concentrated on it, controlling himself.

Nanwyn said, "What a tragic pity it would be to lose Alderich after all this time, after all this waiting, to a simple nun and her wiles. What a loss that would be for us all."

The burning turned to acid within him. "Dammit! I am not going to lose Alderich! You don't know what's going on!"

"No, I suppose I don't. Why should I, when my own son does not deign to inform me of his plans, his life—of anything at all, really?"

He was leaving. He would not stay to listen to this, her meticulous vivisection of him. But his feet did not move.

"So many years have passed," Nanwyn went on, exquisitely condemning. "The brave Leonhart stayed off fighting the wars of others, so busy in his wild life. Did you spare me a thought, Rafael, ever once?"

Rafe made a rough gesture. "How could you even ask me that? What did you think, that I left because I wanted to?"

"Yes," she said.

"I left for you! To give you the things you said you wanted!" He indicated the room, the lush surroundings. "Look at all this, Nanwyn. How did you think you came by it—was it pixies who granted you the spoils of battle?"

She did it at last, the thing he dreaded most: her eyes teared up, her face began to crumple. It could break him, and she knew it.

"We are done here," Rafe said, walking to the door.

"I still want you to go home, Mother. Gather your people and go back to Leonhart. I'll summon you when it's safe to return."

"But what of your captured maiden?" she asked. The threat of tears still glimmered in her eyes.

"What of her?"

"I'd like to speak with her."

"For what purpose?" he demanded.

"She looked lonely." Now Nanwyn gave a small smile, infinitely sad. "I recognize that look very well."

Rafael felt something in him snap.

"Excellent. Do it. Keep her company, guard her from me, if that's what you want, or me from her. Dress her in finery and drape her in rubies, if that pleases you. I care not."

"Why, Rafael, if I've somehow angered you—"

"Angered me?" he interrupted, incredulous. "Do you have the slightest idea of what you've stepped into out here? I have a madman locked in a castle, doing his best to destroy what's left of these lands. I have a demesne of people terrified that in a few days the world will burn up, or the heavens will fall, or what will you—and I have a woman that's barely holding this all together somehow—through witchcraft or sorcery or just plain courage—I don't know!—and now you stroll in with your retinue and perfumes and want to play queen of the manor! Fine! Just let me be!"

Nanwyn looked suddenly small amid her luxuries. "I only wanted to help."

"Splendid," he replied, going to the door. "Be of help. I only hope you brought plenty of food with you. Good day to you."

---

*F*OR YEARS SHE HAD NOT BEEN TOUCHED.

Until now Serath had not truly contemplated it, the lack of physical warmth that had marked her life. There had been so many other struggles to face: obedience, meekness, hunger. Silence.

She had not realized that touch was even gone, which seemed strangely laughable to her now. When had she slipped past noticing her life was barren of the feel of another living being? When had she become so dead to her own existence? Serath had no idea.

It was a remarkable thing, never to feel another person; so much time had gone by when the only physical contact she had encountered had been stinging slaps, or the brief, impersonal grazing of arms in prayer or work. To be touched now—so suddenly and so completely, after years of denial—left her feeling raw, horribly unprotected. She did not know herself in these moments.

One truth shone bright at her, overwhelming and bittersweet: when Rafael held her, she did not want him to ever let go.

She remembered Morwena's hugs, the complete happiness of being in her arms. The last true touch she had received must have come from Raibeart, after Morwena's death, but Serath could not recall even that, her brother's final embrace. And then after he died—nothing.

She had been starved for a thing she had forgotten had ever been, and to have it returned to her now by the man who was, after all, her true enemy, was a thorny and painful dilemma.

When he touched her, her body acted without her consent. Her fingers clutched at him, every bit of her wanted to curl close. Serath wanted to taste him, to inhale him, to press herself into him and feel the tightness of his hold around her. If it hurt, it didn't matter. If it shamed her, she wouldn't care. Rafael alone had reached out and rapped against her defenses: like a statue of glass she had shattered before him.

Now what was left of her? Nothing strong, only weakness. Want. Desire. Fear and shame and absolute captivation.

She was unworthy of her family. She was unworthy of even the memory of her brother.

The fire in her hut did little to dispel the chill that had settled into Serath's bones. She had changed her gown yet again, back into the first one, which was at least dry, and then bundled herself into her cloak. Yet it felt like a thin barrier between her and winter.

Snow would come soon, leading them to that final day, the birthday of Christ and the new year together . . . and then—what?

For the first time in her life Serath allowed herself to doubt the stories of the coming end with the new millennium. It seemed sharply blasphemous to even consider such a thought, but certainly Leonhart and his men acted as if it were so. And if they were right and everyone else was wrong . . . she supposed that sooner or later Jozua would be forced to follow the law and hand over Alderich. And she, no doubt, would be returned to Saint Basilla's. Annihilation by God seemed almost better than that.

Serath huddled on the floor near the fire, staring morosely into the flames. The tattered smoke hole above allowed a dripping slide of raindrops to trickle down, few enough for the fire to stay lit, but enough to keep it sizzling.

A knock came on the door.

Not Rafael. He never knocked. She looked up with little interest as the door opened. A darkened figure hovered there.

"Would you mind . . . ?" came a feminine voice, very cultured. Serath stood.

The lady swept into the room with just the barest evidence of distaste, holding her skirts a shade too carefully away from the floor, looking around with that pinch to her lips as she entered.

His mother. Serath could see the faint resemblance now, the subtle coloring of the hair, the shape of the eyes. That was all, really. While Rafael was all muscle and hard edges—nothing but virile power—this woman was willow thin, polish and gentility in every stroke of her.

"Forgive me," said the woman, her look at last coming to Serath. "I wonder if you might indulge me. My name is Nanwyn. I wished to meet the famed Serath Rune."

Everything about her told Serath the lady was unimpressed with what she saw. Serath resorted to the prioress's lofty look again, and this time Rafael's mother glanced away, stiff.

Serath did not bother to curtsy. "You have found me." It was the pinch to Nanwyn's mouth, perhaps, that made her add, "Shall I conjure up an imp for you, my lady?"

"I pray you will not," the woman said, stifled. Her eyes had still not returned to Serath's face, which meant that Serath was free to examine her as Nanwyn slowly walked the perimeter of the room.

Great pride, Serath noted. Nervousness. Strength beneath it.

When she came closer Serath had a whiff of something that reminded her of a kept garden, blossoms and leaves. Nanwyn's eyes drifted down to the brooch at Serath's throat, only partially hidden by her cloak.

"Well. I see you already have rubies."

Before Serath could reply to this strange comment

Nanwyn had looked away, shaking her head. Furrowed lines appeared on her forehead, pure worry.

"I fear I must be blunt," she said now, giving Serath a hard stare. "What are your designs upon my son?"

Touch, taste, kiss, so miraculous—

Serath stood up straighter, turning this quick, secret betrayal of herself into a pose of indignation. "I have no designs upon him. Mayhap you should be asking him about his plans for me."

"I have," said the woman. "But it is not Leonhart who is a stranger to me, and who might fool me with lies."

"Your son abducted me," retorted Serath. "I am not here of my own will. Perhaps my lady bothered to notice the guards outside my door? The only designs I have are to leave this place."

They faced each other only a few paces apart, nearly matched in height, though Serath had a slight advantage. She could tell that this lady was not ready to back away, that something in her could not allow it. Nanwyn stood still and tight, her fingers clenched white over the folds of her gown, emotion playing across her face. For an instant Serath caught a glimpse of Rafael in her; it might have been nothing more than the stubborn slant of her jaw. Whatever it was, it took Serath aback, and it was she who softened her pose, bringing her arms up to hug herself, close to a shiver.

Nanwyn noticed. Her dark eyes became shuttered, thoughtful.

"I saw your mother once," she said quietly, surprising Serath. "Aye. I did. We were both traveling, and by chance both desired to stay in the same inn for the night. Did you know that, Serath Rune?"

She hadn't, but she wasn't going to give this woman

the satisfaction of saying so. Nanwyn offered a tense smile at her silence.

"Fair, she was—I had never seen a woman so fair as Morwena. She was with a great group of your people, all traveling from Fionnlagh. Of course, it took very little to discover her identity. I doubt she noticed me at all. I had only a few attendants."

Nanwyn looked away at last, her eyes going to the wall behind Serath, as if the vision she described were playing out across it.

"But the inn was full, you see. Your mother arrived only just after I had, and I had taken the last chamber. So I knew there was no room for her. She seemed very calm about it—even gracious."

"She would have been," said Serath.

Nanwyn arched one brow. "Indeed. And the inn-keeper was quite beside himself, apologizing. Morwena smiled at him and charmed him, and just as she was leaving she turned back, and pointed to the roof of the building. I heard her words clearly. 'Have a care,' she said. 'We'll have lightning tonight, and your roof is so dry.' "

Serath took a heavy breath, rubbing her arms. The room was too cold, that was the only reason she felt such a chill.

"And that night," Nanwyn continued, "the storm came as she said, just heat and thunder, no rain at all. And the lightning struck the inn, and the roof blazed, and three men lost their lives, including the innkeeper. I survived. But the inn burned down to ashes."

"It means nothing," Serath said, her stomach wrenching.

"Do you think so?" Nanwyn smiled gently. "I always wondered, you see. Perhaps those men might be alive today, if only I had traveled a little slower, and Morwena had beaten me to that inn."

"A story, that's all it is!"

"True life, my lady."

Distressingly, Serath felt tears in her eyes, pain for her mother. "You can't say that. You can't say she did that. She was good and kind! It was not her fault."

Her voice had begun to shake too much; she choked back the rest of her words, glaring. Nanwyn grew very still, examining her, shadows softening her face.

"I don't know what you are," she said after a while. "You seem very young. Yet the things I've heard . . ."

The fire spat and sizzled beside them, water dripping into it with monotonous regularity.

"I want you to know that Alderich means a great deal to my people," said this woman from Leonhart now. "We have waited many years for it."

Serath swallowed the last of her tears, finding her control again. "So I've been told."

"It is ours by right," Nanwyn said, almost imploring. "Do you understand that? We do not come to take something that is not ours. History has decided that we shall inherit."

"Your history seems to differ vastly from my family's," said Serath. "To the people of Alderich, you are invaders. You are thieves."

"My son has the right to rule here! It is the law!"

"Perhaps it *will* be the law. But it is not so yet."

"Does a witch even care about the law of the king? Why would you seek to thwart us?" Nanwyn's voice rose to an impassioned cry.

"Ask a witch that," Serath said coldly.

"I would not normally dare ask a witch anything! I would not wish to tempt the devil in such a way." Nanwyn held her skirts even tighter; wrinkles spread like cobwebs through the fine material. "But I am desperate!"

It would be of no use to argue with her, Serath knew.

The lady had already decided that the rumors were fact—
and truthfully, Serath could hardly be surprised. All the
world thought her a witch, her mother's daughter. Why
bother fighting it any longer?

Yet it was a heavy thing, sorrowful really, and she had
to raise a hand to her head, rubbing her temple to ward
off the ache that wanted to come. "What is it you wish of
me, Nanwyn of Leonhart? I am tired. I want to rest."

But the other woman said nothing now, seeming
caught in some struggle within herself. Her frown came
back, aging her, but her eyes stayed fixed on Serath,
strangely bright, lit from within. Serath returned the look
testily, then began to turn away. Nanwyn reached out and
caught her by the elbow.

"I have a bargain for you, Serath Rune."

"I do not bargain with anyone from Leonhart."

The woman's eyes glittered. "I think you'll want to
hear this one."

Her hold was firm. Serath subsided, curious in spite
of herself.

Nanwyn said, "I will help you in your goal, my lady.
I will do what I can to free you from this place. I will
petition my son to release you."

Serath let out a caustic laugh. "*That* is your bargain?
You think he will listen to you? He won't release me."

"Nevertheless, I promise you I shall try. You say this
is what you want, so I offer it to you. I'll do whatever I
can."

"And in return for this grand favor?" Serath asked,
envisioning all kinds of ridiculous things; a love spell,
most likely, or a hex for revenge against some slight—

The lady leaned in close. "Leave my son alone."

The laughter in her faded away. Serath said, "I beg
your pardon?"

"Leave him alone. Do not bewitch him. Do not engage him. Do not harm him. Leave him be."

Her mouth opened, too many protests rising through her at once, and all Serath could manage to say was, "*Harm* him?"

"I do not know you—I admit this—and I think at times I barely know him. But he is my son, child of my body, and part of me lives in him. I saw him with you this morning. I saw you in the field. And then, when I looked upon his face—" Her grip grew harder. "I saw something there I have never seen in him before. And it was you, Serath Rune. You have enchanted him already."

Serath pulled back, shaking her head. "You are mistaken."

"Am I? I hope so. But let us suppose I am not. If you are a witch, I would think that it was an easy thing for you to fly away from this place. You would not need to stay. So your plan would not be to leave at all, but to steal him somehow—"

"You are crazed," Serath interrupted. Her heart was beating hard with guilt. "Get out."

"—and if you are not a witch, then so much the worse. For either way I see you keep'in him, and either way it means disaster."

"Out," repeated Serath, pointing to the door. Anger gave her hand a flutter.

"Please," begged the woman. "Just leave him be! There are other souls in the world, there are other men who would lie at your feet—"

Serath placed her hands over her ears, going to the door, yanking it open.

"Remove her," she told the startled guard, who peered into the cottage, trying to see behind her.

"Stay!" commanded Rafael's mother, and to Serath's

fury the guard did, not entering. Nanwyn put her hand on the door, shutting it quickly.

"I did not mean to offend you." Her voice was anxious now, lowered to intimacy. "I swear to you, Serath Rune, my offer is genuine. I *will* help you. Just please . . . grant me this one favor."

Serath shook her head again, but the woman's desperation was impossible to ignore. She felt a reluctant kinship to it, looking into Nanwyn's eyes, seeing the unfeigned concern there.

"I do not care about the land, or the castle—not any of this," Nanwyn whispered, fervent. "I would forfeit it all if it meant his safety! All I care about is Rafael."

His mother, Serath thought, and remembered the brief but absolute devotion of Morwena.

"I would not harm him," Serath said.

"Promise it. Swear it."

Serath found the woman's hand, thin and very cold. "Yes. I swear it."

Nanwyn seemed to collapse in on herself, slumping down, growing paler, and Serath reached for her in alarm. Yet the lady recovered in time, blinking rapidly and pulling back. She gave Serath a tentative smile.

"I will keep my end of this deal, Serath Rune."

Serath only nodded, and then watched Nanwyn leave, out into the freedom of the rainy day. The door closed; she walked back over to the fire.

Nanwyn might choose to think she had sway over Rafael, but Serath knew better. No matter how much she wished to deny it, her heart had found the echo of his, a compatibility of sorts, unwanted but very real. She had recognized from the very beginning the wilderness that lived within him. No one could command him. It made the winter around her seem a little colder.

The fire continued its sizzling song, the heat of it vanishing up to the ceiling, and then to the sky beyond.

———————— ⟲൝⟳ ————————

$\mathcal{T}$HEY MET IN HIS HUT THAT NIGHT, THE BEST OF his soldiers, Abram and Nils and seven others, all of them seated at his table, Rafael standing near the head of it. It was a council of war, and each of them knew their parts.

Food had been long finished; the jug of wine was empty. They had come to discuss the day, to plot and talk of the future, and the emotions in the room were running as dark as the rain outside.

"It was dishonorable," Abram was saying, sending his deliberate gaze to each man. "Jozua Rune has proven himself capable of anything. He would salt his own fields to rid himself of us. I say we act now to rid ourselves of *him*."

A few muttered "ayes" resounded around the table, heads nodded.

"Who can say what he might try next?" asked Gerold. "Archers hiding in the woods, mayhap. Ambush!"

"Aye!" Nils pounded one fist down on the table. "A secret attack!"

The men agreed again, with muttering and speaking looks.

Only Rafael remained silent amid them, his back against the wall, allowing the shadows of the room to take over his form. Eventually the men quieted, one by one looking over at him, until at last Abram asked, "What think you, my lord?"

Slowly Rafe straightened. "I think," he said, making his words very clear, "that Jozua Rune is fully capable of any black deed."

More nods came at this; unified agreement.

"That salting the fields was only the beginning," Rafael continued. "That a man such as he would not hesitate to kill any one of us—all of us—to get what he wants."

"Then you agree, my lord," said Gerold. "We should act now! Gather our forces, bring over more men from Leonhart, and attack the castle—"

"No," said Rafe, cutting him off, and his men fell into silence, staring at him. He met their looks evenly.

"I'm certain Jozua Rune anticipates such a thing," he said. "And it would well displease the king, mayhap enough so that he would rethink the decree that gives us Alderich. Fionnlagh Castle is not yet ours, not even to seize, as tempting as it may be. Losing control of this situation before the new year is the last thing we should do."

And now the silence had a new feel to it, alarm and dawning agreement.

Rafe leaned over and placed his palms on the table, intense. "We are very close to the end. We are only days away from achieving all we have wanted. Everything—I say *everything*—is falling to us. If we wait out Rune until the new year, we will still have the might of the law. And we maintain our strengths in this campaign: a valuable hostage; being here now, fortifying ourselves in this land."

"Rafe." It was Abram, the only man who ever dared to use his given name. "I won't say you're not right. But mayhap you overestimate our advantage. Rune doesn't give a damn about the king's decree, that much is obvious. And as for our hostage—it seems she is of no value at all. Indeed, I think she is far more of a liability."

Rafael did not reply to this, motioning for his cousin to continue.

"Jozua Rune appears to care nothing for her. If that is so, then having her with us means naught. Or, if it is just pretense, if he *does* care for her, then she must know it, and perhaps she acts now to trick us. To foil whatever plot we may consider. She might even be his spy!"

"She isn't," Rafael said, instinctive. He took a breath and continued more slowly, masking his defense of her. "How could she be? She has no means to see him, save if we take her up to the castle. A very impractical spy, I would say."

And Abram, who knew him better than anyone, stared over at him with unspoken consternation and worry in his eyes. Rafe nodded to show he understood his objection, even as he dismissed it.

"Serath Rune can still be of use to us. There is one sure way to prove it." Rafael gave a faint smile now, one that every man in the room recognized. A few leaned forward on their elbows, watching him intently.

"I swear it now—Alderich *will* be ours, and Jozua Rune *will* succumb. If not by the turning of the century, then by my very hand. We will be prepared for whatever Rune may plan for the new year. We will be prepared, in fact, to do what we do best." He looked again toward Abram. "And our hostage is going to help us."

Chapter Ten

*R*EPENT!''

A lunatic had come to the village.

Serath was the only one who called him that, at least in her head. To all else he was simply Zebediah, a wandering preacher, one of the many sprouting up like mushrooms across the countryside, come to speak of doom and sin and God's wrath in these final days.

"Are you saved, children of God? Are you blessed by Him?"

A few of the vanished peasants had begun to trickle back to Fionnlagh, dusty, weary, speaking in hushed voices of the vast emptiness of the world they had encountered. All of them mentioned ill tidings of the future, eerie tales of the end signs: schools of fish floating dead upon the lakes. Children speaking in tongues. Two-headed serpents overrunning villages, wild animals falling from the sky, showers of blood coming down while the righteous ascended to heaven. . . .

The most innocuous of things became an omen—
although it was turning sharply colder, snow would not
fall at Alderich, not even this far into December; it was
said that winter itself was bowing down to God's impend-
ing arrival.

With each new group of arriving peasants, the stories
continued, growing bleaker, more distressing.

There weren't many people returning, not yet, but
Serath knew that Rafael had hopes of more coming. They
reappeared mostly in bedraggled families, shame-faced
and hungry, wanting to spend their final days back at the
place they knew as home. With the last group of them
had come Zebediah.

Rafael had seemed to accept the preacher's presence,
albeit grudgingly, once he had determined the man had
no weapons—indeed, nothing at all, it appeared, save a
worn brown tunic and head full of warnings. And the
serfs had embraced him, in their apprehensive way, feeding the traveler and offering him shelter in the tavern as
they listened with fascination to his frequent sermons.

"The Lord is watching us!"

Serath had overheard Nanwyn telling her son and a
group of his soldiers that such men were becoming more
and more common everywhere, emerging from the
woods, a few attracting followers. Some had even gone to
Leonhart.

"The Lord knows your true heart!"

Initially Rafael had wanted to send the man away,
Serath knew that. But Calum had intervened, speaking of
the fear and need of his people, and in the end Rafael had
acquiesced, although with warnings that the moment the
preacher disrupted the peace, he must leave.

"Repent, I say to you!"

Her own peace was certainly being disrupted. For
some reason Zebediah had chosen the area right outside

her cottage as his favorite preaching ground, and no matter how many times her guards chased him off, like a
stubborn cat after milk, he would return.

"Beware of sin," he was saying now, his voice carrying to her past the walls. "Beware of demons, incubi and
succubi that come in the night to drain away your very
souls. . . ."

Serath sighed, lying back on her pallet, trying not to
listen. She spent a great deal of time alone in her cottage,
and Zebediah's constant doomsaying was wearing. She
knew the end approached. She did not need to be reminded of it every waking moment.

And the one man who might convincingly dispute
this fact was nowhere near her, and had not been for days.

Since that morning in the salted field Rafael had put
distance between them and kept it firmly in place. She
was allowed out every day at some point, to walk with her
eternal guard, to see the sun, or the clouds, whatever the
day had to offer. Four times now she had been in-
formed—via her guard—that she would be needed to
help with the animals that were still meandering back, and
she had done her work without complaint.

Sometimes she would see Rafael, close but not too
close, in a hut or with a group of his men, sometimes
even with some of the villagers. But most often he would
be standing alone, solid and musing, a leader lost to his
thoughts.

In these moments Serath would steal quick looks at
him and feel her skin grow hot, and her stomach would
float. It was a deliberate self-torture she was unable to
resist. There he was, her demon-man, always near but
never near enough, and he would catch her sliding looks,
and his face would turn to stone before her.

Then, either he would turn away or she would.

Well, what had she wanted? His aversion to her was

part of the natural world, Serath knew that. It was the way
it was supposed to be, he of Leonhart, and she of Alderich. Indeed, she should be echoing his emotions. They
had been enemies before time—before even the death of
Raibeart. A few kisses would not alter that.

Her hidden fantasies, her shameful daydreams, were
nothing to that.

Noontime bells tolled from Fionnlagh, her grandfather's persistent marking of the time, reminding each and
every person within hearing distance that the end of the
year was creeping closer.

"Our Lord is like the shepherd, high upon the mountain. We are His flock, alone, astray. Seek Him! Climb up
to Him! Heed His sweet counsel to you!"

Serath draped one arm over her eyes, sighing again.

Perhaps Nanwyn thought it was she who was main-
taining this distance from her son; last night one of her
serving women had arrived at her cottage with greetings
from the mistress of Leonhart, and a selection of gowns
for Serath to wear.

"For the winter," had said the handmaid, and then
transferred them gingerly to Serath before fleeing.

A reward, surely, or a bribe. A rather obvious move,
Serath thought, but decided not to disdain the gift. Her
novice gowns had not been designed for this weather, and
she had grown tired of the gooseflesh covering her.

So today Serath wore secular clothing for the first
time in her adult life, sturdy wool that was soft and fine, a
gentle blue that reminded her of forget-me-nots. It had
long sleeves that felt remarkable against her skin, and a
hood that warmed her back. The skirts of the bliaut were
loose and flowing, layered above a long undertunic of
cream.

And nestled amid the gowns she had discovered a
wide scarlet ribbon, included by design or accident, it

didn't matter. She had used it to tie her hair back, weaving it down through the mass of it until she could knot the ends together. Nuns did not wear ribbons—nor anything so fine as this forget-me-not bliaut—but she seemed to remember her mother styling her hair like this on occasion. The moonstone brooch glowed silver and gold against the blue, the rubies bright, fitting just exactly right at the center of her collar.

After she had finished with the gown and ribbon and brooch, Serath stood alone in her room, marveling at the beauty of such simple and wonderful things.

"The Lord will speak to you, if only you may listen, my children. Fear not His words in these most dark of times, for His faith in you will—"

Zebediah's preaching ended abruptly, cut short with barely a protest.

Her door opened. Rafael stood there, finishing a conversation with someone she could not see, his face averted, his hand on the latch. When he was done he came into the room absently, leaving the door ajar. Then he looked up at her.

Serath rose from her pallet, striving for calm, for poise. She almost raised her hand to smooth her hair, but didn't.

He had stopped to stare at her, unmoving, stone again. But now, in this light, she could see that she had been mistaken about that: he was not stone. He could not be, not with his eyes so savage, a tumult of gray.

She felt slightly faint. She felt too warm, and then too exposed.

His stillness fell away; he tore his gaze from hers. Something about him spoke suddenly of violence, tightly reined, but it was gone before she could fully take it in.

"My lady," he said to her, composed again. "I require your presence outside."

She lifted her skirts and passed by him to the door. Every inch of her skin prickled, heat or alarm or she couldn't name what. She felt him move behind her, and the prickling turned to sharp warmth, the sensation of Rafael close to her back.

Daylight blinded her, and Serath had to squint against it. By the time she could see clearly he had come up beside her, silent, and gestured to a gathering of soldiers and peasants by the tents. The people were looking back at her, waiting. She went to them.

Rafael did not attempt to take her arm, as he used to do. Instead he remained in her shadow, a vague air of menace about him. Her foot struck a loose stone—she stumbled and he steadied her, his hands large on her shoulder and arm. She felt the iron strength of his hold, secure for just a moment. He released her almost immediately.

They walked past the center of the village, people noticing, talking. When she looked out to the countryside she could see dots of men on horseback, sentries he had posted in the fields, patrolling. There seemed to be so many of them, these warriors from Leonhart.

The mass of soldiers broke apart, deferential, as they approached, and when Serath hesitated just outside of their circle Rafael put his hand on the small of her back, guiding her forward again.

There was a large leaf of paper on the ground, rocks holding down the corners of it. The paper had drawings of some sort on it, blackish lines and circles and squares, and arrows pointing to different parts.

Solar, she saw scratched in one of the squares. *Great hall,* in another. *Buttery. Motte. Ramparts.*

It was a map of Fionnlagh Castle.

Men closed in behind her, surrounding her, and Serath stared down at the paper and tried to pretend she did not know what it meant.

"We have pieced it together from the reports of the villagers," said Rafael, standing beside her, studying the map. "But there is disagreement on a few areas. Most of the serfs here have not been above the main floor, where the family would dwell, nor to the turrets. Those few that have cannot seem to recollect the exact layout."

"What do you want of me?" Serath asked. Her mouth was very dry.

"Tell us what you remember," said a new man, Rafael's second, opposite her. His name was Abram. She did recall that.

Serath glanced around at the soldiers, thick and well armed, more people from the village drifting close, curious.

"I don't remember very much of it," she said. "It's been too long."

"You must remember some," said the same man. "It was your home."

"I . . ." She gave the paper a frown, as if her memory faltered. "I'm not sure."

Abram exchanged a look with Rafael, heavy with disbelief.

"Anything," said the demon-man, his arm now against hers as he pushed her nearer to the paper. "Look carefully, Serath."

Storeroom. Second passageway. North tower.

"Why would you need a map now?" Serath asked. "You'll have the castle soon enough. Why not wait until then to map it out?"

No one answered her. More people had come out from the village, men and women both now. Everyone stared at her. She saw Nanwyn in the crowd, pale and alert. She saw the village leader, the wandering preacher.

Everyone watching her. She glanced down at the map again and found the chamber that used to be the nursery, a tiny half circle near some stairs.

"I really can't remember," she said. "I'm sorry."

"She's lying!" burst out Abram. "You know she is!"

Rafael raised his hand, almost leisurely, and the other man fell back with his lips clamped shut, dissatisfaction radiating from him, his stare at Serath boldly hostile. A few people in the back of the crowd began a whispering buzz that quickly rose and then fell.

"Look again, Serath," invited Rafael smoothly. His hand cupped her elbow, drawing her downward to the ground, until they both knelt before the map. "Try to remember. It is important."

"No. I don't—I suppose it all looks fine. I don't know."

He leaned in closer and Serath felt a dark panic begin in her chest. He would see that she was lying. He would know. He would force her to tell him what was wrong with this map—that some of the rooms were too small, and some too long, and some not there at all. Nearly half of the upper story was empty space, and Serath remembered, with such clarity that it might have been yesterday that she roamed those halls, what rooms were there, what hidden vestibules, what places where guards might be.

"No one wants a massacre," said Rafael, the warlord in him manifested again, emotionless. "I dislike bloodshed, Serath, and I especially dislike unnecessary bloodshed."

"You mean to seize the castle," she said dully.

"If it comes to it. If I must. A warrior should be prepared for any event, my lady. You may be certain your grandfather will be bracing for this, should he truly plan not to let go of Alderich."

She swallowed, the dryness again overtaking her, and

the lines of the map became blurred, blended together. What would he do, if she let him? How many people would he kill, aided by her?

He stayed so close to her, his shadow overlapping her own, heat and solid muscle against her arm, her shoulder. She was desperately afraid he could read her thoughts.

"I cannot help you," Serath said.

"The more I know of it," explained Rafael patiently, "the quicker and easier it will be, and the less people will die."

"You cannot seize it until after the new year." She looked up at him. "It's not yours till then."

After a moment he nodded, assessing her. His night-cloud eyes gave away nothing.

Serath said, "Ask me again on December twenty-sixth, demon-man. I might remember more then."

Abram made a sound of disgust, prompting the like from the soldiers around them. Once more the people began to talk, louder than before, their voices worried, harsh. Somewhere in the background the preacher began to rant again.

Serath had not dropped her gaze from Rafael's. She could not. She would not falter now, and become mired in her false bravery before him. His own expression was severe, unwavering. Pale sunlight lit his hair to burnished brown, slanting along his cheek to show her the stubble of new beard.

It was Rafael who broke the moment, standing and then offering his hand to help her up. Serath took it, brushing the skirts of blue and cream back into place, ignoring the corner of the map in her vision.

"Perhaps we should visit the keep again, and your grandfather." Rafael had not yet released her hand. "Perhaps that might jar your memory, my lady."

"I doubt it much," she said. "Perhaps you might

grow wings and fly over the castle for your own view, my lord, instead of asking mine."

He did not smile, but she had a sense of it anyway, the way his eyes glinted and his hand tightened for a second on her own.

"Astute advice," he said, sounding serious. "I'll consider it."

Danger, to have him reduce her fear to banter, to feel a relaxation within her at just the hint of his favor. She pulled her hand free, looking out to the trees. People milled around them now, the group dispersing slowly, although quite a few of his men lingered near. The map trembled with a low breeze, still pinned in place by the rocks.

"Good day, my lord," she mumbled, and tried to walk off.

Rafe stopped her before she could go far, catching her by the hand again, giving her a gentle tug back to him. He did not know why he did it but that he wasn't ready to have her leave him yet. He felt starved for her, even in this very public moment.

For days he had fought this. He was well aware of what Abram suspected, and Nanwyn, as well. He knew that his treatment of his hostage had crossed some invisible line long ago—that she had become less of a prisoner to him than something else, something that could well be dangerous to them all.

They did not trust her, and perhaps they had the right of it. She was the granddaughter of Rune, after all. It was the reason he had taken her. It was the reason she was still here.

And yet, despite all logic and reason to the contrary, Rafael knew, deep in his heart, that she was not the foe everyone believed her to be. When he looked in her eyes he saw nothing of Jozua there, but only goodness, and caution, and anguish for her position now.

He could not help that, any more than he could help the fact that the smartest thing to do now was pressure her, to use her knowledge of her kin and her former home to his advantage, before the year ended.

He regretted what he had to ask of her. The memory of her tears that terrible night weeks ago still haunted him, bringing forth a sharp remorse whenever he thought of it, that time he had forced her to follow his will, and keep the people of Fionnlagh bound to the land through their fear of her.

Rafael knew that a competent leader could do no less than to seize every advantage that came to him. It was the only proper way to rule. And he wasn't going to give Alderich anything less than the best of him.

Hidden behind the facade of his leadership, however, was something even worse than the remembrance of Serath crying—the hunger for her, the burning deep inside of him that drove him half-mad with longings for what could not be.

And so, while he had made his plans for Alderich, Rafe had kept his fair hostage locked away from him, out of his sight but never, ever from his mind. He had entrenched himself in forbiddance. He had remembered his honor, and hers, as he planned his careful takeover of her grandfather's home. He had tried to think of nothing but what he must soon do, and how best to do it. Even if it meant hurting her. Even if it meant she hated him for it.

Hell, she already hated him. He should not forget that, that she blamed him for the death of her brother. It was perfectly clear that there was nothing he could say or do to convince her otherwise.

It pained him to think that; a deep wound in a place that—if he did not know better—he might call his soul.

Aye, it hurt to think what she believed of him, when he thought so well, and so often, of her.

Absurd to feel pain for her at all. Insane. She did not matter to him. She could not.

Rafael had always known that Serath was of a different world than his, a place of sorcery and faerie dust, half-remembered dreams that left him empty, aching for more. He did not belong there. He never would. Best to let go of any promise of her cool magic, and simply use her as he had always meant to do.

But here she was before him again, and like an addict Rafe knew he had not been cured of her, that the denial of her had only weakened him further, heightened the craving for her all the more.

Rafe tugged again at her hand. Serath took another step toward him, tense.

It was so easy to control her like this. He wondered if she had any idea how malleable she was to him, and then thought that probably she did not.

If she did, she would not allow him to maintain his hold on her. She would not allow him to touch her so easily and keep her with him, palm to palm, an unassuming grasp. Serath could not know what even such a simple thing from her could do to him, how it clouded his mind with visions of her, his senses overflowing with just the promise of her. It seemed to Rafael she had to know, it consumed him so—but she did not.

Not in her mind. But her body . . . that was another matter.

Rafe recognized the signs, so slight, so elusive and guarded that were he not already fixated on her, they might well have slipped by him. How her breathing became fainter when he drew too close. How she would not look into his eyes for too long a time. How she moistened her lips with the tip of her tongue when she grew too nervous, sending his desire spiraling outward, quickening in waves.

He should release her hand. Let her go. Get her out of his sight again, guard her virtue and his future plans, allow this constant need in him to subside.

But he knew it would not. The proof of it was this very moment—even though she had remained secluded in her cottage, the need for her seared through him, knowing she was so near, and ultimately, so available. He felt as if he had not slept for days, waiting for this, the chance to be close to her again.

Her fingers curled up around his, just that; Rafael felt his willpower sinking away, down to the churning depths inside him.

Let her go. Let her go.

"My lady," he said. "I think perhaps we should dine together tonight."

Now she did look up at him, plainly unnerved, caution and trepidation on her face.

No, argued the last bit of him that was sane. *Don't do this. . . .*

"We need to talk," Rafael said. "There are things I want to ask of you."

"I told you, I do not remember the castle—"

"Other things," he clarified. "And perhaps tonight, with further consideration, you might remember more in an effort to minimize this war."

Her look turned downward again, to their clasped hands.

There was a ribbon in her hair. Deep crimson, complement to the ebony locks it encircled in generous loops. It came to him then that with it she was marked with his own colors, red and black. The thought of it sent a streak of lust kindling through him—here, in this small way, he could imagine she belonged to him. That the bloodred of

the ribbon was deliberate, an unspoken message to him:
she was his. Every bit of her, eyes and body and hair. His.

He imagined unwrapping the ribbon from the bundled softness, twining it around his fingers as he went, her
hair flowing free, smooth waves against his skin. The ribbon would stay in his fingers, combing through the
strands. Red and black, satin on silk, sheen and luster and
erotic thoughts . . . what it would feel like against his
bare chest, his stomach . . . lower. . . .

"I will have nothing to say to you tonight that I have
not yet said today." Serath raised her eyes but gazed off to
the distance, a hunted look.

"Then you may tell me again what you have said
before. It's only a meal, Serath."

And he meant, with desperate determination, to
make it truth. It would only be a meal. Only that, to have
her next to him for a short while. He could ask her again
about the map, about her grandfather. He would give her
another chance to prove herself to him, that his faith in
her was not misplaced. Surely no harm would come of
it. . . .

"I will see you then." He released her hand and she
almost darted away from him, black hair and blue skirts,
the red ribbon fluttering behind her. Her guards rushed
to follow.

"Tonight," Rafael murmured to himself, and felt the
slow burn of anticipation spread through him.

HIS HUT WAS SPARE. VERY SPARE, SERATH THOUGHT,
but still finer than her own abode, since it at least had
benches for sitting, and a table for eating, and even a
cupboard to hold his things—leather belts and metal scab-
bards, a few knives, folded material that might have been

tunics, or hose. His hauberk took up an entire shelf, gleaming metal. His sword lay flat along the base of it, his shield tilted up against the side.

And, of course, his pallet, larger than her own, composed of a wood frame and neatly folded blankets, all pushed up against one of the walls. Serath kept her back to that.

He had escorted her in with nary a word, not bothering to begin this important conversation he claimed to want tonight. She had her doubts he would remain satisfied with her silence on the matter of the map, and even greater doubts that she would be able to maintain that silence in the face of his increasing pressure. But what were her choices? To side with him, and give in to the gnawing suspicion that all he had said was right—that if the first day of the new millennium really did dawn, better to take Fionnlagh Castle as quickly and painlessly as possible, better to save lives than what might be simply her own pride. She was as certain as the rest of them that Jozua meant to keep Fionnlagh as long as he could, no matter what happened.

But to betray her grandfather, last of her family, even after all that had happened between them . . . how could she convince her heart to do such a thing?

It was a bedazzling quandary, and she had no solution to it.

Worse than even that was her clandestine delight in being here with this man, despite all her dread for what he might say or do next.

He stood with his back to her now, giving soft instructions to a man outside the door; Serath found her gaze resting again upon his pallet, piles of pillows and blankets beyond the fire, before she realized what she was doing and looked rapidly away.

No one had stared at them as he had walked her here

from her cottage, as she had feared. No one had talked. Serfs and soldiers alike had bowed their heads and turned away from them, in fact, as if the sight of their lord and the witch were a harmful thing to see.

But gossip was nothing to her. Gossip had followed her all of her life, and she had learned how to skate around it, or ignore it. No doubt Nanwyn would not be pleased when she learned about this dinner, but Serath could hardly be faulted for it. Far more hazardous than gossip was the peril of what was happening right now.

She was alone with him, late at night, in the place where he slept. No one would dare interrupt them, not even Nanwyn.

Oh, aye, Serath knew it was perilous, in every single way imaginable. She knew it full well, and had since this morning—standing before the map, his hand on hers, his eyes holding an intensity she could feel down to her toes.

Perilous to have even the tiniest delight in this moment. She must not consider it. She must not let it linger, nor even live.

The firepit here was slightly larger than her own; she walked over to it and held out her palms to the flames.

His conversation with the other man was done. Rafael closed the door, shutting out the cutting cold of the night. She felt the breeze from it stir her skirts. The fire flickered and bowed, then swept back.

"What is it you wished to discuss?" she asked him, nurturing the faint hope she could leave this place soon.

But all he said was, "Are you hungry?" Serath heard him move across the room, behind her.

"No."

"I am," he said, in a voice that deepened her peril.

Her hands were growing too hot. She lowered them and then turned, finding him seated at his table, facing her. He indicated the space next to him, a platter already laid out.

"Come eat," he said.

"I'd really rather not," she replied. "Pray begin your conversation, my lord."

"Pray sit and eat first," Rafael said. "And then we may talk."

When she did not move, he added, "Or shall I bring the meal to you? Either way, you will eat, Serath."

He gave her a smile then, that fearsome one, so she crossed to him and sat at the farthest edge of the bench, arranging her skirts with great care. Rafael shifted beside her, picking up and then holding out a loaf of bread to her, waiting.

Serath took it and broke off an end, placing it on her plate. She remembered, with excruciating detail, the last time she had eaten bread before him.

"You needn't be nervous around me, Serath."

But when she glanced at him she saw every reason to be nervous: his sharp attention on her, the firelight against his shoulders and hair, the masked look to his eyes.

She ignored the bread, selecting instead a portion of sliced apple. "Let us eat, then."

He kept up his stare a moment longer, then nodded, turning to the food.

It was not better fare than she was used to getting, nor was it worse. Meat and bread, cold apples with pine nuts, a few stewed vegetables. Plain but filling, perfectly ordinary. Yet it had no taste to her, not any of it. Even the tartness of the apple melted away on her tongue.

"Have you recalled anything further about Fionnlagh Castle, Serath?"

She kept her chewing even. "Alas, no."

"A pity," Rafael said. He speared a chunk of meat with his knife. "I had high hopes for your cooperation."

"You expect much from a hostage, demon-man."

"Perhaps," he agreed. "I do of you, in any case."

"A strange expectation—to think I would betray my grandfather for you."

"Do not think of it as betraying him, but rather more as saving him."

"Saving him?" she echoed, contemptuous. "And will it be saving him when you force him out of his home— the place where he was born, and has lived all his life? Will you be saving all the people of Fionnlagh Castle in such a way, my lord?"

Rafael continued eating. "He will be alive, at least."

"Oh, yes. How fortunate for him! The devil of Leonhart decides to spare his life—for what? Where will he go then? Have you considered that?"

"Let him go to Leonhart," Rafael suggested, indifferent. "Let them all have a taste of hunger to see how well it pleases them."

He looked over at her extended silence, and something about her must have affected him, for he tossed down his bite of meat and said, "What an unfavorable opinion of me you must have. I would not allow him to go without, Serath, nor any of them to suffer. Every single inhabitant of Alderich is welcome to stay on—provided they give me their oath of allegiance."

"And if they do not?"

He smiled now, a cold look. "Then they may find hunger to their liking, after all."

Serath thought of her grandfather, so old and frail, and of all the people who might still be up at the castle, planning for the end of the world.

"A finished map of Fionnlagh Castle would please me well, my lady," murmured Rafael.

"Why should I help you?" she flashed.

"Because you are intelligent," he said casually, again

picking over the food. "Caring. Charitable. And wise, I think. All of these things tell me you will have the same goals as I in this business, my lady. To finish it as well and as quickly as may be."

She sat immobile, as jolted by his words as she might have been if he actually had kissed her again. Had she heard him correctly? Had he truly said those things, had he meant them?

Serath had spent most of her life without praise of any sort. This fact had become merely another inequity she had grown used to; over the years she had concluded that most of what the prioress said of her was true. She *was* stubborn. Willful. Thankless. She had believed these things, even embraced them. Part of her still did—for to feel any other way about her life at the convent would have been a lie.

But now this, coming from him. . . . Such simple words, so lightly given. They engulfed her, they filled her up and rushed to a place in her heart she could not even consider, it was so new and so fragile. The feeling spread throughout her limbs, and finally she was able to put a name to it: gratitude.

Tremendous, delicate gratitude, barely there above her fear of having it crushed. Serath was afraid to look at him again, to see the mockery on his face.

"You must think me very gullible, my lord," she said to the apple in her hand, swift defense against this remarkable sensation.

"Not at all." He had stopped eating. "I merely think of you as like me."

"Like you?"

"Aye. You appreciate the truth. So I offer it to you."

She had to look at him now, to see his face. His expression appeared sober and sincere, nothing of jest or even quiet irony.

"I will always tell you the truth, Serath," he said. "You may count on that."

The last bit of apple slipped from her fingers, down to the plate. She scowled at it as if it offended her, and then brought both of her hands down to her lap, unable to take another bite. It was too warm in here. She felt too warm.

After a long moment, Rafael said, "You do not like to eat around me. Why is that?"

"Mayhap because you always plague me with questions. I cannot enjoy my food."

"Ah." He propped one elbow on the table. "I thought perhaps it might have been because I kissed you once when I saw you eat."

Serath felt herself blush bright pink. "You are impertinent."

"Truthful." She could imagine that wicked smile on him.

Another stretch of silence lingered between them, charged with awareness. She flattened her hands against her lap, never looking up.

"You have not apologized for kissing me," Serath said.

"For which occasion?"

"For either!"

"Because I am not sorry. And that is another truth, beautiful Serath."

She felt a hot vexation at this, cornered, not knowing how to respond. But it seemed she did not have to answer him—he did not want her words. His hands came up and cupped her cheeks; Serath lifted her head to him, helpless to stop what she knew would come next.

His lips felt cool against her own, soft and not soft, a deliberate shaping of her mouth with his. It was like kissing starfire, fierce cold and hot together, a confusion of things that could not be, yet were. The gratitude of before changed within her, turning to something more fluid, sensual. Her arms reached up and curled around his shoulders instead of away, as they should have done.

Rafael made a sound at this, encouragement, perhaps, a hum against her lips. His body came closer to hers, his arms wrapping around her, pulling her into him, and this time the bench was not in the way, and there was no rain to blind her, but oh, Serath felt blinded anyway, by this heat and coolness racing through her, coming from him. She was twisted sideways to feel him; the table was a hard barrier pushing into her ribs. When she moved to escape it he brought her even closer to him, drawing up one of her legs to crook over his lap, her skirts tousled between them.

Serath turned her face away from his, her breath ragged, but he murmured something to her she couldn't make out and pressed his lips to the curve of her neck, his tongue tasting her skin, from her jaw to the hollow of her throat. The world turned dark and dire.

He kept one hand at the small of her back, holding her near him, while the other traveled a lazy path down her side, her waist, her hips, to the leg that was bent half across him, awkward. His touch altered, became an urging behind her knee, pulling and tugging until she had to move to keep her balance. He guided her with his rough kisses, his teeth against her skin, until before she knew it she was centered over him, both legs on either side, a position both immodest and appallingly wonderful.

Serath pulled back, sucking in air to combat the shock. His face was inches away from hers, nearly even, intent eyes, a roguish curve to his lips. He kept her there with both hands, trapped between the table and his body, his embrace now tight, chest to chest, lap to lap, her shins against the wood of the bench.

"Stop," she whispered, finding her voice. "You cannot—"

"I can," Rafael said, and did something that brought back the starfire, a slow squeezing pressure of that most intimate part of her against him, all hard and strange under her. She had to close her eyes to hide from her pleasure in it.

"So beautiful," he was saying, spreading kisses across her cheek, his fingers tangled in her hair. "My Serath. . . ."

She must be feverish. It was the only answer to this, the way she felt now, faint and excited and shamefully wanting. It would explain why she did not fight so hard to free herself, why the sensation of him between her legs— only her skirts and his tunic between them—had become a yearning in her, something to be satisfied only by him.

He found her lips once more. His tongue slipped into her mouth just as he did that tantalizing movement again, pushing up against her. Pleasure flowed from their connection, keen and bright. Serath could not catch her breath, she could not even think. He did it again, and now it was she who made a noise, a small whimper caught in her chest.

She was lost to him now, there was nothing she could do to stop this. Rafael showed her the rhythm and this time her body responded to it, flexing against him; her reward was his hands scraping hard down her back, his fingers tightening against her. Her name became a hoarse whisper, his body stilled, close to trembling. His eyes were closed, his face taut.

But the starfire made her bold. She leaned forward and touched her tongue to his lips, her arms around him for balance. He was frozen, lips against hers, his breath held. She flexed again, feeling the hot and cold delight rise through her, controlling.

Rafael exploded into motion. Before she could react he had lifted himself up from the bench, one arm securing her, the other sweeping behind her. Serath heard dishes clatter and fall, metal hitting wood, clanging to the ground. Then she was on her back on the table and he was above her, shadows and firelight, gray eyes to match the night. Her legs were still spread and he was between them, moving them both up at a slant across the wood. She had one leg on the table and the other dangling, no purchase. It was sharply uncomfortable, and for one gasping moment Serath found her reason again, coming free from her trance, opening her mouth to protest.

He consumed it, capturing her doubt and erasing it under the bruising heat of his lips. His hips moved against her, familiar motion, even closer now, more urgent, exciting. She felt his hand enclose her breast, his fingers finding her nipple, teasing it, rubbing, and the starfire burned from his touch through her gown, shimmering into her skin. She arched into it and Rafael growled his approval, the hard shape of him relentless against her, masterful.

His hand shifted, skimming down her side to the mess of her skirts, bunching them up and aside. His palm brushed across the skin of her thigh, rough calluses against smoothness, and then he leaned away and found the place that burned hottest in her, a soft touch that nearly made her weep for longing and fear.

She heard him exhale near her ear, shaking.

"Ah, Serath," Rafael said, barely audible. "I—"

A scream stilled them both, shrill and long, echoing outside the hut.

Every bit of her clenched, a jerking reaction, and then Rafael was gone, a sweep of shadows, just the view of the ceiling where he had been. Serath was left scrambling to sit upright on the table, fumbling with her skirts with uncertain hands.

Someone was calling Rafael's name, very close outside. Another scream came, and then another.

He was already at the doorway. "Stay here," he commanded, with one brief, frustrated look at her. Then he yanked the door open and was gone, engulfed by the pandemonium of the night.

Chapter Eleven

———— ⟨∞⟩ ————

OF COURSE, SERATH DID NOT OBEY HIM.

As soon as she could contain the wild quaking that had taken her limbs, she walked out of his hut and stepped over the threshold of madness. A babble of voices assaulted her, a furor of shapes in the dark of the night. People were emerging from their homes, running about, everyone talking at once, and she couldn't make sense of any of it.

"The eastern pen!" she heard a woman cry. "I saw them! I did!"

She caught the arm of the nearest person, one of Rafael's men.

"What happened?" Serath asked.

"The devil!" snapped the man, and pulled away from her, moving off into the village.

She took a few steps into the crowd, and now the words were beginning to come through to her, growing clearer:

Demons in the village!

In the pen!

Animal sacrifices!

Devils, monsters are among us!

Serath pressed back against the wall of Rafael's hut, observing the nighttime figures stumbling by her, confusion, panic.

Now, she thought. *Leave now.*

She moved forward, not away from the eastern pen of sheep and goats—where the commotion seemed to be focused—but toward it. Past her own little cottage prison, past the dark edge of the village, people still crying and shouting over the nervous bleating of the animals. A chicken squawked in front of her, a frantic flutter of wings as it rushed out of someone's path.

Serath walked instead of running, feeling the most curious sensation of floating above herself, removed from this moment. Someone bumped into her, then darted off again. She hardly felt it.

Sprinting steps behind her, coming up very close.

"Serath Rune!"

She turned to see the preacher towering over her, tall and bearded, his thin face cratered with moonlight. One of his hands reached toward her from beneath his robes; Serath pulled back.

"The Lord has a special message for you, Serath Rune," said Zebediah, his voice lowered, almost sly.

"What?" She took another step back.

"My lady!"

It was a new man, Abram, beside her in an instant, glowering at the preacher.

"You're to come with me," he said, taking her arm.

"Have you confessed your sins, Serath Rune?" Zebediah stared down at her with a peculiar smile, ignoring Abram. "Are you ready for the Lord?"

She didn't know what it was—the furtive timbre of his voice, or the way his smile showed gaps of teeth, such a crafty look—but Serath felt a deep shudder run through her, repulsion.

But then Abram was dragging her away, into the chaos. When she threw a look over her shoulder the preacher still stared after her, his face unchanged.

"Confess!" he shouted after her, raising his arms to the sky. "Confess, my children, so the devil and his minions shall not harm you!" Two peasant women ran up and threw themselves at his feet, weeping.

"Babbling idiot," muttered Abram beside her, still pulling her along. "Ought to throw *him* to the demons."

"Aye," agreed Serath emphatically, earning her a measured look from the man.

A wolf's howl broke the air around them, not so very far away, from the forest. Another followed it, punctuated with yipping cries. More people yelled out in a panic; the restless calls of the sheep grew louder.

The eastern pen was the farthest from the town, a flat, empty expanse of dirt neatly encircled by a long wooden fence. It could hold up to two hundred head of sheep easily, although right now it was nearly empty, the gate hanging open. Several men were standing around it, arguing. She saw Rafael in the middle of them, framed against the sky and the jagged line of the blackened forest just beyond. To the far left of him rose the mountain that held Fionnlagh Castle, a glimpse of pearled walls amid the trees.

"I don't care whose fault it was!" Rafael was saying. "I don't care if it was demons or God's own angels that opened the damned gate—just find the animals and bring them back!"

"But my lord—the demons might still be out there!"

A villager, speaking for many, obviously, since most of the men nodded. "They'll be waiting for us!"

"It was not demons who let the animals free. It was mere men. You were deceived."

"We saw them!" cried someone else. "They were *not* men, my lord—but black devils, with horns, and flames for eyes, driving the sheep from the pen—"

"Drinking blood, they were, chanting spells—"

More people were approaching, more soldiers, some holding lamps of horn that did little to penetrate the darkness. A few women from Leonhart were scattered on the fringes of the crowd, clinging to each other in a bevy of whispers. As she was taken closer Serath noticed Nanwyn nearby, surrounded by her people. Their eyes met. It was Serath who looked away.

"I need everyone here to keep his head!" Rafael shouted, topping the commotion. At last the noise began to weaken, although even Rafael could not quiet it completely.

"Spread out in groups of two or three," he instructed, brisk authority. "Do not go alone. Gather up the animals and herd them back here, as quickly as you can."

"The demons—" a woman whimpered.

"There are no demons!" Exasperation crept into his voice.

"I saw them myself." Calum pushed forward. "I did, my lord."

"As you saw the demons who salted our fields. I know." Rafael scoured the crowd with his gaze. "Just as before, those were not demons you saw, they were men— the men of Jozua Rune! He is seeking to destroy your livelihoods, don't you understand?"

A wolf howled again, closer than before, and the people moaned with it.

"Groups of two or three!" Rafael shouted again. "No

less than that, and do not stray too far. Go quickly! We need those animals!"

His soldiers broke away, splintering the crowd, but most of the serfs stayed huddled and frightened, shaking their heads, covering their faces.

"Go!" commanded Rafael once again. "Unless you wish to starve to death next year, go!"

Serath heard them mumble, "Demons—by our souls, they were demons, awaiting us—"

"God's blood!" Rafael stood with his hands on his hips, the indigo sky behind him. "Are you so blind to the truth that you allow Rune to cripple you with fear? Care you nothing for your families, for your bread and homes? I say to you, *it was only him*. Not the devil. Only Jozua Rune!"

"Go," said Serath now, raising her voice to them, clear and resounding. All faces turned to her, their expressions veiled in the night. "Follow Leonhart's orders. I will protect you from any demons that think to come here. They would not dare touch my own."

She had surprised everyone, even herself. Conjecture raced through them, a thin fragment of hope, but still they did not move.

"Do you doubt me?" she called out. "Do you think I cannot stop such simple fiends? You know who I am!"

"My lady," said someone. "They hide, waiting for us!"

"Pah," she said, with a dismissive gesture. "They are gone already. Demons are cowardly creatures, afraid of the light, and of goodness. You are safe from them. Go on."

She waited a moment, watching them in the weak moonlight and silvered shadows. She saw Nanwyn again, her face closed, and then Rafael—naught but a dim outline against the stars, a notion of a man, ghostly.

"I will lead," Serath said. Abram had long ago let go

of her arm, so she simply walked away from him, from them all, over the level, grassy ground into the woods.

It was like entering a cave, all cool obscurity, the limbs of the trees closing in, the air heavy with the scent of night things, mystery, the unknown—

"Hold up." Rafael was there, his hand at her waist, pulling her to a halt. She pushed away from him, out of his grasp. He did not seek to restrain her again.

"You want them to hunt for the sheep, my lord," Serath said, striving to sound impersonal. "Then you will need me to do this. They will not heed you otherwise."

She wished she could see him. She wished she could see the expression on his face now, instead of this murkiness, his true self hidden by the dense night.

"I said, in groups of two or three," he responded, just as dispassionate. "You're not to go alone."

"Very well." Footsteps sounded behind them, people beginning to follow. "Send some of them with me."

"I don't think so." Rafael took her hand—not hard, not imprisoning, but lacing his fingers through her own, as a sweetheart might. Suddenly she was glad for the night, to hide her reaction to this: guilty longing, an unwelcome reminder of all that had just happened between them in his hut.

Rafe felt her stiff resistance to him; he raised their coupled hands and let his breath warm her knuckles, a light, gentle touch of his lips to her skin.

"I desire my personal witch beside me tonight," he said softly.

It was not the right time or place. He knew that. But so much had happened at once—what was supposed to be a meal swiftly turned to a seduction, now tattered to shreds—that he felt compelled to try to recapture her somehow, even if it was only with this clumsy insinuation.

He heard her rapid inhalation. Before she could respond to his brashness other people were upon them, and Rafael lowered their hands, blocking them from view with a slight shifting of his body while he issued further instructions. But he did not release her.

"Your mother should stay with us," Serath said carefully, before the group could disperse.

Rafe gave a knowing smile to the air ahead of him. "Nanwyn has returned to her cottage."

Her fingers tightened over his for a second, perhaps an involuntary response.

"Calum," Serath called out, looking past Rafe's shoulder.

"My lady?" The serf bowed to her.

"I think it good you walk with Leonhart and me," Serath said. "My protection will work best for your people with you near."

Calum ducked through the villagers until he was close, bowing again, silent. Serath pulled at her hand. Rafe straightened his fingers, and her own slipped away.

Very shrewd, he thought, conceding her victory. She had turned away from him, as if to examine the night. And since no one else was looking, Rafael closed his eyes, indulging in a second of secret torment.

He had held her and kissed her and she had responded to his touch as he had dreamed she would, with softness and sighs, every bit of her hinting of surrender, vivid pleasure. He had come that close to quenching his hunger for her, to regaining his feet again in this world of earth and woods—and now this. Their spell had broken. He would not find Serath so open to him again, and he knew it.

And he was left hanging between this world and hers, not a part of either, desperate for both. God help him.

"Yes," Serath said, in her voice of tempered calm. "This will work best. Shall we go, Leonhart?"

Rafael opened his eyes again, bracing himself against the loss.

"Aye. We're off."

They moved away into the groups he created of them, spreading to different areas, following the distant calls of the sheep. Serath walked with Calum on the other side of her, womanly grace and catlike steps, probing deeper into the thick of the trees and brush.

The wolf cry came again, forlorn, and so help him, Rafe felt his heart echo it.

"There," Serath said, hushed, and the three of them paused, listening. A small sound came from up ahead—a lamb baaing, or a goat, perhaps.

"This way."

She moved ahead too quickly, a nimble figure sliding in and out of the trees. Rafe was hard put to catch up with her, Calum crashing along beside him. When he caught sight of her again she was stopped in midstep amid a patch of moonlight, arms lifted to halt him, staring at what was before her.

"Serath," he began, but the expression on her face cut him off. He looked to see what she was looking at in the small clearing ahead.

It was not a lamb which had made the noise—not anymore. It was, in fact, a child, a boy with blond hair that shone in the moonlight, crumpled on his knees in the moss and leaves. Muffled breathing came from around the fist he had shoved against his mouth. Beyond the boy was the body of an animal, phantom-white wool, black spatterings that had to be blood. And beyond the ravaged animal crouched something else—something very much alive, a flash of feral eyes in the darkness. A low, warning growl.

Sweet Jesu. Rafe looked from the wolf to the boy, who was close enough to reach out and touch it, rocking in place on the ground, still whimpering.

Where there was one wolf, there would be more—a pack of them at least, each one cunning and fearless, perhaps surrounding them, closing in. . . .

Calum had crept up behind him. The muzzle of the wolf turned at the disturbance, and Rafe saw glinting fangs bared. The growl stayed steady.

Slowly, slowly Serath reached out her hand to the boy, voiceless command, but although the child's eyes flickered to her, he did not rise from the ground.

Calum made some sound of distress, coming closer, and Rafe had to grab his arm to stay him.

The wolf snarled again, lowering its head.

It only wants its meal, Rafael thought, wanting to shout it at the child: *Let it have the lamb! Get up!*

He had no weapons against this—not arrows, not a shield, not even his sword, damn it all. Everything had been left behind in his hut, in preparation for a warless night, a night without wolves, a night with her. . . .

Serath inched closer. When Rafe moved to stop her the wolf sprang to its feet, taking one stiff step in their direction. Rafe halted again.

Not Serath. She kept walking, one step at a time, but the wolf did nothing further, only watched her with its glowing eyes, one foot on the carcass of the lamb. When she was near enough Serath bent down to one knee, her hand still reaching for the boy. The child stared up at her, no longer rocking. He shifted but did not take her hand.

When the boy moved Rafael noticed something new on the ground, revealed behind him. And then he realized why the child would not leave.

Another child lay there, a small girl, it seemed, quiet in the dirt, skirts rumpled. One small, pale arm outflung.

Calum was mouthing something to himself, a prayer, Rafe thought, and heartily wished to join him. Somehow he had to get between Serath and the danger. He had to protect her—all of them.

Rafael began to maneuver around Calum to block the wolf, sweating with the agony of his slowness, while his whole body was screaming at him *hurry hurry hurry!*

Serath had bent forward around the boy and taken hold of the girl's arm, still so cautious, and begun to drag her backward through the leaves. The boy sat stupefied, apparently, not trying to help. When she could Serath used her other hand to grasp him, as well. She began to rise, still holding on to both children.

A loud exclamation to the right of them shattered the delicate balance of truce, and the clearing turned into a blur of motion, too many things happening at once to sort through.

Rafe heard Calum moan something, a plea, a prayer.

He saw the wolf bound forward, startled and furious, leaping straight to Serath.

He heard his own voice shout out a denial, pro-longed, nightmarish.

And he saw Serath hit by the wolf, releasing both children and rolling with it, her scream piercing his very heart.

He could not move fast enough. He was not quick enough, everything was too slow except the wolf, which tore and bit with infernal speed. Serath held her arms up against it, covering her face, somehow managing to hold it off, and Rafael was skidding over the ground to get to her, losing his footing, a howl of his own coming from his throat.

Something came between him and his view: the shape of a man, arms raised, then striking down. The wolf gave a treble cry, whining away to nothing. When Rafe could see clearly again he saw that the man was Abram, and that the wolf was dead at his feet. A sword jutted from its ribs.

Abram was helping Serath up, and more people were crowding close, including a woman who leaped upon the two children, her cries matching the single shriek that had provoked the wolf.

"Why did she not bewitch the beast?" he heard Calum saying, over and over to the others. "Why did she not bewitch it?"

Serath was standing with Abram's support, swaying, and Rafe could see the dark tears along her arms, her chest, deep scratches, blood sliding down her hands and splattered on the front of her gown. Her eyes were dazed, her breathing uneven. He took her from his cousin without a word, examining her closely, fighting the feeling that he might be suffocating beneath the frantic beating of his heart.

Her head tilted back against his shoulder.

"It only wanted its meal," she whispered to him, plucking the thought from his mind, and then her eyes rolled up and she went limp in his arms.

———————⟨⟩———————

SERATH BROKE AWAY FROM THE SMOKY LAYERS of sleep to find herself in a strange place—not the clean, stark enclosure of her cell, but a darkened room of sod and thatch, and a pallet loaded with furs. Not the convent . . .

It seemed she had been caught between a dream and wakefulness for a long time, dull pain lancing up her arms, hands touching her, voices coming and going. At times she even thought she heard music, a lilting play of strings.

Angels, Serath thought groggily. *Angels play music.* . . .

But it was not angels at all. It was a woman in rich skirts with a lute in her hands, tucked back in a far corner of this unfamiliar room. Her head was bent over the lute she held, following her fingers and the complication of notes. A long veil covered her hair, floating like thistledown over her shoulders.

". . . away," the lady was saying, over her music. "She'll do better with the proper medical attention."

"No," said another voice, a man. Serath knew it—

"A dead hostage is a useless hostage," the woman said. "If you will not return her to her convent, better to send her to Leonhart, at least. Old Jens is still alive and healing our people. He may tend to her there."

"No," said the man again.

The melody of the strings altered, becoming shorter, harder notes.

"Really, Rafael," said the woman. "You're not making sense. You have no need to keep the girl here any longer. You said yourself Jozua Rune would not bargain for her, and she refused to help with the siege. Unless you mean to force her, send her away. She is not vital to us."

"She is vital to me," said the man. "Her wounds are not grave enough to warrant sending her away. She will heal well enough here. And she *will* help with the siege."

The woman's response was muttered under her breath. "At her own convenience, no doubt."

Serath remembered why this place was new to her. From beneath her lashes she could make out Nanwyn again, seated on a bench in that corner of the room. And then Rafael, opposite her, like a sentinel standing guard.

A new voice came to her, less perceptible than the others.

"Confess! Come back to the Lord, climb up His mountain, repent your sins—"

The music stopped. "At the very least, send away that tiresome preacher," Nanwyn grumbled.

"The people enjoy him," said Rafael mildly, in a tone designed for baiting.

"The people can do without him," Nanwyn retorted. "They have enough to consider right now without him threatening them with damnation. They should be tending to their offspring."

"I'm certain they are."

"Ridiculous children," Nanwyn was saying. "Such a fuss over an animal. They might have been killed—they might have gotten *you* killed—and for what? Some fancy over a pet lamb!"

"They are merely children, Mother." Serath heard Rafael move toward her; she closed her eyes again. His touch came down on her forehead, light, barely there. "They did not know better than to follow the lamb into the woods."

"They might have known better than to confront a wolf over it!"

"The girl fell and hit her head. Her brother would not leave her." He paused, and then said, "It was an admirable thing."

Nanwyn gave a soft, deriding laugh. "Admirable—to risk their own lives and yours? I think not, Rafael."

"No one was killed but the wolf."

"No thanks to them!"

His fingers moved to stroke Serath's cheek. "Thanks be to Serath," he said quietly.

"To your cousin Abram, I believe you mean," said Nanwyn sharply. "Or am I mistaken in understanding that it was he who killed the wolf?"

"Nay. He killed it. But it was Serath who faced the

danger without a weapon. It was Serath who moved to save the children in spite of that. I think she might have done it, had the mother not screamed."

"A bold witch, indeed."

"She is no witch," said Rafael, and Serath heard what might have been a warning in him.

Nanwyn must have heard it, as well. The strings of the lute made some muted, discordant sound, perhaps from being set aside. "We should go. Let her rest."

Rafael straightened. "Aye."

Noise and movement, the creak of the door opening, and then shutting again.

Serath opened her eyes to the dimness, brought up her hand to her cheek. She touched the place where he had stroked her, feeling the lingering warmth of his caress.

"Do not succumb to wickedness," berated Zebediah, still outside her cottage. "Do not give in to the devil's lure!"

Serath shook her head, lowering her hand. The flash of white on her forearms startled her—with both hands outstretched she could see the bandages wrapping up her arms, all the way up to her elbows. She wore a simple gown of sea green, not blue. That's right, because the blue gown would be ripped and bloodied beyond repair. She had fought off the wolf—aye, she remembered that. The sour breath of it, yellow eyes, tearing fangs . . .

But she was all right. She felt fine. A little dizzy, but fine.

"Hear the Lord! He speaks to you! High on His mountain, He watches over you!"

Her furniture had been replaced, the benches of before, the table.

Serath stared over it, feeling the blood begin to pound through her.

The table.

Shame washed over her, remembrance bringing no sweetness to her now—how she had responded to him. How she had invited his kisses. The food and drink swept to the ground, and she had let him lay her down on his table to be used like a—a tavern wench—no better than that!

How easy it had been for him. How simple she must have seemed, so eager for his advances, so receptive to him that she had kissed him back, and clutched at him, and welcomed him with every bit of her body.

If he had asked then about his terrible map, no doubt she would have finished it for him in her own hand, if it meant he might love her again.

A bitter burning rose in her throat, knowledge of what he could have done—what he might have, but for the timing of Jozua's plot to let loose the sheep. She had nearly become the whore of the devil of Leonhart—dear God, exactly what her grandfather had branded her. She deserved it! It would have happened, it so nearly did! Her heart and her sense had turned against her, against all that she knew was right—

As if he had heard her thoughts, Jozua's bells began to peal, punctuating the words of the preacher.

"Come to me! Hear His counsel to you! He awaits your confession, He offers a special message to you—forgiveness! Redemption!"

Serath sat up, fighting nausea, pressing a hand over her eyes.

And how she had *liked* it! Sweet heavens, she felt as if she had come to life beneath Rafael after an eternal slumber, awake at last, feeling him, tasting him, and holding him against her. What was wrong with her? How could she have given in to such baseness?

"Our Lord on the mountain seeks you, His flock, flesh of His flesh, blood of His blood. . . ."

One particular phrase from the preacher filtered past her distress, encircling her thoughts, echoing the bells, still tolling.

Our Lord on the mountain . . .

Her hand lowered, revelation spreading through her.

"Be ye faithful only unto Him. Fear His justice, yes. Respect His word. Accept Him, and you will be rewarded. The end will be merciful and swift."

Serath staggered from the pallet, fighting the dizziness, over to the door of the cottage. She swung it open, ignoring the surprised face of the guard posted there, staring only at the preacher nearby, people gathered at his feet. Zebediah met her look across the stretch of the village courtyard, and then slowly nodded his head.

"Our lord is high on a mountain," he said to her, in the most lucid voice she had heard him use. "But I know the path to him, daughter of Rune. Do you wish to confess to me?"

"Yes," she said faintly.

"Here now," said the guard. "You're not to be up, my lady."

"No," Serath protested. "I—I must confess."

"Do not interfere in the Lord's work," said Zebediah, walking over to them. He stood in front of the guard, challenging, but although the man looked uneasy, he did not move. Serath solved the situation by putting her hand on the sleeve of the preacher and pulling him into her cottage, then rapidly closing the door.

Immediately she put as much distance between herself and Zebediah as she could, backing away from him. He crossed to the table, not sitting, and his look to her made her skin crawl.

"Daughter of Rune," he intoned with mock solemnity. "What is your confession?"

"You are no man of God," Serath said warily. "Who are you? What do you want of me?"

Zebediah smiled. "I am a man of certain services, girl. My skills are unique, and appreciated by the most noble of men. I told you before that the lord had a special message for you. Are you ready to receive it?"

She tucked her hands under her arms, nervous. "Yes. Give it to me."

"Are you certain?" he asked now, coming closer. "It is not a message for the fainthearted, girl. It is not a missive for a soul in doubt. It is only for the faithful."

"Just tell me!"

He gave his gap-toothed smile down to the folds of his robe. "My lady insists. So here it is."

Fear was crushing her chest, and Serath compensated by breathing through her teeth, watching the man's bony hands reach into his robes, a secret pocket, and pull out something held tight in his fist.

"Come see," beckoned the preacher, still with that crafty smile.

Her feet dragged across the floor, taking her to him even as her fear doubled over, and the sound of blood rushing in her ears became strong. Without warning his free hand shot out and grabbed hold of her own; Serath let out a small cry but then stifled it, gazing up at him.

Zebediah took his fist and placed it over her palm, pressing into it something long and warm and hard. When Serath dared to look down at it, she saw that it was a vial of some kind, dark glass encased in pewter, a design of vines or tendrils encircling it. Thick wax sealed it closed.

"What is it?" she asked, but she knew in her heart the answer.

"Never mind that," said the preacher. "Never you

mind. You know what to do with it, girl. He said you would."

The vial weighed heavy in her hand. She could feel the liquid within it rocking in the glass.

Zebediah whispered, "Here is your message, girl: The devil of Leonhart does not deserve life. The murderer of your own brother is not worthy of this demesne, not even for one hour—not one second. He defiles the very land by being here at all. The Lord of Alderich knows this. So do all the children of this place. And you are one of them, are you not?"

Her throat worked. She could not say a word.

"Are you not?" rasped the preacher.

"Yes," she said, barely a sound.

"I was told it is to be your redemption," said the preacher, looming over her, bent very close. "The lord has put his faith in you, his granddaughter. His hopes rest upon you. Do not fail him. Rid Alderich of this filth before the new year. Let the Last Days end with naught but goodness dwelling in this land."

The glass gleamed black at her. The pewter tendrils looked ominous, choking, their hold so tight around the vial. The shadow of the man before her fell across it, darkening it further.

"In the ordinary way of things, I would finish this duty myself. But the lord said it must be you who delivers it to Leonhart, and I have been charged to hand the vial to none but you. Your task is vital to the peace of Alderich."

In the ordinary way, the preacher had said. But Serath, with muddled wonderment, could think of nothing ordinary about this moment.

"I offer you a lesson, girl; listen carefully. An essence as pure as this"—he tapped the vial in her hand—"is rare on this earth. Two or three drops will do the job. Four if you must be certain. It has no taste, no odor. It blends handily into food or drink."

She began to shake her head, but Zebediah spoke before she could find words.

"It will be a simple task, for one such as you. You dined with him last night, Serath Rune." His smile turned to a leer. "I am certain you may find your way to such a situation again."

"No," she said. "I won't."

"Is it so? Did the devil worm his way into your confidence last night, then? Did you tell him what he wanted to know?"

Serath drew in her breath, that distanced wonder of before turning back to fear. "No."

Zebediah took a step closer to her, smiling his terrible smile. "The flesh is weak, daughter of Rune. The man desires you—all know it. Beware his wicked tricks. Beware honeyed words, and sweet lies. He will kill you when he has what he needs from you. Do not doubt it. Best to kill him first, and save your honor and that of this land."

"But—poison . . . I'm not . . ."

"Why, lady, have you such a foolish heart? Would you show such mercy to the animal that slew your brother, and the rightful heir to this land?"

She looked down at the black glass and pewter, shuddering. Remembering.

"Then know this, as well. My potion works fast and certain. A heavy sleep comes to you. A cold and lasting sleep, that's all. And then nothing else, evermore." Zebediah's voice turned sly. "One final caution. In case of danger—of discovery—the Lord of Alderich has secured you enough of this elixir for two people."

Serath tore her gaze from the vial, back up into his sunken eyes.

"The end is coming, and it shall be merciful and swift," said the preacher, a familiar refrain, but now how appalling. He began to back away from her. "Yet only for the faithful, Serath Rune. Do not allow the world to end with the devil of Leonhart still fouling this land with his presence. The lord says to tell you to do what you must—but do it, and do it soon."

He opened the door and stood there, light seeping in around his form. Serath saw the guard lean in to listen, curious.

"It is truly the end of all, my child," exclaimed Zebediah, raising one hand to the sky. "The end of sin, and of mortal weakness. Be prepared for it. The lord is watching you. Redemption may be yours." He smiled again at her against the closing of the door. "Trust in him. Obey his will—and you *will* be saved."

The light had vanished. She was alone again.

Her fingers tightened around the vial, the metal pressed into her flesh. Here it was in plain fact, the poison Jozua had threatened. But he had chosen her for the burden of it. He had chosen her to implement it, after all.

Serath turned and dropped the pewtered vial onto the furs of her pallet, unable to hold it a moment longer.

The next morning, the preacher was gone from the village.

Chapter Twelve

*T*HE SOUNDS OF THE TAVERN WERE CHEERFUL and bright. Rafael's own people lunched here now, men and women both, and the atmosphere was nearly festive. It was a striking contrast to the mood of the rest of the village. The closer they came to the new year, it seemed, the more vibrant the people of Leonhart grew, and the more despondent those from Alderich.

Serath Rune was no exception to this. She lay alone in her cottage, mending from the wolf's attack, and whenever Rafe came by she watched him with eyes so large and serious that she reminded him of a marble saint in a church, judging him for his faults. Sorrowful, because he was so unworthy.

But now he had something to cheer her.

Rafael sought and found the small, hard lump tucked away near his belt at his waist. He held up the moonstone brooch Serath had guarded so jealously, examining it in the beam of sunlight that made its way past the tavern window.

The brooch had been torn away in her battle with the wolf, lost amid leaves and ferns, and only Serath's anguished pleas to be allowed to go find it had motivated him to return to that little clearing in the woods this morning, searching for what she so clearly desired. He would not have gone back otherwise. He had wished to never see it again, the place where she had nearly died.

But it would be worth it, Rafe decided, admiring the way the rubies caught the afternoon light. It had not taken long to discover the brooch in the scuffed dirt. It had come to rest beneath a pile of old autumn leaves, a speckling of dried blood dotting their curled surfaces. That had bothered him, more than he liked; he had not known if the blood was hers or the wolf's.

The wolf's, Rafe decided. Whether it was true or not, that's what he would believe. It would not be Serath's blood, lost to the cold earth.

The brooch did not appear to have been too badly damaged in the attack, save for a warping of the pin. Rafael now removed the battered swatch of blue cloth that had been torn away with it, and carefully began to shape the pin back into place.

How delighted Serath would be to have this again. How . . . grateful.

Vivid thoughts took him, all the ways she might be willing to express her gratitude. How her eyes would at last light up, heavenly blue. Her lips would curve into that secret smile she sometimes had, shy sweetness, delicious taste, her soft tongue, her hands on him, touching him as he wanted to touch her. . . .

Ah, God.

He wasn't going to fight it any longer.

Rafael had tried. God knew it. He had tried to fight

his attraction to Serath with his very soul. He had wres-
tled with it, felt it smother him, hindering him, turning
his limbs to clumsy thickness, his blood to oil. It didn't
seem to matter what he did, the ache for her would not
diminish.

He had fought enough battles to realize when one
was irrevocably lost. He had simply never thought that
such a loss could occur within him, against his own good
sense and what he knew of right and wrong.

He wanted her. He was going to have her.

It didn't matter if it was in a bed, or a field, or in the
castle itself. His very being was turning deranged with
wanting her, and he had to assuage this hunger in him for
her or else go mad with it.

Rafael was a realist. He must not go mad, there were
too many things he had yet to accomplish. So really, there
was no choice. He would bed her. After that—

He didn't know. He didn't care. She would need
appeasement of some sort, gifts, jewels or furs, whatever might soothe her—or even a place near him—in
Fionnlagh Castle, perhaps, a connecting room to his own.
Aye. There had to be a connecting room to the master's
chambers . . . perhaps it had been on that map. . . .

He had a vision of Serath in the gown of blue that
night he had held her in his arms: curves and hints of her
revealed to him, the white of her skin against the neck-
line, the fall of her hair over one shoulder, wrapped in the
red ribbon.

Her eyes, echoing the blue, but truer, softer, like the
sky at twilight.

Her lips, the dusky shade of roses. Her touch, the feel
of her skin, between her thighs—

No. He would not dwell in this madness.

He would do it. He would not wait.

Rafe pushed aside the remains of his luncheon, listening with only half an ear to the conversation of his soldiers around him. The end of the meal was winding down, talk turning from attack plans and weaponry to more mundane matters. Accommodations. The villagers. Family back at Leonhart. Wives and children, waiting to come to Alderich. The new millennium, the bountiful times ahead.

A few of the men's wives were already here, his mother's ladies-in-waiting. Most of these women seemed painfully young to Rafael, yet were obviously devoted to their husbands. Rafe had asked Abram to ensure that these men had huts of their own in the village. It seemed a small enough concession. And it was not his imagination that since then there was a marked brightening of their attitudes, and a cocky swagger to their walks.

Such a contrast to the hardened gait and bleak faces of the men he had led and fought beside for these past years. And the wives here now, seated beside their spouses, were flushed and smiling, nearly joyous. It was an interesting change of pace for Rafe, used to quick repasts over talk of war, of battles past and future.

A woman in the room laughed; it reminded him of his childhood, some innocuous memory of happier times. He glanced again to Serath's brooch.

The moonstone took the sunlight and absorbed it in shades of silver and dove gray, lustrous. The sheen was nearly perfect, an earthly stone of stellar mystery. It suited her well, he thought.

Despite her somber mien she was healing quickly. Rafe knew it because he made certain to find out. Most of her wounds had been remarkably shallow. Poultices and rest were doing the job of mending her. She would be well soon. She had to be.

And then . . .

He would wed her.

All the noises in the room vanished in just one heart-beat, drowned beneath the rush of this sudden and amazing idea.

Rafael felt notion expand through him, as welcome as the dawn over a shadowed valley. He leaned his head back, grinning at the ceiling, the hand holding the brooch slowly lowering to the table in front of him.

Aye! It was so simple, so perfectly obvious, why had he not considered it before? He would wed her, and keep her, and no one could say aught of it! No one could deny her to him. That hunger for her, that madness in him could be assuaged for the rest of his days.

It was perfect. It was a magnificent idea, and, by God, he would do it!

She was native to this land—the serfs listened to her, surely enough, and that was a blessing no lord should overlook. She was noble, bright, and virtuous. Marrying her would only further ensure his own reign over Alderich. Their children would be of both bloods, born of the old rule and the new. Her virtue would be satisfied, while he . . . ah, he would have every night to find his own satisfaction in her.

Aye. It was a perfect plan.

Rafe clenched the brooch in his fist, still grinning. He would wed her. And then she would be his forever.

"What ails you?" Abram, seated next to him at the table, gave him a disgruntled look.

"Not a thing," Rafe replied, the elation within him undaunted.

"You look remarkably cheerful for a man in your position," Abram said, taking a stab at a slab of mutton before him.

"What position would that be?"

Abram almost threw his eating dagger down on the table, rounding on him. "A good portion of the animals

are still missing. We have wolves roaming the land, growing bolder by the day. Many of the fields have gone fallow, their crops unharvested—and we have no way of
knowing if removing the salted dirt from those that were
tainted will save them or not.

"In just three days we are supposed to inherit this
land, but Jozua Rune is still locked in his castle, and we
are still down here, struggling to catch up with whatever
plot he stews up next. His granddaughter has got half of
Alderich fearing her witchcraft, while the other half is
praising it. She has enough power now to sway a good
many people of this land—and you may be certain that if
she does not realize it now, she will soon enough. Is that
not enough of a position for you, Rafe?"

Rafael studied his cousin. "Your wife is still at Leonhart, is she not?"

Abram let out a sigh, gloom again. "Did you hear
anything that I said, my lord?"

"I heard you. The animals are missing, the fields are
ruined, the madman still rankles us . . . I know it,
Abram. I've known it for months now. But we are working to regain the animals, and the fields. We have plans to
deal with Rune. And there is never any knowing what
may happen tomorrow, anyway. So I don't see the point
of worrying excessively over it."

"You failed to mention the effect of Serath Rune,"
Abram pointed out. "There's not much you can do about
her, I wager."

"You're quite wrong," Rafe replied. "There is something very specific I plan to do about her."

Abram closed his eyes, shaking his head glumly. "No.
Don't tell me. I can tell by your voice that I don't want to
know."

Rafael waited, picking up a sliver of cheese and eating

it thoughtfully, staring off at the far wall. Abram opened his eyes again, the look of a trapped man.

"Very well. Tell me."

Rafe said, "I am going to take her to wife."

"To *wife!*" exploded Abram, and then—looking around them—quickly lowered his voice. "Have you lost your senses?"

Rafe found another wedge of cheese. His appetite was returning along with his good mood. "Not at all. In fact, it's the most sensible decision I have made in years. Think on it, Abram. She is a daughter of the very home we will inherit. She knows the land, the serfs, the life here. And the people listen to her, you know it as well as I. It's a sound choice."

"It is the choice of a fool!" hissed Abram. "You don't know what you're saying! She is the blood of Jozua! Her loyalty will always be to him—it's only natural, if such a word as 'natural' could ever be used for a family such as theirs."

"Her blood might be his, but her heart is stronger than that. She won't be ruled by him."

"How do you know?" Abram asked, leaning in closer. "How can you be certain?"

Rafe shrugged. "I only know."

His cousin rolled his eyes. "Even if you're right, and even if she is not a witch—by God, Rafe, surely there are better choices out there for you! Go to Leonhart! Find yourself a maiden there and wed her. I promise you the people here will be the better for it."

"I am sorry to say again that you are wrong. The people here will be the better for having Serath as their mistress. Think past your emotions. You know that I am right."

Abram subsided with a hunching of his shoulders,

shaking his head dourly at his food. Rafe narrowed his eyes, studying him.

"You yourself saved her life. If you were so certain of her loyalty to Jozua, why would you do such a thing?"

Abram hunched his shoulders even farther, scowling now.

"You did not have to do it," Rafe noted softly. "You might have merely stood back a moment longer, and let the wolf have her. I was too far away to do anything about it. Yet you did not—you saved her. Was it merely instinct?"

"Mayhap," said Abram, still scowling.

"How noble of you." Rafe's voice was dry.

"What do you want me to say?" Abram burst out, low and tormented. "That I saved her for *you*? So that you might *wed* her? I did not, Rafe!"

Rafael watched him, unmoving. Waiting.

"Mayhap she is not a witch," Abram said at last, calmer. "And mayhap she *is* the granddaughter of Rune. But I did not think she deserved to die in such a way. She cannot help who she is."

"True enough."

Abram looked up at him, his eyes troubled. "By my word, Rafe, I don't know what to say. It might be a spell of hers, I know not, but—I find myself thinking she's the victim of us all. Of you, and I . . . *and* Jozua."

Rafael slowly nodded his agreement.

They sat like that a moment longer, understanding between them, that unity of thought that sometimes came over them both. Another feminine laugh rang out across the room, a woman's happy tones, a man's gruff response.

"You truly mean to wed her?" Abram asked, staring straight ahead.

"Aye."

"What makes you think she'll even have you? She

thinks you killed her brother, Rafe. I doubt she's forgotten it."

"I will convince her of the truth," Rafael said, very determined.

Abram's look was cynical.

"She will believe me. She will."

She has to, he wanted to add. So much depended upon it.

Abram sighed. "Your mother won't be pleased"—as vast an understatement as Rafael had ever heard.

"Nanwyn is never pleased."

"This," predicted Abram, "might be the final act that renders her insensible."

"I doubt it. She's got too much nerve for that."

"You are a madman."

"Well, then." Rafe stood up, pushing away from the table. He picked up the brooch again; the glint of silver and gold crept past his fingers. "There will be two madmen in this land—at least for three more days."

THE AIR WAS BRISK ON HER FACE, BUT IT FELT refreshing as Serath walked through the field that days ago she had labored to cleanse of salt. It was her first outing of any significant length since the wolf attack, and even in the cold she cherished it.

An examination of the soil showed her nearly nothing. The rain had melted away the crystals that had been barely visible before. She could not say exactly how much of the land they had managed to salvage—nor even if it mattered.

Her guards paced behind her as Calum walked at her side, staying silent, clearly worried. She felt for him suddenly, noting his strained look around the fields, the prospect of hunger no farther away than the ground beneath their feet.

"You said you found the sea holly," she said to him, trying to use a clement voice. She had discovered that if she spoke too quickly or too abruptly that the man would edge away from her. So she kept her movements small and predictable, her words soft. Slowly it loosened the hold of fear over him, enough so that he walked beside her almost at ease now, the farmer in him turning with her to the problem of the soil.

"Aye, my lady," said Calum. "We got a fair amount of whatever was left at the shore. It wasn't much."

"It needn't be too much now," Serath said. "The seeds of just a few will bring about many new plants. And we may find more later. You took the roots, as well, did you not?"

"Aye." Calum gave a small smile. "Some of them as long as a man, it seemed. We had a time of it digging them up in the rain."

"I'm certain you did. But that was good thinking, Calum. With the roots we could—can—do cuttings in the springtime. And if need be, some might be eaten this winter."

"Aye," said the man again, pensive.

Serath stopped. "Do not fear. I am certain that one way or another, Leonhart will find enough food for all of your people."

Calum nodded, silent again, and Serath resumed her walking. He did not have to speak for her to understand his worried look. It was not so much the prospect of next year's hunger that troubled him so much as it was the approaching finish of this year.

Today was a day embedded deep in the winter, Christmas close at hand. Whether they wished it or not, soon everyone would know if her grandfather was right, and the end was coming—or Rafael was, and all that would come would be the spring.

To the dismay of the villagers, they still had no snow, but Serath hoped she recognized the cast of the clouds above them, thick as carded wool. The leaves from all the trees but the pines had blown away weeks ago, leaving bare branches and bark exposed to the elements.

It was a day meant for lingering inside, in the shelter of a place holding a warm fire, perhaps with mulled wine, and a hot stew. At Fionnlagh Castle it used to be a day for idle pastimes, as Serath recalled—this close to Christmas and the new year there had been chess matches for amusement, games of hoodman blind for the children, and gambling with dice for the adults. The kitchen would produce special sweetmeats and tarts, begging to be stolen. Musicians would play ballads and dancing songs. Often there were riddles for guessing, and gossip traded about. . . .

A glance up at Fionnlagh today revealed nothing of such pleasantness to her. It sat shrouded in woods, a light fog beginning to drape the lines of it. Would the inhabitants today be doing all those things she hazily remembered? Were they even there any longer?

The only person she could say for certain lingered in the castle was her grandfather. He would not abandon Fionnlagh. He would never leave willingly. He would stay up there forever if he could manage it—and he would do anything to manage it. She understood that now.

Calum interrupted her thoughts, hushed, uncertain.

"My lady—forgive my boldness—I . . . something has been bothering me, my lady, and I . . ."

She gave him a sideways look. "Speak your mind. You have naught to fear from me."

"My lady." He let out his breath in a beleaguered sigh, stopping with her in the meadow before the town. His voice was so thin she had to struggle to hear him.

"That night, in the woods, and the wolf . . . I don't understand it. It was so—fierce, my lady." He looked up at her suddenly, stronger. "Those were the children of my sister. They would have died that night, I know it. But you came."

Serath did nothing, listening. The wind swirled around them again, pushing at the folds of her cloak.

"Why did you not bewitch it?" Calum asked her, close to anguish. "It would have killed you as well—but you did not bewitch it!"

"I had no power over it," she said to him.

"But a wolf! My lady—a wolf heeds a witch, it is well known. . . ."

"Aye," she said. "Mayhap. But I had no power over that animal. Do you understand me?"

"Was it charmed already?" he asked desperately. "Was it not a wolf at all, but some wicked spirit?"

"Calum—it was just a wolf. And I was only trying to get to the children."

He stared down at her, and she could see now, for the first time, doubt shading him. Her breath caught in her; hope came alive in spite of her efforts to crush it. But he only looked away again, his fears and suspicions unresolved. Serath let her breath out, accepting the loss of the moment.

Calum was gazing up at the castle now, at the evergreen woods and rising mists. The apprehension in him seemed undimmed.

"My lady. Do you think it true, what is foretold? Do you think it will be the end of the world come the new year?"

"I don't know," she replied, as honest an answer as she had. She hesitated, then added, "I hope not."

The man nodded, silent. Serath glanced back toward the village and saw the people moving about, a few of them staring down at them, but most busy in their own worlds—peasants and soldiers and nobles from Alderich and Leonhart, each with a life that intersected the others, woven together now—and forever, she supposed. However long that might be.

"Why don't you show me the holly you found," she said lightly to Calum, not looking at him. "And we may see how much more we will need. It feels like it might snow soon, what do you think?"

He did not reply but followed when she moved, trudging up the hill with her.

At the top they waited for the guards, then began to walk toward one of the buildings at the other end of the town, winter storage for grains and herbs.

Was it her imagination? Were the people not so stilted with her as they had been before? Instead of mothers hurrying their children out of her sight Serath saw them merely pause before her, watching, their youngsters gone quiet as she passed by. There was still the rise of conversation after her, but even that seemed less agitated than before.

Calum, his steps broad and plodding, did not slow as Serath wanted to do. He gave no outward sign that anything had changed—but for the way his bearing altered. He did not keep his gaze pinned to the ground now, but rather looked up and around them, not fearful. Almost searching.

She watched his face brighten at something ahead. Serath followed his look and saw the blond boy and his dark-haired sister run out from one of the cottages, laughing, carefree as only the very young or innocent could be. They showed no signs of their earlier ordeal, no hesitation at all in running straight to Calum and Serath—

Rafael stepped out of the shadows of the tavern ahead of Abram, saying something to him over his shoulder.

Neither of them saw the children until the boy smacked into Rafael's legs, a hard enough blow to send the boy to the ground, and Rafael staggering back a few steps.

Everyone around them stopped in midmotion, staring, appalled. Only the little girl moved—she ran up to her brother, sprawled on the ground, and threw herself over him, emitting a long, thin wail.

Serath knew what they were all thinking. To insult a lord, even in such a careless way, was a dangerous thing. There were men who ruled lands where just a cross look could bring imprisonment to the offender. Her own grandfather had been known to enact some of the harshest of judgments against men—or whole families—he merely suspected of wrongdoing, or lack of loyalty.

How much more fearsome was it to insult the devil of Leonhart?

Calum rushed forward, his arrival coinciding with a woman just behind the children—their mother, Serath presumed—both of them converging on the place where Rafael stood over the children.

Rafael saw them coming toward him; he bent over and picked up first the girl, still crying, then the boy, until both were standing.

"Please—my lord—" The woman was huffing as she ran, and Calum was speaking over her, trying to take blame for the accident.

"I told them to come! They did not see you, my lord!"

Serath joined the scene as Rafael was brushing off the boy and trying to stop the little girl from throwing herself around her brother again. Then the mother was there, snatching up both children, clearly too frightened to run away. Calum placed himself between Rafael and his family, speaking quickly.

"Forgive them, my lord—they are just children—a simple mistake—"

Rafael gave Calum an irritated look. "I know it was a mistake, man." He turned to the mother. "I wanted to ensure the boy was not harmed."

A growing crowd surrounded them, tense, nervous faces. The girl still cried, softer now, peering with one eye at Rafael from behind her mother's shoulder.

"Hush," Serath admonished her. "Be brave. Your brother will not be punished."

The girl turned her gaze to Serath, hiccuping into an astonished silence. Rafael gave Serath a long, measuring look before turning to the boy.

"Were you hurt?" he asked the child.

The boy shook his head, mute.

Rafael glanced to the mother. "Your children seem to have a propensity for adventure, mistress."

"My lord," the woman mumbled, trying to curtsy while still holding her daughter in her arms. "I beg your pardon, my lord, it will not happen again."

"Merely an observation," said Rafael, moderate.

"Yes, my lord." She dipped another curtsy.

Abram, who had been silent up to now, waved his arms at the gathered crowd around them, shooing the people off, and they dispersed immediately, even her guards, after Rafael nodded to them. Calum and the mother exchanged looks, however, and then the woman approached Serath in nearly sideways steps, birdlike, ready to bolt, Calum behind her.

"They wanted to thank my lady," said Calum, nodding to the children. "For the other night. Did you not, Argus and Clady?"

Both of the children agreed in tiny voices, faces downturned.

"You are welcome," Serath replied, at a loss. She

waited a moment, then said, "Well, off with you, then." The girl wiggled free of her mother, joining her brother, both of them rushing away.

"My lady." It was the mother, standing beside Calum, white-faced and determined. "I wanted to thank you, as well. Thank you for your protection of my children."

Serath met her eyes, open and sincere in spite of her trepidation, not the sort of look she was accustomed to receiving from the villagers. She said, "I am pleased they are well again."

"Aye." Calum cleared his throat. "Children have short memories of distress."

"Sometimes," Serath said.

A hand was placed lightly on her arm; she found Rafael standing beside her. He gave the other two his measuring look.

"Pray excuse us."

Calum and his sister immediately withdrew to the eaves of the nearest building, and then to shadows and hidden alleys, along with everyone else, it seemed. Only she and Rafael were left in this portion of the village—even Abram was walking away from them without a backward look, shaking his head at nothing.

"You're feeling better," Rafael noted. His hold changed to push back the sleeve of her gown. He lifted her arm, skimming the bandages there with his fingers.

"Yes." Serath stood immobile beneath his touch, watching his hand, the tan of his skin against the material that bound her. He had the hands of a warrior—no doubt about that—large and toughened, meant to hold a sword. There were calluses on his palms . . . she remembered that, how they had felt against her skin, such rough delight.

"I have something for you," he said now, very near.

He reached into his tunic by his belt and pulled out something in his fist, holding it out to her so that she could not see what it was.

In an instant she was back in her cottage, and it was the canny preacher who stood over her, too close, clutching his lethal vial.

She took a step away, short of breath, but Rafael opened his fingers to reveal only the glow of her mother's brooch, secure in his palm.

"Oh," she cried, relief and joy, moving to take it from him.

Before she could pluck it away his fingers closed around her own, trapping her hand in his with the brooch between them. She looked up at him, chagrined.

"Serath." His eyes were serious, darkened and beautiful to her, slate gray with deep brown lashes. Strange how she had not noted it before, how the color of his eyes could give such a gentle contrast to the rest of him, so hardened and masculine. She felt herself come adrift in this moment, surrounded in this unexpected splendor, drawn to him.

"I need talk to you." His fingers stayed closed over her own.

She blinked, freeing her gaze. "So. Talk."

But he did not speak, continuing to stare down at her. Serath felt the power of it but did not dare to look up at him again, and risk losing herself to the storm of gray. She tugged at her hand.

"Talk—or let me go, my lord."

"No," Rafael said in a peculiar voice. "I can't do that."

"What?"

"Perhaps we might walk together."

"I am busy," she prevaricated, with another pull of

her hand. "I must—visit the storerooms. I told Calum I would inspect the sea holly he found."

"We will go together."

Instead of releasing her, he took her arm and looped it through his own so effortlessly that she did not realize it was done until he was walking beside her, his pace matching her own.

She slipped the brooch into the pocket of her cloak, keeping her fingers warm around it. Still he did not speak—and Serath would not give in and break the silence first. It left her to gaze stubbornly at the buildings they passed, many still abandoned. Occasional whispers reached her through some of the walls—faces glimpsed in the underlit interiors, quick peeks before vanishing again. Some of the faces were women in colorful veils—not serfs at all.

Serath wondered where Nanwyn was.

The buildings around them now were composed entirely of stone, precious warehouses for the food and seed meant to last through the winter. Rafael led her to the door of the largest storeroom, opening it for her, and Serath entered into a world of musty air laden with spices, piles of grain and vegetables and dried herbs stored in wooden bins, rows upon rows of them. She paused, adjusting to the darkness, trying not to breathe too deeply of the pungent smell. Rafael began to close the door behind them.

She stopped him by placing her hand on the outer edge of the panel.

"I need the light," she said, which was only partly true. There were lamps lined up along the floor by the door. But Serath did not want to be shut in this space alone with him. She did not trust what might happen— what he might think to do. How she might react.

Rafael acquiesced with just a small nod, hiding the

glint to his eyes, and she could not tell if he sensed her disquiet or not. Serath moved away from him, toward the nearest bin. Inside was what appeared to be a golden mound of barley, shucked free from its husks. Out of habit she dipped her hand into the seeds, letting them sift through her fingers.

She heard the sound of flint striking stone. Within seconds a faint, warm glow cast shadows before her. He had lit a lamp. The hinges on the door groaned slightly as he closed it. Her breath caught; she released it slowly, striving for calm.

"It appears you have begun to woo the population of Alderich to you, my lady." The direction of Rafael's voice told her he was still near the doorway.

"What, do you mean just now?" She picked up a seed, inspecting it. "I would hardly term that wooing."

"I would say that Calum has become your man. And that woman nearly fell to your feet with gratitude."

Serath let the seed fall back into the bin, lost immediately amid all the others.

"She was relieved for her children. That was all."

"Ah." He did move now, approaching behind her; his shadow fell long and blurred across the bin. "Was that it?"

"Certainly. One simple act would not serve to sway the opinion of Alderich, demon-man."

"But what an act it was," he said quietly.

She looked down at her hands, where the tips of bandages still showed beyond the green edge of her sleeve, and then shrugged, uncomfortable. Rafael took a step nearer, so Serath moved on to the next bin—hazelnuts, a great many of them in all sizes, basking in a faint, reddish glow from the light. She touched one, and it fell from its place in the pile with a hard clacking sound, knocking into the wood at the bottom of the bin.

"How did you know I would not punish the child?" Rafael asked her.

This time she did look up at him, caught off guard.

"How did you know?" he asked again.

"Why—" She considered it, and her discomfort became more acute. "I'm not certain."

"No?"

"No. I suppose it was that—simply that I knew you knew it was an accident."

"Even so." He hung the lamp on a hook nearby; now he walked up to the bin with her, picked up one of the nuts. She found herself staring at it, the curve of his fingers around the hard shell. "It was still an affront to the master of this land. It might have been justly punished." He held up his other hand in front of him, staying her protest. "And I know that I am not yet the master here, Serath. But I believe you understand me."

She turned her back to him, thinking furiously, and pretended to be distracted by the contents of the next bin.

"Here is your sea holly, demon-man," Serath said. "Not enough to last the winter, I'm afraid. You should have let me go with Calum. We might have found more."

"Serath."

"It's not too late. There is most likely still some left at the shore. But I should leave as soon as possible for it, before the weather grows any worse."

"Serath. Do not avoid my question."

"I don't know how!" she exclaimed, facing him. "Mayhap because you don't seem to be such a monster that you would harm an innocent child!"

She stopped, hearing her own words, realizing what she had just said.

Rafael merely gazed down at her, nightclouds and unsmiling lips, silhouetted against the dusty light.

She made some wordless sound, maddened, throwing

her hands in the air. "Or mayhap I divined it with my witching powers! Or mayhap an elf whispered it to me! Or mayhap—"

"Marry me," he said.

Words fled from her; she was left gaping at him, hands still aloft. Rafael tossed the hazelnut aside and grasped both her hands, bringing them down between them.

"It is a fitting affiliation," he said, sounding perfectly reasonable, not at all like a man who had just turned demented. "This is your home, as it now is mine. You belong here as well as I. And I think you like Alderich— even love it, despite what you've said before. You have a feel for it."

A chill took her, sweeping from his touch all the way through her body. She began to shake her head at him, still wordless, unable to laugh or scream or even flee, as she should.

"I have need of a wife who has sway with the people here," Rafael continued, determined. "A wife who can take control of the castle after Rune is gone, and have a good grasp over the ways there. A wife from Alderich will be best—better even than from my own land. You suit all of my needs, Serath."

He stepped closer, so that her skirts brushed against his legs, and she found herself staring at the column of his throat, strong and thick.

"All of them," he murmured down to her, moving their joined hands until her own were behind her, creating an arch to her back. "In every way. . . ."

His kiss was not tender or soft now. It was a mark of possession, branding her, rough and tasting of the room, and the air, and of him. He released her hands to hold her to him, just as rough, and the desire he emitted enveloped her, smothering. He became all sensation to her: his hands roaming her back beneath the cloak, a hardness between them, his lips over her skin, and the world turned and tilted around her, senseless. Serath had to cling to him to keep herself steady, and still felt as if she might splinter apart, her fragile hold on restraint undone.

"Kiss me," Rafael said, against her lips. "Kiss me, Serath. As you did before. . . ."

There could be no denying him—not now, with his tongue teasing her, and his body ardent against her own. Not now in this room of grain and dust, when he seemed to become an extension of her own life, starfire gracing her in circles that expanded like the ripples over a pond.

He groaned with her response, her slow surrender, her softening into him. Serath found his shoulders and then his hair, loose and silken beneath her hands—and then his face, lean cheeks against her palms. He felt hot, ungentle, a warrior who plied her with kisses, and that starfire of his that made her drunk with his touch.

He stroked her breasts as her head leaned back, revealing her neck to him, the loosened collar of her gown. She felt him pull against it until the material was taut over her front, outlining her; one hand slipped past the cloth to her bare skin, over her shoulder, lower, creating a tingling path across her back. His other hand cupped her buttocks and lifted her into him, a quick pressure that turned her insides to liquid. He maneuvered them both until her back was against a broad support beam between the bins, and his weight against her became something more exquisite, a rhythm she knew. Her own hands dipped lower, down his sides, hard muscles and sinewy tension.

"Yes." His voice husky, as if the air were too thin. "Touch me there, Serath."

Rafael guided her hands to him, that part of him that had changed and pressed against her through his tunic. When she hesitated he wrapped his hands around her own and held her against him.

It was a strange and wild thing, a manly heat, an urgency that pushed back at her. His eyes closed, his breath became a hiss against his teeth. It frightened her—her first taste of dread in this moment, when dread should have come to her long minutes ago.

Serath snatched her hands away, panting with fear and passion both.

Nightcloud eyes opened again, alive with intensity. He said nothing to her sudden stiffness, only held her as he had before, her back to the beam, all of him hard against her. Her hands curled up into fists; she pressed against his shoulders.

"Tell me you will wed me." He stayed against her, unyielding.

She shook her head, pushing harder.

"The convent is no place for you. You know it, Serath." He did not release her but the fine tension in him lessened somewhat, taking away what had been close to pain in her, part of this spinning, unfamiliar world. His hands shaped her hips, his forehead dipped down to touch her own.

"In the dark of the night, that longing you feel—that's me, Serath. You long for me. And I know it."

"Baseborn churl," she whispered. "You know nothing of me."

He proved her lie with just a slight movement, his rigid rod still stiff against her, that mixture of cold and heat swimming through her blood.

"I know you very well," Rafael said to her, his hands so firm. "Mayhap better than you know yourself. I know what your body wants, my love. And I know how to satisfy it."

"Release me," Serath said distinctly.

To her sudden dismay he did, stepping back, leaving her to sag alone against the beam. He did not turn away, the light around him shading his face until she saw only the outline of a man. But she did not need the light to comprehend the certainty in him—nor the panic lodged deep within her.

"You killed my brother," she said, a familiar weapon, but even to her own ears it sounded like a falsehood.

"No."

"You did! I know you did!"

"You know that I did not, Serath. I could not commit such a crime. Look into your heart. You know it there."

And horribly, awfully, she was afraid she *did* know it, that his persistent denial was the truth. That Jozua had lied.

She moaned, bowing her head, brimming with fear and this deep-rooted dread.

"I have done many things, my lady," Rafael said to her, not moving to embrace her again. His voice was solemn and sincere, dark with emotion. "Many terrible things, I would say, over the years, and through all the wars. But not that. Never that, Serath."

He had aided the little boy who ran into him. He had soothed the crying sister with not a drop of anger—she had seen nothing of such evil in him there, a man who would condemn a child to death.

"Trust in me, Serath."

"I cannot!"

"You can. I know you can."

"Liar," she scoffed, but her scorn was thick with tears.

"I know you can, because I know *you*," Rafael said again to her, so very gentle. "You're going to marry me, Serath Rune. You're going to grant me my desire." He gave a sensual smile. "And I shall grant yours."

She pushed off the beam and rushed past him, out the door, into the clouded glare of the day. He caught up with her in just a few steps, staying her with a strong hand on her shoulder.

"I'll escort you back to your cottage, my lady," Rafael said, perfectly controlled. "You may think upon what I've said there until the morrow."

"And then?"

His touch changed, became a curving caress. "The new year comes in just days, Serath. We may bring a peace to this land before that."

"Demon," she said, the only insult that still came clear to her.

He gave her his wicked smile. "Witch," he murmured back to her. "But you are *my* witch, Serath. Know it now."

"God's truth, you drive me mad," she blurted.

"Lady—I know it," he said, and kissed her hand.

---

*R*AFAEL OF LEONHART YET LIVES, MY LORD."

Jozua Rune did not look up from his meal at the news, his hands methodically tearing apart the carcass of a pheasant on his plate.

"She fails me," was all he said, eyes on the torn flesh before him. He spoke quietly, as if the other man in the room was not there.

Olivier said, "Mayhap she has not had the opportunity, my lord."

"Opportunity! Why, I could have found a thousand opportunities in such a time!"

"Mayhap," Olivier ventured, "she has lost the vial—"

"Quiet!" Jozua flicked his hands clean; bits of meat landed on the table. "She has failed me, because she is all I feared she was. I have granted her mercy enough."

Olivier watched him, stoic, recognizing the set of his

master's face. Jozua sat back in his chair, his gaze distant and thoughtful.

"It seems the devil of Leonhart will not die by the new year, after all. So we must ensure that he knows what he would inherit here—naught of Alderich."

"My lord? Surely he will know it, when the century turns, and the end comes?"

"Surely," agreed Jozua easily. "So let us greet him in some other fashion. Let us prepare a proper welcome for him, and for the end of the world."

Chapter Thirteen

*S*ERATH WAS VERY USED TO HIDING THINGS.
She had spent hours and hours contemplating the hidden about her:

Her mother's brooch, tucked away behind a loosened floor stone of her cell at the convent, shielded from any who might take it from her.

The loss of her childhood home, a buried hurt within.

The fear of the vast world, such a strange and capricious place, where delicate happiness could be destroyed with a single blow.

Her faith in her family, her grandfather, long soured. . . .

. . . the black vial of poison, now concealed amid the thatch of her roof.

And her heart—the most hidden part of all of her—locked away so deeply and for so long that now that she had found it again, she did not recognize it at all.

How could she respond to Rafael of Leonhart? How could she feel for him?

How could she ever believe him?

Yet to her dismay, Serath found herself wanting to do just that—abandon her upbringing, and all that she had been taught of the devil of Leonhart, and look to the man himself, warm eyes and firm touch and a smile just for her. He embraced her and she felt blessed. He could say her name in a tone that made her entire spirit rise in jubilation. And he had said he wanted to wed her.

It was her secret musings brought to life, a forbidden daydream manifesting beyond her control, all the more terrifying for becoming so real before her.

She wanted to believe *in* him, Serath realized. Because there was so much more at stake than even the transfer of the lands, and the hope for the dawn of a new century. It was her very existence she was contemplating now—what might be her future:

Alone, abandoned, a nun or a recluse, locked away in solitude forever, keeper of her family's tradition of hatred.

Or with him, a partner, a home in the place she had once loved. Finding trust again, and mayhap even a family of her own . . . to replace the one she would betray.

There was only one thing left to do, and only hours left to do it in.

The knock came just when she had expected it to. The door opened; a slight figure lingered there.

"You sent word you wished to speak with me." Nanwyn did not attempt to enter.

"Please, come in." Serath motioned her to one of the benches. The other woman glided forward, that pinch to her lips ever evident. She did not sit, but stood in front of the bench and table, arms at her sides. Her look was a combination of disapproval and caution.

"I know you dislike me," Serath said. "So I will not keep you long, my lady."

"Dislike you?" Nanwyn sounded perturbed. "Why-ever would you think that?"

Serath gave a little laugh, unable to stop it.

"It is not dislike," said Nanwyn. She looked flustered for a brief moment, her hands brushing her skirts, then spoke again, slowly. "I would like to think that I have learned something of people over the course of my years. I would hope that I might not judge so hastily as I have done before. I would even like to think that the time I have endured without my husband or son has taught me things about myself." She shook her head, rueful. "But all I have learned, child, is that people tend to become what is expected of them, whether they mean to or not."

Now Nanwyn looked up at her. "And *you* are Serath Rune, granddaughter of Jozua, daughter of Morwena," she finished, as if that explained everything.

Serath supposed, with a sinking heart, that it did.

"Nanwyn of Leonhart, we have a bargain, do we not?"

"Aye," said the lady, intent upon her.

"Then it is time for you to fulfill your end of it."

"As you have done yours?" suggested Nanwyn, a caustic edge to her now.

"I have not harmed your son."

"Have you not?"

"Of course not!"

"Tell me this, Serath Rune. What is it, then, that makes him protect you so? What is it that keeps his eyes on you whenever you are near? What is it about you that distracts him, that allows him to put aside all other concerns—very real concerns—until you might be content? Oh yes, I've noticed. I think that *all* have noticed."

Serath felt a sliding guilt pull at her.

"I have done none of it," she said, suffocated. "It is not due to me."

"I think it is." Nanwyn must have sensed her advantage; she came forward now, bolder. "It must be."

"It is not witchcraft, my lady!"

And now Nanwyn stopped, close enough so that Serath could see into her dark eyes, hooded, almost sorrowful. "Truth be told, child, I do not believe you need witchcraft to bespell him. I see your face, your fairness, and it is a wonder to me that half the men of this place are not making themselves fools over you."

Serath was taken aback, not knowing what to reply to this.

"But that is hardly of consequence, is it?" Nanwyn folded her arms over her chest. "I speak only of my son. And here is my true fear: I think it might be too late to save him from you."

"I would not harm him," Serath said, a plea or a promise, she didn't know.

"Perhaps not. Perhaps it would not be deliberate. Perhaps you are all that I am afraid you might be, and all that I hope—an innocent, caught in your grandfather's scheming game. Even if it is so, how little would it take from you to shatter Rafael, and change the man he is from leader to a lost soul? I've seen it happen to other men—strong men, other leaders, broken by a woman. What small thing would it be from you? It might be as simple as the fact that you cannot remain beside him."

There—Nanwyn had uttered the truth that Serath herself had feared to face. *You cannot remain beside him.* Not as a wife, not as a lover, not even as the most chaste of companions. His proposal had been madness, she had known it all along. She knew it even as her blood turned to ice, as a winter frost spread from her heart and began to deaden her whole body, freezing her.

But she asked, "Why not?" past numbed lips.

"Why, child!" Nanwyn's hand reached up, a gentle grazing across Serath's cheek. Her voice reflected the sorrow of her gaze. "You know who you are. You know where you come from, the history of your family—and ours. The legacy between us is naught but betrayal and grief. None of that has changed, nor ever will. How could you possibly think that you have a place beside the leader of Leonhart?"

Serath felt her hopes float free from her, cut loose with Nanwyn's devastating simplicity. Of course she could not be with him. How naive to even dream of it.

"Then I am certain you will recall your part of our bargain," Serath said.

Nanwyn nodded.

"Listen," said Serath, and began the careful plot that would free her from this place, and the man she so wrongfully coveted.

--------- ᧁᴜᴜᴐ ---------

That NIGHT, AFTER THE EVENING SUPPER BUT before Rafael would visit his hostage, three women from Leonhart paid call to her.

Nanwyn brought two of her attendants, gentle ladies with wide eyes and miserable expressions, trailing her like chastened hounds. Serath could guess why the waiting women were so unhappy, but she could not allow herself to feel too badly for them. Time was short.

"This one," she said, pointing to the darker-haired of the two. The other, a brown-haired lady carrying a lute, cast a terrified glance to her friend.

"Come, I won't eat you," Serath said, impatient. "We must hurry."

Nanwyn went to the door, ensuring it was shut completely. "Play for us, Helsa," she said in a voice only slightly louder than it should be.

The brown-haired maiden held the lute slack in her hand. Nanwyn scowled and waved her hands at the woman, who at last began to play, singing in a soft, trembling voice.

"Come, my love, delight in me. . . ."

Serath and the black-haired woman—Kasen was her name, she whispered timidly—began to disrobe. Belts. Bliauts, tunics.

Helsa's voice grew slightly more confident, though her eyes were still very wide.

"The night hath passed and my heart doth grieve. . . ."

Serath and Kasen paused, facing each other, matched in height and hair color. It would be enough, Serath thought. She picked up Kasen's undertunic.

"Who would hear my song to thee?"

The sizes were right, not too large nor too small. Nanwyn had judged well in choosing which of her women would be most like Serath physically. The undertunic slid over her head, soft as down, and then the gown, a dark plum with rich blue trim. The belt was knotted satin, swinging low over her hips.

"But the hawk in the mews, and the hart in the trees. . . ."

It had taken less time than Serath would have thought, but here they were, still looking at each other, and now Kasen stood in the green gown, twisting her hair back the way Serath had her own.

Helsa finished her song with a small flourish, and then looked up at them, smiling. But her smile faded as she took in the two of them, Serath shaking her hair loose, not bothering with the tiny side braids Kasen had worn, looped back. If anyone came close enough to her to notice such a difference, all of this would be for naught, anyway.

"Lovely," said Nanwyn, her voice gentle but her eyes sharp. "Now something slower, I think, Helsa. Play a ballad for my lady."

Helsa bobbed a curtsy and began strumming something new, more morose, rich with notes that did not quite seem to fit together.

"Oh, long have I wait-ed for his dear face, so far from me, so far. . . ."

Nanwyn approached, scooping up the cloak that Kasen had discarded, draping it over Serath's shoulders. She adjusted it until she was satisfied, then pulled the hood over Serath's head. The world became narrowed; only Nanwyn was visible, a crease in her brows as she studied her.

"It will do," she said. "I think it will."

"It must," Serath replied.

"Are you ready, child?"

"Aye."

Nanwyn nodded, then walked over to Helsa. She produced a dagger from the depths of her skirt, and although Helsa's eyes grew, if possible, even wider, she did not cease her song. Nanwyn reached for the lute with her blade.

"A-way to the bat-tles so he went, oh, glory for—"

Nanwyn swiftly cut one of the strings, producing an uneven *twang!* Helsa faltered into silence.

"Oh, dear," said Nanwyn loudly. "Such a pity! And we were so enjoying your song. Run off, both of you, and fetch my own lute from my cottage so that we might continue."

Serath had gathered what she needed already, so she strode to the door. Helsa stood motionless, holding the useless lute. Nanwyn tossed her cloak at her. "Go on!"

she said, steel underlying her words. "Don't delay, child! And make certain you bring the cherrywood, not the beech. Go!" She ended with a small, silvered laugh, mirthless.

As Helsa ducked into her cloak Nanwyn put a hand on Serath's shoulder.

"Go in peace," the woman whispered, "and God grant you mercy."

"And you," Serath returned.

Nanwyn stepped back, and Serath opened the door. Nanwyn pushed Helsa past the doorway first, calling out another cheerful instruction for the sake of the guard, and then Serath was just behind her, following, both of them moving quickly away from her hut, out into the pitch of night.

---

*W*HERE IS SHE?"

Nanwyn did not flinch at the outrage in her son's voice.

"She did not say where she might go."

Rafael clenched his fists to his sides, battling the urge to smash apart the simple hut. He paced in circles, the only outlet for his rage.

"When?" He threw his mother a burning look. "When did she go?"

Nanwyn only inclined her gaze to the ground, silent.

Rafe stopped pacing. "Were you anyone else, I would kill you for this."

She offered no response, no defense, merely sat there, pale as a lily, studying her folded hands in her lap. She looked nothing at all like someone who had just deliberately destroyed his world.

He had walked into her trap so unsuspecting, just a

few minutes ago. He had entered Serath's cottage expecting to find her waiting for him, ready with her acceptance of his offer.

Or maybe, he had thought, it would not be that easy. Rafe had gained quite a few stolen moments of pleasure imagining what he might do to cajole Serath into agreeing to his proposal, how he would speak reason to her again . . . but that would fail, because reason and Serath did not often seem to be easy companions. So he would start with merely holding her hand, his thumb perhaps stroking her skin as he spoke to her. And Serath would listen as that fine blush that fascinated him would rise to her cheeks, and her blue eyes would peer at him from beneath her lashes, and he would dream that she was thinking what he was, of kisses, and bare flesh, and hot, sensual pleasure between them.

And if his words did naught to convince her, he was going to try a surer way—the way he knew she could not help but respond to. He would show her how her body wanted him even if her words denied him . . . how the truth was there, just waiting to embrace him, and grant him such sweet solace that he would make the whole of the world right between them, if only she would have him. . . .

Aye, Rafe had spent long hours today planning his strategy. He had allowed her the time he had said he would, and then some, to be more than fair. So that Serath might know he was a man of his word, that she could trust him. He had made himself stay away from her until the night, using the constant distractions of the problems of Alderich to shore up his resolution—feed, animals, the serfs, the castle, Christmas coming, the new year—a myriad of problems and decisions demanding attention.

But all the while he had daydreamed of her, and of this night. Of when the time would turn in his favor, soft light and the languor of supper to aid him. It turned out he missed the meal with her—at suppertime he had been in the middle of a strategy meeting with a group of his men. By the time it was finished, Rafe had pictured Serath relaxed on her pallet, perhaps drowsy, in sweet repose. He washed quickly and found a clean tunic, anticipation quickening his steps.

He had walked into her hut and seen Nanwyn first, seated at the table. Serath was across from her, her back to him, and for a moment he felt nothing but mild alarm, thinking of what possible business his mother might have with her tonight.

But then Serath had turned to him, and Rafael had seen that it was not his love there at all but another woman, dressed as Serath had been, her hair arranged the same way. She had not looked at him but instead kept her face lowered, bright with shame.

He felt, for the first time, a sickness rise through him, a realization of what he was seeing—the betrayal before him now.

Nanwyn, apparently, felt no remorse. She had dismissed her handmaid from the room and sat there, stoic, as Rafael railed at her.

"I cannot believe it," he heard himself saying, over and over. "What you have done—"

"It was for you."

"What?" He took a step closer to her, so near violence, and had the satisfaction of at last seeing her react, shrinking in her chair.

"For you," she repeated. "I did it for you, my son."

Rafael felt the anger in him go rippling to his fingertips, closed so tightly into fists.

"Don't bother to lie to me, Nanwyn. You did this for yourself—none other. Although I cannot fathom your reasons—she was nothing to you. She was no threat to anyone, or anything."

"Can you tell me in truth she meant nothing to *you*, Rafael?"

He paused, staring down at her.

"You cannot," Nanwyn said. "And we both know it."

"That's why you did it?" he asked, staggered. "To hurt me?"

"To *save* you!" she cried, rising from the bench. "To save you from her! She is the granddaughter of Jozua Rune! Her blood is bad—it cannot be any other way! She would only destroy you!"

He could not say a word, the anger and surprise locked tight in a battle within him; he felt as if he might break apart with the slightest move.

"Sooner or later," Nanwyn said, calmer now, "it would have happened. I know you care for her, son. I see it on your face even now. But she was not for you."

"That was not your decision." Rafe was amazed at how controlled his voice sounded.

"I am your mother!"

"Aye. But allow me to inform you who *I* am, Nanwyn." His fingers unclenched, supple anger flowing free now, powered with determination, cold will—familiar strengths. "I am the master of an extensive land, about to be made more extensive in a few short days. I have killed men, and borne witness to horrors that you cannot even imagine. I have lived and survived and made my own decisions for many years now. And I do not accept your interference in my life—not for any reason!"

Her eyes teared up. "But—Rafael—"

"Enough!" He turned to the door. "By God, I don't know why I ever thought you had changed! You are as arrogant and manipulative as ever! Nothing has ever pleased you!"

"I am pleased with *you*," she said, very small.

He hesitated, hearing what she had just said, feeling it drift through his mind with a kind of bafflement. Rafe looked back at her, caught by her words despite his ire.

"You are my son," she said helplessly. "And I love you." Her head lowered again. "Forgive me for wanting to protect you, however I might."

His rage spread thin and began to vanish, vanquished beneath the glow of her forehead, the neat part in her brown hair. Rafe brought up a hand and rubbed his eyes, weary, unable to think.

"We are too much alike, I think," she said to him now. "Stubborn. Proud. Certain of what we want."

He shook his head. "You have the mettle of a harpy."

"And what does that make you?"

Rafe paused, then said, "A demon, I suppose."

And he felt a smile come over him, in spite of all this insanity. When he looked up, Nanwyn wore a subdued expression—not apologetic, not really, but remorseful, which was the closest thing to an apology he had ever seen from her.

"All I wanted was to defend my own," she said. "I did not desire to hurt you. That is—the very *last* thing I wanted for you."

He believed her. God help him, he did.

"Perhaps you have changed, after all," Rafe said slowly. "I'd like to think so."

She only looked back at him, great dark eyes and a face marked with concern. It tugged at him, bringing back his balance, his sense of what must happen now. A tinge of shame came over him, that he had raised his voice to her, despite what she had done. He had to believe that she meant well, that the source of this disaster had been good intentions.

He could salvage this. He could.

Rafael crossed to her, taking both of her hands in his. He kissed the backs of them, bowing, and then released her, walking to the door.

"Where are you going?" Nanwyn asked.

"Where do you think?"

"But you don't know where she went!"

"I know where she went," Rafe said. "And I'm bringing her back."

AT FIRST SHE HAD THOUGHT IT WAS SO EASY. How remarkable it was, to stroll away from all this, from Fionnlagh and captivity and Rafael, from that starfire he had conjured in her.

Serath had merely slipped into one of the alleys just before Nanwyn's cottage—Helsa had not even noticed her go—and with a great deal of stealth and no little luck, she had made it to the rim of the village, past an empty field, and into the eastern woods, which would hide her as she went to where she needed to be.

The meager light of the village was gone almost instantly, and then Serath was half walking, half running, feeling the strangest combination of elation and despair rising through her.

There was a path to follow but she avoided it; the surest way to be caught now was to remain in the open. She shadowed its progress from the cover of the trees instead, moving close to it only when she had to, when the brush was too thick to pass, or a gully or stream meant she would get too wet unless she used the bridge.

And it all went well. No mishaps, no serious frights—

although once, when a wolf howled in the distance, she did have to stop and catch her breath. But she felt curiously safe, not even very rushed, as if she traveled in a protective bubble, and no harm could come to her.

Eventually she stopped running entirely and just walked, warm in Kasen's cloak, sometimes taking a sip from the leather wine sack she carried, but otherwise moving, moving. Only the nightsounds of the woods surrounded her; she heard no pursuit, no rumble of galloping horses, no voices echoing over the distance.

The night held passing clouds, no threat of snow yet in the air. Part of her worried it truly *was* a sign of the end. But even if it was, the end was not here yet. She had hours, and miles, to go before it came.

So many years building up to this—these final days, the new millennium beginning. And she would fulfill her dream. She would reach the ocean before the turn of the century, snow or not. She would find her peace.

Serath wondered if Rafael had noticed she was gone yet. Probably. If he had meant to come and see her on this night, then yes. It was well past the time for sleeping, and he would not have waited much longer than the finish of the evening meal, knowing him. But perhaps Nanwyn had delayed him. Or even convinced him to give up on her, to allow her to leave freely.

This was a thought that almost made her falter; a dank and depressing thing, to think that his favor might be so fleeting, that what had passed between them could be easily begun anew with some other woman.

It was a sign of how turned around she had become, Serath thought angrily, that she would risk so much to leave him behind and yet grew so melancholy that he would not be near her. She was a heartsick fool, indeed, to care about such a thing.

Mayhap he was searching in the wrong direction.

Aye, that might be it. There were endless places to go, a hundred ways to get to even where she wanted to be. He could not be so attuned to her as to know her most private plans, this secret path she followed now.

It should have gladdened her; instead she was left even more deflated. She had a vision of his face, the light in his eyes when he had astonished her with his proposal—his *demand*—that she wed him, a cross between heat and amusement. He was like nothing and no one she had ever known, and her response to him only confused her further.

What might it have been like for them? What would it have meant, to be his wife, with no thought of the history between them? To have the comfort of his touch every day and feel no guilt overriding it? To be able to meet the gray of his eyes and simply feel delight in it, an honest pleasure, swimming in that warming to him? Starfire and kisses, every day.

To live beside him, at Fionnlagh Castle, most like. To stay at Alderich and be accepted there, to be needed. Useful.

To have his children, boys and girls both, laughter and games and sticky hugs, pride in watching them grow. She would take them up to the towers as Morwena had done with her. She would tell them about mermaids, and show them nature's beauty, and they would all cling together against the rain. What might it have been like, such a dream. . . .

Too many thoughts plaguing her. Serath came out of her reverie, sighing deeply. There were too many options to regret, and she had already spent so many of her years mired in regret, and a slow deadening to life.

But not right now. Not in this moment, her true freedom at last, wind and night and the brush of winter against her. The air was bluntly cold, her feet were beginning to ache, and she was nowhere near her goal, but Serath was still devoutly glad to be where she was, even alone.

An owl called out overhead, followed by a rush of wings, a shadow sailing over her. Serath watched it rise to the starlight, gliding, and then it was gone.

The land was growing softer, the trees farther apart, the soil less compact. She could see much more of the sky now than she was used to, a sweep of sparkling stars with a sliver of a moon, the blue of the heavens so deep it looked to her like the color of angels, mayhap, or a benediction from God.

The wind grew brisker, and she could catch it now: the taste of brine on the breeze, tangy and unmistakable. Serath took a deep breath and allowed it to refresh her, an old promise, an old memory revitalized. When she turned her head into the wind she could hear it now, as well—mermaids singing, faint storms far out, and the call of endless waves.

When she encountered the first of the sand she paused, bending down to touch it, to feel the grit of it against her skin. In this light it paled to match the stars above, countless grains falling from her palms in a faint glitter to the ground.

Serath walked on.

The last of the trees were thick and gnarled, bent sideways to avoid the wind, pines with sharp needles that still bristled in the cold, tufts of thrift and dry sea grass around them, dotting the sand in obstinate patches. She lingered by one of those old pines, then sat at its base, watching the ocean push its way up the shore . . . advance . . . retreat . . . a steady and endless cadence that would surely continue, she thought, even past the end of time.

She closed her eyes and let the rush of sound take her,

so soothing, filling the ache in her until there was no more room for bitterness, and tears fell past her lids, washing it all away.

Here, in Morwena's place at last, Serath could hear her mother's voice clearly, speaking to her as if it were only yesterday that they had parted.

Don't be sad, my daughter. Don't choose to live in sorrow. Life is for enjoying, Serath. Life is magic. Love it, and love it well.

When she could, Serath opened her eyes again to see the very beginning of the dawn, a band of green and periwinkle over the sea, rising to pink. It turned the waves to opal, living stone disguised as water, shimmering with color.

A man was walking toward her on the beach, a shadowed shape with hair that blew freely in the wind, and a stride that sank deep into the sand with each step. He left a solitary path behind him on the beach, a line that led straight back to Fionnlagh.

Choose love over sorrow. Believe in it.

Serath watched as he drew closer to her, framed against the pink and coral of the new sky, stars fading over his head. He came near and stood over her, silent, haloed in light. Finally, he spoke.

"I've brought a tent," Rafael said.

She looked past him to find the figure of a horse on the beach, distant and sturdy, its head bowed. Rafael reached out a hand to her.

Her future was lit by the sun before her, two ways illuminated, two worlds she might embrace: Love and life, the risk of believing; or empty safety and numbing loss.

With the final dawn of the century sweeping over them both, Serath made her decision.

She took his hand and rose to her feet, sweeping the sand from her skirts. Together they began to walk.

Chapter Fourteen

———— ⚬〰〰⚬ ————

*I*T WAS NOT A GENTLE PLACE.

No fairy-tale land, this; no smooth waters and tame waves, no soft sand the color of the sun. No, Serath's shore was a place of churning turmoil, with rows of sea-green waves rolling toward them in long, glassy curls, crashing violently to the beach—nothing peaceful at all. Yet Rafael could not deny it had a primitive appeal for him, this ocean and stretch of sand with its vibrant, endless energy, green and gold and white merging to create a kind of stormy rapture with the new day.

Serath walked beside him quietly, no hint of distress at seeing him, and oddly enough Rafe felt relaxed himself, removed from his troubles and hers, as the sun rose and began the slow blueing of the sky.

He took her to his steed, packed with the tent and food and water, all the things he had thought to bring with him in the haste of his departure from the village. He had listened absently to Calum's instructions on the quickest way to this place, imagining her travels, plotting how long it would take him versus how long it would take her. But there was never any doubt in Rafael that he would find her again. All he had to do was listen to his heart.

And sure enough, she was there, beneath the branches of a massive tree, calm and serene, a faerie queen at rest, perhaps. Gladness lightened his spirit, also a calm thing, and when she took his hand Rafe felt as tranquil and unhurried as the gilded clouds stretching across the sky.

She waited as he pitched the tent, choosing a nook in the rocky shore where the sand turned finer, trees to either side for his stallion, sheltered from the worst of the elements. She sat and watched him work with sunlit eyes, her hair streaming down her shoulders and arms in heavy curls.

Rafe noticed that the bandages on her arms had been removed; from here he could see faint lingering scars from the attack, already fading. Her skin was white and lovely to him, a temptation by itself. He had to turn away from her for a moment, adjusting the pegs in the sand.

When he looked back to her she was standing, still watching him. As if she had been waiting for his attention, she turned and headed for the ocean, picking her way past the stones and broken shells of the beach. He followed, drawn to her slight figure braced against the wind. Her hair now snapped and danced in front of him, black midnight loosened here in the day.

Serath glanced back at him and Rafael saw her as an intricate part of their surroundings, as natural as the water itself, her cheeks flushed with the salty air, her eyes alight. She smiled at him suddenly, free and glad, and Rafe felt something inside him lose itself to it—a sharp, stabbing pang.

God, she was so lovely. How he wanted her.

A distant part of him noticed the change in the coast beyond her, far, far down the waters. How the land became flatter, and the vegetation disappeared. Even the tint of the sand seemed altered, bleached to the color of bone. Over the years of his youth he had walked that remote shore more times than he could count—fishing, hunting, escape from his parents. Each of those times, he had never failed to turn and stare at Alderich. Not once had he dreamed of anything greater than being its master.

But now that he was actually here, Rafael discovered something mattered to him beyond even that: being beside Serath. Seeing her smile at him again.

She was gazing out at the water now, eyes narrowed. He admired her profile against the sky and her hair, dark and wild. A pair of gulls soared by, dipping and floating over the water, exchanging cries between them. Rafe turned and they watched them together, a winding aerial courtship that grew smaller and smaller as the birds flew farther out.

After a long while Serath spoke, breaking the silence she had held since he found her.

"They would not let me sing at the convent."

He sensed immediately the loss in her, that this was something that had hurt her deeply, though he could not imagine why it was so important.

Her look back at him was veiled. "They would not let me speak, either."

"Not speak?" He didn't understand her—how could she not have spoken? It seemed too outlandish to believe. But then Rafe remembered her first words to him, how her voice had been so rusty, rasping. How he had abducted her, and ridden with her, and then struggled with her, and she had remained completely silent—until he had forced her to speak.

"No," Serath said, reflective. "Not for a very long time. Years."

"How many?"

"Oh—seven, I think."

Astonishment flooded him, quickly followed by outrage for her, for what had been done to her. He had countless questions, too many to voice at once, and before he could say any of these things—*why? why? barbaric, jealous cats*—she had that smile again, the one that nearly blinded him with its freedom.

"But now—now I can sing forever, if I wish. Perhaps I will."

And she shrugged off the cloak she had worn, allowing it to fall in folds to the sand, kicking it away from her. She lifted her skirts and walked away from him, right to the froth of the ocean and then into it, and all that Rafael could do was watch her go.

Because she was singing now, and he had never, ever in his life heard a sound more haunting.

He didn't know the words to her song; he couldn't really even make them out over the cry of the wind and the roar of the surf. But what came to him was celestial and thin, a sweet soprano, pure and aching. Hers was not a perfect voice—he had heard courtesans sing with more drama, and madrigals with more cheer. But if this was how she had tried to sing at the convent, he better understood why those fearful women would wish to quiet her—it was heavy magic, mystic power. It raised the hairs on his arms and made him want to silence the rest of the world, just to hear her.

The ocean surged around her figure, darkening her purple skirts to black, but she didn't seem to notice. She simply stood there, up to her knees in frigid water, hands out, sound pouring from her. It seemed she had found the pitch of the waves, a harmony to her tune. The wind brought him snatches of her verse, something of seasons and storms and love, and the sea echoed her, heady with the potency of their mutual song.

In this moment Rafael could believe that there had been truth in the rumors all along—Serath Rune, his lovely lady, was a witch. But instead of being a fearful thing, it was a celebration of her, something good and kind and blameless.

Eventually her song ended and she merely stood there, swaying slightly with the pull of the current, staring out. Rafael walked to her side, splashing through the water, intent on drawing her back to the dry shore. When he reached her Serath was looking down at her hands. The gleam of silver and gold shone at him—her brooch, loose on her palm.

"It's all I have of her," she said.

"Who?" he asked, over the rhythm of the water.

Serath smiled. "Morwena. Everything else was burned or taken away—her clothing, her medicines, her books. Just this was saved, and only because my brother thought to hide it before it could be found. It was a bridal gift from our father."

Rafe said nothing. Together they gazed down at the silvery stone, the cabochons of rubies.

Serath's voice dropped, nearly disappearing against the sound of the waves. "I thought I had lost myself. So many years locked away in silence . . . I had nothing to believe in any longer. There was only this to remind me of who I once was. I needed it for that—to believe in goodness. To remember it."

She lifted her head and raised her arm; Rafe stayed her hand before she could complete the arc of her throw.

"What are you doing?" he asked her, surprised.

"It's what she would want." She faced him, blue eyes

deeper than the sky. "It's for her, don't you see? It belongs to her, and this was her place."

Rafael looked at her, then at the moonstone and its rubies, perhaps as much as a whole month of food for his people held there in her fist, ready to be tossed away into the water.

"It's what she would want," Serath said again, entreating. "My mother. It's my tribute to her."

Rafe released her hand.

But instead of throwing it Serath hesitated, then slowly lowered her arm. She held out the brooch to him, an offering, sea foam sliding between them.

"No," he said, closing her fingers around the stone again. "Do what you must."

She did not hesitate again. Rafe watched as she stepped back and flung the brooch over the waves, high and then low, far from them, just a small, sparkling splash marking its fall. He heard her whisper, "Be free, Mama."

Rafe put an arm around her shoulders and they stood there together, half-soaked and blinded with the new sun, and he felt a peace steal over him like he had never known. More magic, no doubt, benign and gentle, bonding them.

But even magic could not stop the coldness of the ocean, and so eventually Rafe urged her back up to the beach, and Serath allowed it, leaving the water behind them, their shadows dusky against the dunes.

The tent awaited them, firmly embedded in the sand, and he took her there and then inside, where he had placed a blanket on the ground. They sat together, huddled close in the small space, untying the soaked laces of their boots with chilled fingers. He could not help but look over at her; layers of damp skirts were folded back to reveal the fine shape of her calves. Her flesh was bluish white in this light, enough to concern him. Without bothering to ask permission, Rafael took her feet in his hands and began to rub them, shared warmth.

Serath leaned back on her hands and watched him, enigmatic. Seawater dewed her, beads of it glistening in her hair. She held his look without shyness, a slight tilt to her head. He had the sensation that she was studying him, trying to reach some conclusion about him, and this made him pause, his palms still warm on her feet.

"You need another gown," he said, rough. "This one is too wet."

She said, "You told me once you would always give me the truth."

Rafe looked down at his hands against her skin, dark on light. "Aye."

"Did you kill him?"

He met her eyes. "No."

"I believe you."

It was the very last thing he had expected from her. Her words made no sense to him at first; it had to have been illusion, a cruel trick of the air, the thunder of the ocean muddling what he had heard. Rafael wanted to ask her to repeat it, but couldn't even manage that. Fear bound him motionless—he was afraid to reach for her, afraid to move, afraid that any gesture toward her would be rebuffed.

Serath drew her feet back from his touch, tucking them under her, then leaned toward him. He caught the scent of her, sea and sorcery.

She said again softly, "I believe you, demon-man."

He grappled for sanity and found the words for the feeling that filled him now:

"Thank you."

She leaned closer still, his faerie queen bejeweled with sea spray, and then touched her lips to his, warm and confident, tasting of salt and sweet faith. Her hair fell forward and clung to him, to their cheeks, damp, tickling softness.

It was a wish turned to reality for him, too astonishing, much too incredible. Rafael pulled away slightly, examining her, trying to verify this moment and her acceptance of him.

"I swear to you, Serath—on my life, I did not harm him."

She placed one finger over his lips, silencing him; it turned into a caress over his chin. "I have said I believed you. I did not lie. I trust you, Rafael."

And Rafe smiled against her touch and then pulled her to him, lowering them both to the ground.

Joy filled him, complete and total joy, but beneath it was a more familiar response, his hunger for her, and soon this consumed him. He adjusted her until she was draped over him, vague thoughts of not frightening her running through him, the urge to comfort her vying with the crushing need for her, to be inside of her.

Her weight was a slight pressure, welcome against the hard desire his body had become. A curtain of jet black shielded him from the outside world. Her face was framed by it, languorous eyes, lips stung by his kisses. Serath turned her head and pressed her lips to his throat. He felt her tongue against him, tasting, making the blood pound through him. Rafe clutched at her, greedy, his fingers pressing into her, and then guided her face back to him, claiming her with a long, deep kiss.

She made a sound, a low whimper he felt go through the core of him. The interior of the tent became a place of wonder for him, rising light showing him the smoothness of her cheek, the length of her lashes, sweeping down low to shade the blue eyes watching him.

"Serath," he said, but couldn't think of what else to add. Her name was lovely to him, as rare and magical as

she was, sunlight through gloom, a lancing brightness that
warmed him. He wanted to cradle her to him all day—
forever. He wanted to see all of that white skin, the contrast of ebony hair against it. He wanted to feel himself
pressed to her, flesh to flesh.

She lay over him with almost trembling stillness, fervent but waiting, and Rafael remembered her inexperience, that her world had been naught but chaste and tame
until he had come.

The thought sent a fresh surge of lust through him.

His hands stroked her, down the curve of her back
and lower, pulling her closer to him, and he was rewarded
with that sound again, her own music, a thrill to his
blood. She seemed to melt against him; her head sank
down and he felt her lips against his ear, teasing breath,
soft on his skin.

Rafe rolled them both over, reversing their positions,
and the blanket twisted beneath her, creases of deep green
against her black hair. He shifted until he rested between
her legs, the purple gown shifting up her in thick folds.
Serath smiled at him, a woman's look, sultry blue that
turned his blood to burning heat.

And it was that look, that beguiling invitation, that
made him pause, that made Rafael truly realize for the
first time the consequences of what he meant to do, and
what it would mean for her.

He had planned all along to have her. The scope of
his future had included her ever since he had first seen
her, revealed to him amid shooting stars atop that convent
wall. He had dreamed of this seduction for endless nights,
of being exactly where he was now, in her arms, having
her willing and soft beneath him—and he could not do it.

He could not dishonor her. He wanted everything
from Serath, Rafael understood that now, in this most
inopportune of moments. He would have had her wed

him, but without such a promise, what he wanted became fraught with danger for her. She had so little already, a novice nun, no dowry, no family to back her. To the eyes of the world the only valuable aspect left to Serath would be her chastity—and his body was stinging with the desire to steal that from her as soon as he could.

It made Rafe want to laugh with self-mockery. Who could have guessed he might have had such a shred of honor left in him?

He loved her. He loved her more than he loved himself. He would not use her so basely. He could not.

But still she gazed up at him, woman and innocence together, waiting. When he did not move, she arched a little beneath him.

"Rafael?"

He dropped his head down and kissed her lightly, agonized, wanting this so badly his hands were shaking. But he could not. Not yet.

"Serath—" He blew her name across her skin, breathing deeply of her, freshness and ocean. "Sweet love—I . . ."

She moved again, reacting to his touch, and his words faded off, his good intentions faltering. Her hands traveled down to his hips, back up to his back, his shoulders, restless.

"Don't stop." There was something almost plaintive to her tone.

He let out a broken laugh. "I don't want to."

"Kiss me," she said, a demand shaded still with her virtue, and when he did not she reached for him and cupped his cheeks, pulling his head down close to hers. Those noble resolutions of his were growing thinner and thinner—seeping past the hazy notion of her honor was hard-beating passion.

Serath slowly lifted her face to him, finding his lips

again, a succulent taste of her, erotic. Her tongue slipped past his lips, tentative, but with his stillness she grew more daring, imitating the kiss he had given her before, intense and longing.

To hell with it. He would marry her despite her protests. He would beg, or plead, or command it—he would hold her hostage and love her ruthlessly until she would agree, until she was so blinded with him she would have no choice—he would not give up this moment—

Rafael felt the last of his restraint dissolve, an intoxicating freedom, and with his new intentions he shifted over her, finding the folds of her skirts and lifting them, her warm skin beneath, her supple heat, a delicious torment to him. Her gown was loose and soft; she lifted her body into a sleek arc and helped him rid her of it. She wore almost nothing at all beneath it but for a thin undertunic, translucent, his first real glimpse of her figure, disguised behind this gossamer shift. Rafe ran one finger down the center of her chest, his hand rising and falling with her breathing, lower down, to the soft roundness of her belly, perfect, then to dusky curls, faint beneath the cloth.

Serath watched his look of intent concentration, her hands curled to fists at her sides. She knew this feeling sweeping over her, the touch of him leaving starfire to spread through her body. She knew the contours of his shape against the tent, the solid lines of him, what the tautness around his mouth meant. She knew that brilliance to his eyes, nightclouds turned to a winter tempest as he looked upon her.

She uncurled her hands and reached for him, a shiver taking her—the cold day, her bareness, modesty at last coming to her. He leaned over her and touched his mouth to hers, fleeting, then drew away from her again. Before she could voice her dismay he was stripping off his own tunic to reveal his torso, finely muscled, his arms raised above his head and lowered again, his clothing tossed aside. Serath lost her nerve and looked away as his hands moved lower, to the ties of his hose. She studied his shadow instead: movement, shifting, an image of him in dusky lavender. And then he was on top of her again, blanketing the chill.

When she looked up at him he appeared so pensive, almost removed from the man who was doing such amazing things to her, touching her again, skimming the undertunic, bunching it upward until it rode above her breasts. His bare skin came down upon hers, searing warmth. She closed her eyes, delighted, and arched her back again as Rafael slid down the length of her, trailing kisses down her throat, the curve of her shoulder. Her breasts, his lips finding her nipple, causing her to take in the cold air too quickly, startling.

The starfire turned to need, causing her legs to rise, cradling him. Rafael's arms encircled her as he suckled harder, pressed against her. When she said his name he came up again, nuzzling her face, and she felt that hard and unique shape of him settle against the most intimate part of her, where the need was strongest. It happened so gently, so smoothly—Rafael moved and that hardness became a pressure against her, and then an advance, filling her.

It was such an easy thing, so natural that the pain of it seemed almost welcome. He held her and whispered things to her that Serath barely heard, intent on exploring this newness, a stinging ache underneath the mounting pleasure, starfire again—but oh, so much stronger now.

She dug her fingers into his shoulders and held on tightly, moving with him now, a sweet tandem between them. Rafael pressed his cheek against hers, his body ardent over hers, guiding her, showing her how to find the pleasure and increase it—rhythm and salty sweat and his heart, beating strong against her own. The last thing she saw before the storm took her was his face, eyes closed, lost in their joining. And then she was lost as well, surrendering to moment, starfire ringing her with luminous waves until she became it, overwhelmed.

Rafael clenched above her, a guttural moan taking him, and his arms tightened convulsively around her, bringing her even nearer to him, until they were both gasping and spent.

Serath didn't know how much time passed. She felt protected from time, safe from all the things outside this tent that wished to grieve her. She thought, drowsily, that the world could truly end right now and she would not regret it—she had found the most blessed thing on earth and had reveled in it, shameless. Let the end come. She had already tasted bliss.

But the only thing that happened was that Rafael kissed her again, gentle against the corners of her lips, and she felt him slip away from her, leaving a burning emptiness behind. He lifted her up so that she sat in front of him, and then hugged her to him again, blocking out the coming chill carried by the wind.

"You're going to marry me," he said, his head bowed over her shoulder. It was not a question, but when she didn't reply he pulled back, looking into her face.

"Aren't you?" he asked now, blunt.

Serath could not meet his eyes, uneasy. The feeling of protection had vanished; she was cold again, awkward with his demand.

"Serath—what's wrong?" He kept her close. "Tell me."

"I don't know," she began, unable to put her disquiet into words. How could she explain it to him, when her emotions were such a tangled mix? *My enemy, my lover, the last day right now, the end of everything tonight, foretold forever, afraid, afraid . . .*

Rafael frowned, gazing at her, and she felt as if she might be made of clear crystal, he read her so easily.

"Tomorrow will come, Serath," he said, very certain. "And I need a bride. I need *you*." But perhaps he knew this was not enough for her, because he added, "You said out there, in the water, that you needed something to believe in. Well, believe in *us*, Serath. I'm going to make it come true. I promise you."

She felt his conviction, the power of it reaching out to her. He was strength and reality before her, he was tangible and dear. Yet even now, it was impossible to overcome the drenching fear of her childhood lessons, hammered into her over and over . . . such vivid stories that she had dreamed of this end countless times—by fire or flood or the hand of God, reaching down to smite them.

But somewhere deep in her heart, she suspected that if ever a mortal man could change the course of fate, it would be Rafael.

He said to her, "I've discovered something since I've been with you, Serath Rune. All those rumors that claimed I had no soul were wrong. I do have a soul. I must—because you touch it."

She wanted this so badly. Never in her life had she felt such a longing for what might be. Serath brought her hand up to touch his cheek, falling into the intensity of his nightcloud gaze, and then offered him the best compromise she could.

"If what you say comes true, if it isn't the end of the world with this new year—then yes, I will wed you."

"Good enough," he replied, placing a kiss on her forehead, and she almost smiled at the satisfaction in his voice.

His eyes closed; he secured her against him again, his

hand smoothing her hair down her back in slow strokes. She wrapped her arms around him, resting her cheek against his shoulder, too filled with amazement and worry to close her own eyes.

The blanket beneath them had become nothing but rumpled disarray. Serath could see their legs intertwined, sand dusting their skin like golden sugar.

Time spun out, languid and unrushed. Only the gradual, creeping cold of the air began to bother her. She did her best to ignore it, savoring this moment.

At last she could not stop the shiver that took her. Rafael kissed her again, then released her. The undertunic shimmered down her in feathery touches, bringing more chills to her skin. Rafael found her gown and shook the sand loose from it, then helped her back into it, not so damp as before, the hem of it dried to stiffness. When she was dressed he retrieved his own clothing, and soon enough he was a warrior again, so formidable. Yet when she met his eyes she saw the man who had loved her, a tender look that belied the soldier aspect of him.

He took her hands, his touch firm, and she could not help but marvel at even this, the smallest link between them that felt so right.

"We should head back soon," he said. "There is much to do before tonight. They'll be awaiting us."

"I don't want to go," Serath confessed.

His fingers tightened. "I don't think I do, either," he said, and gave her his wicked smile. "But I'm afraid I did not bring enough food to last us long."

"Not even until the end of the world?" she asked, a gentle teasing despite her fears.

"Never that long. Not even until supper, I fear."

Inspiration took her; she was up and tripping from the tent, smiling back at him now, offering reassurances when he tried to keep her inside. The day had turned overcast, clouds tumbling in from over the sea. But she found what she was looking for quickly, kneeling and digging at the sand with near childish glee.

She returned to him carrying the root, still smiling, and Rafael watched her from the entrance of the tent, arms crossed, shaking his head.

Serath presented it to him. "Behold your sustenance, my lord."

His look took in the sea holly, crusted with sand, ungainly with long tendrils trailing from her hands.

"You want me to eat *that?*"

"It's tasty," she assured him, serious, but then ruined it by bursting into laughter.

His look turned warmer, back up to her face.

"You boil it," Serath added helpfully. "Put it in stews." He reached for her, pulling her back inside the tent as she said, "Goats *love* it."

And they laughed together, the first time ever, she realized—a bittersweet thought. Rafael took the root from her and dropped it to the sand, his arms enfolding her. But the tent was too shallow for standing, and so they sank to their knees together, a kiss beginning, and then they were lying side by side on what remained of the blanket, and the kiss wound on, less urgency than before but still so nice, peace and that ripple of starfire, just simmering between them.

The ocean murmured past the walls of the tent, steady reverberation, sounding to her like an ancient promise, a blessing here with them, this moment, the sand and the tang of the air and their embrace. It was enchantment around them again, isolating them from every other thing in the world.

"I wish we might stay here forever," Serath said, against his lips.

Rafael gave a small sigh, more of a heavy breath,

stroking her hair once more. She knew what his reply would be, and so kissed him a little harder, stopping the words. When his hand moved to find the nape of her neck, she spoke again with hushed persuasion.

"It might be the end. Tonight might be our final time together in this life. Why not spend it out here, in the open? Why not witness the last of the world from this place, just you and I?"

"It will not be the end, Serath. I've told you—I won't allow it." He rocked her closer, his words spoken against her hair. "It cannot end like this. You are going to be my wife. It's too late to think to change it, my lady."

"I would not change it," she said, grave. "But who knows what may happen when midnight comes, and the century ends? Only God, I think."

"When midnight comes, all that will change is my place in this land. I will rule here. Anything else is as likely as . . ." He paused, as if trying to think of something suitably impossible. Serath placed the flat of her palm against his chest, feeling the steady beating of his heart.

"As a demon-man turning into a prince?"

He gave a quiet rumble of laughter. His voice deepened with the lazy spell of this place. "I *will* be the prince of this land at midnight, Serath, out here among these hills, this shore. And you will be my princess."

"Prince of Alderich," she said softly. "Best not tell the king."

"The king will have forgotten us, my lady. I cast a charm over him; Alderich is naught but mist and dreams to him now. We'll rule here of our own will, out here in the wild. You'll see."

"I hope so."

"You will," he promised. Rafael leaned up on his

elbow, smiling down at her. "I will seal my vow with a kiss."

Serath lifted one hand and held him off. "Kiss me at midnight, demon-man," she said, less jest than heartfelt wish. "We will know it then if your spell succeeded."

"I will kiss you then, as well," he replied, and overcame her hand easily, until she was on her back and returning his ardor with all the hope and fear that lived in her, burning bright.

Rafael lifted his head. "Mayhap you're right," he said huskily. "We should stay."

This time it was Serath who let out her breath, releasing what she could of that fear. "No. We should get back to the village."

She sat up, looking around, the pearly light everywhere, the reality of the day all around them.

"Tomorrow is a new year," she said. "And I must work on your map for you."

He nodded, as solemn as she, and kissed her just once more.

By the time they had gathered together their belongings, the morning clouds had amassed in charcoal tiers, hanging low in the sky, blocking out the sun. As Serath mounted up in front of her lover, the first winter's snow at last began to fall, coming down around them with silent spectacle.

Rafael urged his stallion to a trot, finding the path back to Fionnlagh. They rode off into the depths of the woods, and the snow fell even here, settling in phantom drifts over pine needles and boughs. Serath pulled her cloak tighter around her and ducked her head against the heavy flakes.

She could not help but pray that it might be the beginning of Rafael's spell.

Chapter Fifteen

⟨∽∭∾⟩

*T*HE VILLAGE OF FIONNLAGH WAS SUBDUED, no hint that Christmas was hours away, a new millennium coming with it.

The only signs of the season that Serath could see were a few bits of greenery over some of the doorways of the cottages. Ordinarily there would be celebrations, a festival at least, even here in the village. The breeze should be laden with the smells of delicious cooking, smoke rising in enticing curls from each home. There should be laughter and singing ringing all over.

But instead there was near silence as Serath and Rafael rode into the heart of town. People bundled in winter clothing began to come out and watch them in the snow; flecks of white coating them, covering their heads and torsos. More and more came, lining the narrow street, a procession following them as Rafael walked the stallion down the lanes. Serath had to keep wiping the moisture from her face in order to see. The air was thick with flakes, and still the people came, surely every resident of this land, wraiths amid the sifting white, ruddy faces, shining eyes. She could catch some of their words, muffled by the snow:

"She's back!"

"He found her!"

"He's brought her back to protect us, our witch . . ."

Our witch.

Outside the stables Abram separated from the crowd, helped Serath dismount. She saw Calum behind him, a few others she recognized. As Rafael and a group of his men began to discuss something in low tones, a woman ventured near Serath, clutching timidly at her cloak.

"My lady, is it a sign from God?" She pointed to the sky, the falling snow. "Are we redeemed?"

Serath hesitated, then met the eyes of Calum. "We are," she said.

Relief took the crowd, several of the people embracing each other, still restrained. She felt Rafael's hand on her shoulder, warm and strong, but resisted his slight push forward, toward shelter.

"It is not the end, then, my lady?" asked a new person, a young man holding the hand of his sweetheart. His face was lined with worry. "Tonight is not the end?"

"It is not," Serath said strongly.

Again there seemed to be a surge of caution and faint hope from them, faces gazing at her so eagerly through the snowfall.

"Listen to me," she said now, searching for the right words. "I know it has been a trying time for us all. Men have come to you and tried to put fear in your hearts, and drive you away from faith. But it is the eve of Christmas, and a new year. We should celebrate it, not fear it." She looked back at Rafael. "Soon Alderich will have a new ruler—a just and wise man. God has not forsaken us. Tomorrow is coming, the same as today did, and all our yesterdays."

"Is it because of a spell of yours, my lady?" asked the same young man.

"Not of mine," she replied.

"Then how do you know it?" called out a woman.

"I know it here," Serath replied, placing a hand over her chest. "As do each of you. I have looked into my heart and found the truth. You may all do the same."

And now she did walk forward with Rafael, trying to smile confidently for the people, who parted for them and began to smile back, just a few of them.

Rafael ducked his head low, whispering in her ear.

"Such faith, my lady."

She matched his pitch, speaking around her smile. "If something could be made truth by wishing it hard enough, then what I said would be as true as anything."

"Your heart had the right of it, Serath." He opened the door to the cottage for her. "You listened well."

She walked into the refuge of the chamber, a bright fire crackling with heat, and just as she realized he had escorted her to his own cottage, and not hers, Rafael was taking her into his arms and kissing her.

His lips were cold now, as cold as her own, but soon the warmth of the room and the starfire conquered that.

Let it be true, thought Serath, somewhere far back in her mind. *Oh, please let it be true, let tomorrow come . . .*

After a long while, Rafael pulled away from her, melted snowflakes dripping off of them both, forming puddles on the ground.

"It's not midnight yet," she said, breathless.

"Practice," he murmured, his eyes full of sleepy warmth. "I can think of something else I'd like to practice with you, fair Serath."

"It's the eve of the new millennium, demon-man." She held him off, and her smile now was regretful. "I should return to my own room, and work on your map."

But instead he took her to the tavern, for the noon-time meal, and it was here that Serath saw the first tentative signs of the people rebounding against their fear. Conversations were close to zealous among both serfs and soldiers alike. Ale was flowing freely, enlivening the laughter, and when a roasted pig was brought out, it was accompanied by muted cheering.

Serath recognized the good spirits striving for life here. More greenery decorated the interior of this large space, holly berries creating small clusters of color—little things, certainly, but still present.

They were echoes from her past, a far more innocent time for her, when she had roamed the castle and this village freely, filled with nothing but trust; when she had been just another part of the intricate web of the land, and the people.

Many were laughing, close and comfortable. Cheerful voices, happy looks shared around the room, warmth and familiarity. She felt suddenly lost amid it all, insignificant—yet somehow important.

No one was staring at her. No one was whispering. It left her feeling odd, though she could not say precisely why.

And then Serath realized what it was she recognized, this chiming in her soul—acceptance. They were treating her as one of them. She felt as if she had truly, and at last, arrived home.

A girl was making her way to Serath past the rows of tables and benches, carrying a platter of food. She placed it in front of Serath and then curtsied, and Serath saw that it was the child from the woods.

"Thank you, Clady," she said, and the girl gave a shy smile, then fled.

"You have a friend," Rafael noted, surveying the food.

Serath gazed around the room, at the people who now paused to watch her, but not in fear—in something rather more like bright promise, and hope.

"Aye," she said. "I think I might."

———— ⚬ɷɷ⚬ ————

SHE CHOSE A GOWN OF RED TO MARK THE PASSing of the century. None would sleep, Serath knew that. Nothing was going to fully erase generations of predicting the doom of this evening. The only proof that the world truly would not end would be tomorrow's dawn.

But as a show of bravery, perhaps, Serath plucked from Nanwyn's gowns one the color of summer poppies, a bold hue meant to bolster herself more than anyone else. It was not until Rafael came to her in her own cottage that she realized what she had done—he wore his formal tunic, red and black, dramatic, the colors of Leonhart. Her gown was the natural complement to it.

He entered her room without a sound, pausing by the door, lit with flickering firelight. Serath, seated at the table, looked up quickly from where she had been studying his map of Fionnlagh Castle.

Rafael of Leonhart stood there, fabled warrior, her old enemy dressed in his fine heraldry. But instead of the dread she used to feel, what bloomed through Serath now was nervous happiness, unsteady. Part of her still refused to believe it could be real, that he was smiling at her, so intimate; that she adored the curl of his hair over his shoulders; that his nightcloud eyes could hold such beauty as they did.

Rafael cleared his throat.

"You look . . ." He did not complete the sentence, simply kept up his stare, and so she smoothed her hands over the paper before her, blushing as she looked down at it.

He crossed to her, surprising her by lifting her up in his arms, pulling her away from the table.

"Red suits you," he said, not kissing her, just gazing down at her with his bright look. "A fortunate thing, since I plan to keep you in my colors, my lady."

"It is your mother's gown."

"I'll get you your own. A thousand shades of red for you, a rainbow of them."

"So many?" she asked, smiling. "You'll grow tired of seeing me."

"Never," he replied, perfectly serious, and Serath found herself staring at his lips, the sensual outline of them, remembering what they felt like against her skin.

He set her a little away from him and said, "Your grandfather has sent a message."

Serath gave a start, thinking of the preacher, the vial.

"He claims to be willing to hand over Alderich," Rafael continued. "Without a fight."

"Really?" Her voice echoed her doubt.

"That's what he said." The calm in his eyes disappeared, turning guarded. "On the condition that you and I go up to the castle tonight."

She pulled away farther, dismayed. Rafael watched her carefully.

"It would mean no need for a siege," he said. "No violence. No deaths."

"But—it's not true! It can't be! He is deceiving you!"

"Aye," Rafael conceded. "Perhaps. Or perhaps he's found reason at last."

"Listen to me." Serath clasped her hands together,

earnest. "He is not a man to give up so easily. He is too proud. He has ruled here too long. It *is* a deception."

"Can we risk not finding out?" he asked her quietly.

She understood his meaning; that many could die if they ignored Jozua's message, that a battle for the castle and the land would be inevitable, no matter what the law proclaimed. She thought of all the people here she had gradually come to know—honest villagers and brave soldiers, even Nanwyn, so fiercely loyal to her son. There would be no easy outcome to this, but Serath tried to find one, anyway.

"I'll go alone," she said. "I'll speak to him."

Rafael shook his head, his face shadowed.

"It's safer this way," she argued. "He is my grandfather. He might listen to me."

"We go together, Serath, or not at all."

She could see the finality about him, arms crossed, obstinate. He seemed suddenly so vulnerable to her, despite what she knew of his skills. It filled her with desperation to think of all the ways her grandfather might try to kill him.

Rafael was nothing less than a miracle to her, this demon-man who had transformed into her mortal lover. He had pestered her and kissed her and touched her in so many ways that she realized that she could no longer remain satisfied hiding away from the world, no matter what the future would bring. Rafael alone had discovered her true self, and then, to her wonder, had rejoiced in it. She could not allow him to sacrifice himself like this.

But if she did not, so many might die.

Serath knew this man, what hard choices he was offering her—what was really no choice at all. She bowed her head, defeated.

"When do we leave?"

She felt his touch on the crown of her head, his palm

sliding down her hair, settling against the curve of her neck.

"Soon," he said. "Too soon."

———————⟨⟨⟨⟩⟩⟩———————

*O*UTSIDE, THE PEOPLE OF THE VILLAGE GATH-ered to see them off, braving the snow as they had earlier today. Only now it was late, less than two hours until the new century, and the flakes gleamed dull silver in the night, coming down endlessly from a blue-black sky.

The dun mare was waiting for her, her mane speckled with snowfall. Alongside her steed were Rafael's soldiers, already mounted and ready to ride, each of them in the colors of Leonhart. There were so many of them. Yet Serath knew that this was only a portion of Rafael's force; that after much debate it had been decided to split his men evenly: half to go to the castle, half to guard the village—in case it *was* another trick, and her grandfather tried to attack the defenseless serfs. It was an unhappy compromise at best, but Rafael had been unwilling to leave the village unprotected.

She walked with him now toward the mounted soldiers, allowing her gaze to fall upon the rows of shields secured to their arms, red and black, a scheme repeated over and over in dizzying sameness until she came to Rafael's shield at the head of the line. His alone had the red dragon emblem of his family upon it.

A teenaged boy in chain mail held the shield ready to be handed up after Rafael had mounted. He seemed so young to Serath, almost a child, his face unlined, his eyes lit with anticipation.

This dauntless youth might be dead within hours. She had to look away from him, from everyone, at the thought.

But Serath found that she met the eyes of a slender woman instead, who gazed back at her with dark tragedy. Serath paused, then broke away from Rafael's escort, making her way toward Nanwyn and her circle of women. People parted before her, bowing, until she stood face-to-face with the other woman, snow drifting between them.

Nanwyn spoke in a voice brittle with despair.

"I see that nothing seems to keep you from him."

Serath hesitated, then placed her hand on Nanwyn's shoulder. "I pledge my life to keep him safe."

Nanwyn only shook her head. She began to turn away, but Serath stopped her, pulling her back.

"I made you a promise once before, my lady, and kept it. Please believe me—I'll do whatever I can to see that he stays unharmed."

And now Nanwyn returned her look, steadier.

"I've done what I could," she whispered. "I cannot fight the forces of fate. I know it."

"I will fight them for you," Serath replied, and gave her shoulder a squeeze.

Nanwyn let out a sorrowful laugh. "Perhaps you may even win, Serath Rune. I begin to think that almost anything is possible. God knows I never thought to see the day when aught of Alderich would be aiding my son. I shall be praying for you." Her look slipped past Serath. "For you both," she amended, quietly.

"Midnight approaches. We must go." It was Rafael, just behind her. Serath turned toward him, then passed by. She heard him say, "God bless, Mother," and a choked, stifled response from Nanwyn. Serath kept walking, and soon he was alongside her again, his pace brisk, his expression emotionless.

She thought she understood that look on him now— he was no dispassionate demon, as she used to fear. He wore this mask to hide his feelings, a warrior's reflex, she realized. It was not that he did not feel, but that he felt too much.

After they mounted she noticed he threw one last look to the villagers, his mother, all the people before them, so utterly dependent upon his success. Serath fancied she saw something slip across his face, there and gone in an instant: pain lived behind his facade, along with intense determination. When he glanced back to her she saw it burning in his eyes still, the will to win. To save them all.

It made her both proud and anxious, and then resolute. It would not be up to Rafael alone to conquer this foe. She knew her grandfather better than anyone here. She must not fail them.

Outriders held up torches against the gloom of night, and standards waved high to announce their presence. No one cheered as they marched off. No one waved. But when Serath looked back at them over her shoulder—just once—everyone had stayed to watch them go, still as marble statues against the fading light.

The trees were illuminated with the moving torchlight, eerie shadows dancing alongside of them, the path hidden and then revealed in golden glimpses. It was as clear a proclamation as Serath could imagine—the new master of Alderich had come. Prepare for the end.

And when they reached the walls of Fionnlagh Castle, she saw that Jozua was also ready for this night. The wallwalks flickered with brazier light, highlighting white snow against white stone, an illusion that left her slightly lightheaded.

There was no pausing outside the walls of the castle this time; the gate was already lowered, the portcullis raised. Rafael led Serath and all the rest into the protection of the bailey, past a scattering of her grandfather's men.

There were not very many of them. As they stopped a serf in plain clothing came forward and took the reins of Rafael's horse, deferential. Rafael dismounted, examining him, and the man bowed deeply. More serfs came up and aided with the horses, equally respectful, although the soldiers from Leonhart eyed them with suspicion.

"Hold." Rafael stopped the first man, who had begun to walk away with his steed. "Where do you go?"

"To the stables, my lord." The man raised his eyes. "I'll take good care of him, my lord."

Serath had been helped down from her mare; she approached them, listening. The man spoke again, his voice distinct.

"There are some of us who recognize what comes, Rafael of Leonhart. Tonight may bring the end of us—or it may not." He looked to his fellows nearby, strained faces, and then lowered himself to his knees, still holding the reins. "We pledge ourselves to you, my lord, if you would have us."

Serath studied the man, his bowed head, the bend of his shoulders. Snow fell upon him and settled against the rough weave of his tunic, white on brown. He seemed genuine to her. He did not have the aspect of a conniving man—nothing at all like Zebediah had been.

Apparently Rafael reached the same conclusion.

"Your name?"

"Harald, my lord. I am the stablemaster."

"I accept your pledge, Harald." The other man looked up, relief clear on his face. Rafael helped him to his feet, then lifted his voice, speaking loudly across the bailey.

"Know this, people of Fionnlagh Castle—the only thing that will end tonight is the rule of Jozua Rune in this place! I will accept the oaths of any of you who vow to serve me. I need good men such as yourselves, and you will be welcome to remain here with me. This is your home, as much as it is mine now. But you may tell any others who wish to serve another in my stead that they will not find it an easy course to follow. Best they leave here now—tonight—than stay to face my wrath."

And the men from the stables bowed again, dropping to their knees, repeating his name. Rafael surveyed them, then nodded. He turned again to Harald and spoke more quietly.

"Know you anything of Jozua Rune's plans tonight?"

"Nay, my lord. He has not allowed many in the keep for days now. Some of us wanted to go down to the village, but we did not dare." And now Harald looked toward an open door in the keep—not one of the main doors, as she had expected, but a smaller side entrance, open to darkness, where distorted shadows in the shapes of men lurked against the stone and wood.

"There will be no need for that now," Rafael said, with a glance at the forbidding summons of that door. "I entrust you with our horses, stablemaster. Guard them well."

"I will, my lord," vowed Harald. He made a clicking sound to the stallion and began to move off into the night, his comrades closing in behind him, soon lost to Serath in the snow.

Abram was beside them suddenly, watching the stablemaster disappear.

"Do you trust him?" he asked.

"There's not much choice, is there?" Rafael said. "One way or another, we shall find out if he was sincere."

Rafael guided Serath forward. Abram stayed at her other side, the rest of the men falling in behind them, small comfort against what she knew lay ahead.

What struck her first about the interior of the castle was the smell—not so much the scent of beeswax and rushes she had expected, but something else, acrid and more subtle, difficult to capture. It was familiar enough to tease her senses, and Serath frowned at the floor, where rushes still lay.

The shadows detached themselves from the walls and became solid men, soldiers armed with swords, a silent escort. No one spoke as they traveled into the depths of the keep, walking deeper into the darkness.

Serath had the otherworldly feeling that she was part of an ancient, pagan drama, where each role had been defined long ago, and every player was chained to his part. She was meant to be here, on this portentous night. She had awaited this moment her entire life, to behold the changing of Alderich, the fall of one man and the rise of another. And she, for good fortune or ill, was tied to them both, by blood and by fate.

Their footsteps echoed down the hallways, just as they had the last time they had come, but now it was so dark—even the vermilion and cobalt of the floor tiles were muted, nearly lost. She could not tell how many of her grandfather's men were with them; she counted to twenty before they shifted beyond her sight, around the corner to a room she barely recalled—an antechamber to the great hall, she thought. Light stretched along the floor from the doorway of it, the only brightness around them.

Rafael pulled her back with just a slight touch on her arm, walking ahead of her, his men close by. She watched his shadow leap to life as he crossed the threshold of the room, and then paused, motionless. But she could not stay blinded out here in the hallway, and so walked past the men surrounding her, approaching the light and the outline of Rafael's back.

It was the antechamber, she had been correct about

that, and then wondered in a distant way if she had remembered to place it on the map.

It was a cramped space, mostly meant for private conversations or secluded meals. There were but two small
tables in it, a lamp set upon each casting fuzzy shadows all
around.

Serath recalled that her grandfather had hardly ever
used this chamber. Indeed, it was somewhat disconcerting
to see the connecting door that led to the great hall beyond closed tight.

Standing next to the lone fireplace was Jozua, dressed
in splendid colors, bright and bold against the small fire.
His men had fanned out around him, the twenty she had
seen before, their tunics of blue and white now clearly
visible. Her mind did the math—twenty men would be
no match to Rafael's forces. Jozua had to have more
soldiers than this—perhaps hiding in the great hall, so
near, waiting for the signal to attack. . . .

"Welcome," said Jozua, unmoving. "How delighted I
am to see you here, devil of Leonhart."

"I'm certain you are," replied Rafael, sardonic.

"Indeed I am." Jozua offered him a smile that chilled
Serath's blood. "You have no idea."

"If you think to attack the village, old man, know
that I have not left it unguarded. You will not find the
people so defenseless as last time. Nor the fields," Rafael
added.

Jozua gave his wheezing laugh. "You discovered that,
did you? A pity. I must confess I am surprised. I had not
thought you such a man of the land."

"I told him of it," Serath said, stepping forward.

And now her grandfather's gaze fell to her, unreadable with the fire behind him, though she thought she
could see a slight tightening in his shoulders.

"Did you?" he asked lightly.

"Aye." She took another step forward, toward him, and Rafael shifted beside her. She knew he meant to hold her back again and stopped him with just a simple look. The pain in his eyes had grown stronger, mixed now with hard worry, the only hint of his misgiving. He dropped his hand.

Jozua spoke again, eyes narrowed. "So you have chosen to support the devil of Leonhart rather than fulfill your duty to your family, is that right?"

"Your hatred is not mine," she said.

Serath thought she had finally reached him; Jozua's face flushed with blood, his mouth stretched thin in anger. But within seconds he regained his control.

"What a pity you proved to be so weak, girl. I should have known it. At midnight tonight, Serath, you shall go to the depths of hell with this devil for your treachery."

"I would follow him anywhere," she replied steadily.

"But not, I think, there," interrupted Rafael, sounding amused. "I have other plans for midnight tonight."

Jozua focused on him. "It is the final hour, Leonhart. You are going to die soon—all of you. All the world."

"I doubt it, old man." Rafael's voice hardened. "And so do you, don't you? Why else salt my fields, if you think the world ends tonight?"

"Mayhap I merely wished to bedevil the devil."

"More like you wished to starve me, and these people too, come the spring. Too bad for you your granddaughter outwitted you."

Jozua smiled again. "Well, she has her mother's face—no doubt she has her mother's evil intuition, as well. She appears to be no better than Morwena, I would say."

"You're right about that," Serath said. "I am no better than she was. But both of us were stronger than you."

"Think you so?" Again Jozua spoke lightly, but she

recognized the tint of anger lurking in his tone. "Brave words from a foolish girl. You could not do even one simple thing for me."

Serath shook her head at him. "No. I *would* not." She reached into the folds of her cloak and brought out the ominous vial, holding it up to the light. The black glass reflected the firelight, the pewter vines shone against it. A few of the men around them began to whisper, staring.

"What is this?" Rafael asked her, coming closer.

"It is the work of a cowardly man," she said, keeping her gaze on Jozua. He was not looking at the vial, but straight at her, rigid with restrained emotion, his face twisted, awful. "My grandfather sent the preacher Zebediah to give me this. I was supposed to feed it to you."

She heard Rafael's intake of breath, the hushed conversation now sweeping the room.

"Weak," spat Jozua. "Simple girl. Just as your brother was. Your mother's blood tainted you both. What I would give to have my son back!"

Without warning Serath threw the vial as hard as she could to the fire—and missed. It hit the stones of the hearth instead with a dull thump, then fell and rolled across the floor, coming to rest, unharmed, near Jozua's feet.

Dozens of men on both sides had drawn their swords at her sudden movement, then halted, right at the brink of violence. The moment hung, suspended, as the steel all around her glowed with the light.

"It is a weak man who sends others to commit his offenses," she said into the silence, to Jozua. "Speak not to me of weakness. I am witness to your own."

"You sent a man to poison me?" Rafael's voice reverberated around the room, strong, honest—all that her grandfather was not. "To have *her* do it? By God, this is too much!"

He had his own sword out now, and leveled the tip of it at Jozua, still across the room. "I was prepared to grant you mercy, Rune—for the sake of the law, and of your own granddaughter. I would have allowed you to stay at Alderich—even at Fionnlagh, should Serath have wished it! But you dare to try to *assassinate* me, to use your own kin to do it! You have forfeited any right to stay. I banish you from this place—from my demesne!"

His words rang off the stones, thundering, and even the flames of the fire seemed to flinch back. There could be no doubt that these were the words of a seasoned warrior—a man born to be the master of this place, and who had the means and will to fulfill his pledge. When Serath glanced up at him she saw the devil of Leonhart before her, righteous fury, unfathomable power.

A few of her grandfather's men lowered their swords, exchanging uncertain looks.

And then Jozua began to laugh. It was so oddly and completely out of place that for a moment Serath truly doubted his sanity—thin, delighted cackles echoing from him.

"Banish me, do you?" He turned to the fireplace, one hand braced against the stone. "Banish me! Indeed!"

"Is it a war you want?" Rafael asked, deadly. "I am prepared to give it to you."

"Oh, I'm positive you are, Leonhart. Brave man that you are, coming to take away my home!" Jozua looked up, facing them again. "But before you begin your grand war, let me tell you something. This supposed poison that my granddaughter brought is only water! She begged me for a poison to give to you, Leonhart. She sent me a secret message, and claimed to want nothing more than your death."

Serath turned to Rafael. "He's lying."

"Why should I bother?" asked her grandfather, still smiling. "I have naught to lose with the truth, after all."

"Then speak the truth!" Serath cried, moving toward him. "Tell him you hired the preacher! That you made him deliver that poison to me, that you alone wanted to kill Rafael!"

"A very unlikely story," reproved Jozua. "There is no sense in trying to deceive him now, Serath." He looked at Rafael again. "She wanted poison, she said, to avenge her brother. But I, Leonhart, am a nobler man than that. Certainly you are no friend of mine, but it wasn't you who killed the boy. It was her. Her witchcraft."

"No," Serath gasped.

"Aye, girl. I've known for years it was you." His look turned mournful. "I defended you as best I could, but the facts were there for all to see. Even as a child you belonged to sin."

"The truth!" she said again, drawing closer, furious. "Tell him the truth!"

"The truth must come now from you, Serath," replied Jozua, unperturbed. His eyes locked on hers, relentless, shining green. "You killed Raibeart. I know not why. A sacrifice, perhaps, to increase your unholy powers. I thought mayhap sending you to a sacred place might save you—alas. I see now I was wrong."

Serath felt a deep and dreadful trembling come over her, stealing up her body, rage and anguish combined to keep her mute, staring at him. The fire seemed dim behind his figure, the rest of the room darkened until it was only her, and him, and this terrible moment.

Jozua's face showed nothing but gentle concern, watching her. He approached her in slow steps, his words falling softly around them.

"Her message claimed to want vengeance on you,

Leonhart. No doubt you'd be yet another sacrifice. I could not risk letting her grow stronger. And so I did not send her poison. Yet I had to send her something, for I knew she would act. It was water, child, only that, all along."

"It's a *lie!*" Her voice was thin and high; he was close enough to her now that she could catch the smell of him, age and perfume, oils turned to musk.

"Is it?" Jozua whispered to her, smiling so sadly. His hands came up, reached for her shoulders. "Come here and convince me I'm wrong."

Something long and bright flashed between them, causing Jozua to draw back with a hiss. Rafael's blade, the flat of it pushing hard now against her waist, forcing her to take a step back.

"Serath, move away from him," he said, just behind her, very calm.

She saw it then—the fury that streaked over her grandfather's face, savage anger. His hands, which had come so close to her, dropped again to his sides, fingers splayed to claws.

Rafael still pushed at her with his sword, and she stepped backward haltingly, unable to look away from the thwarted scheming in Jozua's gaze. The pure malice there, aimed at her.

And then it was gone. In the blink of an eye he changed completely, now showing nothing but smooth calculation. But she had seen it, sweet Mary, she had.

He hated her. *Hated* her, when all her life she had only tried to love him.

Her breathing was constricted, strained. The room seemed to shimmer around her.

Rafael had her beside him again, his warm hand now placed where his sword had been, holding her next to him. She was shaking so violently that she had to grit her teeth, clenching her hands tight over Rafael's arm.

"Serath," he said, his head bent close to hers even as he watched Jozua. "You know I believe you."

Jozua laughed. "You believe her body, I suppose. If she's whored with you, you might well believe anything she said."

"I believe," said Rafael in the same cool tone, "that I have heard enough of your slander, old man. I hope you are ready to leave. Because you are going now."

"Only a fool would trust a witch, Leonhart!"

"I trust Serath. Never you."

"There is a ready way to prove my words." Jozua turned to the line of soldiers along the wall beside him. "Olivier!"

From the darkness stepped a man, his blond hair gleaming with firelight. He approached Jozua, and bowed.

"My lord?"

Jozua indicated the vial at his feet. "Drink it."

The blond man seemed to blanch. "What?"

"Drink it," repeated Jozua, impatient. "Do not fear. No harm will come to you. It is only water."

The soldier did not move, staring at Jozua. His mouth worked, but no sound emerged.

"Do you doubt me, Olivier?" asked Jozua quietly. "You, of all people?"

The other man glanced around the room, blinking rapidly. "My lord—I—"

"Drink it!"

"Don't," said Serath to the man.

The look on Jozua's face grew dangerous. Still the soldier hesitated.

"Is that the way of it, then?" he asked him gently. "Is that what these final hours come down to, that you would listen to her over me?"

Olivier held out his hands, pleading. "I beg you, my lord, do not force me to—"

"Whom do you obey, Captain?"

"I have done all that you have asked of me, my lord, without question! I have worked for you, planned with you—I would give my life for you!"

"And so you shall," replied Jozua. "For the end of the world is indeed at hand."

Jozua moved, quicker than Serath could follow. Before even Rafael could respond, something streaked between the old man and his second, a metallic gleam, silver and red. Men exclaimed, voices echoing from both sides of the room. But when it was done the man named Olivier merely stood alone, hands clutching at his ribs, a startled look upon his face.

Jozua stepped back, holding the dagger aloft now; blood dripped from the blade, oozing down his hand.

Everyone in the room seemed frozen. Only Olivier moved.

"My lord!" He sounded only slightly flustered, as if he had just suffered some mild insult.

"There is no room in my realm for the faithless," said Jozua softly.

The blond man's face went slack and pale. He toppled to his knees and then to the ground, the material of his cape unfurling across his body, settling slowly over him. Blood seeped through it at a rapid pace, darkening the blue to black.

Jozua turned back to Rafael and Serath, still brandishing the dagger before him. "Now," he said, in a very pleasant tone, "there is something I want to show you, Leonhart. You and your whore."

Someone was bending over the fallen man, turning him, feeling his neck. It was another soldier from Fionnlagh.

"He's dead!" said the man, stunned.

"We shall all be dead soon, soldier," said Jozua, walking to the door, a trail of blood behind him. "The final moments of the millennium are upon us."

Rafael let out his breath. "By God, Rune, you *are* mad!"

And this time there seemed to be agreement among all the men here, the men in blue and white backing away from their master, edging toward the other end of the room.

Jozua appeared not to notice.

"Perhaps I am," he said. "Perhaps. But you will want to see my surprise for you, in any case, Leonhart."

A deep, black foreboding lodged in Serath, snaking around her in tight spirals. She had an overwhelming feeling she had been here before, in this place and this moment. Something awful was about to come, something even worse than before. . . .

"All I am interested in seeing is the back of you, leaving my castle in chains," said Rafael, wintry.

"Not yet," replied Jozua. "You do not rule here yet, I'm afraid. I have a fragment of time left as Lord of Alderich. And you—my honored guest—will have to indulge me."

He was at the connecting door to the great hall, pushing it open so that only a sliver of darkness showed beyond. Still clutching the dagger, Jozua picked up the lamp from the table nearby. He looked up at them then, his back pushing against the door.

"I offer you your inheritance, devil of Leonhart!"

The door creaked open all the way, and he slipped through it.

That peculiar smell Serath had noticed before rushed at her again, more pungent now, sharp and familiar. She had to cup a hand over her mouth to block it out, but moved forward into it anyway, fighting the foreboding, unable to resist seeing what lay ahead in the great hall.

Rafael stood in front of her, already in view of the doorway, stopped dead. The pale light from the other room showed her his face, harsh and fixed. She looked past the opening.

At first she could not make out what was before her. It was so dark in the massive hall, yet she saw that many things filled the room. A pile of things, in fact, and coming closer she saw that it was a small mountain of goods, great and marvelous items heaped upon each other: bejeweled plates, goblets, chests open to reveal coins, scattered jewelry, furs, dozens of crumpled rolls of rich cloth, ivory and silver and gold glowing through it all.

Sweet heavens. It had to be all of the treasure of Alderich gathered here in this room, tossed carelessly together into a pile of glittering wealth.

Jozua had walked over to the base of this amazing collection, holding his lamp high. Only then did Serath see what Rafael must have noticed all along—the source of that bitter odor.

It was pitch, a great deal of it, black as night, spread along the floor, around the treasure.

"The devil has indeed come, as it was foretold," intoned Jozua with his unnerving smile.

"No." Serath could only shake her head, because her feet were frozen with fear.

"What are you doing, old man?" asked Rafael cautiously, beginning to inch toward him—but her grandfather was too far from them, Serath could see that.

"So it is indeed the end of time," Jozua continued, looking straight at Serath, ignoring the man approaching him. "The end of everything, as I have always known it would be."

"No—" Serath said again, stronger, and now her grandfather laughed at her, turning to Rafael.

"Welcome to Alderich, devil of Leonhart!" he exclaimed wildly. "Long may you reign!"

And then he hurled his lamp to the pitch-covered floor, and the room erupted into flames.

Chapter Sixteen

———— ⟳ ————

*I*NSTANTLY SERATH WAS BLINDED BY THE EX-
plosion of light. She raised her arms to shield her face,
turning away from the shock of it. Heat pushed at her,
rushing past her ears in a roar. It nearly drowned out the
shouts of the men behind her, terror and consternation.

When she could see again the world had turned to
insanity: fire spread in shooting flames across the great
hall, circling the mound of goods, catching on the rolls of
cloth to creep upward. A pair of dark shapes darted and
twisted in front of the light, clenched together—two
men, fighting each other or the fire, she could not say.

"Rafael!" she cried, stepping into the inferno, toward
them. But a black wind tore at her—someone had managed to open the main doors at the other end of the hall.
Fresh air fed the fire to new heights, and Serath could no
longer see them. The world had turned to orange and
yellow, and thick, acrid smoke.

"Rafael!"

"Serath!"

A figure moved through the flames, there and gone again, obscured in the violently changing light. She thought she had run toward him, but when she stopped there was no one to be seen around her; the black smoke ate up the room, and the cries of the men seemed very distant. Serath began to cough.

Where was he? She found herself next to a man who was beating at the flames with his tunic—blue and white against the flames. Another man did the same with a blanket, and another—all of them strangers to her, faceless, intent on fighting the fire. A cloud of black billowed in front her; Serath lost her bearings, turning left, then right—the fire was spreading too quickly. Her eyes stung so badly that even the brightness was becoming a blur of color to her.

"Serath!"

Behind her—his voice had come from behind her, and she turned too quickly. Her foot slipped on a stone wet with pitch, and Serath fell sideways, a hard jolt.

Feet rushed by her—someone pulled her up, she could not see who, and began to push her toward what might have been the door. She twisted against his hold and saw it was Abram, his face streaked with sweat and soot.

"Get out!" he was yelling at her, still pushing. "Get out of here!"

"Wait! Where is Rafael?"

But Abram did not answer her, instead nearly throwing her toward the main doorway, where the smoke curled in a massive funnel, moving out into the cold night.

"Out!" he shouted again, and then he rushed back into the great hall.

She could not catch her breath very well, but people

were lifting her, pulling her from the entranceway. The clamor of the bells tolling was painfully loud—sounding the alarm of the fire, quick ringing peals.

More and more men were shoving past her, going back inside the castle. Water sloshed from buckets as they ran, shouts filled the night. She heard women screaming now, as well. Farther out in the bailey a great many forms knotted together in a frightened mass, faces lit with distant gold.

She did not need to look closer to know that Rafael would not be among them. He would be inside, fighting to save Fionnlagh. Perhaps injured. Lying on the floor, his clothing quick with fire—

———————— ⟋⟋⟋⟍⟍ ————————

$\mathcal{S}$ERATH BROKE AWAY FROM THE MEN AROUND her, running back into the keep.

She knew what to expect this time and still it did not help her. The heat singed her lungs, and her coughing turned to choking. But she bent over and continued deeper into the hell of it, holding the edge of her cloak over her face and breathing through her mouth.

Many figures rushed about, water passed between them, but none of these men resembled Rafael—none had his hair, the shape of his shoulders. She saw Abram again, throwing water furiously over the flames. Other men, other faces . . . he had to be here. . . .

The wind shifted once more, winter and inferno swirling together, right into her face, and Serath was forced to bend double, hiding from the blinding smoke. A new brightness came at her: the hem of her cloak had caught fire, yellow flames swarming up, toward her skin. She pulled frantically at the clasp, ripping the cloth, her hair tangled in the metal—and then it was off her, fallen to the ground, blazing merrily.

Serath staggered away from it, gasping. She could not breathe. The air was too bitter, too thick and hot to fill her lungs any longer. Where was the fire now? She was so turned around . . . it seemed to be everywhere—all around her, belching virulent smoke. Everything was so dim. It was truly the end of the world, after all, and she was not ready for it, she had never been ready for it . . . what a ghastly way to die. . . .

Oh, Rafael!

Serath felt the hardness of stone beneath her hands, her cheek, and realized she was lying flat on the floor now, slightly below the smoke. She had no sense of time or place; the fire still burned, and shouting still filled the chamber. But the air was better down here, below the noxious cloud that churned just above her. She could breathe again. She could see again. She was still alive.

She struggled to her hands and knees, gulping the air, and the world began to clear. Serath realized she was looking at a booted leg, flat on the ground. When she crawled toward it she saw that it was connected to a fallen man, one with a face that showed no life. She had seen such emptiness before. . . .

Raibeart!

No—it was Rafael. His eyes were closed, not open and blank. One arm lay perilously close to the burning treasure, yet he did not stir.

Serath ran frantic hands over him, feeling for the knife wound he had to have—but did not find it. The only blood came from a gash to his head. A deep, black smudge of charcoal streaked across his temple, mingling with scarlet to run down the side of his face. He did not respond to her rough touch.

A portion of something long and heavy lay near him,

alight with flames; a mahogany walking stick, the end of it touching the fire, smoldering in red-hot embers. Beyond that she thought she saw Jozua's dagger, tossed deep into the flames of the fire.

"Rafael!" She shook him, very hard, but his eyes remained closed, his face vacant, grimy with soot and caked blood.

Her only hope, her only love, dead, dead, dead!

"No, no," Serath was saying, and took hold of his arms, trying to pull him away from the fire, from the heat that seared her skin.

A solid shape blocked the flames then—a demon!—looming over her, tearing loose her grip. Its hands snarled in her hair, yanking her away from Rafael. She was pulled off balance and fell again to the stone floor.

"Let him burn!" commanded the creature, and it had her grandfather's voice, if nothing else—the shape was charred and twisted, monstrous. White hair had burned short, boils and welts disfigured his skin. But now she could see that the demon had her grandfather's eyes, as well: pale green, frenzied.

She fought the Jozua-demon, kicking at it, and the thin, wailing sound that surrounded them was coming from her, from the depths of her panic. The fire was growing. Rafael was too close, too close, unmoving.

"Let him burn, I say!" screamed the demon. "It is up to me to do what you and your brother could not! He must die!"

"No, stop—" Serath was crying, fighting, making incoherent sounds. "Rafael, no! Raibeart!"

"The boy was an idiot!" The Jozua-demon was dragging her away from the man on the ground, infernal strength, his hands tight on her. "Couldn't—do—one—simple—thing!"

She swiped at its face and felt blood and gore, but the demon still pulled at her.

"One simple thing!" it screeched now, bright red and black, green eyes shot with blood. "One simple death! And he could not do it—both of you so weak! He could not even live long enough to reach the devil's home, to do as I told him to do—to use stealth, and cunning—"

Serath kicked out and found the demon's weakness— her foot connected with its knee, and it buckled over. She tore away from it at last, scrambling to her feet, half-blinded with smoke and tears. She could almost make out the shape of Rafael—

—Raibeart—

—before her, so close to danger and death, the fire raging nearby. Debris was beginning to fall from the burning mountain, rubble tumbling down toward them. Flakes of burnt cloth sifted through the air, black snow, hellish. Something round and rolling bounced off the pile of fire and swept just past his head, metal heated to cherry red, a trail of sparks behind it . . . it might have been a chalice—

Almost there. She would do it this time, she would save him. . . .

The demon was still behind her, its breath a hiss against her back.

"Morwena!"

Abruptly her feet were hobbled, bringing her down again to the floor. Her chin struck sharply against the stone, snapping her teeth closed, barely missing her tongue. Blue lights exploded before her, stunning and bright.

When she could see again it was Jozua standing over her, her grandfather, burnt and crazed. But it was him, it was, holding her by the shoulders, pulling her to sit upright. She could see the reflection of the fire dancing in his eyes. Such a fierce fire. . . .

"Girl," he was saying, shifting his arms under her shoulders. "Comely witch—"

"I loved you!" Serath wept, trying to hold on to him. She could not feel her hands or feet. She could not make them work. "Don't you know—I always loved you—"

Jozua was almost calm now. It was as if he did not even feel his wounds, that immense fire so close behind him. He had her securely now and began, one step at a time, to drag her backward, toward the greedy flames.

"My daughter," he said, sounding so normal. "My pretty girl. Come with me. You belong to me."

More fragments fell from the pile, a shower of cinders, settling over her skirts, scorching little black marks into them. There was something she was supposed to do, something important. What was it?

Raibeart was nearby, he needed her help!

But no, that wasn't right. Raibeart was dead. He had been dead for a long, long time.

The heat of the fire began to hurt too much, they were too close, but Grandfather was showing no indication he meant to stop.

"You must burn," he murmured to her, lovingly. "It is your fault; you have bewitched me. But if it cannot be, you will burn."

One of the cinders on her skirts began to glow. The material—*bright red, poppies*—around it started to smolder. Another cinder landed on the back of her hand, searing. She felt *that,* and shook it off.

"The fire, the fire!" Grandfather sang happily. He stepped on a chunk of burning wood and seemed not to notice. But Serath did, watching with horror how the flames instantly gathered on the cloth of his shoe. She jerked away from him.

"Grandfather! Your foot!"

He reached for her again, and the fire was crawling up his leg now, racing along the bottom of his tunic, emblazoning the bright colors of it with burning gold.

"Grandfather—look!"

Serath found her feet again, but the cinders were still falling, lighting her own gown with little yellow flowers, tiny splendors of color. She tried to beat them down with her hands, spinning around, frantic.

"It's been so long, Morwena—don't fight me," Jozua said, his arms stretched toward her. "If you will not have me, you must burn. One kiss, my daughter."

She looked up, ducking away from him, from the fire that was consuming her and him and everything. Jozua took a lurching step forward. The fire on him was beginning to encircle his arms in ripples of blue and orange. His voice rose, shrill.

"One kiss! Or you will burn, I promise it!"

"Grandfather!" she cried, anguished.

"Burn, then!" he shrieked suddenly, raising his hands to his head, clawing at his hair, his skin. "Burn, witch!"

And the fire roared over him, leaping from his sleeves to his face, engulfing him.

Serath screamed, running away from the hideous sight of him wrapped in flames. She ran and stumbled and ran some more, choking, past shapes in the smoke—men, water.

"Moor-wen-aaaa!"

It was a death cry, long and drawn-out, resounding past the fire, the smoke, and Serath stopped to cover her ears and close her eyes, hiding from it, from what it meant, close to sobbing.

She had to leave this place. She had to escape! She could not remain here, with what she knew now—ghosts and treachery, the most foul of crimes. . . . She would die here if she stayed—but she had forgotten something, so vital. . . .

Oh, God, she had left Raibeart behind her!

No.

It was *Rafael* behind her. The realization came with bright calm, a bead of clarity amid the panic.

Rafael had been hurt. She had to save him.

Serath turned around, rushing back to where she hoped he was, waving her hands in front of her to fight the clouds of smoke, searching desperately.

There! Rafael was there to her left, on his side now, crawling away from the fire, one hand at a time. His head was lowered, bent to the floor. He did not see her, did not seem to feel her as she tugged at him, trying to help.

"Rafael—stand up—"

One hand grabbed at her skirt; she took hold of the other, pulling at him with all her might, until he was on his knees before her, heavy, clinging to her.

"Up!" she grunted, straining against the weight of him. "We have to leave, you must stand *up*—"

And somehow he did, swaying, his arm over her shoulder, and together they staggered away from the flames, through the soot and smoke, until Serath was touching the mortar of the wall of the great hall. They followed it, cool stone a relief to the brutal, scalding air, until suddenly more men were upon them, aiding them, dragging them out into the night.

Cold air embraced her, clean and fresh. The bailey was full of people, so many people, surrounding them now, exclaiming. They pulled Rafael away from her and she had to let them, because all her strength had fled, sapped away by the cold, mayhap.

Serath felt her knees give out and dropped, uncaring, onto the dirt. Arms supported her, preventing her from falling back completely. She had a glimpse of the sky above her, rolling indigo, dots of snow still falling down all around her.

A man's face broke the vision. It was Abram.

"My lady! My lady!"

He sounded so worried. She wanted to reassure him. She wanted to tell him she was fine, just tired, so tired, but instead her eyes closed, shutting out the worry of his face, and that was all right. That was good, too, because there was nothing to bother her now. . . .

In some other world, some faraway place, bells were chiming, a pair of them, tolling in fair harmony.

"Serath."

It was a strange voice, raspy and broken, nearly un-recognizable beneath the pealing of the bells. But she opened her eyes to it anyway.

Rafael was above her, dirty, bloody, and so beautiful that it made her want to weep again.

"Is it midnight yet?" she whispered.

His face broke into a weary smile. "Aye, my love," he said, and bent close to her, placing his lips over hers.

The last ring of the bells echoed over them, dwindling away to nothing, taking all the noise in the world with it. But Serath barely noticed; she was lost in the kiss, Rafael's promise come true. It tasted of smoke and fire, and precious, precious life. When he lifted his head she sat up with him, gazing around in wonder.

The snow still fell, drifting lazily upon them.

People still huddled together, red and black and blue and white mixed together, nobles and soldiers and serfs, women and men.

The world became a perfect, endless hush, as the final seconds of the century died away.

Many were watching the skies, waiting, and so Serath looked up as well, but all she saw were the same clouds as before, distant and dark. No heavenly wrath was descending. No thunder, no showers of fire—at least not here. No portents at all, in fact. If there was a blood moon, it was safely hidden behind the thick of the night.

A miracle, she thought with hazy surprise, her mind still clouded. *Rafael did it. He did. The spell worked. . . .*

He helped her to her feet, and Serath turned and scanned the sky in the other direction, just to be certain. Still nothing. It was as calm and quiet as could be. Even the fire from the keep had waned at last, only blackened tails of smoke left to rise up to the sky, blowing away.

He did it!

She wanted to laugh out loud, to scream and cheer and celebrate Rafael's miracle—it wasn't the end, it wasn't! But her body was too tired to obey her careening emotions, and so Serath clung to her lover's arms, dizzy and thrilled, and let the excitement wash over her.

The last of the men appeared at the main doors, limping out to the bailey, dazed, fatigued. Others rushed to help them, but still without speaking. It was as if no one dared break the moment of silence, as if this might be the lone thing staying the hand of God.

Serath dared. She had come too far, and survived too much, not to.

She gathered her strength, pulling away from Rafael, and then turned to the crowd.

"It is a new year upon us," she called out to them, her own voice husky and cracked with the remnants of smoke. People jerked their attention to her, startled, wide-eyed.

Serath spoke louder. "No end at all, but a beginning! A new century, and a new millennium! And behold—the new Lord of Alderich!" She took Rafael's hand, raising it as high as she could. "Who among you will not swear allegiance to him?"

And there she stood, motionless, still holding his hand

high, and the snow blew gently around them all, between her and Rafael and the rapt faces before them.

One by one, the people in the bailey began to kneel. It began with Abram, the closest to them, and then the men from Leonhart, his own soldiers going to their knees before him. More and more men followed; soldiers in tunics of blue and white dropped down as well, drawing out their swords, placing them flat on their outstretched hands, heads bowed. Others copied their pose, the women, the serfs—Serath saw the stablemaster of before near the back, other people in the livery of the castle, everyone kneeling, saying his name, awed.

She looked over at Rafael, and he turned his head and looked back at her, his gaze unreadable beneath the streaked soot and blood, his hair blowing in the breeze.

Serath released his hand and slowly, carefully, went to her knees, as well. Her hair fell loose around her bowed head, trailing in the snow.

His hand came down upon her shoulder.

"My lady," he said, and she looked up.

Rafael was close now, giving her a sharp and guarded look, helping her back up to her feet. He did not seem pleased. For a moment she felt her heart sink, afraid she had offended him with her impulsive plan. But he pulled her to him and kissed her again, in front of everyone, hard and passionate.

"I love you, Serath Rune," he murmured, and before she could respond to that, Rafael turned away, addressing the crowd.

"I accept your pledges to me, good people! Rise, all of you, and rejoice in this new year!"

Everyone rose and let out a cheer, soft at first, growing louder and louder, until it reverberated all around them, deafening, and Serath and Rafael could only stand still amid it, clasping hands. He gazed out at the people again—*his* people, she thought, and she watched the caution on his face slowly transform, becoming a ferocious smile.

"I love you," she said to him, knowing he could not hear her, but saying it anyway, because her heart was so full.

---

*T*HE PHYSICIAN SAID YOU'LL HAVE A SMALL SCAR, my lady."

Rafael, perched on the edge of Serath's chair, tilted her head up and back to gain a better look at the mark beneath her chin, where she said she had hit the floor while fighting the fire. He held his lamp closer to her, trying to see the cut more clearly.

"I don't mind about the scar," Serath said to him, keeping her face where he directed her. "If you don't."

"I don't," he said, very sincere.

They sat together in some unnamed room of Fionnlagh Castle, chosen because it had no damage from the fire, and contained chairs and torches and very little draft. He had brought her here from the bailey, after that remarkable show of fealty that Serath herself had maneuvered into being.

Rafael had at first intended nothing more than to hide her away and kiss her again, to seal the magic around them on this night. But then he had caught sight of all the blood on her.

The wound had been cleaned thoroughly; he had carefully watched the man who claimed to be the castle physician do it, scrutinizing. Thank God she hadn't needed to have it sewn closed. He didn't know if he could have handled that.

Rivers of blood, Rafe had seen. Battles that had left

countless dead. Atrocities of war and the greed of men, he had endured—even this night, the most violent and amazing he could remember, or even imagine—and yet he knew that watching the needle pierce Serath's skin would haunt him forever. Just the small cut that it was hurt him deeply; far more, he was sure, than it did her. He had had to leave the room for a moment, collecting himself, speaking to Abram and the rest for distraction.

Immediately he had been swarmed by worried people—all asking about Serath. Every one of them had been covered with soot; every one of them had stopped what they were doing to inquire after her. They included many of his own men, and even a contingent of the villagers who had climbed up the mountain when they had seen the fire turn the sky from black to gold. Calum had been there, others Rafe knew, and it had taken him quite some time to assure them all that Serath was indeed going to be fine.

He supposed he had repeated it so much that eventually he was able to believe it himself, which was a good thing. The thought of Serath *not* being fine was unbearable.

It was easy, in that moment of lingering smoke and ash, to see that his was not the only heart she had won. As unlikely as it might have seemed, the villagers of Fionnlagh, who weeks ago had hidden from her, now clamored to be near, wishing her well. Despite her history with them, Rafe could not wonder at such a marvel; of course she had won them over. Serath Rune, with her fey clarity and her generous heart, could warm the hardest of souls. Witchcraft or no, Fionnlagh had never had a chance—and, Rafael reflected, neither had he.

Thank you, God.

The light from the lamp showed him a cut that

looked too tiny for all the blood it had produced. Yet it still sent a chill through him, the thought of her pain.

Serath lowered her head now, smiling at him. "A trifle," she said, perhaps reading his thoughts. "I can't even feel it."

"That's strange," he replied, trying to smile back. "Because *I* can."

He remembered very little of the events of this night. His nemesis, taunting them with fire. Rushing forward, trying to prevent it, and being too late.

The dagger in Jozua's hand; knocking it aside, and then Jozua, as well. Calling her name past the inferno. Hearing her shout out to him—but he could not find her, she was lost to the flames. His desperation, his fury. And then Jozua again, coming up beside him and felling him with the burning stick.

After that things grew hazy, his memory confused. He thought he heard Serath cry out again—his own name, even her brother's. And Jozua's response, chilling, something about burning, which of course made sense, because it seemed to Rafe that *everything* was burning, the world, the sky. . . .

He had tried to move, to reach her. All had turned grotesque before him: fire of gold and blue and orange, metal glowing beneath it, shrunken shapes of things kindling to black lumps. At one point he could have sworn he caught sight of Serath struggling against a demon—a wildman, screaming at her.

When he had tried to lift himself to his feet to get to her, blackness swelled up around him, emptying him. And that was the end of it.

But Serath had found him. Abram told him of it, how he had tried to keep her safe but she had rushed back into the keep anyway, and then later—much later—had returned with him in her arms, the two of them looking, Abram said, like nothing so much as an overdone dinner.

Rafe wanted to smile at the recollection but didn't. All he had to do was look down at Serath's hands to see the results of this night, pink marks dabbed across her skin in the shape of rose petals, reaction to the ash and cinders that had rained upon them. He knew who the wildman she fought had been, and what it must have cost her to break away from him.

Abram had also told him that most of the treasure Jozua Rune had set to destroy, remarkably, was salvageable. All the cloth had burned, most of the wood, but the jewels, the coins, and other metal pieces seemed unharmed.

But whether or not the most precious treasure of this land—the lady seated before him—had escaped this night unscathed was what worried Rafael the most.

"My love," Rafe said to her, to the deep blue of her eyes. "I have something to tell you. Your grandfather is dead."

"I know," she replied. The corners of her lips turned down, her only distinct reaction.

"I'm sorry," Rafe said, not because it was true, but because he *wanted* it to be, to feel sorrow over the old man's death, if this would comfort her.

Serath nodded and patted his hand in an absent way, her gaze distant. After a moment, she said, "He was a very ill man. It is better this way." A heavy sigh took her. "His hatred consumed him. It was not rational . . . very little about him was ever rational, I think."

Rafe left his perch on her chair, finding now a seat in the one opposite hers. Outside the room he could hear his people talking, Abram's voice, directing the cleanup of the great hall, picking apart the ravaged pile of goods.

"Do you want to tell me what happened?" he asked her, low, as gently as he could.

Her lips kept their downward turn; a frown puckered her forehead.

"No. Not yet," she said to her lap. "Someday, though. Someday I will."

"All right." He came forward, wanting to hold her, to hug her and let her hide against him—or let him hide against her. But he contented himself with just placing his hand on her knee, light, reassuring.

"I love you," she said.

He looked up, wondering if he had actually heard that.

Rafael had confessed his love for her in the bailey because he had to, because the moment had demanded it—his pride in her, his gratitude and wonderment of her had no longer been containable. But he honestly had not thought—had not even hoped—that she might feel the same toward him. It was enough that he had her beside him, her hands warm in his, sharing in his dream.

Serath met his look of startled inquiry now, the cloud of memories in her eyes dissolving, turning to something brighter, celestial.

"I love you," she said again. "Rafael of Leonhart, my own demon-man—I love you."

It winded him, so much so that he could not reply to her as he wanted to. The elation sang through him, pounding through his blood, overflowing in his heart, and all he could do was go to his knees before her, burying his head against her neck, squeezing her.

She began to laugh around his hold, breathless, her hands light on his back. "You have a promise to fulfill, my lord. But you won't be able to wed me if you smother me to death first."

He released her, pushing her back into the chair,

careful with her chin, kissing every other part of her that he could reach.

"Love you," Rafe whispered, inhaling the scent of her, so happy that he thought he might drown from it. "I love you, Serath. Thank you . . . thank you. . . ."

And she met his lips now, holding him, giving back to him what he needed, her touch, her vow, the goodness of her saturating him, consuming him.

Yes, he thought, and, *thank you, thank you, all my love, for you, forever. . . .*

He was feverish with the need to be with her now, devoutly wishing they were anywhere but here, in this open room, people passing by, no chance of privacy between them. . . .

Serath pulled back at last, her breath warm and quick on his neck. "Has the dawn come?"

"Almost," he replied, tracing the curves of her ear with his lips. "I think."

"We should go." She broke away from him, leaving him cold and wanting, then stood up, looking around her.

"Wait, Serath." He stood as well, glancing again to the door. No lock. Damn the luck. "Go where, my love? It's still a cold night out there."

"To the village," she said.

"Tomorrow," Rafe said, and brought her back to him, overcoming her resistance until she was pliant and warm against him, his sweet Serath. He spoke down into the smokiness of her hair. "We'll have a forever of tomorrows to go out. I've already sent someone down to tell them we are safe. Tonight, you need to rest . . . there must be a room in this maze of castle where we can rest. Where is that cursed map?"

"No, it has to be tonight," she said into his tunic. "There is still one more thing that must be done."

"Aye. But not done only once more."

She gave a buried laugh. "Besides that."

"What could be more important than that?" he asked her, his hands at her waist. She fit so perfectly against him. Oh, God, he needed her so badly.

"Just one more thing," Serath persisted, leaning away, searching his face.

He could feel the determination in her, recognizing the pressure of her fingers against him, the tone of her voice.

"Tonight, then," Rafe agreed helplessly, and then kissed her once more, putting aside his reservations and that hot desire. *A forever of tomorrows,* he reminded himself firmly.

Outside the room, he borrowed someone's cloak and secured it around her shoulders, already worried for her. But she merely smiled up at him, and together they walked out to the stables, finding Harald and their steeds, saddling and mounting. People trailed them as they always did, and Serath rode out the gate of the castle slowly enough that they could be followed. Calum was there again, Abram, a whole line of men and women behind them.

He had no idea what she was about, but in the end, it hardly mattered. Rafael felt his good fortune was bountiful; he was humble and amazed by it all. He trusted her. Serath had led him to so many great places already—her home, her heart. He would support her wherever she wished to go next.

It was a new beginning for both of them, here in this land. In a sense, Rafe thought, they had both been away from Alderich too long. How grateful he was that they would be able to establish new lives here together.

The clouds had thinned and begun to scatter, revealing patches of stars, the snow all but gone. Bands of blue and gray paled the eastern sky, luminous. Serath and

Rafe picked their way down the path of the mountain, still slow, and when he looked over at her she was looking back, her face clear of distress, a small smile curving her lips.

It was going to be a spectacular day. Rafael was suddenly certain of that.

At the base of the hill was a new crowd of faces, the rest of the villagers and his men, Nanwyn and her retinue, everyone almost exactly where they had left them hours ago. They pressed close to the gravel of the path, the day rising around them.

He caught his mother's eye and nodded a greeting to her, smiling. Her hands came up to cover her mouth, and then lowered—showing him her own tremulous smile in return.

Serath drew close to the people, Rafe beside her. Behind them he could hear the hushed voices of the castle folk, the responding murmur of the villagers. He could see the wonder on the faces of everyone, growing stronger as the sun rose.

He watched it for a moment, this day of a lifetime of dreams finally dawning, the clouds becoming drenched in orange and purple, a hazy glow melting to pink at the edges.

Serath raised her voice.

"People of Fionnlagh, welcome to our future!"

Rafe noticed how everyone stilled to watch her, engrossed in her, a faerie queen of sapphire and midnight among them. Her arms lifted high into the sky, graceful.

"Our new century has arrived, a miracle come true! And so I now break the curse that was laid upon Alderich, and place instead a blessing upon you all, this land, and all your houses! A blessing upon all the people of Leonhart and Alderich, united as one!"

Exclamations rose around them, a sensation of sound,

delirious with joy. It spooked the horses but Rafael controlled them both, because now he was leaning over his saddle, bringing his soon-to-be wife as close to him as he could.

Her face was bright, her eyes glowing. She brought her hands down and caught his chin with her fingers, laughing, placing a quick kiss on his lips.

It was more than he had ever hoped, sweet beyond even his most lofty dreams. He had Alderich now—and more importantly, the love of Serath Rune, his own mystical, magical, beautiful witch. Great blessings, indeed.

Rafael stood up in his saddle, waiting until it was calm enough for him to speak, until everyone was watching again.

"Good people, I present to you—Serath Rune, past, and *future* Lady of Alderich!"

And the crowd roared its approval as the sun finally appeared over the horizon, spreading warmth and light over them, crowning this glorious new day.

Epilogue

───────⟨∞⟩───────

*T*HE WIND SWEPT BY THEM IN TEASING GUSTS, carrying the scent of the sea up high to the top of the turret. A thunderstorm was approaching over the ocean, whipping the steely blue waves to froth as far as the eye could see.

"I saw one!" came the excited cry, a girl of no more than six years, tugging at her mother's sleeve. "I saw one, Mama! A mermaid!"

"Did you, love?" Serath squinted into the wind. "Where?"

"There, there!" The girl bounced up and down with excitement in her mother's arms, pointing to the rows of waves crashing to the shore far below them.

"I saw it too!" exclaimed a boy, about four. "A pretty mermaid, Mama!"

"Well, that's a lucky sign," Serath said to them, holding them close. "The mermaids have favored you, my angels. Mayhap they'll leave their seashell necklaces on the beach for you later."

"Mermaid!" shouted out a third child, a little boy of two, nestled between his siblings.

The wind blew stronger, and off in the distance the thunder picked up, a rumble that could be felt through the stones of the turret. Lightning lit the heavens over the water, a haze of rain falling just where the sea met the sky.

"Listen!" Serath lowered her voice, a conspiratorial whisper. "Can you hear them? The mermaids are singing for us. They're laughing, too!"

"Are they playing games with the fishes now, Mama?" asked the girl.

"Aye. Silly games, and the fish always win, because they can swim fastest."

"But all the mer*children* are resting far beneath the waves," said a new voice, coming up behind them, "eating their suppers, which is what some children I know should be doing right now."

And with a smile Serath released her sons and daughter as they squealed and ran to their father, even the little one, clinging to his legs as Rafael laughed and bent down to hug them.

"Go on," he urged them gently. "Your food is waiting. Even mermaids don't like their meals cold."

Serath walked her children over to their nursemaid, a smiling young woman who gathered them close and led them to the turret door, toward safety and soft beds and a nursery of playmates.

Serath and Rafael watched them go, and it wasn't until the door closed after them that they looked to each other, the wind still dancing between them.

"I had a feeling I might find you up here," Rafael said, coming close, taking her into his arms. "Watching the water. I think if it were up to you, you'd be down at the shore now, looking to frolic with the mermaids in the rain."

"It was only that once," she said, laughing. "And at least it was a summer rain."

"Aye, and I spent nearly a week in bed recovering from that summer chill, the one I got while fetching you back."

"Was it so awful, a week in bed, my lord?"

"Only whenever you left it," Rafael replied, and brushed a kiss over her temple.

Serath wrapped her arms around his waist and leaned her head against his shoulder, gazing out again at the water, the coming tempest.

"It's a fine show," she said. "You should stay and watch with me."

"Mayhap I will."

But he was not looking out over the battlements of the turret. He was fumbling with something in his hand, and at last Serath looked down to see what it was that he held. His fist was closed, hiding it.

"The mermaids have sent you an offering," Rafael said, and then opened his fingers.

Slowly she picked up the brooch he held, feeling something hard and tight in her throat.

It was a moonstone—cut round, instead of the rectangle that her mother's had been. And instead of rubies bracketing it, only a few simple gold clasps secured it to its pin. But most striking of all, it had a carving upon it: an exquisitely scaled dragon with wings and a long, coiling tail. Carefully etched beneath its feet were the initials *R + S*.

The moonstone picked up the light of the storm, turning the depths of it to shimmering silver, enhancing the dragon's sinewy lines.

"Call it a bridal gift," said Rafael, so warm next to her.

She gave a tearful laugh, overwhelmed. "I have not been a bride for many years, my lord."

He closed her fingers around it, and Serath looked up at him, her cherished husband, his nightcloud eyes more vibrant than the storm.

"You'll forever be my bride, beautiful Serath," he said. "I've charmed you with my magic, sweet witch, and now you're bound to me until the end of time."

Her laugh was freer now, the wind whipping up her hair around them both, black ebony against the violet-blue clouds.

"You managed to cast quite a spell, Rafael of Alder-ich—for a demon-man, that is."

"Aye," he replied, his lips coming down on hers. "I did."

Author's Note

The idea of celebrating the new year on January first arrived in Britain with William the Conqueror in 1066. Before that, Anglo-Saxon England combined the birth of Christ and New Year's Day into the same day, December 25.

Various sources cite wildly differing versions of the final days of the year 999 in Europe. Some texts state that most places were peaceful, the new century arriving with no more and no less fanfare than any other. But other (more interesting) sources tell stories of the terrible omens that plagued the lands—rains of blood, stars showering the earth, animals dropping dead, famine, locusts. Many landowners supposedly really did release their serfs and livestock, hoping to impress their coming Lord with their newfound virtue. Wandering preachers really did traverse the countryside, predicting death and doom and retribution for mortal sins.

Naturally, I considered this latter version of events to be a much more compelling background for Serath and Rafe. I hope you enjoyed following their love through this exciting period as much as I did.

One more thing. I beg you, please do not write to me to protest that the new millennium would have actually begun in the year 1001. I have considered the arguments both for and against this date until I developed a rather severe headache. Suffice it to say that whatever you want to think, I will agree with it, and we will both save our postage.

But really, who could resist the lure of all those zeros for a new beginning?

—S.A.